Johnny Romanek: The Start of an Era
A Story of War, Family and Securing Workers' Rights
© by Frank L. Golon, Sr.

To my children, grandchildren and great-grandchildren, who encouraged me to finish a story I started writing nearly forty years ago.

I'd also like to thank Bill O'Dea, who guided me through the publishing process and to my editor, Raviya, a true professional.

And finally to the memory of my wife, Anna. I had the privilege of her love and devotion for 72 years. I miss her every day.

Chapter 1
Year 1964

The evening was cold and damp as the sun started to set behind union headquarters. Large oaks sheltered buds beginning to burst with the coming of spring and at the northeast end of the building languid weeping willow trees dipped their long branches into the river.

The landscape echoed the restlessness of the men standing, their shoulders hunched, their coat collars turned up to ward off the wind. They waited impatiently for the doors to open so they could witness the outcome of the local union election.

Some stood on the riverbanks drinking beer and skipping rocks, causing a rippling effect over the surface. They separated into groups, those supporting Don Byrne, the incumbent president, and those supporting Johnny Romanek, the young maverick who campaigned so vigorously to upend the present leadership.

On the fringe others gathered, detached from either party but interested in who would be the leaders of the union for the next two years and also curious about the reaction of the losing candidates and their supporters. Many past elections spurred rumbles between both parties.

An hour passed since the polls closed. Joe Kleppard, chairman of the election committee, came to unlock the doors, raising his hands for attention.

"Men, I know you're cold and want to get downstairs," Joe said. He held his ground against their pushing. "Hold it, no one's going to get in until you hear what I have to say."

He told the group that three tables were set up in the center of the hall. The one in the middle was for the secretaries and the election committee responsible for counting the votes for each of the candidates. The first table was reserved for Don and his supporters and the last table was for Johnny Romanek and his group.

The members in the rear surged forward but were restrained.

"Come on guys," Joe shouted over the noise. "Ease back. You in front open up and let Romanek's group go through first and then Byrne's group."

The crowd separated, allowing both groups to enter and then followed quietly down the marble steps, through the foyer and into the auditorium. The election committee was pulling the voting machines from the wall, circling the three tables. A rope hung in front of the machines was meant to keep unauthorized personnel away except for challengers in each party and Joe Kleppard.

At the opposite end of the hall, other election members emptied paper ballots from sealed containers, used for district union committeeman, and dumped them onto a table. The ballots were distinguished by different colors for each department and were sorted into separate piles.

Johnny walked in with the cocky stride of a winner. His World War II trench coat flapped behind him. He was a trim, good-looking man of medium height. With rugged features he still bore the etchings around his eyes and nose from his early fighting years but these only added to his appeal. Aware of his effect on women, he winked and flashed a grin as he walked by the secretaries.

Johnny was elected to the body shop, consisting only of the toughest men in the auto plant because of the heavy and hard laborious work involved in the department. The company assigned the biggest and strongest men to the large gun welding machines. They were required to carry and install the doors to the body of the car, weld the body parts to the unit and handle the large grinding machines to smooth out the bumps and bangs on the outer surface of the body. Johnny Romanek soon gained all of his constituents respect by the positions he took in their defense.

After serving in World War II, he attended college and made it a practice to read all the umpires opinions and memorandums dealing with discipline. Whenever any of the members from his department were summoned to labor relation for discipline, he was prepared and was successful in defending them because of his knowledge of the contract.

In the body shop, temperature was the problem there because of enormous heat generated by the welders especially in the summer months. Whenever the temperature entered into the 90's, Johnny immediately met with the company to get a short day. He pointed out that the heat was a threat to the workers' health since they could suffer from heat exhaustion. Many times the company agreed with him and knocked off production for the day. There were other times the company disagreed with his request because of sales, so in turn he advised workers to walk out of the plant. This was in violation of the company contract but the men always stood behind Johnny because they knew he was concerned about their health. Other departments followed suit, looking for Johnny to take action when temperatures soared to extreme levels of heat.

After the walkout, company labor relation representatives summoned the violators to the office for discipline. The workers always defended Johnny. The members throughout the plant recognized his talent and devotion, urging him to run for the presidency. When he agreed, he presented a ten-point program stressing benefits and a substantial wage increase. He campaigned tirelessly by walking the assembly lines and if he missed folks, he would catch them at the hot coffee machine or in the company cafeteria or in the parking lot. The opposition laughed at his idealism, calling it "pie in the sky" but his followers believed in him and Johnny's mission.

On election night Johnny removed his coat and draped it over the back of his chair. Johnny's supporters assembled at his side including ex-fighters standing at attention behind him with their arms folded across their chests, forming an impressive yet silent entourage. Johnny picked up a tally sheet and asked Pat Fager to keep score at the table. He glanced around the hall to see how the members lined up with the candidates, noticing the anti-union radicals off by themselves at the far end. Most of them sported shoulder length hair with bandanas tied around their forehead, some with unruly beards and others with earrings and elaborate tattoos.

"Johnny, I thought Rocky was right behind us when we came in," Pat said as he picked up the tally sheet. Pat was running for recording secretary. "I'll hold this chair open for him," Pat said. "He probably got held up bullshitting." Rocky Durango was a candidate for vice president.

Don Byrne, the incumbent president, was heavily favored to win and had a large group of supporters around his table. He stood up on his chair to get a better view. He was a short and immaculately dressed man, of middle age and overweight with a receding hairline, which he tried unsuccessfully to disguise by combing the remaining few top hairs crosswise. He had served as the local president for the last 10 years but recently his popularity dipped with new members who grumbled about being assigned to the night shift permanently. They circulated petitions for a rotation of shifts. Assessing the crowd, Don jumped down from the chair and turned to George Plassard.

"It's all over except for the counting," Don said. "I've done too much good for this local to have them go against us. The first machine will tell us the story."

George had been local secretary-treasurer for twenty years and the most powerful vote getter of the local. Considering that he was in his fifties, he was still well built with only a slight paunch developing around his midsection. He handled all the members' health problems, pensions and unemployment claims as well as administering the local union funds. The treasury was in the red mainly due to the heavy spending during the election but there were no outstanding debts. The union building was free and clear and valued at over one million dollars. They had the most modern and-up-to-date office equipment. George never hesitated to assist any member and had grown popular, facing only minor opposition.

"George keep score," Don said, passing him the tally sheet. "I'm too nervous."

"That's some motley crew standing around Johnny," George said, observing the big men surrounding Johnny. "They look like watchdogs. God help this local if Johnny ever gets elected president. He's a hothead. He'd have this plant shut down at the snap of his finger. We'd be living on the street."

George stood up to get a better view. "I don't see Rocky at Johnny's table," George said. "I wonder why?"

"He's standing in the doorway with those radical bastards," said Don, pointing toward the rear of the hall toward Rocky.

"How could he stand those slimy bastards?" George grumbled. "Some of them haven't taken a bath in a month. Oh well, better him than us. My hope is that he strictly campaigned for himself and not for the ticket. If Rocky gets elected along with Johnny, he'd cut Johnny's throat in no time. Rocky is unhappy since his supporters wanted Johnny to run for the presidency instead. If Rocky becomes vice president we're going to have to watch him closely. No matter who gets elected president, that person is in for trouble. All his years as committeeman, Rocky never took a position on a hot potato. He always passed the buck."

"Right," interjected Buddy Mackenzie, the incumbent vice president, who had born the brunt of Don's mistakes. "Everywhere I campaigned, the members made no secret that they were supporting Rocky. He works strictly for himself and dropped hints that he could work with Don if he was elected."

Buddy reached over and nudged Don with his arm. "You'll get elected again but you'll have to watch that bastard full time," Buddy said.

"Soon as we get re-elected, I'll assign that bastard to the grievances they dumped on us during the campaign," Don said. "He'll have to shit or get off the pot because they have no merit to them. Our biggest job is to keep him away from the membership. He's a master of rapping everyone while they're behind the racks."

Pat became restless as he bantered with Johnny across the empty chair. He stood up to get a better view of the hall.

"Here I'm saving this chair for Rocky and he's standing with those crumbs that always broke our balls in the plant," Pat said. "Why?"

"I'm not sure," said Johnny as he shrugged his shoulders, also concerned by his absence. "Let's hope it's only a case of nerves."

"I never trusted him," Pat whispered. "I knew we needed the Italian vote but dammit he never walked with us during the election in the plant. He walked strictly with Carter. I know fucking well, they didn't campaign for our ticket."

"We'll find out soon enough," Johnny said. "Kleppard's ready to open up the first machine."

"Let's have your attention!" Joe shouted over the noise in the hall. "I'm going to open each machine as I come to it. I'd like to have the two challengers standing right behind us so they can see the number of the votes as I call the numbers of the vote. I'll read the numbers very slowly for each candidate so the counters can register them. If there is any doubt to the number I call out, please stop me and I'll go over the count. We have all night to go over this, so there will be no rush."

"Joe, I'd like you to call out all votes cast on each machine before you call out the count, for each candidate," Don asked. "Do you know what I mean?" Joe agreed to that protocol.

Johnny and Don took their places behind the machines as Joe called out.

"The total votes on machine number 1 is 621," Joe bellowed. "For president, number one is Don Byrne with 281 votes."

Joe paused as he allowed the counters to write down the numbers.

"Number two is Johnny Romanek, 251 votes," Joe said.

A hush came over the crowd as Joe continued to read numbers.

"For vice president number three is Jack Mackenzie, 221 votes," Joe said. "Number 4 for vice president, is Rocky Durango, 403 votes."

The hall burst to life. While some candidates whispered, others looked surprised at the amount of votes that they got. All eyes turned toward Rocky who stood there with a happy grin on his face as his supporters pounded on his back in jubilation, shouting and raising their arms up in the air in a gesture of victory.

"I knew it," Pat grumbled in anger. "We supported that son of a bitch and he had his supporters bullet vote for him only. Johnny if you get elected, you better get a steel jacket to protect your back."

"Simmer down," Johnny said, a look of concern spreading over his face. "We got nine more machines to go. Maybe we'll get lucky on the next machine."

"I hope you're right," Pat said, fuming as he watched Rocky's supporters making a spectacle of themselves around Rocky.

The hall was buzzing over the voting results but quieted down when Joe's thunderous voice boomed.

"For financial secretary, number five on the machine, George Plassard 273 votes," Joe said. "For financial secretary number six on the machine, Larry O'Brien, 221 votes."

The voting trend reflected that the membership was ignoring the party lines and were voting independently.

"That's no surprise," Johnny whispered as he leaned closer to Pat. "George was always a high vote getter. Some of our people are beholden to him for the favors he did for them over the years."

Across the room, Rocky took Al Carter by the arm and led him to the far corner of the hall away from the crowd.

"We fucked-up at that last caucus meeting," Rocky fumed.

"You're damn right, we never should have let Johnny head our ticket," Al said. "Look at the votes you're piling up compared to Johnny. You're up more than 150 votes over him and this is only the first machine. We fucked-up when we gave in too quickly."

Johnny and Rocky were inseparable members of the caucus for the last ten years. It was during their caucus meeting that Rocky nominated Johnny to head the ticket to upend Don. Everyone was satisfied that the combination of Rocky Durango and Johnny Romanek was unbeatable. Everything ran smoothly until some of his Italian supporters insisted that Rocky head the ticket. A special caucus meeting was called to select the remaining positions on the executive board. Since Rocky was an officer of the Italian Social Club, he was able to get the use of their hall free of charge. During that special caucus meeting Johnny and Rocky had taken a table in the corner of the hall to discuss the remaining positions for their ticket.

Rocky, a party animal with smoldering dark eyes had a lifestyle many envied. Most of the men were bogged down with family responsibilities and high mortgages. They only looked forward to getting a better position in their various jobs. Rocky, on the other hand, lived the life of a prolonged bachelor. He had season tickets to all of the Yankees baseball games and New York Giant football games. He considered these events a perfect venue to show off his girlfriends and make an impression on his friends. He often double-dated with Johnny and his wife but he never brought the same girl. He was an effective committeeman whose biggest concern was to keep 50 percent of his constituents happy. He knew everyone on a first name basis and whenever he was approached with a difficult problem, he had a knack for being able to change the subject, distracting the member who walked away eventually happy. When it was of a serious nature, he always pushed the problem over to the bargaining committee who were the only ones who were blamed if the results weren't favorable.

"Johnny a lot of the caucus members are breaking my balls to head the ticket rather than you and have you run as the vice president," Rocky had told Johnny during that meeting. "They feel I have a better chance of dumping Don and taking the entire board along with us."

"What brought this on?" asked Johnny, a surprised expression on his face.

"Half of the membership is of Italian descent and they're solidly behind us," Rocky replied, nervously moving his drink back and forth across the table. "They've been after me ever since we announced that you were going to head the ticket. They want you to step down to the V.P. spot."

"We settled this months ago," Johnny countered with a touch of anger. "You're the one who nominated that I run for the president job. A change now would show a sign of weakness and we'd all go down."

"Johnny, this wasn't my idea," Rocky insisted. "Most of the guys think I'm the only one who can dump Don. I wanted to alert you to what's going to happen when you open the caucus. I promise you on my father's grave that I will support the caucus in whatever they decide. I'll be a hundred percent behind the ticket no matter who heads it."

"Rocky, I hope you're not referring to all the new people you brought to the caucus today," Johnny said. "You know they're not members of the caucus and have no vote."

"I know that," Rocky said. "All of them work in the plant and all of them are members of the union and social club. They just wanted to see how we operate. We always advocated an open caucus and any member of the plant could join."

Rocky was sitting down facing the hall. He could see his followers sitting at each table, talking to the members about Rocky taking up the leadership of the caucus.

"Looks like everyone is done eating, we ought to get started with the meeting," Rocky said to Johnny.

Johnny nodded and walked to the head table. He rapped the top of the table with one of the glass ashtrays to get their attention.

"I call this caucus to order," Johnny said, after everyone had settled down. "Everyone knows that I was elected to head up our ticket for president and Rocky for vice president. Well today I was informed by Rocky that there are many who feel we made a mistake and are looking to make a change. I'm shocked and disappointed that no one mentioned this to me before today. I personally feel making a change at this late date would be a sign of weakness and all the campaigning we did in the past will be for naught. In spite of my feeling, I'm going to open the floor."

"Johnny, before we discuss any changes, I'd like our recording secretary to read the names of all our dues paying members," Pat said. "Our by-laws state that only dues paying members have the right to vote on selecting our candidate to represent our caucus."

Many at the meeting began booing.

Johnny rapped the ashtray on the table to restore order.

"Pat has the floor, let him speak," Johnny said.

"I noticed that a lot of new brothers are here that aren't members of the caucus," Pat said. "I'm not going to be swayed by any new members to change what took us months to put together. I make a motion that only dues-paying members be allowed to speak."

Boos continued to rise. Some started to bang their drinking glasses on the table to gather attention.

"I also add to the motion that these new comers have no right to vote," Pat shouted over the noise.

A second cry rang out from the floor. Rocky stood so everyone could see him.

"Members of the caucus and friends, I feel that everyone in this hall has the right to speak and vote on whoever is going to head our caucus," Rocky said. "We always advocated an open caucus and I don't think it's fair to invite new people to the caucus and deny them the right to participate in our discussions and selections of our candidates. Everyone here is a member of our local and is politically aligned with our caucus. I say we allow everyone here a right to vote."

Pat shouted before anyone responded.

"We paid for this privilege for the last year and we don't intend to give up this right," Pat yelled. "I look around the room and I see a lot of Rocky's friends that never showed any interest in helping any of the caucus candidates during the campaign. Now they come out to one meeting and want to take over. It takes two-thirds of the dues paying members to change the rules. So let's get on with the vote."

"Is everyone ready to vote?" Johnny asked when he restored order in the hall. "All in favor of the motion raise your hand."

He stopped to count the vote.

"We have 28 in favor of the motion," Johnny said. "Now raise your hand to oppose the motion. I received a count of 23 opposed. The motion is carried."

Johnny picked up his papers and placed them into his briefcase.

"I'm going to turn this over to Pat until the vote is taken to determine who will head our ticket," Johnny said. "After that, the chosen person will be our candidate for president and will chair our meetings."

Pat got up and began to pass out blank slips of paper and pencils to the dues paying members.

"The blank slips are for voting," Pat said. "Write in the name of the man who will head our ticket. It'll be either Johnny Romanek or Rocky Durango. I gave out 51 slips of paper to the number of dues paying members that are here. When you're done voting each of you will deposit your vote into the hat on the table before me." The hat was in plain view and Pat stood behind the table to watch each member cast his vote.

Each member walked up to the table and put his vote into the hat, then returned to their seats to wait for the result. Pat and Larry O'Brien, who was going to run for financial secretary, unfolded each voting slip and displayed each vote to Johnny and Rocky who were standing in back of the counters. They were standing in a position that each could see every vote cast clearly. The final result was 26 for Romanek and 25 for Rocky.

"Johnny will head our ticket," Pat said. He then turned to Rocky and stared at him.

"Unless you want a recount of the ballots," Pat asked, testily.

"No, Pat," Rocky said. "We saw every vote and the count is correct. Congratulations Johnny. It was fair and Democratic, so let's get on with picking out the rest of the ticket." He sat down with a relieved expression on his face. Rocky never wanted to head the ticket but his Italian friends wouldn't take no for an answer.

The caucus members stood up to applaud Rocky as he resumed his seat next to Johnny. Meanwhile Al Mannino walked in and inquired what was going on. As soon as he realized he shouted to cast a vote for Rocky.

"We have a tie vote, so who's going to head the ticket now?" Al asked.

While Al was speaking, Bummy Harris walked in and heard what was going on.

"I want to cast my vote for Johnny Romanek," Bummy interceded.

Rocky didn't want to see a split vote in the caucus, which would cause all of them to lose. He stood up so everyone could see and hear him.

"Mr. Chairman, the caucus voted fairly that you head the ticket so be it," Rocky said. "I make a motion that all voting be closed and we get on with other business."

That special caucus meeting had been the beginning of the friction that would plague Johnny and Rocky for the remainder of their partnership. Rocky thought back to that night and just shook his head.

"There is nothing we can do now," Rocky said to Al, who was pacing back and forth. "Another thing, did you get rid of all those slate tickets?"

"We only had 500 made up," Al said. "I gave them only to our faithful followers with strict orders that they were to hand them out on the sly and to destroy the ones not used. They were told to only hand them out in Don's strong hold. We're clear as far as the cards go. Don't worry about them."

Over at his table, Don fingered the tally sheet nervously as he turned to his vice-president.

"Buddy, it looks like Rocky is going to win by a landslide," Don said to Buddy. "What hurt you was that slate ticket that came out supporting me and Rocky as my vice-president. You know that we didn't have anything to do with that, right? Car delivery members were buying that. It was done late last night just before they came out to vote. Rocky had to be behind that or knew his followers were doing it. He's one sneaky son-of-a-bitch."

"The total votes cast on machine number two is 480 votes," Joe's booming voice called out. "For president, number one on the machine is Don Byrne, with 233 votes. For president number two, Johnny Romanek, is 182 votes. For vice-president, number three on the machine is Buddy MacKenzie with 180 votes. For vice-president, number four is Rocky Durango with…" He stopped to wipe his eye glasses clean to be sure of the count. The hall was in complete silence.

"Durango got 300 votes."

The entire hall erupted as Rocky raised his arm in a salute to the crowd. Many walked over to Rocky to offer congratulations, others slapped him on his back. Rocky's supporters jumped up and down, hugging and embracing Rocky. It was a positive sign that Rocky would win in a landslide. The voting trend also indicated that Don would be re-elected to another two-year term as president and building chairman of the local.

"Look if you don't hold down the noise, I'm going to get the police to escort every one out except the candidates," Joe said. The crowd quieted down.

"For financial secretary, number five on the machine, George Plassard, got 250 votes," Joe announced. "For financial secretary number six on the machine, Larry O'Brien, got 126 votes."

Another commotion erupted, this time at Don's table. His supporters stood up on their chairs to proclaim him the winner. The taste of victory was theirs, except for Buddy, who sadly conceded defeat. Joe was annoyed but he wasn't ready to call the police. He recognized the tensions were high and there was nothing he could do about it. He resumed the count on the rest of the machines and walked over to the third machine. The members were pushing to get a closer look at the count. Joe stopped and looked at the crowd. Everyone knew he wouldn't continue the count until they settled down. The crowd quieted down for the next announcement.

"Machine number three has a total of 380 votes for president," Joe said. Don Byrne has 215 votes and Johnny Romanek has 155 votes."

Bedlam broke loose at Don's table. His supporters pounded the table with everything that made noise. Many in the rear came over to shake his hand while others just pat him on the back. Police came forward to restrain the crowd and order was restored but only for a moment. Shouts were heard throughout the hall.

"We want Byrne! We want Byrne!" his supporters shouted.

Don beamed with joy and a hush came over the crowd when Rocky approached him with an outstretched hand.

"Don, it looks like you and I are going to get elected for the next two years," Rocky said. "I'd like to be the first one to offer you my congratulations. I'm sure we'll be able to work as a team."

Don accepted his hand and lifted it up to show unity for the coming years. The members cheered as disappointment settled around Johnny Romanek's table. Buddy also showed his displeasure.

"Quiet!" shouted Joe "I still have results to announce and I need absolute quiet." He took a moment to wait for the crowd to quiet.

"For vice president, Buddy MacKenzie, with 134 votes and Rocky Durango with 251 votes," Joe said.

Rocky's supporters began marching around the hall with hand-made placards displaying Rocky's name in bold print. The police immediately restored order and Joe began the count again.

"For financial secretary, George Plassard, 216 votes," Joe said. "For financial secretary, Larry O'Brien with 154 votes."

There was no holding back Don's supporters. They marched around the hall waving cards and banners showing Don as number one. The reminder of the hall joined by whistling and rooting for Don with the exception of Johnny. The marchers pulled Don and George to join in the march along with the beaming Rocky. The police hustled them all back to their table.

Don then stood up on his chair to address the crowd.

"I appreciate your support but quiet down so we can get on with the count," Don said. He then assumed his seat next to George.

"I was really worried about the election," Don whispered to George. "If it took place a week sooner, I'd have been a dead duck. Johnny was getting to the membership and I thought for sure that the night shift would come out strong to dump me."

Don was referring to a special membership meeting that was called by the local union a month prior to the election. The night shift circulated a petition demanding that the local union rescind the agreement freezing all shifts. They demanded that all shifts be rotated every two weeks to allow the newer workers the right to work day shifts. The meeting was called on a Sunday to allow the entire membership to attend because there was no production scheduled then. The meeting was scheduled at a nearby theater so everyone could attend to express the views.

At that meeting, Don was the president and had called the meeting to order. A member who called for a special point of order then interrupted him.

"What's your point of order?" asked Don.

"Mr. Chairman, we came to this meeting for a special purpose," said the man. He was an older man but new at the plant and a member of the night shift. "We are here to hear your regular report. So I make a motion that we dispense with the regular order of business and get into the petition that was circulated at the plant for the last few weeks about rotating the shifts."

Hands flew up in the air from all parts of the theater as members fought to express their views. Don pointed to one.

"I'll recognize the man with the black sweater waving the white card," Don said. "Give us your name, number and the department that you work in and what shift."

The man worked in the maintenance department on the night shift. He was told that he only could work the night shift. He shared his name and that he was 38-years-old, with three small children.

"My shift starts at 3:30 in the afternoon and I have to leave an hour before my shift to get to work on time," he said. "My kids are in school at that time and when I get through with work, they're fast asleep. The only time I see my children is on weekends and that's not fair to my wife and children. With this agreement, I'll be stuck on the night shift for the next ten years. If we could rotate the shifts every two weeks, I could be helping my wife to bring up our children. I don't think we're asking too much from the old timers to rotate the shift with us newer members. Most of them have children all grown up, I appeal to the membership to support this motion."

Many of the members began to hoot and holler that they supported his position. Don rapped his gavel to bring the members back to order.

"Now I'll recognize a member who is against this motion."
Hands flew up again. "The man in the front row with the brown
suit."

The man worked the day shift and said he worked over 20
years.

"I took my lumps on the picket lines to win the right for
seniority," he said. "We're not going to let some young punks
come in and say that seniority doesn't matter. They just started
here and should be thankful that they got a job here instead of
trying to change the rules. Mr. President, seniority is the backbone
of the union and if we lose that we got nothing. I say we vote this
motion down."

"I'll recognize the man waving the white placard, if he's
for the motion," said Don.

The man worked nights and opened up his statement
agreeing that seniority was the backbone of the union for
promotions but didn't feel it fair to bury union members on the
night shift forever.

"I happen to be single and I'd like to take girlfriends out
on a date, dinner or a movie,"
he said. "I can't do this except on weekends. With this kind of a
set up, I'll never be able to get married. You all know that the
young girls want to go out on dates during the evenings not only
on weekends. I'm new here and this working strictly nights is a
bitch. You guys have to give us a break. I ask for your support of
this motion."

While another member was talking, George leaned over to
Don.

"Why don't you recognize Johnny as the next speaker?"
George whispered. "Put him on the spot. He'll have no choice but
to go along with the day shift. This way we could get the night
shift pissed off at him also."

Don nodded in agreement and rose to continue the
meeting.

"We've been listening to the rank and file speak express
their views," Don said. "I'd like to get the views from some of the
elected union officials. I'll recognize Johnny Romanek,
committeeman of the body shop on the day shift."

Don smiled as he pointed to Johnny.

Johnny looked up with a surprised expression but responded immediately. He grabbed the microphone and cleared his throat.

"Thank you, Mr. Chairman," Johnny began. "For the benefit of the new members of the local, my name is Johnny Romanek. I've represented the body shop and the maintenance department for the last ten years. The first thing I want to point out is that our local agreement was passed unanimously six months ago when we had volunteers manning the night shift. To rescind this motion, our bylaws state that it takes a two third vote by the members to make any changes in our local agreement. Both sides have expressed their views clearly but this meeting should have taken place six months ago when only a majority was needed to make any change."

Johnny paused before looking over at Don.

"Mr. President, you should have asked the leadership that question six months ago not today," Johnny said. "Look around and you can see the day shift outnumbers the night shift by a vote of three-to-one. Everyone knows this motion could never muster a two-third vote now, nor at anytime in the future."

A loud round of applause followed Johnny's speech. The hall erupted with shouts calling for a vote on this motion. Order couldn't be restored until the chair recognized their demand.

The move backfired on Don. He rapped his gavel.

"All in favor of this motion signify by saying 'aye,'" he said.

Five hundred people stood up to vote in favor of the motion. When he asked for those against, the remaining members numbered more than 2,000. They stood up shouting against the motion. The motion to rotate the shifts was defeated overwhelmingly. That meeting was adjourned and the issue was put to bed.

During election night, Joe's voice brought everyone to back reality. They were still awaiting the results of the next machine.

"Machine number four has a total of 666 votes cast," Joe said. "For president, Don Byrne has 303 votes." Applause erupted from Don's supporters. Don stood up to quiet his supporters down.

Joe took his time and began to clean his glasses and slowly looked at the chanting group.

"Now I want all of you to hear this loud and clear so you realize that this election isn't won until the last machine has been counted," Joe said, stepping closer to the machine. "For president, Johnny Romanek with 353 votes."

All of the members were confused. A trend had been established, there had to be a mistake. Could Joe have made a mistake and misread the numbers? A call from Don's table asked that the number be repeated. Joe and Don and Johnny's two challengers moved closer to the machine.

"Don Byrne got 303 votes, and Johnny Romanek got 353 votes," he said. He turned to their challengers.

"Is that the right numbers that I called?" Joe asked them.

Don's challenger stepped up close to the machine to get a better view and nodded his head in agreement. Timmy Larkin, Johnny's challenger, put two fingers up in sign of victory and had the broadest smile on his face, anticipating a possible change in the voting trend.

Joe assumed his position behind the machine, calling out the vote for the remaining candidates where the same trend continued. Now the members were only interested in the count for the presidency. The hall was so quiet one could only hear the deep breathing from those in attendance. They all moved closer to the machine.

"Machine number five has a total of 600 votes," Joe said. "For president, Don Byrne got 264 votes." He paused. "For president, Johnny Romanek, got 311 votes."

Johnny's table sprang to life. They were behind in the vote but the pattern was changing, clearly. Many members began to gather around Johnny to wish him good luck. Johnny, however, was concerned by the erratic vote and stood up on his chair to get Joe's attention.

"Joe, I want you to station a cop behind the machines so no one can tamper with them," Johnny said. Johnny then turned to Timmy.

"Was the last count correct?" Johnny whispered to him.

"It sure was," Timmy said with a huge smile.

Joe stopped the count while he placed a policeman by the open machines with strict orders that no one was to go by the machines, not even to look. This election was too critical and he was making sure no one would disrupt the election, since he was elected to head the election year after year.

During the lull, members totaled the votes for presidency, which showed Don still in the lead. As Joe approached the next machine members started to push to get closer to the voting machine.

"Come on you guys, stay clear," Joe said. "All you're doing is holding up the count. I'm not going to open the next machine until all of you move back." Anxious to hear the count, they shuffled back and waited anxiously for Joe to continue.

"Machine number six has 630 votes cast," Joe said. "For president, Don Byrne has 207 votes." Joe stood still refusing to call the next number until everyone moved back and became quiet. Excitement was in the hall and the election could go either way. "For president, Johnny Romanek got 343 votes."

At this midpoint, Johnny took the lead. Hysteria broke loose as a fistfight erupted in the hall. The police immediately broke up the ruckus and dragged the troublemakers out. Johnny stood up on his chair and called his supporters to get around his table.

"Cool it," Johnny said. "There are four more machines to go. We're back in the race, so let's not blow it."

Don did likewise.

"Quiet down," Don ordered. "All the screaming and fighting isn't going to change anything. The votes have already been cast and nothing's going to change now."

Don motioned to his supporters to gather around.

"Look, we took the first three machines so the race is going to be closer than we thought," Don said.

"Hey Don, which side is Rocky on now?" a voice from the crowd called out. Everyone laughed and looked toward Rocky. "He was marching in your victory parade around the hall fifteen minutes ago, whose side is he on now?" the voice continued. Rocky was bewildered but made no move as he stood there talking to Al.

Joe opened up the next machine as the hall fell completely silent.

"The total votes on machine number 7 is 592," Joe said. "For president, Don Byrne got 292 votes. For president, Johnny Romanek got 300 votes."

Thunderous applause came from Johnny's forces as gloom set in at Don's table. Everyone was aware that the vote on any machine could change the course of the election.

While the count continued, Don leaned over to George.

"Something is wrong here," Don said. "I can't figure it out. If I end up winning this election, I'm going to personally burn Rocky's ass. He took a lot of votes away from us when he put out that phony slate ticket. I feel a lot of Buddy's supporters got pissed and didn't vote for me. They felt I deserted Buddy and I can't blame them. I've never seen a trend change like it's doing here, before. What pisses me off most is that Rocky is getting more votes than you, and he never did anything constructive for the members like you did."

Rocky was self-conscious about his previous approach to Don's table.

"These fucking bums behind us put me in a bind with Johnny," Rocky whispered to Al. "I was positive Don had the election locked up. We better hope Johnny doesn't find out about our little plan or someone's ass is going to get kicked. He's got all those fighters backing him up and they'll do whatever Johnny wants."

A commotion erupted near the entrance of the hall as a huge black man named Bummy Harris dragged another man by his coat collar along the floor toward Johnny's table. Bummy spun the man toward Johnny.

"I caught this bastard with a stack of cards linking Don and Rocky as a team against us," Bummy said. He kicked the man in the ribs as he lay on the floor with his hands covering his head.

"This bastard is in our caucus," Bummy said. "He walked with Rocky during the election but never with us, now I can see why. He's one of our caucus members who's cutting our fucking throat."

The police rushed over with raised clubs. Johnny stepped in, keeping the man targeted by Bummy, named Jack Roberts, and the Bummy apart.

"Officer, these men are both in our caucus," Johnny said. "I'll see that they settle their differences amicably."

"Keep your hands off him, get it?" the officer shouted at the black man.

"Yes sir," said Bummy Harris, an ex-professional fighter who didn't want any confrontation with the police. He smiled as he crossed his hands in front of his chest and sat down next to Johnny.

"I was standing in the doorway when Roberts came in," Bummy said. "He got cocky when he heard that Rocky was way ahead in the election. Then he took the fucking cards out of his pocket and shouted, 'we did it!' That's when I took the cards out of his hands to take a look."

Johnny took the cards to examine them closer. The rumor that the cards circulated the plant was now a fact.

"We'll get together with Rocky when the election is over," Johnny said. "Sit with us until the counting is over. We're ahead by a few votes, maybe we'll stay that way."

Jack Roberts got up on his feet and walked over to Rocky with his head down.

"Rocky, I fucked up," Jack said. "When they announced you were way ahead, I jumped up and down and the cards fell out of my pocket. Bummy was standing right next to me and picked them up. When he saw them, he was pissed and grabbed me before I could get away. I know that that black bastard is going to kick the shit out of me when he gets me alone, what should I do?"

"Son-of-a-bitch," Rocky roared. He turned to Al.

"I thought you told me that you got rid of all the cards?" Rocky snapped. "This drunken fuck got us in a bind. Get him out of here before someone beats the living daylights out of him. I'm going over by Johnny to see if I can set things straight."

Al and the supporters filed out of the hall quietly so as not to alert Johnny's forces of their leaving. Rocky approached Johnny with the eyes of the whole hall on him.

"Johnny, I just heard what happened with Roberts," Rocky said. He put his right hand up in the air.

"I swear on my father's grave I had nothing to do with those cards," Rocky said. "I heard about it for the first time last night when some of Don's supporters came over and showed me the slate card. There was nothing I could say except I only campaigned for our ticket. You know Don hates the both of us. I know I did a stupid thing when I went over to congratulate him and I'm sorry about that. I want you to know that I never double-crossed you. We're a team and we have to stick together."

"I'm glad you're back where you belong," said Pat as he relinquished his chair so Rocky could sit alongside Johnny. "Rocky, let me be the first one to congratulate you on your victory as vice-president."

"Machine number eight has 621 votes," Joe called out. Now the attention of the entire hall was centered on the coming count. "For president, Don Byrne got 290 votes. For president, Johnny Romanek got 341 votes."

Johnny's supporters took up to march around the hall carrying placards with the words "Romanek Number 1" and throwing pieces of paper up in the air like confetti. The police broke up the demonstration and the marchers gathered around Johnny to congratulate him. Bummy Harris sat at the table with a huge grin on his face and raised his right hand up in the air in a black salute. Johnny winked at him to acknowledge the gesture.

"Johnny, let me be the first to congratulate you as the new president of Local 3001," Rocky said as he pulled Johnny into a bear hug. He raised both of their hands up in the air as a sign of victory and the crowd reacted by cheering, with the exception of Don's supporters, who were scowling.

Johnny pushed Rocky away.

"I don't need your congrats now," said Johnny. "You went through the same motions with Don an hour ago."

"No Johnny, Don did the hand raising, not me," Rocky protested. "I'm here where I belong and we're going to win this election, you'll see."

"Look at that Rocky," George said to Don while watching the exchange at Johnny's table. "He's hugging and practically kissing Johnny, yet a short time ago he was kissing your ass when he thought you were the winner. What will he do if the voting swings back to you? I got my fingers crossed and if a prayer will help, you'll make it."

Joe continued with his count.

"The total vote on machine number 9 is 530," Joe said. "For president, Don Byrne got 250 votes. For president, Johnny Romanek got 280 votes."

Mayhem broke loose around Johnny's table and the police rushed in to restore order. A hush came over the crowd when they saw Jack stagger over to Johnny's table.

"Johnny, Bummy got me all wrong, I found those cards on the floor when I came in," Jack cried. "I'm with you and Rocky all the way."

Bummy was being restrained by some of the caucus members, but broke away and charged at Jack. He hit him across the side of his jaw, sending him skidding across the floor and into the center of the hall scattering the members.

"You fucking liar, I was there when you took the cards out of your fucking pocket," Bummy thundered.

Johnny circled his arms around Bummy, pinning his arms to his side and calling out to Larry O'Brien.

"Larry get him out of here before the police come to arrest him," Johnny said. "We'll be meeting at 711 club after the election count is over."

Johnny pushed his way through the crowd that was trying to help Jack, who was still as he lay on the floor. A policeman came over and asked what happened.

"He got carried away and he slipped on the wet floor," Johnny said. Jack was shaking his head to get rid of the dizziness as Johnny wrapped his arms around Jack.

"Right Jack?" Johnny looked to Jack for agreement. Jack nodded his head but the officer pushed his way closer to him and could see that Jack's jaw was broken.

"Johnny, call for an ambulance, this guy got a broken jaw," the officer said. "Meanwhile look around to see if someone has a broken hand. We don't want to have the ambulance make two trips."

Joe called to have the police nearby in case of any disruption as he went through the final machine. He waited until the cops had the medics assist Jack out of the hall. He made sure both challengers were standing next to him so they could see the count clearly. He put his glasses on to make sure he didn't misread the vote.

"Machine number 10 has total votes of 421," Joe said. "For president, Don Byrne has 194 votes." The hall was in complete silence. "For president, Johnny Romanek got 227 votes."

Everyone gathered around Johnny except Don's supporters. Sweat glistened on Johnny's forehead and his mouth broke into a half-grin.

"It's all over," Johnny beamed.

Don came over to shake hands and offer his best wishes. "Don, let me know if you guys need anything," Johnny said. The rest of the count was anti-climatic and the crowd moved out of the hall restlessly.

"We took control of the executive board by one vote," Pat said. He handed the final tally sheet to Johnny. "If Rocky goes over to the opposition, we're dead."

Johnny analyzed the outcome, scanning the sheet.

"We have to get some of their guys on our side, we can't trust Rocky," Johnny said. "He's too ambitious but we got to keep him close to us if possible."

Johnny broke away and walked over to Rocky who was surrounded by all of his well-wishers.

"Rocky we're going over to the 711 club for our victory celebration," Johnny said. "Are you coming over?"

"We finally got it after ten years, this victory smells sweet," Rocky said. "I might come over for a drink. I'm busted after all this. I promised Dolly that I'd take her out for dinner right after we found out the results of the election no matter what. So I'll see you later."

Truth was, Rocky was reluctant to face the caucus after his actions at the hall and knowing what Bummy did. With a few drinks in him, Bummy might go after Rocky, too. It was best not to show up at the celebration.

When Johnny entered the club, the party was in full bloom. They all stood up to pay him respects, offering to buy him a drink to his victory. Johnny waved to acknowledge their offering and walked over to Pat who was mulling over the final tally sheet.

"Something was wrong with the first three machines," Pat said. "I talked to Larkin and he said he never left the machines except on two occasions. Once to take a piss and he came right back. The other time he took a lunch break and Carter relieved him for an hour."

Pat stopped talking and looked around the room.

"Is Carter here?" Pat asked.

"No," a member replied. "I saw him drive off with Rocky when they left the hall."

Johnny swallowed hard, anger written all over his face. He looked for Timmy Larkin and spotted him eating a slice of pizza at the end of the table.

"Timmy, don't go into work tomorrow, I'll notify the company that you'll be working at the local and we'll pick up your lost time," Johnny said. "I want us to have a conversation with Al Carter. Someone tampered with the first three machines.

The total vote for the president doesn't jive with the total machine count."

"I wondered about that but you can never tell in a union election," said Timmy with a confused expression on his face. "It looks like Rocky was getting votes from both sides, maybe they bullet voted just for him."

"Let's get to the bottom of this tomorrow," said Johnny. "Carter had to be involved with those three machines in some way."

Johnny trusted Timmy implicitly who was beholden to Johnny for getting him off of the moving line and transferred to General Stores, which was one of the better jobs in the plant. Timmy worked tirelessly to get Johnny elected.

Johnny tapped Pat on the shoulder.

"Pat, keep this party going for as long as our guys are having a good time," Johnny said. "I'm out of here. I want to go home and surprise Ann and the kids."

Johnny took a leap and jumped on the table to talk to his supporters.

"I want to take this opportunity to thank all of you for your support and help," Johnny said. "Without you guys, I'd have never made it. Thanks again, I'm on my way to tell my wife the good news. She's been so supportive in all my ventures."

Chapter 2
Early 1900's

The young man stopped plowing the field when he saw Russian horsemen riding hard down the dirt road, toward the small farmhouse. It was unusual to receive visitors during the plowing season and when the farm hands were ready to seed. He pulled a large red handkerchief out of his rear pocket to wipe the sweat off his brow. He recognized the riders as elite Russian Cossacks. It was too early in the year to take inventory of the livestock or to collect taxes, so he wondered why they were there. Eight of the riders rode toward the house while three peeled off and rode toward him. They scuffed over the freshly plowed ground and pulled up next to him.

"What's your name boy?" one of the riders asked, a sneer on his face.

"Frank Romanek," he said. Frank casually removed the reins from around his neck and placed them on the handles of the plow, showing annoyance at them for trampling on his freshly plowed field. White foam bubbled around the horses' mouths as they shook their heads and shuffled their legs while standing.

Frank was an arrogant young man who didn't like the Russians.

"What do you want?" he asked.

"We're looking for Alexander Romanek," replied the sergeant. He dismounted and stood wide-legged in front of Frank.

"Where is he?" he asked, shoving his gun into Frank's chest.

Frank immediately knew that they meant to harm his brother. His mind raced ahead about how he could warn him. He continued wiping his forehead with his handkerchief.

"He left early this morning," Frank said. "Why do you want him?"

The sergeant resisted slapping the sarcastic young Polish boy but was eager to get to the house where his brother might be. He jumped on his horse.

"Get back to your plowing and stay there," the sergeant said. "Hurry up before he gets away," he beckoned to his comrades.

They rode off at a gallop toward the house.

Frank quickly draped the reins over the horses' necks so they wouldn't drift away from the field and ran as fast as he could over the plowed field, which was difficult until he reached the solid ground.

Dashing through the front door, he saw the soldiers holding his father, George Romanek, by his hair and slamming his head into the table, demanding where his son Alex was. George kept repeating that he didn't know where his son was while the soldiers continued punching him in the stomach, another soldier kicked him in the groin while others restrained his mother on a kitchen chair as she tried to get away to help her husband.

The house was one large room that was sectioned off. In one corner, hay was placed on the floor where the children slept. The kitchen table and chairs were placed near the fireplace where Mary Romanek's kitchen utensils clustered on the hearth. Upstairs was the loft that served as the parents' bedroom.

Frank was stunned and angered to see the soldiers tossing around the bedding and clothes every which way looking for something. It was obvious that Alex couldn't be hiding there. Frank rushed forward to help his father only to be struck in the head with the butt of a rifle.

The officer holding the elder Romanek continued pounding his head.

"Tell us where Alex is or we're going to apply the same treatment to your wife," the officer snarled.

George looked up at the soldier, blood running out from the open wound on his head and into his eyes. All he could make out was the large curly mustache and brown stained teeth.

"Please believe me, I don't know where he is," George pleaded. "He left early this morning to sell a pig so we could get money to buy seed for the planting. He should be home in a short time."

The officer slammed his head onto the table again. George's face was swollen and the blood flowed freely from the open cuts above his eyes.

"Alexander is a good boy," George cried. "Why do you want him?"

"Liar!" the officer shouted. He swung his arm into the elderly Romanek's face, opening another cut below his right eye.

"The whole village knows that Alex is the leader of the resistance," the officer screamed. "They've been planning action against the government for months. Now you better tell us where he is or we're going to work on your wife and son who's lying unconscious by the door."
The officer leaned over and grabbing the old man's hair, pulling his face next to his.

"Tell me where he is or your wife is next." He threw a haymaker at his head, knocking him off the stool.

George lay on the floor with his hands covering his head to protect himself.

"I swear I don't know where Alexander is," he whispered, his voice barely audible.

The soldier standing over Frank noticed him rousing and kicked him sharply in the ribs. "Where is your brother, or your mother is next," the soldier said.

Frank spat on the soldier's pants and was kicked again. Frank bit him on the leg and the soldier slammed the butt of his rifle against the side of his head.

"Please, he's just a small boy!" his mother cried out. "We told you the truth, we don't know where Alexander is. He took a team of horses and the wagon with the pig to sell. He could be anywhere right now. Soon as he sells the pig, he'll come home."

She pleaded to the officer who was standing over her husband.

"Do what you want to us but leave the young boy alone," she said. "He's no threat to anyone. I beg you to have some compassion."

A soldier came down from the loft, carrying some papers. He went over to the soldier in charge.

"Sergeant, I found a letter addressed to Alexander Romanek from the florist in the village," he said. "Looks like he works there."

The sergeant snatched the letter to examine it closer.

"Does Alexander work at the flower shop?" he asked

"Papa, don't tell them anything," Frank said, as he regained consciousness. "They––"

The soldier standing over him slammed his rifle butt to the side of his head. Blood gushed out of the open cut when he was knocked out.

Mary Romanek wrenched herself free from the soldiers' grasp and ran to her son who was lying unconscious on the floor, she fell to her knees and lifted her son's head to her bosom and wiped the blood with her apron.

"Let her be," the sergeant said, waving his hand dismissively. "Let's go get the revolutionist."

He moved toward the door and beckoned to the soldier standing there.

"Stay here and keep watch," the sergeant said. "I'll leave another soldier out in front. If Alexander happens to come back and we missed him on the way, hold him here and if he resists, don't be afraid to shoot him."

He pointed to the others.

"If they try to do anything to stop you, shoot them," he said.

The remaining soldier backed up to the door and placed his stool against it. He sat watching the family with his rifle on his lap and his finger on the trigger. Mary tore her apron in strips and applied a compress to her son's open cuts. She placed her sweater under his head as a pillow. She then walked over to her husband to tend his wounds.

Meanwhile, Polish partisans were summoned to assist Alex and drove their wagon hard toward the village, whipping their horses to get there faster. The local partisans who were employed at the Russian consulate told these partisans that an

By Frank L. Golon, Sr.

order was issued to arrest Alexander Romanek and deport him to Siberia.

They stopped their horses in front of the flower shop and one of the youths ran into the flower shop looking for Alex. He spotted him waiting on a woman customer and rushed up to him, not bothering to excuse himself.

"Alex, you have get out of here right away," the boy panted, catching his breath. "The Russians are coming to arrest you. They sent soldiers to your house to pick you up and they'll be here shortly. You have to hurry, we have a wagon and a fast team of horses to take you to the German border."

Alex knew it would be some time before the soldiers could find him. His farm was ten kilometers away from the village. He placed his arm around the youth to calm him down and slowly walked to the wagon.

"We have too much work to do before I leave the country," Alex told the partisans. "I'll hide in the forest up by the lake, they won't find me there. I can get food from the villagers around the cabin. They're members of our group."

"You can't stay," said the oldest partisan, coming to place his hand firmly on Alex's shoulder. "Someone in our group informed on you and we don't know who it is. He'd soon find out and inform again."

The man handed Alex an envelope.

"Here is your steam ship ticket to America and enough money to pay for your expenses," he said. "You'll be met by one of our patriots who will find you a job and a place to live. Everything is written in the letter. Hurry now before the Russians soldiers come. Simon will drive you to the forest, there's a path marked with red paint on every fifth tree at the base that'll lead you to a place at the German border where no sentry is posted. At the start of the path, the first tree will have a 'no trespassing' sign. Follow that path, while looking on the right side for the markings."

He helped Alex up into the wagon and hugged him.

"Alex, God bless you for all that you did for us," the old man said. "We'll get the rat who informed on you. Now go."

Alex reached down to hug each of the partisans. Then he summoned Simon to ride. They rode off in a cloud of dust making their way across Poland toward the German border. They drove all day and stopped only to water the horses and rest them for a short while.

Alex, a tall quiet man in his early twenties, had a fury toward the Russians. It ran counter to his placid exterior, which hid the rage inside. After years of watching the Russians bleed and abuse his people, Alex devised a plan to outwit them.

Most of the farmers were poor and raised just enough to feed their families. Each year at harvest time, the Russian government came to collect part of their livestock and half of their crop as taxes. It was so unfair, no matter how poor the crop was due to the weather conditions or the drought, they took half. There were many times the farmers would have starved if it weren't for the neighbors who helped each other.

For months, Alex rode on horseback to each of the farmhouses proposing a system to combat the tax. At harvest time the partisans posted a sentry on the only road leading to the village. They had prepared in advance to cart the livestock into the forest, hiding it, leaving only the stock that was registered with the Russian government.

The Russians threatened to burn their homes if they didn't increase their livestock production but the farmers cried that they had too little food to feed their family and livestock.

The Russians suspected trickery and sent an agent to investigate. The agent mysteriously disappeared and when the thaw set in they found his body frozen to death alongside his dead horse. No explanation surfaced and the Russians felt even more suspicious.

At dusk, the wagon reached the forest. They both dismounted the wagon and looked around carefully, making sure no one was around. The area was clear. Alex placed his arm around the youth.

"Simon, be careful," he warned. "Don't use the same road going back." He took the envelope from his pocket and pulled out some money.

"Here are some rubles to buy a few sacks of potatoes from the first village that you come to," Alex said. "If you're stopped by anyone just say you're delivering them."

Simon placed the rubles in his pocket as his eyes filled with tears.

"We will miss you Alex," Simon said. He mounted the wagon, yet hesitated to leave.

"I'll write as soon as I get to America," Alex said. "Thank everyone for their help and please get word back to my parents that I'm safe. I know that they will be worried about me."

Alex then turned and disappeared into the forest.

Alex found the markings which led him safely into Germany. Farmers going to the market gave him a ride in their wagon. His fluent Russian, Polish and German skills helped when agents stopped him as he was about to board the ship. He showed them his ticket along with his passport and they allowed him to board.

As soon as he was on board, he went to meet with the kitchen staff and asked if they needed his help. They gladly took him on, relieved to get someone to do the dirty work, such as the dishes, peeling the potatoes and cleaning up after the cooks. Alex was able to get money to cover his expenses while crossing the Atlantic Ocean.

After landing in America the passengers were taken to Ellis Island to be examined physically and mentally and to make sure their passports were in order.

The agent took his papers from Alex's hand to examine them. After reading them a moment, he tapped Alex on the shoulder.

"Pick up your bag and look outside where the visitors usually wait," the agent said. "I have to talk to your friend or relative to get more information and the address of where you'll be staying."

Alex was worried. What if his friend didn't get there? There was so little time to get the information to him. He looked around at the people standing there and recognized a huge man standing outside the gate. He had on blue coveralls and a wide brim straw hat with a red band around it. He gave a sigh of relief as he approached the man.

"I'm Alexander Romanek," he said in Polish.

"Welcome to America, I'm Wadlock Retkowski," the man said. They shook hands and Wadlock addressed the immigration officer.

"I'm here to take Alexander Romanek to Morristown, New Jersey," Wadlock said. "He'll be working for Mr. John Shelton."

Wadlock took the papers from his pocket and handed them to the immigration officer.

The officer examined the papers thoroughly and handed them back to Wadlock, telling him everything was in order.

"Welcome to America," the officer said to Alex. "I hope you find what you're looking for here. Good luck."

The officer shook Alex's hand. Alex was so excited, he hugged the officer.

Wadlock took Alex's small cloth bag and led him toward his wagon that was parked outside the gate.

"Alex, I've been waiting several hours here and was afraid that you might have been caught before you got out of Poland," Wadlock said. "I received a letter from my brother-in-law, Paul Kwasniewski and he explained all the good work you did for the people. If there is any way I can help while you're in America just let me know."

"Paul is one of my most trusted patriots," Alex said. "He's the only one working the farm since his father got sick. You know his brother left home and is a sailor on a Greek freighter. In spite of all the work that was dumped on him, Paul came to almost every meeting to help."

Alex paused before continuing.

"We'll never be free until we get rid of the Russians."

They crossed the Hudson River on a ferry and rode through New Jersey. They rode on the dirt roads, passing many flourishing farms.

"Wadlock, is the farm that I'll be working on is as large as that one?" Alex asked, as they passed by a large, sprawling farm.

"Mr. Shelton's farm is much bigger but you'll be working in the green house," Wadlock said. "Mrs. Shelton enters all kinds of flower shows in New York City and wins all types of ribbons. I told her that you worked as a horticulturist and she's anxious to have you run her greenhouse. She's very proud of growing the best flowers in America. Most of them are rare flowers and cost Mr. Shelton a lot of money."

"I know everything about flowers," Alex said, relieved. "I'm sure I'll be able to help the lady. Are there many Polish people nearby?"

"Your Aunt Martha runs a rooming house for Polish people that come to this country," Wadlock said. "Maybe some of them are from your village. It seems like every Polish immigrant that comes to this country are told to look up your aunt. She's helped a lot of people. The rooming house is in Wayne Township, which is about fifteen kilometers from where you'll be working and staying."

Alex recalled that the last time he saw his mother's sister was when she was leaving for America. They were all so proud of her, leaving her home for a new country, not knowing anyone there and unable to speak the language. He looked forward to seeing her again.

Mrs. Shelton met them as they pulled up near the barn. She was immediately impressed by Alex and took him to the greenhouse to show him her flower collection. Alex, in turn, was impressed with the wide selection of rare flowers. He walked by each flower, touching the soil to feel if they had enough water and turned to her nodding his approval. She knew instantly that he would be a great addition to her farm.

Alex worked tirelessly to please Mrs. Shelton. As a reward, Mrs. Shelton spent hours teaching him how to read and write English.

Alex existed on bare necessities and his only luxury was to visit his aunt and his Polish friends. The Sheltons allowed him to use the wagon and a team of horses every Saturday and Sunday so he could visit his aunt and on occasions visit New York City.

In the city he would marvel the enormous buildings and sit with a cup of coffee in Washington Square, watching people enjoy their day off. He saw people playing bocce ball and others sitting at tables playing dominoes. He watched lovers walking by holding hands in the filtering sunlight, young children careening in and out of the crowd chasing one another.

Everyone was so relaxed. It was so different than what Alex experienced in Poland. But someone watching him would say he was relaxed here, too. Here he found the freedom that he sought all his life. He yearned to share this freedom with his whole family. He planned to put money in the bank every month until he had enough to bring his brother over. Then they would pool their money and bring the whole family to America.

Initially, Alex thought Patrick, his eldest brother, should come first. However Patrick had gotten married and didn't want to leave his pregnant wife with his parents, who were struggling to make ends meet from the meager income from their small farm.

Instead, Patrick suggested that Frank come to America first since he had no such commitments.

Frank had fully recovered from his head wounds and his hatred for the Russians became deeply embedded. Time and time again, he tried to join the partisans but they refused because the Romanek family was always under Russian surveillance.

George Romanek was sickly and working the farm became Frank's responsibility since Patrick had left home after he got married and rented a small farm nearby. Their brother John was inducted into the Polish military and their only sister, Mary, was planning for her wedding in the coming fall. Steve, the youngest, was only 10 and could only help with light chores.

George Romanek was dependent on Frank to keep the farm going and initially wouldn't allow him to go to America. They argued constantly because his father refused to give Frank the ticket for the ship and the money that Patrick had left him. Finally after arguing constantly, one day his father threw the ticket and the money on the floor.

"Take the ticket and money," George Romanek yelled. "I'm tired of fighting with you but you promise that you'll wait until your mother comes back."

Mary Romanek was just outside of Warsaw at a prayer retreat. Warsaw was quite a distance from their farm.

"Father, she knows the ship is sailing in two days," Frank said. "I told her before she left that I might be gone before she got back and she understood. I have to leave for Gdańsk tomorrow."

"We'll leave at dawn tomorrow," said his father, sighing from resignation. "Pack up the clothes that you'll need. The wagon is loaded with supplies and that has to be unloaded now. When you'll be ready to unload it, Steve will help you. Now get going."

The following morning, they drove in silence. It was emotional for George Romanek because he felt like his family was breaking apart. Steve had tears in his eyes as his brother took him in his arms to hug him for the last time in many years. They embraced again and kissed each other on the cheek. Frank placed both hands on his brother's cheeks.

"Alex and I will work hard to get enough money to bring all of you to America," he promised. "It took Alex a year to get enough money to bring me over, so it should take us only six months to bring you." He hugged his father and kissed him on both cheeks as he blinked away the tears. "Papa, we'll have you and mother over with us before you know it."

His father shook his head.

"I don't think so, son," George said. "We're too old to travel that far. Write often, mother will be so worried. Give Alex our love and tell him we pray for him every day and that we miss him so much."

The elder Romanek turned and walked back to the wagon.

Steve started to follow his father but suddenly ran back to his brother. He hugged Frank again before joining his father in the wagon. They both waved as they drove off.

* * *

Still an attractive woman in spite of having born six children, Mary Romanek kept herself trim by working on the farm and taking care of her grown children. She was a devout Catholic who traveled many kilometers with her female neighbors to attend yearly prayer retreats on the outskirts of Warsaw.

The Russian government outlawed the people's right to worship, yet in spite of that, many officials turned their backs when the women went to mass.

The church was a small white building with a steeple and a cross on top. It consisted of one large room, with folding chairs facing a table that served as an altar. The Catholic priest was in his 60's and frail, suffering from arthritis. He survived on the bare necessities that the parishioners supplied him with which included fresh vegetables, meat and used clothing.

Mary entered the church searching for her young friend, Ann Pupek. She enjoyed talking to her. Ann was only seventeen and full of excitement that she was going to America. Ann waved at Mary, pointing to an empty seat next to her. It was the last day of the retreat and the women were preparing to return home.

Suddenly an interruption occurred during the mass. A rowdy group of Russian Cossacks stormed the church, cursing and flailing their whips at the women. One of them carried a bomb and set it on the floor in the center of the room next to where the women were sitting. There were no men attending the church services. The men were back at their farms tending to their work or working in the factories near Warsaw. As they caught sight of the Cossacks, the women began panicking, scattering out of the church as they were whipped by the Cossacks on their legs and butts. During the intrusion, the old priest ran toward the bomb to remove it only to be hit on the head with a rifle butt, rendering him unconscious.

Mary and Ann stood there paralyzed with fear, hearing only the ticking of the bomb. Mary rolled the rosary between her fingers.

"Let's get this thing out of here before it goes off killing the priest and destroying our church," Mary said. In shock, they carefully picked up the bomb, carrying it past the unconscious priest. They took it outside of the building and brought it to the center of the field that was surrounding the church and gently placed it on the ground and sprinted back to the church. They just got into the church when the bomb exploded, shaking the countryside and spewing debris like an erupting volcano. The women clung to each other, dodging the rubble as it spewed around them.

"Can you believe we did that?" Mary asked, the adrenaline leaving and making way for shock. "I'd never forgive myself if we were killed."

"I wouldn't forgive you either," Ann said. They both burst out in nervous laughter, still in disbelief that they took such action and were alive. A special bond that was never unbroken was formed that day.

The women made their way back to the church, stepping uncertainly over the now disrupted landscape. They clustered around the old priest, dabbing his wounds and reassuring him.

When the priest came to, he asked them a question.

"How could you both be so brave?" he said. "You two were wonderful."

"I came here to ask God to watch over my sons, Alexander and Frank and for the whole family to reunite in America," Mary said. Mary was worried about Frank who had a deep hatred toward the Russians. She feared that he would soon be arrested and sent to Siberia. She prayed that her husband would understand and let Frank go before they lost him forever.

"My family and I live in such fear," said Ann. "I've been saving my money that I earned cooking for the rich people in Warsaw. As soon as I get enough money to buy a steamship ticket, I'll be off to America."

"How are you going to live there not knowing anyone there and not being able to speak the language?" asked Mary, a sadness entering her at the thought of her friend leaving.

"Look at your sister," Ann shrugged. "She went and is doing fine. I'm not afraid of hard work and I'm a good cook. I'll work for the rich like I did here. Maybe I'll go to New Jersey to see your sister and get some advice on what to do."

"I'll write to Martha and ask her to help you, maybe by that time my Frank will be there," Mary said. "He's such a handsome man and I'm sure you'll like him."

The two women hugged one another before separating, never to see one another again.

Ann lived on a small farm with her parents on the outskirts of Warsaw. She was an only child and did most of the housework. She also helped the family by feeding the livestock and cleaning the barn. She was a talented cook who was called on frequently by the rich to cook the meals at parties or rich merchants when they entertained. Every Friday evening and Saturday morning she cooked and did manual chores for a rich family. Whatever she earned her parents allowed her to keep. Every ruble she collected she placed in a small wooden box, looking for the day when she would be able to buy a steamship ticket to go to America.

She refused to be distracted by any young man, fearing that she would fall in love with someone who didn't share her dreams. She had no formal education but taught herself how to read and write. She constantly gathered books from the schoolhouse to learn all about America, reading in between her daily chores and in the evenings. Often she'd run to show her mother pictures of beautiful large homes and farms with abundant crops and barns filled with livestock. The pictures she showed captured women standing in front of beautiful homes and dressed in gorgeous dresses, parasols and beautiful feathered hats. She wanted to share in that rich and beautiful life.

Her parents were frightened by her desire for a different life, but they knew she was doing the right thing. They were in constant fear of the Russians, who thought nothing of raping or killing anyone who went against them. When the Russians came to collect their taxes, her parents hid Ann in the forest. Her father always stayed home when the Russians came to protect his wife from them. For protection, Polish farmers depended on the patriots who patrolled the area to warn them in advance when the Russian soldiers were coming.

* * *

The trip to cross the Atlantic Ocean to America took more than three weeks. Frank spent most of his time leaning over the rail, retching and throwing up everything he ate, suffering from persistent seasickness. He was miserable during the entire trip and was glad when they arrived at Ellis Island.

After getting off the boat, Frank was standing next to the immigration officer, confused and overwhelmed by the flood of people searching for families and loved ones. Then Frank saw his brother standing nearby. Immediate joy entered his heart.

"Alex, I'm over here," Frank said. Alex broke into a huge smile and ran over to his brother. They embraced and Alex pushed him back at arm's length.

"Frank, you grew quite a bit since I last saw you," Alex said.

Alex also looked different to Frank, with longer hair, a mustache and he was dressed in a black suit with polished shoes. He looked more muscular than Frank remembered.

"You're going to love it here," Alex said, grabbing Frank's few items. "It's much different than Poland."

As they walked to the car, Alex mentioned a job at Shelton's farm. While they were riding through New Jersey, Alex gave him the lay of the land.

"Mr. Shelton is very rich and is a good man to work for," he said. "Over here is not like it is in Poland, you have to work hard but the pay is fair. You'll find Mr. Shelton a considerate man but he expects everyone to do a fair day's work. It's nothing you can't handle.

He stopped talking for a moment to study his brother whom he hadn't seen for over a year.

"You've grown a lot since the last time I saw you," Alex said, eyeing Frank. "You'll be paid thirty dollars a month with room and board included. The food is good and we sleep in a small house behind the barn. Every month, I put aside $25 to save so I can bring the rest of the family here."

Frank seemed to not listen and was admiring the countryside instead.

"You're not listening to a word I said," Alex said.

"I just can't get over the beauty of this country," Frank explained. "It's nothing like Poland. Alex, I heard every word you said. I won't let you down. We'll double what you put away. My needs are few."

Alex slapped the horses with the reins to hurry them along. He was amazed to see how much Frank resembled their father.

"We'll have a good time while earning money," Alex said. "At Aunt Martha's you'll meet many friends. I buy a bottle of vodka that we all share at Aunt Martha's house and Mr. Shelton allows me to use the wagon and team of horses to bring fresh vegetables to her. He heard about a lot of good things Aunt Martha has done for our people."

Frank interrupted.

"I almost forgot," he began. "Zachary Ktezewski told me they got the informer who ratted you out to the Russians. It was Ed Kraski who works in the livery stable. He had an accident with one of the horses going wild and it stamped him to death before anyone could come help him."

Alex nodded his head and kept steady hands on the reins. His old life in Poland felt so far away.

They arrived at the estate just before dusk. Turning the bend of the road was a large white house surrounded with shrubbery and flowers, with a deep green lawn extending right up to the road. Behind the house stood the glass greenhouse where his brother worked. On the other side of the road stood a large red barn with both doors wide open. He saw the cows munching on hay, the pigs wallowing in the mud and the chickens chuckling away on the rail fence. A farmhand was unloading a wagon full of hay and stopped a moment to wave to them. He was using a block and tackle to haul the bales of hay to the upper loft of the barn.

The front door of the large house opened and a beautiful woman came out to greet Alex. This had to be Mrs. Shelton. She was tall, in her early 40's. She was wearing a long black silk skirt, with a lace white high collar blouse tucked in at the waist, accenting her hourglass figure. On her feet were black high heels. Her brown hair was swept away from her face and a fancy hat sat atop her head. Her smile was bright and warm as she walked over to greet them. Frank had never seen such a beautiful woman.

Alex stopped the horses and jumped off the wagon.

"Mrs. Shelton, this is my brother, Frank," Alex said.

"Welcome to America, Frank," Mrs. Shelton said, displaying her even, white teeth. "I hope you'll be happy here with us. "

Frank didn't understand a word she said but assumed she was greeting him. He replied "thank you" to her in Polish as he took her hand to kiss it.

Alex translated and Mrs. Shelton smiled with a slight blush reddening her cheeks.

"I'm sure your brother is going to do just fine in America," she said. "He must be tired after his long journey. Set him up in the bunkhouse and get yourselves something to eat. You both must be starved." She turned gracefully and walked into the house. Frank was impressed by how beautiful, rich ladies conducted themselves.

They rode to the barn and Frank unhitched the horses and began to rub them down while Alex went to get the feed and water. The bunkhouse was similar to his home in Poland. There was one large room with bunk beds lining the wall and a large table in the center of the room with chairs set around the table.

Alex placed Frank's meager belongings on an empty bed,

"You'll sleep here and I have the bed next to you," Alex told his brother. "We'll place your things in my trunk when we get back after supper. I'll show you around and where you'll be working tomorrow."

He raised the lid of his trunk. He had very few clothes in spite of the fact that he was here over a year. They walked in the field, the corn was starting to husk and the beans were ready to be picked. The trees in the orchard were laden with fruit.

"I can't believe that so much could be grown on one farm," Frank mused. "We'd be millionaires if we had a farm like this back home."

"There are many small farms around here that have a high yield of crops," Alex said. "In America, the weather is ideal for all kinds of crops. If you think this farm is big, you should see the ones in the Midwest of the country. They're ten times as large. We are in New Jersey, which is mostly known for dairy farms. When we visit Aunt Martha's house, we'll see many large farms on the way."

From the outset, Frank worked very hard from early morning till dusk. Some of the farmhands complained to Alex that Frank worked like a bull and were afraid that the Sheltons would expect the same from them. Alex managed the situation diplomatically, understanding that his brother had a strong desire to be successful in America but wanting to avoid tension with the others. Alex was able to transfer Frank to a job where he worked alone and everyone was satisfied.

Every Sunday, the brothers visited Aunt Martha's home. It was there that Frank met Anna Pupek. Anna remembered her good friend Mary Romanek telling her about her handsome son, Frank. Mary was right. It was love at first sight for the both of them.

Anna was successful in obtaining a job as a chef at the hotel located in the center of the town. Initially the waitresses would give Anna orders in English and then Martha would translate. Eventually Anna learned English and was able to understand the orders on her own. She was known for her flair for seasonings, preparing meals to perfection.

All available bachelors in town wanted to date Anna, but she had eyes only for Frank Romanek. He grew into a handsome young man. He was over six feet tall, and with a sculpted and muscular body from all the hard work from his day job. He could drink with the best of them and during the Polish dance festival, he'd do the polka with Anna. Everyone enjoyed watching the couple dance. Both Anna and Frank were accomplished dancers in their own right. The crowd would step aside to watch Frank swing Anna over his back and bring her down gracefully. All the dancers clapped when the dance concluded.

This was typical of the life they lived in America. Existing on bare necessities, but enjoying life when not working.

Frank put away 25 dollars monthly toward bringing the rest of the family to America. In less than a year, Alex and Frank saved enough money to be able to bring Patrick and his family to America. When they met their brother at Ellis Island, Patrick explained that the rest of the family refused to leave Poland. John was discharged from the Polish army and was working the family farm. Mary got married and was living happily on a small farm.

Patrick suggested that Alex and Frank continue to pool their money to help the family to buy more land and livestock because they barely had enough to live on. All the brothers agreed.

Frank and Anna met every weekend for dates. They'd go on picnics or to the lake. Soon after they were married at the

Catholic Church in town and had a reception at Aunt Martha's rooming house. There weren't many guests but there was plenty of food and drinks for everyone. They even had an accordion player so they were able to dance.

After the wedding Frank took his bride back with him to the Sheltons who had provided them with a small, furnished house and all the food they needed. Frank continued to work for a small salary but was restless with his job as a farmhand and wanted to give Anna a better life. He heard the factories were paying a good wage and wanted to make a change.

One Sunday afternoon while visiting Aunt Martha, Frank took Alex aside.

"The Sheltons have always been good to me but I have get a job that makes more money," Frank said. "I can't expect Anna to live like we are now. She's expecting a baby in six months and we need so many things. I know that I'll make three times as much if I work in the city."

Alex realized that this mean Frank would have to quit working for the Sheltons, but he was supportive.

"Frank, you do what's best for your family," Alex said. He knew for months that his brother was destined for better things. He put his arm around his younger brother.

"I have a trade that pays me very well," Alex said. "I knew for a long time that you weren't satisfied working here so I took it on myself to meet with Mr. Shelton and ask him to give you a job in one of his factories. He agreed and has a job opening for a fireman's job in the boiler house that pays 100 dollars a month. When you get the engineering license it will pay a lot more.

Frank was elated and grabbed his brother in a bear hug.

"I'll take the job, when can I start?" Frank said.

"We'll talk to Mr. Shelton first thing in the morning," Alex said.

Frank had been turning over a major portion of his salary to Alex and had very little money in the bank.

"You'll have to live in the city," Alex told Frank. "You have no furniture to set up an apartment. What will you do? "

Aunt Martha overheard her nephews talking. She offered Anna's old room, which was still empty until Frank had enough money to set up their own apartment.

When Frank got home he sat Anna down in their kitchen and explained everything he had done. She was thrilled with the new job and a place to call their own. The following morning, they met with Mr. Shelton who put him to work at his factory that was walking distance from where Anna and Frank were now living. Life was good in America, and it was getting better day-by-day.

Chapter 3
Year 1964

The day after the election, Johnny Romanek strolled into the empty union meeting hall. It was a mess; littered with empty beer bottles, coffee containers and union literature. Talley sheets, slate cards and campaign promises were scattered all over the tables. The strong smell of beer and cigarettes lingered. He glanced at the voting machines, still locked securely in the center of the hall.

He couldn't help but wonder why the first three machines favored Don. His first thought was that he peaked during the last week of the campaign and was on his way down but he dismissed that idea as he began to study his campaign pledge. He promised members fully paid medical insurance, paid drug prescriptions, improved working conditions and even more benefits.

Johnny was hired into the Ford Motor Company before there was a union. There he studied each of the previous president's demands for the contract. Most advocated a large wage increase but no meaningful benefits.

Walter Reuther changed that thinking when he became the president of the United Auto Workers Union. In 1950, he challenged General Motors until he won the first pension at an industrial company. Walter realized that Social Security could never support a family when the worker retired. Walter also secured health insurance benefits for all autoworkers and a cost of living clause that guaranteed employees a raise.

Johnny spoke in favor of this proposal at a membership meeting. He realized the necessity of this through the eyes of his father who was approaching retirement age and his need for a supplement to Social Security to provide a stable life with his wife.

Johnny campaigned for six months before the union election. He spoke to each member working the line, while taking a coffee break, in the cafeteria, in the parking lot and outside the plant. He listened to the members' complaints about the high cost of doctors and hospitals bills. Many bought homes when they got home after World War II and complained about high taxes. There were a few members that blew most of their paychecks on drinks and some gambling. Many of them didn't have enough to take care of their family needs.

Johnny realized that protective benefits were essential. When he presented his ten-point program at his caucus meeting, many opposed it and favored a large wage increase. He convinced them that his program was a tax saver with security and protection for the member's family. Many dubbed his program "pie in the sky" and only a gimmick to garner votes.

The day after winning the election, Johnny knew better. He climbed the stairs of the union offices. He walked through the double glass doors, Betty Morrow, the union secretary was typing the results of the union election to be mailed to the International Union Office in Detroit. Everything was business with Betty. She was efficient with her desk organized with filling cabinets with separate drawers for grievances, seniority lists, classifications and rates for every job in the Assembly Plant. She was completely devoted to her job. She was a beautiful redhead in her early thirties, with eyeglasses on the top of her head and a pencil stuck in her hair. Today she looked up from her work with a proud expression on her face.

"Congratulations," she said to Johnny. "I know you're going to be great as president." After all, he was her favorite union official over the years. He was soft-spoken, considerate at all times and showed the greatest respect whenever he came to the office. She looked forward to working for him for the next two years.

"I'm sure going to need all the help I can get with this split executive board and only one committeeman on the day shift elected from my caucus," Johnny said. "I'm going to be looking to you for a lot of help, you'll be my right hand here at the office."

He picked up her report and reviewed the results of the election. He asked her to get in touch with all the elected officers and committeemen to notify them of a meeting he scheduled for that day at 2:30 in the afternoon.

"If anyone says they can't come, please let me know," Johnny said.

He headed for his office but hesitated.

"Betty, Don Byrne will be coming in to get his personal stuff," Johnny said. "When he gets here, tell him to come to my office. I want to meet with him for a little bit. Another thing before I forget, contact whoever does our office cleaning to come in right away. That hall downstairs stinks to the high heavens."

Just as he was about to enter his office, Don came in. Johnny waved for him to come into the office.

"Congratulations, wish you a lot of luck, you're going to need it," Don said.

Johnny smiled.

"I want to talk a little politics with you," Johnny said. "First, I'm planning to put you on union business for the next two weeks to give you time to set up a job at the plant or to do whatever you want. If there is a job in the plant that you want, just let me know. I'll do everything I can to help you. I'll authorize the lost time to be paid by our local at your present rate or the newer rate if it's higher. I know it's not going to be easy for you to go back working in the plant after being president for so many years. If any of my guys try to give you a hard time, let me know and I'll put a stop to that immediately."

There was a knock on the door, Betty entered with a tray of sweet buns and a pot of hot coffee.

"I know you have important things to discuss but I thought you both could enjoy having some coffee," she said.

"You're a darling," said Johnny, grabbing the tray. "If anyone comes to see me, including Rocky, don't interrupt us. "

When it was just the two of them, Don turned to Johnny.

"Johnny, I'm going to lay my cards on the table," he said. "Last night when Bummy broke Jack Robert's jaw, we knew Rocky was playing both sides against the middle. He wanted to make sure that he got elected. I was told that Al Carter made those phony slate cards with Rocky's consent but I'm not sure of that."

Don took a moment and gulped some coffee.

"I'm not trying to drive a wedge between you and Rocky," Don said. "I just want you to be aware of who your friends are. Another thing. Be careful with how you deal with Tony Rodgers, he's a bastard. He commented that you have a short fuse and he could provoke you at will. Watch your step when you're dealing with him. He takes pride in making the union look bad."

"I'm well aware of Rocky and his tricks for years," said Johnny, chewing on a sweet bun. "And Tony, I know him well, too. Whenever I went to see him about any issue, he wants you to know, he's doing you a favor. I'd like to ask you a little about Lou Sargent. I know he has a hatred for me because I beat you in the election. Do you think he'll play along with the company to make me look bad when we're in negotiations? "

"Lou's not that way," Don said, swallowing the last bit of coffee. "He hates Tony Rodgers more than he hates you. Tony tried his best to get him fired when he had a fight with one of the foreman last year. Don't get me wrong, if you ever make a mistake, Lou will take advantage of that. You got to remember that you did some job on him during the election. "

"He didn't treat me with me with any kid gloves," Johnny said. "I still have the scars on my back to prove it.

Don nodded.

"It was a rough election but you got to understand that he feels like he lost his right arm when I lost."

"I realize that," said Johnny. "It's going to be an interesting two years."

"Before I forget, the current grievances are in the top drawer of the cabinet and the communications with the International Union and the Ford Motor Company are in the second drawer," said Don. "Betty set up the filing system so if you get stuck just ask her."

He got up from the sofa to shake hands with Johnny.

"Thanks again for the leave, you didn't have to do that but I appreciate it," Don said.

Rocky was standing near Betty's desk as Don took a somber walk out of the union headquarters. When Don was out of earshot, Rocky turned to Johnny.

"I hope you convinced him to line up his forces behind us when we take on the company," Rocky said. "We're going to need a lot of help."

"No such luck but we did talk a little politics," Johnny said. "I'd like to discuss this combined meeting we're having this afternoon."

Rocky helped himself to the coffee and buns and sprawled out on the sofa.

"I called this meeting to unite both forces to get the most from the company," Johnny said. "I need your help to neutralize Lou Sargent. See if you could convince him to go along with our thinking. If he tries to hurt us, I'll cut his balls off."

Rocky nodded his head in agreement as Johnny continued.

"The board is split down the middle but we have control with the presidency," Johnny said. "I'm sure we'll get our way most of the time but if they go along with our program, it'll make our job easier."

Johnny walked to the front of his desk and sat on the edge.

"Those first three machines bother me, once the voting trend is established, it usually follows the same pattern," Johnny said. "I asked Timmy if he left the machines at any time during the election. He said he had on two occasions but each time he had Al Carter relieve him."

He watched for any reaction from Rocky, seeing none he continued.

"Timmy assured me that no one went near any of the machines on his watch," Johnny said. "I'd like to get together with Al to see if he noticed any irregularities while he was watching."

"Oh," Rocky began. "Uh, as a matter of fact, I talked with Al about those machines. He mentioned while he was watching he got a phone call from George's office but when he got there, no one was on the phone. He wasn't gone but a couple of minutes. There was no way anyone could tamper with the machines in that short time."

Rocky nervously moved his coffee cup in his hand.

Johnny sensed that some thing must have happened for Rocky to admit that Al had left the machines unattended. He knew that Rocky and Al were inseparable in and out of the plant. He rose from his desk, brushing the hair from his eyes.

"I'm going to set up an investigating committee to see if there was any wrongdoing taking place during the midnight shift at the polls," Johnny said. "I have a list of the workers on duty from the ballot company. We'll question them separately to get an idea of anything unusual happening. What are your thoughts?"

Rocky looked visibly disturbed.

"Why open up a can of worms and possibly get the election results thrown out?" Rocky stuttered. "We both won so why take a chance of having the election committee rule for a new election? We'd be the only losers then."

"I guess you're right," Johnny acquiesced. "Let's put our focus on the board meeting."

"I'll get to work on Lou to try to get him to cooperate," said Rocky, looking relieved.

Rocky got up from the sofa and quickly headed to the door.

"I'll see you at 2:30," Rocky said.

Pat entered the office as Rocky left.

"Looks like Rocky was in a hurry to leave," Pat said. "What's up?"

Johnny recapped his conversation with Don and Rocky.

"I don't think Rocky was involved with rapping the voting machines," said Johnny. "If he was, he'd never have said anything about Al leaving the machines. I still think we're going to have to watch him very closely."

Before Pat could reply, there was a knock on the door. Betty called out that Timmy Larkin and Al Carter were there to meet.

Timmy walked in and dropped himself down on the sofa looking relaxed. Al followed with a worried expression.

"I've been a union member for over 20 years and this is the first time I've made it to the president's office," Timmy said. "Nice piece of furniture, that mahogany desk. And I like the pictures of Reuther, Bannon and Gerber. If they visited here they'd be proud of your set-up. You're living in the big leagues now."

Pat was about to leave but Johnny asked him to stay.

"Stick around," Johnny said. "What we're going to discuss could be of importance to you."

Pat held the tally sheets in his right hand.

"Timmy, it's those first three machines," Pat said. "There's no doubt in my mind that they were rapped by someone. Did you ever leave those machines unattended?"

"No one got near those machines while I was watching," Timmy said angrily.

No one had ever questioned his integrity before and he resented the question.

"I was away from those on three occasions and each time I had Al relieve me," Timmy said. "Twice I had to take a piss and I was right back. The third time, Al asked me if I wanted to take a lunch break which I took for about an hour."

He turned to Al.

"Did anyone come near the machines while you were watching?" Timmy asked.

"No one came near the machines while I was watching," Al mumbled. "I never left them unattended. It was three o'clock in the morning and there was no one around."

"Huh, that's funny," Johnny said, rubbing his chin in thought. "I talked to Rocky about this and he said, Al, that you had a phone call while you were watching the machines. Was he bullshitting me?"

Johnny looked Al right in the eye.

"Oh…yes, I remember now," Al stuttered, turning red. "Someone came from upstairs and told me I was wanted on the phone. I went upstairs for a couple minutes and came right back."

"Al, who came downstairs to call you to the phone?" Johnny asked.

"I don't remember," Al said, fidgeting on the sofa. "It was three o'clock in the morning and I was half asleep."

"Yeah, you keep mentioning that," Johnny said. "Isn't it strange to get a phone call at three in the morning? And at the same time you relieved Tony to watch the voting machines?"

"Well…I guess, now that you mention it like that, it does seem strange," Al said. "I was upstairs only a couple of minutes and I came right back. No one could rap those machines in that short time."

"Rocky told me that you were offered a drink while you were there," Johnny said. "Did you take it?"

Al got up from the sofa with the realization that he had been trapped in a lie.

"Yeah I…I remember now," Al said. "George was in his office and offered me a drink so I had one with him and I went right back to the machines. But when I went back, no one was around the machines."

"Al, I need you to think hard," Johnny said. "This only happened last night. Rocky told me a lot more than you're telling me now. How many drinks did you have and how long were you away from the machines?"

Al began pacing the floor as Johnny stared at him.

"I remember now," Al said. "I had a few drinks with George but the hall was deserted."

Johnny shot up from the sofa in a flash and stood next to Al.

"Who called you from upstairs to the phone?" Johnny asked. "I want that name now."

"I swear, I don't remember who it was," Al cried. "I swear I don't remember."

"Al, I want that name right now," Johnny thundered. He placed his arm around Al's shoulder.

"Al, we put a lot of money and time into this campaign," Johnny said. "We're going to have a lot of unhappy members when they find out that someone tried to steal our election. We got some rough guys who don't like to be taken advantage of. Think hard, this only happened yesterday."

"It was Pete Rodney, the guy who was the watcher for Don's caucus," Al blurted. He was trembling with his head cast down toward the floor.

"How much did they pay you to take a walk?" Johnny asked.

"Johnny I swear to God, I didn't get any money," Al said. "I just had two short drinks with George and went right back."

"How many votes did they rap on those first three machines and how much did they pay you?" Johnny asked. "And don't you lie. I was told that you were the one who set up that phony slate card putting Don and Rocky as a team together. "

"They gave me 300 dollars, a dollar a vote," Al said. He began sobbing.

"Al, I expect you to do the right thing," Johnny said.

Al gave him a look of confusion.

"I want you to go over to the plant and resign," Johnny said. "If you don't, I'll turn the whole caucus on you. How long could you last with 300 caucus members after your ass?"

"Johnny, please, I need this job," Al pleaded. "Where can I get a job to take care of my family?"

"You should have thought of that when you were selling us out," Johnny said. "What burns me is that you were one of our key players. Was Rocky in on this with you?"

"No, he didn't know anything about this," Al said. "I swear. I'm sorry this ever took place."

Al took out a handkerchief from his pocket to wipe the tears from his face.

"Pat, why don't you go over to the plant with Al to see that he does the right thing," Johnny said, unfazed by Al's tears.

Johnny then turned to Al.

"If you have any idea of changing your mind and sticking around, you'll be the sorriest son-of-a-bitch," Johnny said. "I'll have the company mail you your check and your vacation time."

Al was well aware of Johnny's background and he was one you never crossed. All he wanted was to get out of the office.

"I'll hand in my resignation to the company," Al said. "I'm really sorry that this happened."

Al left the room abruptly.

"Wow, I never thought that he was that kind of a guy," Timmy said. "For a few bucks, he blew a good job and all the goodies he would have received especially from Rocky who depended on him for advice. I know Rocky would have placed him on a good job. It doesn't pay to get greedy."

"I'll lay odds that he had them add votes for Rocky along with Don," Johnny said. "Rocky was his bread and butter. What a fool."

Johnny had to wonder if Rocky was clean in this whole affair.

"What are you going to do about Pete Rodney?" Timmy asked.

"Bummy and I will have a little chat with that character," Johnny said, drumming his fingers on the mahogany table. "He won't be working here long."

"Johnny, be careful," Timmy said. "Don't do anything rash. There's too much to lose if you go overboard."

"Oh, I'll be careful," Johnny said. "Let's forget about this little incident and I'll tell Pat to do likewise. What people out there don't know won't hurt them. We know Al isn't going to go around bragging about what he did."

Johnny placed his arm around Timmy.

"Thanks for all you did for me and our group," Johnny said. "Now take that worried look off your face."

"Johnny, everyone knows that you have a bad temper so don't blow your top," Timmy said. "You're president now. We need you. Don't blow this whole thing over one bad apple."

"I got it Timmy," Johnny said. "I'm in complete control."

* * *

The board members, committeemen and bargaining committee filed into the meeting hall. Some to listen to Johnny's projected programs, others just to put stumbling blocks into his agenda and others came out of sheer curiosity. Johnny ushered all of them into the large conference room across from the auditorium. There were pads and pens placed in front of every chair around the table for everyone to take notes as required.

Johnny lightly tapped his gavel on the table to call the meeting to order.

"I scheduled this meeting so we could all discuss and evaluate the plans that I outlined during the election to bring to the local over the next two years," he said. "It's important that you understand my policies and we are unified when we present them to the membership. The membership elected us to do our job regardless of our political affiliations and now that the election is over, we're obligated to concentrate on our dealings with Ford. We have our work cut out for us. I need the help of all our officers and committeemen to gain our objectives. I intend to incorporate some of Don's points into my program and each of you can have the opportunity to voice your opinions and ideas at this meeting. It's important that we speak with one voice and only one voice when we meet with management. They must see that we're united."

Johnny's supporters felt unity was absolutely necessary, while Don's caucus were plotting to get Johnny on the company's bad side without alerting the membership of their intent. Johnny could read them like an open book but he was going to do his utmost to win them over.

He started the meeting giving the men his background history. He shared how he started at Ford before there was a union.

"Back then we couldn't talk to each other without the security men coming over to tell to do our job," he said. "They were programmed to make sure workers wouldn't talk about organizing a union after United Auto Workers was successful in organizing one for General Motors."

Johnny told the men he was at Ford when the union was built after organizers successfully won the case before the National Labor Relations Board. He mentioned his great support for labor union leader Walter Reuther, and would similarly fight for the benefits Walter secured for autoworkers.

Johnny mentioned the need to increase the time for bathroom breaks, giving workers three days plus pay when an immediate family member dies, improving pensions, and making sure present and future retired workers obtained the same medical coverage. He told the men he was going to be pushing for these demands at the next council meeting. He asked for their feedback on this.

"Johnny, I agree with a lot of your ideas that the benefits are sorely needed but I still feel the number one issue has to be increasing our wages by a substantial amount," George Plassard said. "Most of our members are young, they've bought homes with high mortgages, cars, furniture, you name it. They need the money to make ends meet."

"George, money is important but the taxes involved on that raise will eat us up," Johnny countered, visibly frustrated. "What I outlined is tax free."

"There's a lot of talk about getting a big raise in the next contract but many of us are griping about the high medical co-payment we have to pay when our family members have to go to the doctor," said Pat Fager. "I'm one of the younger men working here and I support what Johnny proposed. He's still asking for a raise, along with new benefits. When we only get money in the form of a raise, the contract looks small but put money and benefits together, it's big and we save money because the government doesn't tax our benefits."

"Let's quit kidding ourselves," Lou Sargent interjected. "We'd have to go on strike for a year to get all those benefits. Our members can't afford to go out on strike at this time. The company lawyers always sit in on contract talks and always watch the cost of any agreement like a hawk. They could hold out longer than us if we went out on strike. They'll fight us tooth and nail. I agree with George since we can get a large wage increase without going on strike. "

"I appreciate your frankness, Lou," Johnny said. "I intend to take my proposals to the United Auto Workers. The assembly line worker is tied to that line and needs that extra 24 minutes of relief plus that extra time will break up the monotony on the job. Today the auto companies are making large profits and they're ripe for the taking. I think we can get all these demands without a strike."

Rocky had his hand up and was already standing. He walked toward the head of the table and stood alongside Johnny.

"Johnny has a lot of new and good ideas," Rocky said. "We got to get behind him on these issues that are important to our members. Our union has to have planners like Johnny to improve working conditions and build protections for our members and their families. I'm 100 percent behind Johnny. I make a motion that we go on record supporting his proposals."

"I second the motion," Pat said, standing.

The motion was carried unanimously to Johnny's pleasant surprise.

Johnny picked up his papers and placed them in his briefcase.

"You guys stick around," he said to Rocky and Lou. "We have a meeting with Tony and Jay at four. We should head there now."

They all met in front of the administration building where Tony Rodger's secretary, Marie, met them. She was stunning, with long blond hair and a tiny waist.

"She's built like a brick house," Rocky whispered to Johnny.

"She your next target?" Johnny retorted.

"You know I never get involved with the girls I work with," Rocky said.

"Bullshit," Johnny said.

Despite their good-natured banter, Johnny was still suspicious of Rocky given the election debacle. But he knew which battles to fight.

"Come in, Rocky, get your eyeballs back in your head," Tony joked. "Most of us here are married. We can look but not touch."

"I sympathize with you married men," Rocky said. "But you sure know how to pick out beautiful secretaries."

Jay Cannon, the plant manager, coughed, clearly uncomfortable with this type of conversation. He was straight-laced and all business.

"Mr. Romanek, I asked Tony to set up this meeting with your bargaining committee here so we could lay the groundwork and get off on the right foot for our future meetings," Jay said. "The union is here to stay and in order for us to succeed, we must have a mutual understanding with each other. I hope you'll find me a fair man and if there is anything within reason that you need, don't hesitate to call Tony or me. I've been told that you are rigid in your demands but I'm hoping we can reach compromises to meet everyone's needs."

"Mr. Cannon, I'm sure we'll get along," Johnny said. "I've worked with Tony over the years and he's tight with the purse strings. I'm hoping you can loosen him up."

It was a known fact that whenever Johnny was denied his contractual rights he simply went to a higher authority to get what he wanted. Rocky wasn't as quick-tempered. He'd negotiate and would often settle. Management was aware of this and knew they had to focus on Johnny, who was tougher to deal with.

Johnny's comment pissed Tony off. Tony was a man of authority married to a former beauty queen. He won an athletic scholarship to Ohio State as a running back in football and a catcher in baseball. He quickly became a star and drew the attention of a vice president at Ford. In spite of the fact that he had no experience with unions and their complex problems, Tony rose through the ranks and secured the number three highest positions in his department. He was six feet tall and his once powerful frame now showed signs of flab, which he covered with perfectly tailored suits.

Since Tony came to Clinton as a manager, he felt that whatever benefits he gave to the union had to serve his interests two-fold. He always looked down on union officials as people with little intelligence who could be easily persuaded to his way of thinking. Johnny's statement angered him but he held his composure.

"Johnny, we've had many meetings over the years where you walked away satisfied," Tony said. "Anything you need we can handle without involving others."

Tony then turned to Rocky.

"Rocky, I always resolved your problems whenever you came to see me, right?" Tony asked, confident that Rocky would answer affirmatively.

"Yes, we were always able to resolve my problems when I came to see you," Rocky said. "I don't know how you dealt with other union officials but you were fair with me."

Rocky was determined to stay on Tony's good side.

Mr. Cannon was a tall man in his early sixties with bushy white hair and heavy eyebrows. He closely watched Johnny's reactions.

"Let's hope you take care of my problems like you did for Rocky," Johnny said. Johnny had too many dealings with Tony to know that he wouldn't give in so easily.

"Johnny, we know your needs," Tony said abruptly, wanting to end the meeting. "We'll be able to work together and we want to wish you all a successful two years."

Lou leaned back in his chair to loosen his tie and open the top button of his shirt. He was a small man who was completely bald from early childhood and shaved his head daily every morning before work. He was a militant leader, respected by his constituents for his competence and daring. Many referred to him as the "bald eagle" but never to his face. He prided himself on the fact that he always took care of his friends and associates in the union.

"Tony, now that Don has to go back to work, where do you intend to place him?" Lou asked.

"Tony, Don is going to be out on union business for the next two weeks," Johnny interrupted. "I think you should place him in an inspector's job."

Don needed an easier job to assuage membership's opinions. If Don was placed on a hard job, the membership would retaliate against Johnny. This had to be settled before the meeting broke up.

"Johnny, the contract is clear regarding when Don has to go back to work," Tony said. "He has to go back to his previous classification after he was defeated in the election, which was a wheel assembler. We'll place him on that and discuss afterward what we can do."

Johnny's eyes blazed with anger.

"Mr. Cannon, that's what I mean about Tony," Johnny exploded. "You just finished saying that you wanted to deal with the union fairly and here's Tony whose quoting the contract and placing an ex-president who was defeated in the election on the hardest job in the plant. Don has a lot of years seniority in the plant and if he were working, he would have been able to bid and get a higher job."

Johnny paused to regain his composure.

"This is Tony at his best, he wants to show our union membership that he can do whatever he wants to any ex-union official," Johnny said. "We can't place Don on a back-breaking job at this point. This is our first official meeting and I have to ask you to intervene."

"Johnny, let's be reasonable," Jay said. "Tony is going by the contract. I'm sure you can come back to see him and figure out a compromise."

"Mr. Cannon, we were elected by the local membership to represent them and their problems," Johnny said. "We have no choice but to come to labor relations to have these problems resolved. Over the years, I've dealt with Tony and Franklin Todd; they're both of the opinion that they're doing us a favor when we come to them and request a resolve for our complaint, whether big or small. I'm not going to sit here and have Don come crawling to Tony's office begging for a job that I feel he's entitled to have."

"Johnny, I don't expect Don to come crawling to my office," Tony interjected.

"Tony, let's put our cards on the table," Johnny said. "Whenever I came to your office with a problem, your famous crack was, 'what am I going to get out of this?'"

Tony tried to respond but Johnny continued.

"Jay, I didn't call this meeting, you did," Johnny said. "While we're meeting I'd like to set up a new procedure to discuss plant problems."

"Jay, called this meeting to get acquainted with the new bargaining committee," Tony said. "We will discuss your new procedure request at another meeting. "

"You were the one who opened up this meeting saying that you wanted to get along with the union," Johnny snapped. "In our future meetings, I'd like to have at least a production manager in attendance who understands the problems of the workers. Tony has no touch with reality when it comes to the workers on the production line."

"That's not true, you've come to me on many occasions to resolve your problems," Tony protested.

"You're right, I did come to you with cases that couldn't be resolved on the floor," said Johnny.

He chuckled sarcastically as he continued.

"Like the heat problem in the body shop, your answer to that was that you couldn't do anything about the weather," Johnny said. "After the body shop workers walked out in protest due to the extreme heat of more than 100 degrees in that department, the problem was resolved. If that's your way of resolving a problem, we are going to have issues."

"That's not true," Tony said. "There were times I did you favors out of the kindness of my heart."

Johnny snorted in disgust.

"Well, I can see that you all want to get this meeting over with," Johnny said. "So are you going to put Don on the inspector's job in car delivery?" He directed the question to Jay, ignoring Tony entirely.

"Johnny, be patient and meet with Tony later to discuss this," Jay said, picking up his papers and sliding them into his briefcase.

"Listen, I'm not going to allow Don to go begging for a job," Johnny insisted. "We'll get it through the grievance procedure."

He turned to Tony.

"You hated the union for years, I guess we'll have to do it the hard way," Johnny said. "Let's go into the plant to do our job. There are many safety violations threatening our members. Let's start in freight department. I know the company doesn't want the tugs and the forklifts polluting the air."

Johnny stood up to collect his things.

"Johnny, I just don't understand why the hell are you so angry?" Jay asked. "You and Tony can agree to a solution before Don comes back to work."

"That's easy for you to say, Mr. Cannon," Johnny said. "Tony loves to play the game of carrot and the stick. You never had to deal with him on a one-on-one basis. You're his boss and he tells you what you want to hear. I don't trust him, period. I need an answer now or we're leaving."

"When this meeting is over, we'll discuss Don's job," Tony said.

"Let's not bullshit," Johnny said. "Give me an answer now. Yes or no. It's that simple. I want Mr. Cannon present when you give us your answer."

"Are you threatening to walk out of the plant if I don't acquiesce to your demand?" Tony asked, his face turning red in anger.

"Fuck no," Johnny said. "We'll just be in the plant to make it a safer place to work in. I know you have the union members at heart and wouldn't want them to work under unsafe conditions. Am I right?"

Johnny stared at Mr. Cannon with a raised eyebrow.

"Tony, Don's been working here for a long time and I'm sure if he wasn't a union official, he'd have qualified for the inspection job," Jay acquiesced. "We discussed replacing two inspectors in car delivery at the end of the month. Why don't you see that Don replaces one of them?"

Jay could see that Tony wasn't happy with this agreement and that he would have to moderate with Tony and the union in the future with issues they couldn't see eye-to-eye with.

"Well then I'd like to fill that other inspector job with Al Carter," Rocky said. "He has over twenty years of seniority."

Tony was taken aback.

"Rocky, we can't do that," Tony said.

"Now what are you doing, pulling the same shit on me?" Rocky asked.

"Rocky, you're misunderstanding," Tony said. "Al Carter came into the personnel office and quit. I thought you knew about this."

Rocky was confused and turned to Johnny.

"Did you know about this?" Rocky asked.

"First time I'm hearing about it like you," Johnny said, feigning surprise.

"Rocky, I would have gladly placed him on the job for you," Tony said, attempting to assuage Rocky.

"Tony, then give the job to Bummy Harris, he has 30 years of seniority and he's a minority," Johnny said.

"I just gave you Don, now you want more," Tony said, his voice raising.

"You gave me bullshit," Johnny said. "Lou Sargent asked about Don and I just followed up. Are you objecting to Bummy going into a lily-white department? He has the seniority to get there legally."

"Tony, place Bummy on the other job," Jay ordered.

He realized there would be justifiable issues if they didn't agree to this, and he didn't want any more problems.

"Johnny you got everything you wanted today," Tony said. "I hope you're generous when we come to you for something."

"Tony, like the old expression goes, you win some, you lose some," Johnny said, extending his hand toward Tony.

Tony ignored the gesture.

"I'll have Bummy spread the news that you wanted to break the color line in car delivery," Johnny said. "They'll be impressed."

Johnny and the plant manager left. Rocky and Lou stayed behind.

"Rocky, I'm sorry about Al Carter," Tony said. "You both were very close friends and I would have given him the inspector's job."

Tony then turned to Lou Sargent.

"I had every intention of giving Don the inspector's job but I had the intention of doing that alone with you," Tony said. "When you're with Don let him know that you were the one who intervened on his behalf. I don't want Johnny to get the credit for the move."

Tony placed his hand on Rocky's shoulder.

"You and Johnny ran together as a team but he's not going to get a fucking thing from me," Tony seethed. "He's going to learn that I hold the bag of goodies and he'll play by my rules."

No one paid attention to the porter who was cleaning the office but was out of sight.

Rocky excused himself and wandered into the office where Marie was typing.

"How about meeting me at the 7-11 Club right after work?" he asked, leaning into her ear.

"Mr. Rodgers frowns on any of us going out with the union workers and that includes you," she said, though she was smiling from interest.

She looked past him to observe what her boss was doing in the hallway. Her voice dropped into a whisper.

"I guess what he doesn't know won't hurt him," she said. "Here he comes."

"Thanks Marie, I'll call my office right away," Rocky said loudly so Tony could hear.

"Fill me in on what made Al Carter quit, I'm curious because he had a lot of seniority," Tony said to Rocky. Rocky nodded his head and winked toward Marie.

Lou was still waiting for Rocky in the hallway.

"I see Johnny has a short fuse," Lou said. "I've never been in any formal meeting with him before. Is he always that way?"

Rocky looked around before replying.

"Johnny is a clever one," he said. "He does everything by the book and knows exactly how far he can go without getting into trouble. Just like he did when he walked out of the body shop because of the excessive heat. That department swears by him and they do everything to protect his ass. "

"I remember," Lou agreed. "The company spent weeks interviewing every worker there to see if someone would admit that he told them to walk out. Even the foreman from the body shop wouldn't admit that he was in the department during the walkout. But he'll slip if he tries to pull that shit in another department."

"You're probably right," Rocky said. "And when he does, Tony will be waiting. You got to admit he has the balls to take the company on. He's not afraid. We could lose a lot of work if he doesn't get his way."

Lou's primary focus was to prevent Johnny from getting too popular with the membership.

"You and I got to team up to slow him down," Lou said. "Today I gave him the opening but that won't happen again. I was talking to George and he's going to give Johnny a hard time about spending the union funds. Don spent a lot of money, sending his supporters on trips as a way to pay them for their support. Our funds are in the red right now."

"I can't see George getting away with that," Rocky said. "He co-signed all the checks for Don. Johnny went over all the vouchers for the last two years and knows that our local is in the red on finances. He knows we're in debt to the tune of $5,000. He's getting the International Union auditors to go over the books. The first thing that Johnny will do is to go to the membership at our monthly meeting and report the reason we're in the red."

"Don't sell him short," Lou said. "George is a master when it comes to talking about money to the membership. He'll cop a plea about the high cost of this election and then explain that the local will have to tighten their belt on spending. That will make him look good and Johnny will be on the spot if he disagrees."

"Well I wouldn't sell Johnny short either," Rocky said. "Johnny spent his nights going to college and he's no dummy. No other committeeman went to college. Johnny is a different breed. He reads a lot and that's why he's so effective. George isn't dealing with a rank and file member."

Rocky shifted gears.

"What does Don think about all this?"

"After we lost the election, we held a private little caucus with Don and the top leadership," Lou said. "We told Don that we would have a tough time trying to get him re-elected as president in the next election in two years, so he agreed to step down in favor of you heading our group and running for president in the next election. If we team up now, we'll control the bargaining committee and executive board. We could make Johnny look bad in the eyes of the membership if we both take the right positions."

"You're bullshitting me," Rocky snorted. "I can't see Don stepping down after being president all those years. I wasn't born yesterday."

"Rocky, I swear on my mother's dead grave that Don agreed," Lou said. "When Don comes back to work, you ask him or better yet, I'll get him to tell you in person. Our plan for the next election is for you to run for president, me for vice-president and Don for my job as plant committeeman. Our plan is to boost you up when we get things favorable for the membership and blame Johnny for everything that will go wrong. The only way we can do this is if we go after Johnny right away and don't let up on him. You willing to join us?"

Rocky's pulse was running rapid.

"I'll give this some serious thought but I have to be careful that I don't lose my loyal supporters in the caucus," Rocky said. "If this comes out wrong and I look like a double-crosser, the membership will sympathize with Johnny. Give me some time to think about this."

"Look at the votes you got," Lou pressed. "You swamped Johnny and Don. If you had run for the president's job instead of Johnny, our whole ticket would have lost. We have to campaign for the next election right now, we can't wait. Don't fuck up like you did when you challenged Johnny to head your ticket before the election. You had the votes at your caucus but he outsmarted you. With us teaming up, we can bury him. What do you say? Will you come along with us? "

Rocky was reluctant and remembered when he was coaxed by Don's supporters to go congratulate Don on his victory when it looked like he had won the election, and then having to go back to Johnny when he won, instead. He convinced Johnny he was coaxed into making that mistake and that he was now with him 100 percent. If he gave Lou an answer now, word would spread throughout the plant and Johnny would lash out against him immediately. He was well aware of Johnny's abilities and feared him. He would go along with Lou for the time being but not commit himself until he evaluated the temperature of the membership toward Johnny.

"I like what you said but I have to meet secretly with my supporters to feel them out," Rocky said. "Let's play it by ear for a while and I'll get back to you. I've got a hot date tonight. I have to go."

Chapter 4
Years 1920-1940

America was in a deep recession and jobs were scarce. Frank Romanek left Shelton's factory and tried several more jobs with the goal of making more money. He finally found a job at the Ford Motor Company in Edgewater, New Jersey, where the work was hard but they paid top dollar. Quickly, his supervisors at the plant recognized his efficiency on the job.

Frank was promoted quickly to be a finish paint sprayer on the cars. He was skilled in the ability to cover up flaws to prevent rejections by inspectors at the end of the line. Since rejects cost the company money, it benefited the plant to have Frank on the job. He took pride in his work and at times he was required to spend additional time on his job even though he was only paid for the regular shift work. Frank and other workers accepted this because of the higher salary.

Rumors circulated in the plant that Ford's Edgewater plant was shutting down due to a lack of sales in the car industry. One day during lunchtime the workers gathered around the bulletin board where the company clerk was posting a notice on the board. The company announced a reduction of jobs due to the economy. They would have to wait until the following week for the company to announce which 1,500 men out of 2,000 were going to be laid off.

Everyone but Frank was concerned about the layoff. His confidence came from the fact that for years he outworked everyone and was considered one of the best workers in the plant. On the day of the big layoff, the superintendent, Mr. Socrates, told Frank that he would still have a job. However, he was also told that he would have to give 10 percent of his salary to the plant manager, Mr. Miller. Frank was a proud man who for 15 years felt he proved his loyalty and worth to the company by the quality of his workmanship. He stared long and hard at Mr. Socrates.

"You know that I do twice as much work than any other worker and I come here every day even on the days I'm sick," Frank said. "While everyone else complained when they stayed late, I did the best I could for you, without complaint. After all I did for this company, Mr. Miller wants me to pay him kickbacks? No matter how many hours I work in this plant, all I get is five dollars a day. So I say no, I won't pay any kickback."

"Frank, don't be rash," Mr. Socrates said. "Five dollars is a lot of money compared to other jobs in this area. Just pay the 50 cents a day. At least you'll have a job to feed your family."

"No, I won't do it," Frank said. "Just give me my money through the day and I'll go home. I quit."

Mr. Socrates shook his head.

"Frank, I'm sorry you are doing this."

When Frank left the plant, sleet lashed at his face as he trudged home through the snow. He wondered how his wife would react when he told her he was out of a job. During all his years at Ford they bought only the bare necessities and set aside savings. He was hopeful this money would tide them over until he was able to find another job.

The moment he walked into the house, Anna knew something was wrong. She took his hat and coat and placed them into the closet.

"I have hot coffee on the stove and I just made that apple pie you like so much," Anna said.

Anna Romanek radiated good cheer, always seeing the positive side of everything after living in hardship all the years. That is what Frank came to love about his wife. She was happy living in her small cold flat and cooking tasty dishes to please her family. From her love of baking, Anna verged on the plump side and the blond braids coiled around her head halved her round face. They had survived the rigors of Poland, nothing could be that bad here.

When she approached the table with the coffee and pie, Frank stood up and placed his arms around his wife.

"Mama I got laid off from my job today," Frank said. "I have to get up early to look for another job."

Anna never doubted her husband's ability to provide.

"We will do all right," she said. "Watch and see, you'll get another job right away. You could always go back to the farm."

"I wish I could be as positive as you," Frank said, hugging her close. "Even farms aren't looking for any help. I never expected to get laid off from Ford. I was working there so long and I worked so hard."

He told Anna how the boss would allow him to remain if he paid kickbacks to the plant manager. He apologized to her for not having a job anymore.

"Papa, you did the right thing and I'm so proud of you," she said. "We have some money put aside for something like this."

Young Johnny Romanek, 12 at the time, burst into the apartment.

"Papa, what are you doing home so early?" Johnny asked. It was always dark before his father came home from Ford except on weekends. Frank was honest with his son.

"I just lost my job at Ford," Frank said. "We're going to have to tighten up our belts until the economy improves and I get another job."

"Don't worry Papa, I'll get a job to help out," said Johnny.

Frank smiled at his son, who had no concept of how bad things were.

* * *

For the next few years the Romaneks struggled to make ends meet. Frank was always able to get enough work to pay his rent and provide ample food on the table.

Johnny grew up to be a large muscular boy. He used his muscular build to become a sparring partner for professional fighters, picking up a few dollars after school at the local gym. He earned respect from fighters and managers for his grace and devastating punches, from either hand, in the ring.

Johnny also worked his muscles at the docks by unloading linseed at a processing plant in Edgewater. He'd make a day's pay and was always selected to work standing out for being huskier and more brawny than men years older than him. He claimed to be 24, but was only 16 at the time. The hiring boss always hired 40 of the best workers in the crowd.

It was a grueling job, and Johnny got only 48 cents an hour. There were times it took 40 straight hours to drain the ship of linseed. His earnings would be 17 dollars or a little more. But he was proud to contribute the money he earned to his mother and father.

"Papa is so proud of what you're doing to help us," his mother would say, tears running down her face. "Johnny you're such a good boy."

During his summer vacation in 1938, Johnny heard that the battery company was hiring. The economy was still in a depression and jobs were few and far between.

When he stood in line to inquire about the job, he noticed many men in their forties and some in their early fifties. Most of the conversations centered on the hazard of getting lead poisoning or severe burns from the sulphuric acid that was used to make batteries. Some mentioned workers who lost their eyesight from the raw acid. The noxious odors of the chemicals drifted into the employment office that was directly above the plant. Many of the men became nauseous and began to leave the line and others were concerned about the exposure to the chemicals. Johnny, instead, took advantage of their leaving and inched his way closer to the office door, hoping to get hired. He needed this job to help his parents.

The superintendent came out to look at the men. He noticed Johnny standing nearby with his arms folded across his strong chest, showing off his muscular arms.

"Hey young fellow, you with the brown short sleeve shirt," the super asked. "You want a job?"

"Yes sir," said Johnny, stepping forward.

"Go in to see the doctor to be examined," he said. "Also, how old are you?"

"I'm 24, sir," Johnny said quickly.

The superintendent smiled, as if he didn't believe Johnny.

"Tomorrow bring in your birth certificate, that is if you pass the doctor's examination," the superintendent said. "You look a lot younger than 24."

"I can't help it if I have a baby face," Johnny said.

From experience Johnny knew if he said he was 20, he wouldn't get hired. Using the higher age always got him the job. He passed the physical and was offered a job at 42 cents an hour. If he could just get through the first day of work, hopefully the superintendent wouldn't need the birth certificate.

At the start of his shift he was taken to the battery-charging department and introduced to the foreman, a man named

Harold Lowen who was in his early 40's but looked 60. He was more than six feet tall and very thin with a tired and defeated expression on his face. He wore steel rim glasses set on top of his nose and a baseball cap that had the Yankees inscription in bold print. He took Johnny to a man who was working between the trays of batteries that were connected to electrical wires which were charging the batteries that would be sent to different stores for sale.

"Jerry, come over here," Harold said. "This is Johnny Romanek. He will be your assistant during the summer. Line him up on how to cap the batteries and show him the other work that he'll be doing."

Johnny was assigned as Jerry's assistant. Jerry warned Johnny on the hazards of the job and took him under his wing like a father. He told Johnny not to panic if he got acid in his eyes or on his skin. He showed him the water hose to clear acid away if it did get on him.

Johnny's back ached and his skin burned from the acid that burned through the rubber gloves. However, he was determined to get through this first day. He gave a sigh of relief when the lunch bell sounded. He was at the hose washing the acid off his hands when Jerry came over.

"Kid, come with me," Jerry said. "We'll go up to the roof to eat our lunch."

"I didn't bring any lunch," Johnny said. "I need to go upstairs to buy food."

"All we have is a vending machine with milk," Jerry said. "My wife always packs me more lunch than I can eat. You can have some of my food."

Johnny was warmed by Jerry's friendly gesture and got to know more about him during their lunch break. Jerry continued to fill him in on the hazards at the plant and what protective measures to take.

After work Jerry offered to drop Johnny off at home. Johnny, spent from a full day's work, nevertheless had agreed to be a sparring partner that night. He would earn a couple bucks and always kept his word.

"I've got to go to the gym to fight," Johnny said.

"I didn't know you were a professional fighter," Jerry said. "You have the build of a fighter but you don't have the face of a boxer."

Johnny replied that he wasn't a professional; he simply kept fighters sharp for upcoming fights. Tonight he was sparring with a fighter name Kid McGreevy.

Less than an hour later, Johnny was at the gym getting his hands taped. He felt a tap on his shoulder.

"I thought you chickened out on me," said Kid. "We've been waiting and you've never been this late."

"I got myself a job and just got done," Johnny said. "But I'm here now. Let's get to work."

Johnny had his trunks on and quickly finished taping up his hands. The manager, Dale Novak, put on Johnny's gloves.

"Alright, three fast rounds," Dale said. "You know the drill."

Johnny stalked Kid like a huge cat, flicking out his left hand with straight fast jabs and hitting the Kid repeatedly on the nose, making sure the punches were light. Kid didn't appreciate being hit and moved in to throw a volley of hard punches that Johnny easily blocked. Johnny countered with a devastating right cross that dropped Kid to the canvas. Kid jumped up, shaking his head to clear it and rushed at Johnny, throwing punches wildly, which Johnny easily blocked.

Johnny then pulled back on the intensity of his punches, since he saw no advantage in hurting Kid. For the remainder of the match, he threw fast punches with no zip on them.

After three rounds, Dale came over to take the gloves off Johnny.

"What do you say, I get you a fight a week and you can clear over 40 dollars," Dale said. "That's more than you will ever make at the factory."

"The fighter life is not for me," Johnny said, ripping off the tape. "I don't want to end up like Kid. Maybe some day I'll be a manager like you. I'll make a bundle of money but never get hit."

In the locker room Johnny ran into an old friend named Spike. He talked to him about the job at the battery plant. Noting his interest, he told him to meet him early tomorrow morning and they would head to the plant together. The plant had just received a big government order and would be hiring more men.

The next morning Spike was there with a few other guys from the gym. They all got jobs. During lunch, they all met in the locker room where Johnny shared his lunch with them. Johnny's mother had put extra food in his bag, supplying him with six large sandwiches. The men all had enough to eat and spent lunch complaining about the hazards of the job.

Johnny and the other guys would put in 10 hours of work at the plant, then head over to the gym for their workouts.

One evening while leaving the gym Spike told Johnny about a birthday party that Sunday. It was for a girl named Sally who Spike was interested in.

The following evening, they arrived at the party a little after eight in Johnny's 1935 Chevy Sport Coupe. Sally met them at the door. She gave Spike a hug and kiss on the cheek.

"Sally, this is Johnny Romanek," Spike said. "He's the guy I've been telling you about. He got me the job at the plant."

"Good to meet you, Johnny," Sally said, extending her hand. Johnny felt himself blushing. He wasn't used to being around girls.

As Sally led the boys into the house she warned Johnny that several of the men were unemployed and might hit him up for a job.

"When you get tired of talking to the guests, please dig into the food," she said. "There's plenty to go around."

A table in the center of the room was laden with cold cuts, salads, drinks and other snacks. Johnny talked to some of the guests and realized most the girls were paired with the guys. He decided he would grab something to eat and head out. He had no other reason to stay. Then he noticed a dark-haired girl walk into the room. He couldn't take his eyes off her as she mingled with guests.

She was of medium height with an amazing figure and tan, shapely legs. She had on a form-fitting black dress, which sparkled with rhinestones and buttoned up to her chin. Around her neck, she wore a single strand of white pearls. She felt Johnny's eyes on her and turned toward him. He was staring at her.

"Is there something wrong?" she asked.

She looked down at her dress to see if something was wrong.

"Is something out of place or is my slip showing?"

"No," he stammered. "Everything I see is perfect."

She laughed, a throaty laugh, which matched the beauty of her physicality.

"I'm Johnny Romanek," he said. "I hope you're not attached to someone at the party."

"Well I'm a little too young for that," she said.

"Could I have the pleasure of taking you home after the party tonight?" Johnny insisted. He grabbed her hand. She looked flustered. He let go of her hand and instead asked her if she was hungry.

"A little," she admitted.

He went to the buffet table and began making her a plate.

"You're a persistent man," she said, smiling up at him.

"When I see something I want, I go after it," he said.

"Wait, you're not putting all that food on my plate are you?" she said, as he handed her a plate laden with food. "I can't eat all that."

"Then I'll eat the rest," he said. She was amused.

They found some seats and she introduced herself.

"My name is Ann Cordone," she said.

"Ann, a pleasure to meet you," Johnny said. "You share my mother's name."

"That's sweet," she said, blushing. "How do you know Sally? I've never seen you before."

Johnny told her about Spike and Sally, and how he had just met Sally for the first time that night.

"I'm glad I came because now I met someone I'd like to take out," he said.

Suddenly Ann's mood changed.

"I've got a lot of friends here who I haven't seen for a long time," she said. "I should go talk with them."

"Ann, please don't get the impression that I'm a wise guy," Johnny said. "I'm not. I fell for you the moment I laid eyes on you. Please allow me the privilege of driving you home tonight after the party."

She paused a moment before answering.

"Ok," she said. "I'll take you up on that offer."

As she mingled with her friends, he noticed again her grace and beauty. He walked up to Spike.

"You see that girl across the room with the dress with the sparklers on it?" Johnny said. "What do you know about her?"

Spike's face furrowed into confusion.

"She's some looker but I never saw her before," he said.

Johnny had an idea. He told Spike to see if he could get Sally to come along to the lookout point off of Route 9W.

"Ann won't go with me alone," Johnny said. "We could all get something to eat and drink. Maybe do some dancing."

"Boy, you really got some crush on her," Spike laughed. "I'll see what Sally says."

Johnny turned his attention back to Ann who was laughing at some joke. He saw her glance at him and coyly look away.

"Sally says she can come but she can't stay out late," Spike said.

"Oh man, I owe you one," Johnny said, suddenly grabbing Spike in a hug.

The party wound down and Johnny found himself near Ann. He asked her about going out that night for refreshments and dancing with Spike and Sally.

"You're really serious about taking me home," she smiled. "How are we going to get there?"

"My car is parked right out in front," he said.

She was surprised since none of her friends had a car or a job.

"Sure," she said. "I'd like that."

He took her hand and they walked over to where Spike and Sally were standing. They were saying their goodbyes to the final guests.

"We'll meet you downstairs," Johnny said. "Car is parked in front."

When Ann saw the car, she was impressed and nodded her head in agreement. The sport coupe had large wooden wheels with whitewall tires and two spare wheels attached to the front fenders. The car was a dark maroon offset by varnished wood paneling. The inside of the car was upholstered with maroon seat covers that Johnny kept immaculate.

Soon after Spike and Sally joined them.

"Beautiful car, Johnny," Sally said, climbing into the back seat.

Johnny took them along the scenic route that overlooked the Hudson River. The moon reflected on the water as the lights from the high-rise apartments glistened, adding sparkle to the New York skyline. Ann relaxed and rested her head against the back of her seat as Johnny drove. When they arrived at the restaurant, the parking lot was full of cars. They walked into the restaurant and heard soft music coming out of the jukebox.

They were seated by a large picture window suspended above the river with the light flickering on the water below. When the waiter appeared, Johnny ordered for all of them. He then turned to Ann and asked her to dance.

"I'm glad I went to this party," Johnny said, holding Ann in his arms. "I was afraid I was going to be the odd man out. Instead the highlight of the evening was meeting you. Ann, I'm not being corny but you're the most beautiful girl I ever met."

"I'm glad you enjoyed yourself," she said, blushing.

They headed back to the table where Sally and Spike were seated. Their meal had arrived. Johnny asked Ann about herself as they ate. He learned that she lived just around the corner from him, in Clinton. He played football against her brother, Springy and had known him for years.

"I can't believe that we live so close to each other and we never ran across each other," he whispered. "Don't you ever walk through town?"

"My father took me out of school after the eighth grade and made me go to work," she said. "My father was a good provider, but he needed more money to provide us with our needs."

"I'm going to make it a point to keep you in sight from now on," Johnny said.

Ann put her fork down.

"Johnny, you've got some sweet lines," Ann said. "You must say this to all the girls you meet for the first time."

"Ann, I'm serious," he said. "When you first walked into the room at the party, I knew you were the girl for me. I know that you said that you were too young to go out steady with anyone but I would like to start dating you. We will have a lot of good times together."

"We will see," she said. "It's getting late. I've got to head back home. My parents will be worried."

Johnny dropped Sally off first, and then Spike. At Ann's house he placed his arm around her shoulders to kiss her goodnight. Ann stiffened and pushed him away.

"You don't think I owe you a kiss for taking me out, do you?" she asked.

"No, not at all," he said. "I'm sorry if I was being too forward."

"Do you still want to date me even though I'm not the kissing type?" she asked.

"I'd like to take you out on Saturday," he said. "I'll pick you up at eight in front of your house. Would that be all right?"

"Works for me," she said. "I did have a lovely evening, thank you very much."

She leaned over and kissed him on the cheek. Then before Johnny had a chance to react, she opened the passenger door and quickly walked away, disappearing inside.

When Johnny got home, he sat in his car and thought of his evening with Ann. Johnny hadn't ever dated and recently he was so busy because he worked ten hours each day, six days a week, then went over to the gym to make a few extra bucks. On Sundays he hung around the poolroom with the football players from the team that he played with. Many of them bragged about going out with girls. Now he knew better.

He took it for granted that girls wanted to be kissed after going out. He also realized that he'd have to change some of his life style. He always gave his entire pay to his mother and only kept money for food and necessities. Now he needed money to properly court Ann. He wasn't entirely sure what it meant to date, but he would soon find out.

* * *

As time went on, Johnny Romanek realized the battery plant wasn't a safe place for anyone to work. Most of the workers were older men who migrated to the United States from Sweden, Norway and Italy and younger workers like Johnny who needed these jobs to support their family. They worked long, hard hours under dangerous conditions, never complaining. Management took advantage of their ignorance, especially those who weren't U.S. citizens. Johnny took it upon himself to lodge complaints on behalf of coworkers.

He pushed requests for the company to provide protective equipment, such as rubber soles to protect their shoes, and rubber gloves and rubber aprons. But management completely ignored his requests. Johnny's foreman, Harold Lowen, was a fair and just man who was sympathetic to the workers' plight but told Johnny to be careful. He was told by Ray Curly, the plant manager, to find fault with Johnny's work in order to lay him off. Johnny took the warning seriously, doing his job to perfection, but continued to complain.

Johnny encouraged Spike and five other workers to go with him to meet with the American Federation of Labor headquarters in downtown Clinton to learn how to start a union at their plant. AFL representatives told Johnny that he would have to get workers to sign a petition to agree to have a union represent them. Once that they had a majority of the workers sign up, they would take that petition to New Jersey's relations board who would then conduct a secret ballot vote.

The following day, they called a meeting in the locker room at lunchtime to explain to the workers the advantage of having a union represent them. They detailed that a union would ensure safer working conditions at the plant and provide them with proper equipment to protect them. Everyone was interested in what was being said until Mr. Curly broke up the meeting. He charged Bing Ryan as the spokesperson and fired him on the spot for interfering with plant operations. Everyone then left the locker room and returned back to their jobs when the lunch bell sounded.

Johnny realized it was illegal to solicit votes to join a union on company property. He changed his approach by meeting outside the plant to explain how a union could protect workers. The first man he approached was Charley Brannagan, a young man who worked at the plant for many years. He cornered him behind a stack of batteries.

"Charley, you've been working here for more than 10 years, how come you haven't been complaining about the unsafe working conditions?" Johnny asked.

Charley knew Johnny was interested in trying to get a union at the plant. He looked around to make sure no one could see them talking.

"Look at your hands and knees, they're infected and scarred from the acid burns," Johnny continued. "This company doesn't give a shit about us. Look at our clothes; they're falling apart. I've been going around like a bum, picking up old clothes to wear while working here to save money. I put patches on my rubber gloves so I don't get burned from acid. The cost of this is coming out of my pocket. The company knows this but they won't supply us with any protective equipment."

"Johnny, you're a young man with a high school education," Charley said. "If they fire you, you'd get another job in a short time. Most of us are getting on in years and jobs are hard to find. Look at most of the guys in the plant. Most can't read or speak English but they're damn good workers. How long do you think they would last here if Curly caught them trying to get a union here? He works the hell out of all of us but with the overtime and Saturday work, we make a fair buck. We're in a deep depression right now and the 32 bucks we earn weekly looks big. Also, your father is out of work and struggling to make ends meet. He'd be pissed if you got fired for trying to start a union here.

Charley needed the job and was afraid to get involved even though a union would help all of them.

"Charley, I know you need this job and how you feel," Johnny said. "I also know that times are bad and this isn't the right time to try to start a union but is there ever a right time to start anything? What good is any job if it makes you sick and disabled? Look at Dutch, he was laid up with lead poisoning for three months with no pay coming in except for unemployment checks. He even had to pay out of pocket for doctor bills and medicine. Charley, that's just not right."

"Johnny, you're trying to do the right thing but I'm getting married in a couple of months," Charley said. "I can't afford to lose this job. All I ever did since I left the eighth grade was work odd jobs and for the last ten years, I got hired here and worked in the charging room. That's all I know about work. What would I do if I lost my job here? I have no other skill and no education."

"Charley, when you get married and your wife becomes pregnant or you get sick, what protection do you have?" Johnny said. "We have no security, no medical coverage and the company ignores every safety rule. Is this the way we're going to work for the rest of our lives?"

Johnny noticed Charley was paying attention now.

"Did you talk to Elphick or any of the other guys in the charging room?" Charley asked.   "No you're the first one I talked to," Johnny said. "I'll get to all of them before the week goes by."

"If you get the others to go along with you, come back to me," Charley said.

Johnny did go to talk to the rest of the workers but to no avail. They all liked what he was trying to do but were afraid of losing their jobs. At quitting time, he sat on the stool in the locker room next to Spike and asked how he made out in his department.

Spike said he got so disgusted that he just went back to his task. He noticed a little while later that Skeeter came back with a cast on his arm. He told Spike that the doctor said he would be out of work for at least six weeks. Mr. Curly called him into his office and offered to pay the hospital bill as well as $12.50 a week.

"I offered to go to the labor board to get more money but he was too scared to do anything," Spike said.

"I'm running into the same thing," Johnny said. "When Bing got fired, he scared the shit out of all of them. I heard Curly was going to call a meeting in his office with everyone to discuss the coming contract. The word is that he wants all of us to sign the new agreement. Let's try to get everyone to ask questions about the safety hazards and what he's going to do to correct them."

The following day, the charging department workers were the first ones to be called into Mr. Curly's office.

"Mr. Curly, this is a new contract," Johnny said.

"Could we get a copy of it so we know what we're getting? And all of us are concerned with the safety conditions here. We had an example of that yesterday when Skeeter was told to climb a rack without a ladder by his foreman and fell and broke his arm."

Curly shouted Johnny down and slammed his papers on his desk.

"Romanek, I was told that you're a trouble maker," Mr. Curly yelled. "By the way do you have another job?"

"No, I don't," Johnny said. "I'm not here to cause trouble. But when our workers get hurt needlessly, by a foreman disregarding the safety of our workers, we have to talk about safety conditions at the plant. You are aware that Skeeter broke his arm because he listened to his foreman who told him to climb the rack without a ladder, right?"

Mr. Curly just grew angrier.

"I can see that you're a wise ass and you're holding up this meeting," Mr. Curly said. "Why don't you go back downstairs to work so I can tell the men what we're going to do for them."

"I can't sign that agreement unless I read it and know what's in it," Johnny said, shaking with anger.

"Go back to work, you wasted a lot of our valuable time," Roy said. "Also, I've decided that you won't be required to sign the agreement."

Johnny stood up slowly and stared at his fellow workers. They sat with their eyes cast down staring at floor. Johnny could see that even though he was speaking for their benefit, they didn't have the nerve to support him.

When they returned to work, Johnny saw Charley going into the bathroom and followed.

"What did Curly offer in the new contract?" Johnny whispered.

"Curly is pissed off at you," Charley said. "We overheard him tell Harold to fire you the minute you did something wrong. He told us not to listen to you because you're a troublemaker and you just want to upset the workers. If anyone listens to you, we will be in the same boat as you."

Charley said Mr. Curly made excuses for such a meager raise, explaining that the company is losing money each year and that is why they could only get seven cents an hour as an increase.

"We were afraid to open our mouths and so we signed the agreement," Charley said.

"How long is the agreement for?" Johnny asked.

"I don't know," Charley said. "He wouldn't let any of us to read the contract. As soon as we all signed the agreement, he rushed us out of his office so he could get the next department in."

Johnny walked back to his job in disgust when he heard the workers signed away their rights for any protection. Now was the best time for the workers to organize a union in the plant since they knew the company wasn't going to give them any concessions.

"Charley, we had him by the balls but you guys wouldn't listen," Johnny said. "I proved to you that when I spoke up, he wouldn't have the balls to fire me. All we got out of this contract was a couple of pennies as a raise per hour and no protection."

When Johnny arrived home that evening he saw his father sitting at the kitchen table reading a paper with a smile on his face. His mother was setting the table with steaming hot dishes of Polish food.

"This is a telegram from the Ford Motor Company asking me to report to work tomorrow," his father said. "I spoke to the employment manager and he told me they were going to open the plant for full production next Monday. They're going to hire a lot of new workers."

"Pop, when are you going back to work?" Johnny asked.

"Tomorrow morning at seven," his father said. "They pay a lot more money then the battery plant. Why don't you shape up at the factory plant gate tomorrow? You would lose a day's pay, but I'll stop in and see the employment manager. Maybe he'll help to get you hired."

The next morning Johnny arrived at the bottom of the stairway from the overpass that extended over the railroad tracks near the entrance of the Ford plant. He was stunned to see more than a thousand men standing around the huge cyclone fence that surrounded the entire plant.

From his vantage point, he observed a tall man in a grey suit walking out of the building with two beefy security guards at his side. As the suited man came to the gate, the crowd became unruly. They began to push and shove to get closer to the gate to be the first ones in to be interviewed.

The man raised his hands up in the air to quiet them but to no avail. Fights broke out as the ones closest to the fence fought to keep their position. The man in charge stopped the guards from removing the chain that held the gate closed. He attempted to reason with the crowd but they continued to shove and push to get closer to the gate. The man in charge got disgusted and walked back into the building.

Johnny was standing still on top of the walk leading from the overpass. He wasn't sure what to do. He could go back to work and be only minutes late. As he started to walk away he heard police sirens blasting as they came over the ramp leading to the factory gate.

The police pulled up behind the unruly crowd and began to shove and use clubs to open a path for them. It seemed the police were trying to organize the crowd.

Johnny ran down the steps two at a time to get behind the police as they approached the gate. He was dressed in a black pinstriped suit, white shirt and a black striped tie. The crowd assumed he was a part of the police force and opened up to let him through. He walked up to the gate and faced the crowd while they waited for someone to come.

The employment manager reappeared and instructed the guards to remove the chain from the gate.

"I will take the first 35 men," he said. "That's all I can handle at a time."

Everyone began shoving to get close to the gate. He raised his hands above his head to get their attention and shouted.

"The office can only hold 35 people so I'll be back when we interview that group and I'll be back to see that everyone will be able to sign up for employment," he said.

They all quieted down and allowed the first group to enter the gate, including Johnny. The clerks in charge of signing up the men were standing behind the counter with stacks of applications in front of them and began to interview the men. The employment manager stood in back of the room watching his clerks interviewing each prospective employee. They were all aware of the crowd waiting outside and were typing up the applications as fast as they could.

The employment manager was a man named Ralph Bradley. He was a distinguished-looking man in his early 50's, with rugged features and a full head of hair turning grey at the temples. He had a stern expression on his face and turned his attention to Johnny.

"Let's start with you young man," Mr. Bradley said. "What's your name?"

"Johnny Romanek, sir," said Johnny.

"You don't happen to be related to big Frank Romanek, from the top of the hill, now do you?" Mr. Bradley asked.

His face softened and broke into a warm smile.

"Yes, in fact he's my father," Johnny said.

"You look husky enough," Mr. Bradley said. "But do you think you could you could handle the assembly line? The line is hard work and very boring."

"Sir, I've been at the battery plant for three hard years of work, stacking batteries ten feet high," Johnny said. "I also worked unloading the ships at the linseed plant. Hard work isn't anything new to me."

"If you're half the man that your old man is, you won't have any trouble working here," Mr. Bradley said.

He picked up a blank application and pencil.

"Fill this out and answer all the questions," Mr. Bradley said. "If you pass the physical, you're hired. When you're through with the application, go through that door into the medical department. And good luck."

The sun was just beginning to rise over the top of the apartment, the sky was clear and not a cloud in the sky. Johnny bounded down the steps of the apartment, where he lived with his parents.

At the door, he saw Spike sitting on the fender of his car, waiting to go with him to work. Johnny's face broke into a smile. He rushed to his friend, picking him up in a bear hug. Spike was confused by his friend's reaction.

"I got hired at Ford yesterday," Johnny said. "I got a gut feeling that Curly is going to be pissed because I took yesterday off."

He slapped the steering wheel with his hands, laughing out loud.

"I'm going to have the pleasure of telling him to stick that job up his ass," Johnny said.

Spike placed his hand on Johnny's shoulder to get his attention.

"Be careful what you say to that bastard and don't tell him that you got another job," Spike said. "If I read him right, he has connections in the industry and can squash your job with Ford. He's the kind of prick to screw you out of a job."

Johnny couldn't help but be in a happy mood back at the battery plant. He whistled as he was changing into his work clothes in the locker room. He slapped other workers on their backs while he was walking downstairs to punch in at the time clock.

After punching in, he threw his apron over his shoulder and his rubber gloves under his arm. He bounced down the stairs two at a time as he approached his job in the charging room.

Jerry was walking between the lines of trays holding the batteries, hooking them up with electrical wires to be charged. He just waved to Johnny and continued working. Johnny waved to the foreman who was standing at the desk that was situated in the middle of the room. Workers were standing around his desk, waiting to be assigned to their jobs. Johnny was walking toward his workstation but was beckoned by Harold to come to his desk.

"Good morning, Harold," Johnny said. He pointed to the conveyor that was carrying the batteries to his workstation.

"The batteries are piling up, I better get started," Johnny said.

"Hold on a minute, I need to speak with you," Harold said.

Harold turned to one of the workers who was standing by his desk.

"Please go to Johnny's work station and place the batteries on the trays," Harold said. "I'll be through with him in a few minutes."

Harold turned back to Johnny.

"I hope you got a good excuse for being out yesterday," Harold said. "Mr. Curly was pissed when you didn't show up. He instructed me to send you to his office when you showed up to work."

Despite his tone Harold placed his hand on Johnny's shoulder. Harold empathized with the workers and didn't approve of the men working under hazardous conditions but his hands were tied. Ray Curly was only interested in getting the work done in cheapest way regardless of the unsafe conditions. Harold needed his job like all members of management did.

"Be careful how you talk to Curly," Harold said. "He knows you're the one who is trying to get a union here. He doesn't approve of anyone trying to disrupt the production."

Harold noticed Mr. Curly walking toward them and stopped talking.

Johnny continued looking at Harold and ignored Mr. Curly when he approached. Mr. Curly was angry.

"Mr. Romanek, you know we have a fucking plant to run every day of the week," Mr. Curly roared. "We lost production yesterday because of your absence yesterday. It took us a half hour before we could get a man released that could do your job. We don't need deadheads like you around. What's your excuse for being absent?" He stood in front of Johnny with his arms folded across his chest and his legs spread apart. He was deliberately trying to provoke him as he stood waiting for an answer.

"Who the hell do you think you're talking to?" Johnny shouted back.

Mr. Curly was surprised by Johnny's reaction and jumped behind Harold for protection. Harold quickly tried to restrain Johnny, pinning his arms to his side.

"Take it easy," Harold whispered. "You're going to blow your job."

"Harold my argument isn't with you but with this no good son-of-a-bitch," Johnny continued. "You can't talk to me like that and get away with it. I want an apology from you or I'm going to kick your ass."

Mr. Curly realized that he made the mistake of demeaning the young man but he was in no position to apologize to him with the whole department watching.

"I don't intend to apologize," he mumbled. "I want an answer as to why you didn't come to work yesterday."

Johnny had never taken a day off all the years that he was employed at the plant. He was still angry and made another attempt to get at Mr. Curly but Harold moved in to hold him back by placing his hands on Johnny's chest. Mr. Curly realized the situation was getting out of hand and began to move backward down the aisle to get away.

"Harold, tell him that he's fired and I want him to leave the plant immediately," Mr. Curly yelled.

The workers in the department began protesting, shouting and booing. Johnny broke away from Harold and went after Mr. Curly who was running toward the stairway. In all of Curly's years as plant manager, no one ever talked back to him and he controlled the workers by having them terrified of losing their jobs. Harold had never before experienced the reaction that Johnny was having.

"Run, you bastard," Johnny yelled at Mr. Curly. "Why don't you stay here and do the dirty work?"

Harold was still holding onto Johnny's shirt but released it when Mr. Curly disappeared up the stairway.

Johnny turned to Harold.

"You're a good foreman and I'm sorry that you had to be part of this," Johnny said. "That old bastard will probably take his frustration out on you sometime in the future."

The workers were still standing around the desk, waiting for Johnny's next move.

"Who's next?" Johnny called out, for all to hear. "Now is the time to organize and protect your jobs in the future. This would never happen if you had a union here. They'd make sure you wouldn't have to work under unsafe conditions."

Harold stood there in disbelief, shaking his head.

"Johnny, you better leave before he calls the police," Harold said. "Even though you're a trouble-maker, I'm going to miss you as a worker."

"No more than I am," Johnny said. "Someone had to tell that bastard off."

Johnny extended his hand toward Harold for a handshake.

"Thanks for everything, I hope to see you around," Johnny said.

They shook hands as Johnny departed with his lunch box under his arm and his regular hand salute.

Chapter 5
Year 1964

R ocky entered the 7-11 club a little after 5 p.m. but couldn't find Marie at the bar. He stood there for a moment as his eyes got accustomed to the darkness when he noticed her waving to him from a booth at the rear of the room.

"Marie, why are you sitting back here?" he asked, leaning toward her to kiss her on the cheek.

"I noticed someone from the plant walking into the men's room when I came in," she said, glancing around nervously as she moved into the booth to make room for Rocky. "Tony has a firm rule that he doesn't want any of the staff fraternizing with any of the union workers. His excuse is that we may be able to tell the union some of the company's secrets."

She stopped talking when the waiter approached the table. Rocky ordered the drinks.

"Also," her voice dropped into a whisper. "Tony has been trying to date me for over a year now. But I have a firm rule against dating a married man."

The waiter returned with the drinks.

"The scotch and soda is mine," Rocky said.

He placed Marie's drink in front of her and Rocky began to sip his drink until the waiter left. He needed information about Tony for the future.

"I heard Tony's wife is quite the looker," Rocky said. "Why would he cheat on her?"

"Why does any man want to cheat and go out with a younger girl?" Marie said. "His wife is in her forties and very attractive. But Tony's always had a wandering eye. He has been going out regularly with a beautiful brunette named Geraldine. Once I asked her what they did on their dates and she said he takes her to swanky restaurants outside of town. He treats her to the best food and drinks. Afterward he buys a great bottle of drinks when they register at a motel. I don't think I'd like to be in Geraldine's shoes with a guy like that. He's only out for one thing and it's not to get married to her."

"Hon, which girl is Geraldine?" Rocky asked. "I thought I knew most of the girls working in the office."

Rocky asked this question for more reasons than one.

"She has only been with us a short time," Marie said. "She works in the accounting office."

She took a sip of her drink.

"You might have seen her walking in the hallway, she's the one with the sexy figure and always wears tight dresses," Marie said.

Rocky nodded as Marie continued talking.

"I talk to her quite a bit when she comes to our office to see Tony," Marie said. "She's ambitious and said Tony was going to place her into the foreman retraining program that she will eventually be in charge of. That'll bring in a salary increase of a few thousand dollars a year."

"I remember her now," he said. "She really flaunts it when she walks by. Why is he trying to make a play for you?"

"Tony's getting a little worried with Gerry," Marie said. "She's always talking about their dates with the office girls and thinks nothing of barging into his office when he's on the phone and leans over to give him a kiss on the cheek. It's now at the point where his wife might find out about his shenanigans. If you didn't know, his wife is responsible for him getting this good job at Ford. Her father is one of the vice presidents. One word out of her mouth and he could lose his job."

They were discussing the very thing Rocky wanted to know about Tony. Rocky could easily use this information in the future if he needed it. He probed further and noticed Marie starting to move into the shadows of the booth. The man who she had recognized earlier from the plant just came out of the restroom and walked past the two of them.

"How about you and I go to the Hawaiian Moon to celebrate my victory tonight?" Rocky asked.

Marie smiled. She was thrilled Rocky was part of the jet set that patronized the most exclusive clubs regardless.

"I'd love to," she said. "It's after six now."

"I'll pick you up around eight," he said. "Nothing starts there until around ten. We could relax there with a few drinks and a nice meal before the show starts. The band plays continuous music until closing time."

He escorted her to her car.

"Marie, wear something dazzling," he said, touching her arm. "I want to show you off to my friends."

He kissed her quickly and waited as she drove off.

While driving home, Marie recalled the office girls referring to Rocky as a womanizer. In spite of this she was excited to go out with him. He was very handsome and fun. She touched her necklace and her excitement was building at the thought of seeing Rocky that night.

Rocky was putting the finishing touches on his appearance as his mother stood by, admiring her son.
"Son, when are you going to get married and give me some grandchildren before I get too old to enjoy them?" she asked. "There are so many nice girls in Clinton who are crazy about you. I'm sure one of them would make you a good wife."

"Mama, what would you do if I wasn't here with you?" he asked, pulling her into a bear hug. "Where could I get all this attention from a wife? I go out every night with a different girl and no commitment. I got the best cook in the world and no one to tell me what I can or can't do."

His mother ignored his words and pushed him away.
"Why can't you marry a nice girl like Ann Cordone?" his mother asked. "She makes Johnny Romanek very happy. There are a lot of Italian girls like her around, she's still a very beautiful woman after having three children. I'd love to see your children running around our house. But the way you're going, that's never going to happen."

"Mom, that's not the life for me," Rocky said, admiring himself in the mirror. "Johnny is up to his neck in bills. He's got a heavy mortgage and three kids to support. His eldest son is ready to go to college, that'll cost him a good buck. I have to admit, Ann Cordone is an exception, she still retains her beauty, but I'm not the marrying kind. I can't see myself sitting around the house every night. I love the life I'm living. Why should I get married and keep one woman miserable when I can keep so many girls happy while I stay single?"

His mother sighed.

"Son, some day you're going to be sorry when you don't have someone to love you," she said. "You'll be all alone and you won't have all the options to find a good woman like you have now."

"No Mom," he said, working on his hair. "I'll still be having a good time even when I get old."

He put his arms around his mother to give her a huge hug. He loved his mother very much. She never stopped fussing over her son. He pulled her away at arms length.

"Besides, I'll always have you to love me," Rocky said.

Despite herself, she shook her head and looked admiringly at him. Rocky was six feet tall with light sandy hair which he parted to one side, allowing his curls to fall over his eye. He was a handsome man and he knew it. His mother always worried that he would get in trouble with some girl who didn't live up to her expectations. He stood in front of his dresser staring into the large mirror attached to it. He was brushing his hair while his mother selected a dark tie to match his pinstriped suit.

"Don't forget, you have to go to a meeting tomorrow so don't stay out too late tonight," she said, handing him the tie. "You got to sleep sometime or you're going to get sick."

"Come on Mom, don't treat me like a baby," Rocky said, putting the tie on. "The meeting isn't until the afternoon, so please don't wait up for me tonight."

He pulled on his suit jacket. Then he kissed her on top of the head and walked out.

Rocky drove over to Marie's house to pick her up and saw her waiting on the front porch of her parent's large colonial home that was located in a very exclusive section of town. Her father was the mayor and a prominent lawyer on Wall Street. She called out to her mother who was in the kitchen.

"Mother, my date is here so don't wait up for me tonight," she said. "I'll probably be late."

She wore a white blouse with two buttons opened at the front and wore a simple gold cross on a gold chain that hung between her breasts. As she walked to his car, her pleated white skirt clung to her beautiful legs. A large black belt she wore around her waist accentuated her slim hips and flat stomach. Her honey blonde hair moved like a spool of ribbon across her back.

Rocky had never seen her dressed-up and was impressed by her beauty. He smiled wide as he caught a glimpse of her. Her clear blue eyes and red lips were parted in a smile, showing off her perfectly white teeth.

"I see you believe in being prompt," she said.

She climbed into the car while he held the door open for her.

"You look so handsome in that black suit," she continued. "I've never seen you in a suit before. You should dress like that more often in the plant."

She chuckled before continuing.

Actually, I take that back," she said. "You should dress like this only when we go out together."

Rocky laughed. He felt good and loved the flattery. He wanted to impress her tonight and was seemingly off to a good start.

"Marie, you're gonna enjoy the Hawaiian Moon," Rocky said. "It's an exclusive club that caters to the younger set. They keep the riff-raff out due to their higher prices. Their food is something different but excellent. They have an outstanding band that plays an assortment of numbers to satisfy everyone."

"I've heard a lot of good things about the club," Marie said. "I know we're going to have a good time."

While they were driving down the highway, he placed his arm around her shoulders and slowly let his hand fall on her right breast. She didn't seem to mind, picking up his hand off her breast and holding it close to her cheek.

"After you left the plant with Lou, I heard Tony talking to Jay Cannon on the phone," Marie said, piquing his interest. "He said that he wished you were the president rather than Johnny Romanek. He feels you are more responsible and understand the importance of getting along with the company."

She glanced over at him to gauge his reaction, and then continued.

"He also told Jay that he was going to put pressure on Johnny to make him realize that management is running the plant, not the union," Marie said. "I didn't hear what Jay said but I gathered from Tony's response that he better be diplomatic about what he does. Jay doesn't want any trouble with the union."

She stopped talking and moved closer to him and began kissing his ear while running her hand through his hair.

"I love the way your curls fall over your forehead," Marie said. "It makes you look so sexy."

"Marie, you better stop that, you're getting me all worked up before we get there and then you'll be in a lot of trouble," Rocky said.

"Now don't get fresh," Marie laughed. "Anyway, we're here."

The valet was standing under the large marquee. He was dressed in a tuxedo and opened the car door to assist Marie. Then he walked to the other side of the car to park it and gave Rocky a card to retrieve the car when they left.

Rocky escorted her through the entrance and was met by the host.

"Welcome to the Hawaiian Moon, Mr. Durango," he said. "We have a special table set up for you and your young lady near the dance floor."

He escorted them through the garden-like room, which had small palm trees growing in large wooden pots spaced ten feet apart. The Chinese lanterns were hung from the ceiling on heavy brass chains.

When they entered the main dining room, a beautiful rippling waterfall was against the far wall with bright lights shining through the sparkling water. The walls were decorated with heavy blue drapes, which were complimented by huge vases with freshly cut flowers.

The musicians were playing a popular love song and many of the guests were dancing. When they got to their table the host pulled Marie's chair out to assist her.

"Enjoy yourselves tonight, your waiter for the evening will be Manuel," the host said. "He's coming now to take your order."

"Thanks Pierre, this table is perfect," Rocky said.

As he reached out to shake Pierre's hand, Marie noticed he handed him a handsome tip.

"Miss, may I suggest that you try one our most famous drinks, the Hawaiian Collins which is our specialty," Manuel said. "It's made with gin and our own special fruit juices."

Marie nodded her head.

"Mr. Durango, you'll have the usual, Chavis Regal with club soda, I presume?" Manuel said.

"That'll be fine Manuel," Rocky said.

He picked up Marie's hand when Manuel stepped away.

"Be careful with that drink, it goes down smooth but it has the habit of creeping up on you," Rocky said. "I don't want to carry you out of here."

She was looking all around the hall, admiring the surrounding beauty. She stood up and pulled Rocky's hand toward her.

"The music is beautiful," she said. "Let's dance."

He escorted her to the dance floor as a few of the dancing couples waved to them, recognizing Rocky. Rocky held her close to him.

"Marie, you look so beautiful tonight," he said. "I see my friends looking at you with envy and I can't blame them. Are you having a good time?"

"I could dance all night long," she said, moving closer to him.

"Honey, you better back off a little before you get me into trouble," Rocky chuckled.

Marie moved away, but had a mischievous smile on her face.

"In about an hour, they'll put on the floor show which is the best in the state," Rocky said. "They're featuring Johnny Apollo as the main vocalist. He's the closest voice I heard that sounds like Perry Como. If you'd like to meet him after the show, I can introduce you to him."

She nodded and pulled him closer.

As they were dancing across the floor, many of the seated couples stared and admired the way Rocky and Marie glided across the floor. Rocky was an exceptionally good dancer and was able to move Marie around so her skirt flared out, showing her shapely legs and radiant smile.

The music concluded just as Manuel brought their drinks to the table. Marie was parched after dancing and started to drink the Collins like a glass of soda.

"Marie, be careful," Rocky warned her. "Drink that slowly or it'll knock you out."

He placed his hand on hers to slow her down. When Manuel arrived to take their order, Rocky ordered for them.

"Manuel, we will have the Hawaiian seafood platter and the New York strip steak," he said.

When Manuel disappeared Rocky turned to look at Marie.

"You are too beautiful," he said, pulling her close and nuzzling her neck. "All the men in the room are watching you with that hungry look in their eyes. You fit in perfectly with the beautiful surroundings."

"It feels like I'm walking on cloud nine tonight," she beamed. "You look so handsome in that pin-striped suit. I don't want this night to end."

She reached over to take his hand and placed it against her cheek and kissed each finger.

In what seemed like no time at all, Manuel brought two steaming plates to their table.

"Sweetie, I ordered two different dinners," Rocky said. "We'll share half of each to see which of them you like best."

Manuel separated the portions and placed a little of each on their plates, starting with Marie.

As Marie started eating, she smiled even bigger. The food was excellent, according to her.

"You know Rocky, I fell in love with you the first day I laid eyes on you when you walked into Tony's office," she said.

Rocky was used to women falling for him, but when they mentioned the "L" word, even he got nervous.

"Well, well, it can't be that easy for me, now can it?" Rocky said, chewing his food.

She leaned across the table to kiss him. Rocky responded to the kiss and was satisfied the night was going so well. He wanted to impress Marie because she was going to be his main source of information on all the happenings that come through the labor relation department. It also didn't hurt that she was a very beautiful woman and single.

After dining and dancing until 2 a.m., Rocky suggested a scenic drive through the Alpines along the highway overlooking the Hudson River. Marie agreed and allowed Rocky to escort her out of the restaurant. The drive to the highway took just a few minutes. Rocky parked between two large trees along the edge of the palisades with a perfect view of the New York skyline, which was brightly lit.

"It's beautiful here," Marie said as she snuggled up close to him. "Watching the sun rise from here must be a sight to be seen. Can we stay to see it?"

She placed her arms around his neck and began kissing him.

"Honey, let's get in the back seat where we will be more comfortable," Rocky said. "I'm banging my ribs into the darn steering wheel."

They moved to the rear of the car where she stretched out her beautiful legs and he took her in his arms.

"Did you have a good time tonight?" he asked, nuzzling her neck.

She was so thrilled she responded by squeezing him tightly and kissing him.

"I'm in seventh heaven tonight," she said. "Everything was perfect. Most of all I enjoyed being out with you."

He pulled her closer as he kissed her on the neck, the cheeks and the mouth. He placed his hand under her blouse and inside her bra to touch her breasts. He gently twisted the tip of her nipples and he felt them harden, she moaned with pleasure.

He continued kissing her and reached behind her to release the snaps of her bra. He took each nipple in his mouth. She felt a tingling sensation between her legs and was gasping for air.

He continued to kiss her and gently placed his fingers under her panties. He moved his finger into her very slowly until she became faint with pleasure. As he kissed her he removed her panties and placed his finger deeper into her. She began pushing him away.

"Please Rocky, I'm a virgin," she said. "I've never done this before."

She lifted herself up slightly to replace her panties and hooked the snaps of her bra. While she buttoned her blouse, Rocky kissed her neck.

"I'm sorry if I pushed you too much," he said. "You are just too beautiful but you're worth the wait."

"I enjoyed this evening so much," she said. "Thank you."

"I'm glad," Rocky said. He helped her out of the back seat and they headed for home. While driving, he placed his arm around her to bring her closer to him.

"Sweetie, I'm going to a sub-council meeting with our union in San Diego," he said. "Why don't you take your vacation and come along?"

"I'd love to," Marie said, leaning into him. "Are you going alone?"

"No, Johnny Romanek and Lou Sargent also are going," Rocky said. "We'll take a different flight and stay at a different hotel at the other end of the city. The meetings are held in the morning. I'll rent a car to get to the meetings while you spend your day swimming in the Pacific or shopping. The rest of the day will be ours. We could go sightseeing during the afternoon and night clubbing in the evening. "

"Wow that sounds amazing," Marie said. "You convinced me. Soon as I get in on Monday, I'll make arrangements for my vacation."

* * *

Johnny walked into the lobby of the administration building and was stopped by one of the plant porters.

"Johnny, can I see you for a moment?" the porter said.

"Gerald what can I do for you?" Johnny asked.

"Johnny what I have to say is only for your ears," Gerald said. "Let's go outside so we can talk in private."

"What's up?" Johnny asked.

Gerald Cleary looked all around to see if anyone was watching them before speaking.

"Yesterday when you left the conference room Rocky and Lou stayed behind to talk to Tony Rodgers," Gerald said. "I was sent by my foreman to clean up the room after your meeting with the company. While I was there behind closed doors and no one saw me, I heard Tony talking to them in the hallway. From what he was saying, it's clear Tony hates you with a passion. Tony told them he wasn't going to give the union anything until you realized that he was the one who held all the goodies to operate the union effectively in the future. He assured Rocky and Lou, however, that he'd give them anything within reason. To me it looks like he's trying to split the bargaining committee."

"What did Rocky say?" Johnny asked.

"He thanked Tony for his consideration and then mentioned something about going to see Al Carter about his quitting," Gerald said. "Tony also said something about how the minute you make a mistake, he's going to hit you with the book. I've been working here in the administration offices for years and I've seen and heard Tony getting people fired that stepped out of line. He's a miserable son-of-a-bitch. Watch out for him. He's the kind that sucks you in and then lowers the boom."

"Gerald, thanks for warning me," Johnny said, shaking hands with him. "Looks like I'm going to have a problem on my hands with my bargaining committee."

"You did me a lot favors over the years," Gerald said. "This is the least I could do for you."

Gerald looked around before continuing.

"I'm surprised Rocky didn't try to defend you," Gerald said carefully. He's your vice-president and from our caucus. If I hear anything around the office, I'll let you know right away. I also clean the waste baskets, so if I find anything of importance, I'll bring it to you."

At the good and welfare meeting, which is a meeting to discuss how to improve the union, Johnny argued vigorously, to the point that it displeased Tony to no end. Johnny threatened to take action against the company if they continued to ignore the union's complaints. Many of the complaints were safety violations that could seriously injure workers.

The company representatives stayed behind to discuss the violations while the union bargaining committee walked into the hallway. A production worker rushed toward Johnny.

"Johnny I just got a call from my mother who told me my father had a heart attack and was rushed to the hospital," the worker said. "I asked my foreman for a leave of absence but he told me that he has too many people going on vacation and he couldn't afford to let me go. "

"Chet, do you have any vacation time left?" Johnny asked.

"No, I used it up a month ago," Chet said. "I never expected this to happen. When I talked to my superintendent about my family situation he said I could go at the end of the month. The way my mother was talking, my dad might not last that long."

"Johnny, Tony just came out of the conference room," Rocky said. "I'm sure he'd approve of the leave if you ask him."

Johnny nodded his head and walked over to Tony.

"Can I talk to you a minute?"

"Yes, what is it?" Tony said, obviously annoyed.

"I'd like to have Chet Owens from the chassis department excused for the remainder of this week and next week," Johnny said.

Before Johnny could explain, Tony interrupted.

"You know I can't do that," Tony snapped, trying to contain his anger. "You'll have to go through the regular procedure. Go see the foreman and then speak to the superintendent. Why come to me? You just got through blasting

me in front of Jay, saying I'm not doing my job and I'm hard to
get along with. Why don't you see Earl Johnson? I'm sure he'll
listen to you."

Johnny was fuming inside as Chet stood by with the union
committee and heard the entire conversation. Johnny knew this
was one of the ways he was going to get back at Tony.

"Tony, I didn't ask you to open up the bag of worms that
you opened with Rocky and Lou after the meeting we held,"
Johnny said, pressing his finger into Tony's shoulder. "I'm telling
you that Chet Owens will be out on union business for the
remainder of the week and all of next week. I merely wanted to
inform you verbally as a courtesy. A written communication will
be in your office this afternoon."

What Tony didn't realize was that since Johnny was
president, he had the authority to place union members on union
business without the consent of management. Tony realized that
he underestimated Johnny. He was annoyed and embarrassed that
he was put down in front of hourly employees and union
representatives.

"I'd like to know what Mr. Owens will be doing on this
leave of absence, before I let him go," Tony said.

Chet was very uncomfortable during this conversation and
didn't know what to do. Rocky leaned toward him.

"If Johnny doesn't get you the leave, I will," Rocky
whispered. Rocky felt he was in a politically strong situation
given that Tony owed him a favor.

"Since you feel you have to know about union business,
I'm going to ask you what does Jay do as the plant manager?"
Johnny asked.

"That's none of your business," Tony countered.

"You're damn right," Johnny said. "And what Mr. Owens
will be doing for the union is none of your business and you better
not forget that. You run your business and I'll run the union."

Johnny turned away from Tony and toward Chet.

"Chet, the company has been officially informed that
you'll be on union leave," Johnny said. "We'll see you back here
in a week-and-a-half. Chet, if your foreman or superintendent ask
you what you were doing, tell them to come to the union office to
see me. We'll see you in two weeks."

"Johnny will you inform my foreman that I'll be gone?"
Chet asked. "I don't want to put him out by me not being there."

"Leave that to me," Johnny said.

Tony was fuming as he watched Chet leave. He turned to Johnny with blazing eyes.

"You'll never pull that shit on me again," Tony said. "We all know Chet is not going on union business. You pulled a technicality on me in the contract. You're going to slip one of these days and your ass will be mine."

"Tony if you think for a minute that I'll come begging you for favors, you're sadly mistaken," Johnny said. "You may pull this bullshit on my partners but not me. Now, I've got to be going. I have work to do."

Johnny then walked away.

"I don't know which one of you told him of our conversation, but what I told you was in confidence," Tony seethed. "I didn't appreciate that scene one bit."

Tony suspected Rocky was the one who told Johnny of that conversation and would have to be careful in future dealings with him.

"I didn't tell him a damn thing," Rocky said. He also was surprised that Johnny knew of their conversation.

"He repeated word for word what I said," Tony said. "If you and Lou didn't tell him, who did?"

Tony stormed into his office, slamming the door behind him. Marie was busy typing but heard the whole conversation. She kept her eyes on the computer screen. She knew Tony was angry with the union and the officials.

Lou walked out of the administration building but Rocky stayed behind to catch Marie's eye. He whispered to her to find out what Tony was going to do but Marie shook her head and continued typing. She was frightened that Tony would find out about her going out with Rocky and she needed to be careful.

Johnny went directly to the union office. He stopped at his secretary's desk to give her a directive.

"Betty, please type this up and get it into Tony's office this afternoon," Johnny said. "I'm placing Chet Owens out on union business for the remainder of the week and next week. It's important that he get this by this afternoon."

She noticed Johnny's tense attitude and realized he must have had an argument with the company.

"Johnny I'll do that immediately," Betty said. "Oh, also, I let Bummy Harris into your office. I hope I didn't do anything wrong. He told me he had to see you as soon as possible."

"You did the right thing," said Johnny.

As soon as he entered the office, Bummy stood up with a smile on his face.

"I got a favor to ask you," Bummy said. "I have to be out of work tomorrow, I got a heavy date with this chick tonight and I know that I'll be in no shape to work. I spoke to my foreman and he told me it was okay as long as I covered his ass with a union leave."

"Bummy, when are you going to get married and become legitimate," Johnny joked. "All those cute chicks that you've been going out with are going to wear you out."

Johnny's private phone rang.

"Thanks Pat," Johnny said into the phone. "If he tries to leave, do something to hold him there until Bummy and I get there. I don't want you to get involved at all. Just leave as soon as we get there."

"What's this all about?" Bummy asked, raising his powerful frame from the couch.

"That was Pat," Johnny said, putting the phone down. "He told me Pete Rodney is over at the Circle Inn drinking with five of his cronies. Rodney has to be taught a lesson that he can't bang the voting machines against us and get away with it. I'm sure Al told him about us finding out."

He put his arm around Bummy's shoulders.

"We might be the ones who will get the shit kicked out of us," Johnny said. "Are you game?"

"This will be like old times again," Bummy said, rolling up his sleeves. "I've been out of shape lately. We'll find out how good I am after our talk with Pete."

"Betty, add Bummy's name to the communication telling the company he will be out on union business tomorrow," Johnny said as they walked by her desk.

They entered the Circle Inn just as Pat Fager was leaving. Pete was sitting at the bar drinking and talking to the bartender. Johnny walked over to him and placed his arm around Pete's shoulders. Pete was unable to mask his surprised and slightly trembling reaction.

"Pete, how the hell are you?" Johnny said. "I haven't seen you since the election."

He called out to the bartender to get another round for Pete and his cronies. Bummy took the seat on the other side of Pete.

"I'll have a gin and tonic," Johnny said. "What'll you have Bummy?"

"I'll stick with the scotch and club soda," Bummy said. He took a position on the other side of Pete and gently tapped his arm.

Pete gulped down his drink and stood up to leave.

"Thanks Johnny, but I can't stay," he said. "I promised my wife I would go home after one drink."

The bartender set the drinks in front all of them.

Pete got off his stool. Bummy accidently pushed him into Johnny who was prepared for the move. Johnny pretended to be caught off balance and inadvertently hit Pete in the nose, which immediately began to bleed. Johnny quickly picked up the dirty bar cloth from the bar and began to apply it to his bleeding nose.

"Pete, I'm so sorry," Johnny said. "Bummy, how could you be so careless? Look, Pete's nose is bleeding."

"Let's forget about this," Pete stammered. "I have to leave now."

Johnny placed his arm around Pete's shoulders and shoved him back on the stool.

"Don't hurt my feelings by leaving so soon," Johnny said. "Look at all your friends drinking the beer I paid for. Stay a while. I have about three hundred things I want to talk to you about."

Pete was more than six feet tall and weighed over 250 pounds with only a slight paunch around his stomach. Despite this, he knew he was no match for Johnny and Bummy. He was in for a beating and his body tensed.

He stood up and threw a right hook to Johnny's head, knocking him clean across the floor and over one of the tables. Johnny was up in a flash but his eye was bleeding profusely. He was at Pete instantly, hitting him with rapid blows to the head. Meanwhile Bummy was off his stool and stood between Johnny and Pete's friends.

Pete attempted to run away but Johnny was all over him. They were exchanging furious punches but Pete was no match for Johnny's speed and strength. Johnny threw vicious punches to the head and body, knocking Pete clean across the room and over one of the tables.

Pete's friends got off their stools to go to his aid but Bummy tore into them with a volley of punches. In a matter of seconds, two of them were knocked unconscious. One of them grabbed Johnny from the rear to pin his hands to his side as Pete hit him repeatedly across the head while Johnny rolled with the punches. Bummy quickly moved to help Johnny, hitting the man who was holding his arms with a right cross behind his ear, which dropped him to the floor.

Johnny was again at Pete in a flash, hitting him with everything he had. Pete went flying back into the pile of chairs on the floor and sat there trying to shake the stars out of his head and the taste of metal from his mouth.

Johnny walked over to Pete and lifted him up by his hair.

"You son-of-a-bitch," Johnny seethed. "This is only a sampling of what you're going to get. Al quit the plant and I expect you to do the same. Either that or you stick around and I'll find many more chances to get even with you for rigging the voting machines."

Johnny drew his right hand back and hit Pete right on the chin, knocking him out cold. He then rushed over to Bummy who was fighting two men at once. Johnny hit the man closest to him, knocking him clear across the floor. The remaining man had no intention of fighting Bummy one-on-one and instead fled.

"Let's get the hell out of here, they play too rough for me," joked Johnny.

He took out a handkerchief and pressed it into his bleeding eye.

Bummy viewed the damage and watched as the men got up from the floor. No one attempted to resume the fight. Pete was still unconscious on the floor with a chair lying on top of him.

"Johnny, you think they got the picture that you're pissed off at them?" Bummy asked, as he and Johnny walked out.

"We'll know tomorrow," Johnny said.

The following morning, Johnny walked into the union hall with a bandage over his right eye. Underneath the bandage the eye was still swollen and bruised. George Plassard met him.

George was always the first one in the office. He was sitting at Betty's desk and looked annoyed.

"I got a call from the bartender at the Circle Inn just a few minutes ago," George said. "He said you and a friend beat the shit out of Pete Rodney yesterday. Johnny, you got to get it into that thick skull of yours that the election is over and you can't go around beating up the opposition."

"George, Pete has some nasty friends," Johnny said. "Bummy and I went there to have a sociable drink. We were attacked by five men and we were lucky to get out of there in one piece."

"Look, I don't know what you're trying to prove," George said. "I talked to Pete about the fight. He told me that you hit him first before he decked you."

It was clear George was angry.

"George, why don't you and I go see Pete and ask him why he decked me," Johnny said. "My intention was to have a sociable drink with him," Johnny said.

"Who the fuck do you think you're bullshitting?" George said. "Pete told me that you forced him to quit today and if he didn't, you'd continue to beat him up."

"George, why would I do a thing like that?" Johnny said. "You forgot that I won the election. I have everything to be happy about. Why don't you fill me in on why Pete quit? I'm dying to know all about it."

George shook his head and started to walk away in disgust.

"You forced Al and Pete to quit, who's next?" George asked.

"George, I thought Al was on my side during the election," Johnny said. "Was I wrong?"

George left the conversation by walking into his office and slamming the door behind him.

Betty came walking into the office through the large glass doors, catching the tail end of the conversation.

"My God, what's George so upset about?" Betty asked. "I can tell I'm going to have a tough day today."

She leaned closer to take a look at Johnny's patched-up eye.

"I heard you and Bummy did quite a job on Pete Rodney and his friends last night," she said. "I can see the aftermath on you, what do the other guys look like?"

"How did you get the news so fast?" Johnny asked.

"You forgot that I live nearby and all the bars know that I work for the local union," Betty said. "Whenever any of the union members get in trouble, they call me to see if I can help."

Johnny told her about the fight but made no mention of the union election.

"It seems George is upset with Al quitting and now he says Pete quit," Johnny said. He was hoping Betty might have some information about someone tampering with the voting machines, but she gave no indication she did.

"You see this eye?" Johnny said, pointing. "George never even asked about it. All he did was rip into me and accuse me of starting the attack. He never made reference to the fact that there were six of them against Bummy and me. Lucky for me Bummy's in good shape or they would have beat the shit out of me."

Betty smiled. She was aware of Johnny's boxing skills and knew the men were no match for him, outnumbered or not.

"I was told that Lieutenant Romeo came over to the bar to inquire about the fight," Betty said. "He questioned Pete at length and asked what he did to provoke you. He began to question the other men involved with the fight but realized they were involved only because Pete was their friend. He asked Pete if he wanted to press charges against you but Pete decided against it. Lieutenant Romeo told the bartender that he was going to come over here to question you about it. If I know the police, they'll be over bright and early."

"It'll be nice to see Tony again," Johnny said, unperturbed. "When he gets here send him right in."

"Another thing," Betty said. "Apparently it took them five minutes to bring Pete back around. You must have hit him real hard."

Johnny just shook his head, feigning surprise. He walked back to his office but before he could sit down, Betty buzzed him on the intercom.

"Mr. Romanek, Lieutenant Thomas Romeo of the Clinton police is here to see you," she said.

"Please send him right in, the door is open," Johnny said. "Betty, could you also please send out for some coffee and buns."

Lieutenant Romeo walked in and was met with a warm hug.

"Tom it's good to see you after all these years," Johnny said. "I've been missing you at the gym. Bummy told me that he and you work out quite a bit."

He motioned Lieutenant Romeo toward the large couch against the wall.

Tom sat down on the couch.

"Johnny you still look good," Lieutenant Romeo said. "You haven't changed much over the years. I can see you're keeping in good shape. How are Ann and the kids? I've seen her driving around town. She's still as pretty as ever."

"Ann's fine and the kids are doing well in school and sports," Johnny said. "How are Maggie and your two boys? I haven't seen them since we were together at the shore. That was a long time ago. They have to be grown men now."

"Maggie is fine and so are the boys," Lieutenant Romeo said. "Tom Jr. is married with a son and Ron is in college studying to be a doctor."

"Well look at that," Johnny said. "Good things all around. Great to see you."

They were relaxed when they heard a knock at the door. Betty entered with a tray of assorted buns and a steaming pot of coffee.

"If there is anything else you need, just buzz," Betty said. "I'll hold all your calls until you're done.

"You got a good-looking secretary there," Lieutenant Romeo said. "Don't let Ann catch you fooling around."

"It's not a problem," Johnny said. "My secretary is happily married with two children and I'm still completely in love with Ann. She's been so good to me over the years. I don't know what I'd do without her."

Johnny poured himself a cup of coffee and took the seat next to Lieutenant Romeo on the couch.

"Tom, I know you're not here to talk about my family," Johnny said, drinking from the mug. "What's up?"

"The same old Johnny," Lieutenant Romeo said. "You know damn well why I'm here. Last night I got a call from the Circle Inn about the fight between you and Pete Rodney. I was there when the call came in. When I was told that you and Bummy were involved, I thought that it was best that I look into this personally. Now what the hell did Pete do to get you so riled up?"

"It goes back to the local union election," Johnny said.

He explained in full detail Pete and Al's involvement in the voting machine rigging.

"I went into the bar to provoke Pete to throw the first punch which he did," Johnny said, finishing up the coffee. "He sent me flying over a table and gave me this cut eye."

"How the hell did he give you that that gash?" Lieutenant Romeo said. "You were always the best when it comes to rolling with the punches."

"Despite his size I thought Pete was soft," Johnny said. "I underestimated his punching power. He was probably a street fighter in his younger days."

"I can see you getting pissed off about what he did but I can't understand why didn't you bring him up on charges before the union board," Lieutenant Romeo said. "I'm sure he would have been expelled from the union and out of a job."

"Tom, I thought about that but I didn't want to take that risk with the election committee," Johnny said. "They might have wanted to hold another election. I won this fair and square. I wasn't going to through another exhausting campaign and the expenses to finance it."

"How about Al, did you beat him up?" Lieutenant Romeo asked.

"No Tom," Johnny said. "I just gave him a choice to quit or go up before the whole caucus. He made the right choice and quit."

Lieutenant Romeo finished his coffee and placed the empty cup on the tray.

"I appreciate you telling me the whole truth about the incident," Lieutenant Romeo said. "Pete told me you were pissed off because he opposed you in the election. He's refusing to press charges against you. You're lucky; you beat him up pretty bad. You better control your temper, you're the president of the local union and you need uphold that position with some responsibility."

Lieutenant Romeo paused to think.

"By the way, what would happen to Pete if he didn't quit?"

"I don't think I'll have a problem there," Johnny said. "George Plassard, my financial secretary who is from the opposition group, claimed that I forced Pete to quit this morning. I don't know for sure if he did but I'll find out."

"I'd appreciate it if you could do that now," Lieutenant Romeo said.

Johnny dialed the company employment office and they informed him that Pete indeed did quit. Johnny nodded his head as he placed the phone down into its cradle.

"He quit this morning," Johnny said. "He told them he was offered a better position with another company."

"Are there others involved with tampering the machines?" Lieutenant Romeo asked. "I want to make sure there aren't any more fights over this issue."

"Not to my knowledge," Johnny said, scratching his chin. "I'm sure there were others who were aware that the voting machines were being hit illegally but weren't directly involved."

"I'm glad to hear that," Lieutenant Romeo said. "I can't afford to have you going around beating up your enemies. One last thing, I'd like to have you and your family over for dinner next Sunday. Maggie would enjoy seeing you and Ann again, also the kids will be there. It'll be like a reunion. There were many times we talked about our vacation down the shore with you, Ann, Spike and Sally. That was some vacation."

"Thanks Tom, I'm sure Ann would love that," Johnny said. "Let's make it a date and if something comes up, I'll let you know right away."

Tom started to leave but hesitated.

"I noticed your executive board listed on the door and saw Rocky Durango as vice president," Lieutenant Romeo said. "Could that be the same Rocky Durango living in downtown Clinton?"

"Yes, do you know him?" Johnny asked.

"Not personally but I know of him," Lieutenant Romeo said.

Johnny could tell the Lieutenant was considering what to say next.

"He's been running the number rackets around town," Tom said. "We believe he's one of the leaders and we're keeping a close eye on him." The number rackets was the illegal lottery.

Johnny was taken by surprise.

"I never saw any indication of that in the plant," Johnny said. "I know just about every bookie there but no one ever mentioned Rocky. He ran on my ticket as my vice president. Turns out now he and my plant committeeman are undercutting me with the company. Are you sure about this, Tom? About Rocky?"

"I can see you don't know what's going on in your local," Lieutenant Romeo said, shaking his head. "How do you think Rocky can afford to go to all those elaborate places almost every night and with a different girl each night? I'm sure you guys don't make that kind of money working at Ford."

"We do fairly well," Johnny said. "We can only put in for overtime when the plant is working, and we average about 60 hours a week. Sometimes we get double-time pay for repair work we do on Sunday. But I agree, we don't make a lot of money to live that elaborately."

Johnny looked Lieutenant Romeo square in the face.

"Tom, I'd like to know more about this," Johnny said. "I have to keep an eye on him from now on. He'd like to be president of the local and he'd cut anyone up to get that. He's one of those politicians who always has to meet behind the racks or where he can't be overheard to downgrade somebody but not in the open. He's always pretending to be everyone's buddy."

"You better watch him like a hawk," Lieutenant Romeo said. "He was responsible for beating up a few of his runners who held out on him. You're right about him being sneaky. We're concerned about the numbers racket in town and how it's eating up a lot of the poor people's salary. Once they set their hooks in you, they don't let go. Rocky's ambitious and would like to get control of all the action in Clinton. His ambition could get him in trouble with the other gangs."

"I can't understand why he'd like to be president of this local," Johnny said, shaking his head. "He has free run of the plant and access to every department as vice president. He has no boss except the membership. If he runs against me and loses to me, he would have to go back to work in a department and be confined there."

"Johnny, the name of the game is control," Lieutenant Romeo said. "As president, he sets the policy of the local and has direct contact with the politicians including at the state level. This would give him the opportunity to use the local as a club to get what he needs."

"Well what can you tell me about George Plassard?" Johnny asked.

"He's a nobody," Lieutenant Romeo said. "His only source of income is what he makes from the union. He's a little bit of a lush and is known at all the bars. He's a heavy drinker when someone else is paying and that's often. That's all I know about him. Listen, I have to get going. I'll see you on Sunday at 2 p.m."

Chapter 6
Year 1939

It was a Friday night, Johnny was shaving in the bathroom, while his mother was washing the dishes in the kitchen sink.

She could hear her son humming as he was running the bath water.

"You sound very happy tonight," his mom asked. "Are you taking Ann out somewhere special?"

"No Mom, Ann's going out with her girlfriends tonight and I'm going over to the gym to see the old crowd," Johnny said. "It's been months since I've been there."

He came out buttoning his shirt and went into his room to search for something.

"Mom, where is my light jacket?" Johnny asked. "The one with the football emblem on the back?"

"You hadn't been wearing it any more since you've been going out with Ann," his mom said. "So I put it away under the plastic cover in your closet. It's at the very end of the hanging rod and against the wall."

He removed the plastic cover off the jacket and pulled it on in front of the mirror. But he wasn't satisfied with how it looked. He brushed out some wrinkles and began to brush his hair.

"Your friends at the gym probably won't recognize you," his mom said. "It's been a long time since you were there. That jacket makes you look bigger than you are. You lost so much weight since you went to work at Ford."

He moved toward his mother in a fighter's pose.

"Come on Mom, put up your dukes," Johnny joked. "I'm in tip-top shape. I weighed myself and I'm at 180 pounds. That's five pounds heavier than what I weighed in the battery plant."

She punched him on the shoulder lightly.

"You'll never change," she said.

He hugged his mother then picked her up around the waist and started swinging her. She squealed and playfully hit him until he put her down.

"Now don't wait up for me tonight, I don't know what time I'll get home," Johnny said. "It's been a long time since I've been out with the fellas. But then again maybe the old gang won't be around any more."

When Johnny entered the gym it was like he never left. One fighter was hitting the light bag at a rapid pace and another was banging the heavy bag, while a trainer was holding it in place. Two others were throwing the medicine ball back and forth to toughen their stomach muscles. Johnny stood there a moment, taking in all of the action at the gym. He noticed two of the fighters were sparring in the ring with protective headgear on. He approached the ring to get a better view of the action.

"Welcome back Johnny," said Slugger, one of the fighters. "We haven't seen you around lately. Did you marry that cute little chick that you brought here a while back?"

Johnny went into a fighter's stance and threw two fast jabs at Slugger, tapping him lightly on the nose.

"Not married yet but I'm working on it," Johnny said. "How are you doing?"

"Just fine, Johnny," Slugger said. "It's nice to see you again. It looks like you're still in good shape."

Slugger pointed with his gloved hand toward the ring. Spike was in there working out with Lieutenant Romeo. They had been going at it for two rounds.

Slugger told Johnny that Spike was going to have his first professional fight at the end of the month.

"Are you coming to see the fight?" Slugger asked.

"Well I'll be," Johnny said, surprised. "Spike always said he was made out to be a manager but never a jock."

"He has the makings of a champion if he were to take fighting seriously," Slugger said. "He doesn't train like you did when you were here. You ran every day while working out but Spike is lazy."

"I'm interested in this upcoming fight," Johnny said. "Thanks for the info."

Johnny went over to the side of the ring to watch the action between Spike and Lieutenant Romeo. The bell rang for the start of the third round and Spike moved out fast, shooting left jabs that were snapping the Lieutenant's head back. He snapped a hard right cross to the Lieutenant's solar plexus making his knees buckle. You could see Lieutenant Romeo wince as he covered up.

Instead of moving in for the kill Spike danced around throwing snappy left jabs to the head. Lieutenant Romeo recovered from the body blow and began to wade in, forcing Spike against the ropes. They moved to the center of the ring and stood toe-to-toe, both landing good blows to the head and body. Neither gave an inch until the bell rang, ending the round. Johnny jumped into Spike's corner, bringing the stool with him. He splashed a sponge full of water into Spike's face and began wiping it with a towel.

Spike sat there panting and taking in deep breaths.

"Long time no see," Spike said. "How's Ann?"

"She's fine," Johnny said. "What's this bullshit that Slugger was telling me? Are you serious about turning pro? You have to be out of your mind."

Johnny lectured Spike about what it took to be a professional fighter. You had to have a killer instinct and not just punch and move away. You had to run more than three days a week to get strong legs. Spike was getting ready for some sparring with Slugger and nodded as Johnny spoke.

"Now take a deep breath," Johnny said. "Remember that Slugger isn't going to be like Tom. He's a professional and he'll rip your head off. And he's coming in fresh and you just went through three grueling rounds. His punches will come in real fast. When you go out there, I want you to throw a hard left jab to his face. He'll open up and be a sucker for a hard right cross. No holding back, understand?"

Slugger was standing in his corner pounding his gloves together and prepping to go. Johnny nodded to the timekeeper that they were ready. At the bell, Spike came out fast, throwing a hard left jab to the face. Slugger began back pedaling but Spike caught him with a crunching right that staggered him, causing him to cover up. Spike threw a series of punches to the head forcing Slugger to drop his guard.

"Now Spike," Johnny yelled. "Throw punches to the head. Make them hard!"

Spike moved in for the kill, throwing smashing rights and lefts to the head. He hurt Slugger bad enough to have him drop his guard completely. Spike hesitated.

"Don't stop," Johnny yelled. "Keep throwing those punches to the head."

Spike was all over Slugger who rushed in to pin Spike's arms to his side.

"Spike, throw both arms up fast," Johnny said.

Spike followed through with Johnny's command and broke the hold Slugger had on him. He then hit him with a hard body blow, making him double up. Prepping for a knockout, Spike moved in with devastating blows to the body. Slugger dropped his guard and Spike crossed with a right hook, putting all his weight against the punch. Slugger was out before he hit the canvas.

Johnny jumped into the ring and ran to Slugger to take the mouthpiece out of his mouth to prevent him choking. He broke a couple of capsules of smelling salts under his nose to revive him. Johnny wiped his face with a wet sponge and held Slugger close as he came to and helped him up onto the stool.

"Slugger, you all right?" Johnny asked.

"Damn you Johnny," Slugger mumbled. "You're back here for the first time in months and you got him to fight like a tiger. Why did you have to come back just as I went into the ring with him?"

Slugger pushed away the smelling salts. They all moved aside to allow the trainer to work on him. He cleaned the blood off his mouth and nose, then lifted him up by the waistband of his trunks to have him move around the ring to clear his head.

Johnny moved over to Spike to remove his gloves.

"You did good in there," Johnny said. "That's the way you should have gone after Tom. As long as you're determined to be a fighter, you can never show your opponent any mercy. You were lucky with Slugger tonight. He was cold when he entered the ring and never expected you to come out fast throwing punches. He's a better fighter than that. Don't get overconfident with this win. In a month, you'll have your test and then we'll know what kind of fighter you are. So how did you come up with this idea to turn pro?"

"Since you stopped coming around, I've been coming here every night to work out," Spike said. "I feel that I'm a lot better than the pros here. So I figured I could get paid for it."

"You don't have that killer instinct," Johnny said. "You only went after it when I shouted to you. You hesitated when you hurt him. But your reflexes are good because you moved in for the kill when you heard me. You got the makings of a good fighter but you got to train a lot harder to hone that killer instinct."

Spike's manager, Chuck Waller, overheard them.

"Johnny I always said you two guy could be champs if you turned pro," he said. "You handled Spike real well from the corner. He looked like the champ that he's going to be. You two make a good team. How about it? Have you considered turning pro?"

"No, Chuck," Johnny said, shaking his head. "I told you before that I'd never turn pro. I'll continue to work out at the gym but that's as far as I'll go."

Johnny was examining the bloodstains on his jacket. He could already hear his mother complaining about how long it took her to get it clean the first time.

"Johnny, what are you doing tonight?" Spike asked, stepping out of the shower.

"I'm slumming tonight," Johnny said. "Ann went out with her girlfriends and I came down to the gym to look up some of the old gang. What are your plans? I'm cool with us getting together."

"Yeah," Spike said. "Soon as I finish my shower, how about we head to Mario's Pizza for some slices and a beer?"

"Okay, soon as you're done come find me in the bathroom," Johnny said. "I'm going to try to get these blood stains off my jacket. It looks like I was in the actual fight."

While in the bathroom Johnny ran into Tom Romeo.

"Johnny, you're the one who should be turning pro instead of Spike," Tom said. "He's good but he doesn't have the killer instinct that you got. He had me in the third round but chickened out. He looked good against Slugger but that was only because you were coaching him."

"Like I told Chuck, I'm not interested in turning pro," Johnny said. "I do hope Spike changes his mind. You're right that he doesn't have the killer instinct. Maybe with a good trainer, he could go all the way. Let's wait and see how he does in his first fight."

"How's that beautiful girl you're dating?" Tom asked. "I've seen both of you driving around town together. She's a doll and comes from a good family. You two serious?"

"She's fine, we decided to go steady but we're both young," Johnny said. "We talked about marriage but with the war going on we're not sure what is the right thing to do."

"What are you doing tonight?" Tom asked. "The cold water should be able to take out the blood stains pretty good."

"Spike and I are going over to Mario's Pizza for something to eat and drink," Johnny said. "How about you join us? We can talk more there."

"Yeah I'll come along if Spike doesn't mind," Tom said.

"Join us," Spike said, walking up. "We both want to hear about Johnny's new job and love life. I hear you guys got handed a union on a silver platter, while old man Curly is still riding rough shod on us and getting away with it."

They drove to Mario's Pizza and parked in the empty lot next to the restaurant. When they entered the parlor, Mario, the owner, greeted them. He knew them as regulars and sat them in a booth at the rear of the restaurant. In no time at all, the place filled up and there were only two tables available.

A group of girls came in giggling and laughing as they chattered on. The guys didn't take notice of the girls until Johnny heard one of them order. He recognized Ann's voice and looked toward the table. Along with Ann he saw Sally, Spike's girlfriend.

"I hope you got money on you because you and I are going to pick up the tab for the girls at that table," Johnny told Spike.

"Like hell, we are," Spike retorted. "They can pick up their own tab."

Johnny winked at Tom.

"Ok then," Johnny said. "I see your girlfriend over there. I figured that I'd help you out with the bill. Unless you're too proud to have me share the bill with you. That's okay with me."

Spike stood up to get a better view of the girl's table and smiled back at Johnny.

"Oh damn," Spike said. "I see Sally and Ann with that group. We'll pick up both their tabs and ours."

"Glad we could agree on something," Johnny said, smiling.

Tom called Mario over.

"Mario tell the girls their meal is on us," Tom said. "Make sure the pies are loaded and they get all the drinks they want."

Mario smiled big and rushed over to the girls.

"Ladies, I was just informed by these fine gentlemen at the next table that the bill is on them," Mario said.

The girls began to cheer and stood up. Both Sally and Ann recognized Spike and Johnny and blew kisses over to them before resuming their seats.

One of the other girls picked raised her drink.

"A salute to these fine gentlemen," she said.

"You guys don't make any sense," another said. "You buy our pizza and drinks and don't even talk to us. What's the catch?"

Ann and Sally exchanged looks.

"Girls I want to introduce you to my boyfriend Johnny Romanek," Ann said.

Johnny stood up and waved.

"And I want to introduce you to my pride and joy, Angelo Marrone, better known as Spike," Sally said.

She beamed as Spike stood up and bowed.

While they were applauding Spike, Ann continued.

"And last but not least, I have the extreme pleasure of introducing you all to the best of the Clinton police force, Lieutenant Thomas Romeo," Ann said. "A fine gentleman and friend."

"Me and my big mouth," Tom joked. "I wanted to talk to you guys and I end up paying for your girlfriends night out."

He paused before changing the subject.

"How's the new job at Ford?"

"Much better," Johnny said. "The first job they put me on was really hard and boring. I was even ready to quit."

Johnny explained that it was a much more interesting job and he wasn't chained to the moving line. The union also was able to secure him a raise and back pay. Johnny said they would probably be flooded with orders due to the war.

"I hope you're wrong but the way the Germans are going through Europe, they'll probably come after us next," Spike said. "I never expected that England and France would be folding the way they are. It's scary. I just hope we're prepared when we get involved."

"How did we get on this subject?" Tom asked. "All I was interested in was how you were doing since you left the battery plant. You look so much better now, you got some color back in your face."

He turned to Spike.

"Now is the time for you to get out of that plant," Tom said. "They're hiring all over the country for defense jobs and they pay a lot more than what you're getting. Fighting in the ring isn't the way to make a buck. You'll end up on queer street like Slugger."

"Things are a lot better since I got this new job and we have a union here to protect us," Johnny said. "Would you believe that we have a committeeman who comes around daily to see that workers are treated fairly? When we have a safety problem, he makes the company correct it immediately."

Johnny changed the subject and told them that the plant was going to be shut down for two weeks, and he knew a guy with a bungalow in Point Pleasant on the beach. He asked if the guys could get that time off to go with him.

"No problem for me," Spike said. "If they don't give me the time off, I'll just take it. Then I'll quit and get myself a better job in a defense plant."

"You guys forgot that I have a wife and two kids not even in their teens," Tom said. "Where in the hell could we go in the evenings? Also, my youngest is three-years-old. Why don't you and Spike take your girlfriends along and rent the bungalow?"

"We can't take our girlfriends along unless your family came also," Johnny said. "Ann's parents are very strict but with you and Maggie along as chaperones, we could all go. There's a teenage girl next door who sits for a half buck an hour and she's very good with children. Tom, your wife would have a ball there. Whaddya say?"

"Well, that's good news about the sitter," Tom said, contemplating. "It's been a long time since Maggie and I had some time together. Sounds like the kids would have a ball also."

"The guy told me that there's an amusement park on the boardwalk with all kinds of kiddy rides and stands where you could win prizes," Johnny said. "And the boardwalk has a lot of other things to do too. When I get back to work, I'll pay the hundred bucks up front for the two weeks and we'll divvy up later. While we're there, we could cook our own meals, so food won't cost us too much."

As Johnny spoke the bill came. They each threw five dollars on the table as Mario came by.

"Mario, we left enough to pay for both bills including your tip," Johnny said. "Thanks for everything."

"The next time you guys come in for pizza, it's on me," Mario said, beaming. "Good night and thanks for the tip."

The following Saturday, Johnny drove over to Spike's house to pick him up for the Point Pleasant trip. Spike was sitting on the front steps dressed in a white polo shirt opened at the collar, light tan pants and white shoes. They buckled the suitcase onto the rear carrier rack of the car.

"Did you bring a dress jacket?" Johnny asked. "You'll need it when we go out nightclubbing in the evening."

"I packed it in my suit case," Spike replied. "Let's go over to Tom's house now. Tom and Maggie should be with us when we pick up the girls. Sally's mother isn't too keen on her going alone with me but when she heard Tom and his wife were coming along, she relented."

They drove over to Tom's house who was busy packing everything into the car. Maggie was dressed in a pinafore with a white fluffed blouse and her hair was pinned up in curlers covered with a red scarf. She was slightly on the plump side but her figure was evenly proportioned.

"You guys got here at the perfect time," Maggie said. "Would you give Tom a hand with the bags while I settle down these two monsters? When you place the suitcases on the overhead racks, put the straps through the handles of the milk box. Our first meal is in that box for when we get to the shore. When we get there, the ladies will go shopping for food."

She ran past them just in time to catch her small son from climbing out the car window.

They drove to Sally's house first where her mother was sitting on the front porch waiting.

"Maggie, keep an eye on the girls," Sally's mom said. "This is the first time Sally is going to be away from home without us."

"Please mom, you're embarrassing me," Sally said. "I told you we wouldn't do anything we would be ashamed of."

Sally hugged and kissed her mother while handing her suitcase to Spike who tied it onto the rear rack. He then helped Sally into the back of the car.

"Don't worry Mrs. Alfredo," Maggie said. "Sally will be just fine and Angelo is a gentleman."

When they got to Ann's house, she was sitting with her mother and sisters on the front steps. Johnny got out of the car and walked over to Mrs. Cordone and kissed her on the cheek.

"Mrs. Cordone, this is Lieutenant Tom Romeo and his wife Maggie," Johnny said. "We're all going to be together in a big house on the beach. Angelo and I will have our own bedroom and the girls will have their own room. Don't worry about Ann."

"I feel better now that I met Maggie," Mrs. Cordone said.

She hugged and kissed her daughter on both cheeks while each of her sisters took turns hugging her.

"You have a nice time and please be safe," Mrs. Cordone said.

The drive to the bungalow took three hours. It was a white one-story building with an open porch facing the Atlantic Ocean.

They walked into the spacious living room. A large sofa was set against one wall with matching easy chairs on the opposite side of the room with a console radio between them. Tom's oldest son immediately put the radio on.

Listening to the music, the boys each sat in one of the easy chairs while the women went to pick out their rooms. The largest bedroom had an adjourning small bedroom attached, and was taken by Tom's family. Ann and Sally selected the room on the other side which had twin beds. The last room was for Johnny and Spike. Johnny carried the girls' suitcases into their room while Spike helped Tom with their luggage. Maggie organized the box of food that they were going to have in the evening.

As soon as they were settled, Johnny noticed the two boys standing in the middle of the room looking bored.

"The first one ready to go swimming will get a prize," Johnny shouted.

The children ran into their room to get dressed into their swim trunks.

"Mom where are my swimming trunks?" young Tommy asked. "I want to win the prize." Maggie abandoned her task to help her son search in the suitcase.

Their other son, Ronnie, rushed into the living room.

"I won, where's my prize?" Ronnie asked.

"That's not fair," Tommy said, scowling. "He hasn't got any trunks on. He can't go swimming in the ocean with nothing on. Mom, hurry up, give me my swimming trunks. I want to win the first prize."

"Okay Ronnie, you win the first prize for being the first one to be ready but there's another prize for the first one to go swimming with his trunks on," Johnny said.

Johnny knew the kids were driving Maggie up a wall.

As Maggie assisted the kids, Johnny went to put his trunks on. When he came back to the living room the kids were standing there with outstretched hands to receive their prizes.

Johnny knelt between the two of them, putting his arm around them both.

"You both won a first prize," he said. "The prize is a hotdog and a soda but not until we all come out of the water. How does that sound?"

They both nodded in agreement.

Just then Ann came out of her room dressed in a black one-piece bathing suit, which showed off her voluptuous figure. She looked beautiful with her long black hair hanging loosely about her shoulders.

"Hold on there, buster," Ann joked. "You're not leaving me behind to go out with those little kiddos for the goodies. I'm the first lady to get dressed to go swimming. I should win a prize also. Right kids?"

Maggie came out of her room carrying a blanket, towels, a sun hat and lotion. Tom had the kids' toys, shovels, pails and a beach ball.

"Let's hit the water," he said. "I think we got everything."

They selected a clean area by the water so they could keep an eye on the children. As soon as Maggie placed the blanket down, the children made a bee line for the ocean with Johnny and Tom right on their heels. When they got to the water, they both dipped their toes and decided it was too cold for them. They turned to run back to the blanket but Johnny scooped up Ronnie while Tom grabbed Tommy. They were both screaming for their mother for help but she sat on the blanket smiling.

A large wave came over their heads, sending them flying toward the shore, head over heels. Johnny scrambled back to his feet and pulled Ronnie out of the water and held him close.

"Let's do it again," Ronnie shouted, clinging to Johnny's neck.

Tom had his hands full with Tommy squirming in his arms. Tommy was more afraid of the ocean than Ronnie was, but then gained confidence, evening threatening his brother. Johnny and Tom kept both boys apart and distracted. When the children had enough of the water, Johnny took Ronnie back to the blanket. Then he made a grab for Ann.

"You had enough of the sun, let's go in the water," Johnny said. "It's warm."

She stood up to put on her bathing cap.

"I'll come but no ducking me under," she said. "I just had my hair set and I don't want it coming down."

"That's what the bathing cap is for," Johnny teased.

He picked her up in his arms and carried her toward the water. Spike and Sally joined them. They splashed at each other and dove into the breaking waves for quite some time until Ann had her fill. She pulled Johnny by the hand.

"Let's give Maggie and Tom a chance to enjoy the water," she said. "We can take the children to the boardwalk for their prizes."

Johnny nodded and agreed to the break. They told Maggie to enjoy the water and they would take the kids to get their prizes.

"Let's go!" the children said in unison.

They ran toward the boardwalk with Ann and Johnny right on their heels. When they got there Johnny took Ronnie's hand while Ann took Tommy's.

The boys settled on hamburgers and French fries with a Coke for Ronnie and milk for Tommy. Ronnie also wanted a red balloon while Tommy wanted ice cream.

The children scrambled back to the table when the counter boy brought the food. They dug in and ate the food rapidly and continued to argue with each other. Tommy kept stealing French fries from Ronnie's packet. Johnny was done first so he went back to the counter to order some more food.

When they got back to the beach, Spike was splashing Sally while she was trying to get away from him.

"Come and get it while it's still hot," Johnny said.

Spike and Sally jumped out of the water, picking up their towels to dry themselves.

"We brought hot dogs and hamburgers," Johnny said. "Ladies first. Guys, you take the rest."

"It's been a long time since I had this kind of service," Maggie said, biting into her hamburger. "Thanks Johnny."

When they were through, the men raced to the water to cool off. The children took their toys and began digging in the sand. The women applied their sun tan lotion and laid out on the blanket. A young man with big arms and a muscular chest walked up to Ann and the girls. He stood over Ann, casting a shadow on her while admiring her. She looked up to see him staring.

"Honey, you're very pretty," he said. "I know a lot of fabulous places where we could have a good time."

Ann turned away and pulled her towel up to cover herself and began to read her book. He continued standing above her while still staring.

"Why don't you take a walk?" Maggie said. "You're bothering us."

The young man ignored Marcy and continued to stare at Ann. He kneeled down next to Ann.

"I'll see you later," he whispered. "Honey, you and I are going to have a good time while you're down at the shore."

The man finally left but Ann was shaken.

A woman sitting next to them said the man had a reputation for hitting on every pretty girl at the beach. He even went so far as to assault some of them. No one dared to go to the police because they were so afraid of him.

Just then Johnny came out of the water. He stood over Ann to allow the cold water to drip on her bare back, teasing her. Ann was in no mood to be teased.

"Uncle Johnny, some big mean guy was just here," Ronnie said. "But my mom chased him away."

"What's he talking about?" Johnny asked.

"Some big dope was just over here bothering us," Ann said.

The woman on the blanket next to them spoke up.

"I warned the young lady that the guy is a bum," she said. "He was arrested many times for assaulting girls, but they were too afraid to press charges against him. I believe the police are even afraid of him."

"What's his name?" Johnny said, trying to remain calm.

"Jim Connors," the lady said. "He lives in that large apartment house."

She pointed to a large building facing the ocean.

Johnny pulled on his shirt. Then he sat on the blanket to remove the sand from his feet before putting on his sneakers. Tom came out of the water and picked up a towel from the blanket. He watched Johnny get dressed.

"What's going on?" Tom asked, patting himself with the towel.

"As soon as you dry off, I'd like you to come with me to the police station," Johnny said. "Some wise guy made a pass at Ann. Some lady familiar with this guy warned me that he's some kind of a nut. All I want the police to do is warn him to stay away from Ann."

"Please John, don't make a big thing out of this," Ann said. "He left as soon as Maggie hollered at him."

She took his arm and tried to pull him toward the blanket.

"Let's forget about it, we're having too much to have some idiot spoil it for us," Ann said.

Johnny shook his head as he sat down on the blanket to tie his laces.

"No Ann, I want to put a stop to this before it gets out of hand," Johnny said. "The police station is close by. With Tom being there, I'm sure the police will listen to my complaint."

"Ann, Johnny is right," Tom said. "We'll be back in a few minutes. We don't need some nut making a pass at you."

As Johnny and Tom entered the station they noticed the sergeant sitting at his desk with a girlie magazine on his lap. Visibly embarrassed he quickly shoved the magazine into a drawer.

"What can I do for you gentlemen?" he asked.

"My name is Thomas Romeo and I'm a lieutenant in the Clinton police force," Tom said, producing his police badge. "We'd like to lodge a complaint against a man named Jim Conners. He made a pass at one of the young ladies who is with us. The lady who was sitting next to us said to us that he's some kind of a bully and is always harassing the pretty girls who come to the beach. We don't need a guy like Jim giving our girls a hard time. "

The sergeant sighed.

"We've had trouble with this character," he said. "It doesn't take much to set him off. Problem is if we talk to him, he might deliberately go after her. Why don't we hold off? He might forget about her entirely."

"Officer, I'd rather you talk to him before we have to do it ourselves," Johnny said.

"It's not that I don't want to talk to him," the sergeant stammered. "I just don't want to trigger this nut."

He took a pad off the desk and handed it to them.

"Please write your name and the address where you're staying at," the officer said.

The sergeant warned them that Jim was the leader of a gang which roamed bars and was always looking for a fight. He loved to provoke people into assaulting him first. He warned them to be on guard.

"If Jim so much as talks to any of your party, give me a call immediately," the sergeant said.

"Please make sure Jim gets the picture that we don't want any trouble from him," Tom said.

They thanked the sergeant and walked back to the beach.

Although Ann expressed some concern, they quickly forgot about Jim and the incident. They began playing volleyball and enjoyed themselves for the rest of the afternoon.

That evening they got a babysitter for Tommy and Ronnie so they could enjoy an evening on the town. The men dressed up in their light summer jackets and slacks while the girls wore light, breezy dresses. They went to the boardwalk to check out the local bars, searching for one that had music so they could dance. They found a cozy little bar that had a four-piece band and a great menu. They began to enjoy themselves. Shortly after Ann noticed Jim walk in with a group of his tough-looking friends. She leaned over to Tom and pointed him out.

"Johnny, that's Jim over there at the bar," Tom said. "He's the one with the black jacket doing the talking." Johnny started to get up but Tom restrained him. "I don't think we'll have trouble but we will keep an eye on him."

While Jim and his gang continued drinking at the bar, Johnny and the group danced and enjoyed themselves. It was almost as if Jim didn't recognize Ann anymore. She finally relaxed and danced the entire evening.

It was after midnight when the group left and piled into Johnny's car to head back to the bungalow.

"I was nervous when I saw that gang come into the bar," Maggie said. "I was sure they were going to make a scene. But I think they are listening to the police and staying away from us."

"Remember, this is a small town where all the people know everything that's going on," Tom said.

Johnny pulled up to the rear of the house next to the kitchen door. They climbed out of the car laughing and telling jokes. Suddenly Maggie spotted a huge man stepping out of the shadows of the house. She let out a loud scream. The man had his shirt open and a large gold medallion shined in the moonlight. He stared at Ann.

"Now you're gonna have something to tell the police," Jim snarled. "You're not getting away until I'm through with you."

Ann screamed and ran toward Johnny.

Jim took out a large switchblade and sprinted after her.

Tom flew out of the car and drew his revolver.

"Maggie, you and the girls get into the house and don't open it until I tell you to!" Tom said. He saw Jim brandishing the knife while pursuing Ann. Five thugs appeared from behind the bungalow, carrying clubs with chains wrapped around their wrists.

"Freeze, I'm a police officer," Tom said, pointing his revolver at them. "Or the next step you take will be your last."

They saw the gun pointed at their heads and immediately raised their hands. Jim ignored the threat and continued to chase Ann. Johnny interceded and pushed Ann into the car and told her to lock the doors.

Johnny braced himself for Jim's attack, who came at him in a run with the knife pointed directly. Johnny hit Jim's arm, deflecting the knife. Jim ran around the bungalow and was trapped by a gate. Johnny kicked the picket fence and broke a wooden slab in half with a nail protruding at the end of the stick.

He watched Jim who was in a crouched position, ready to make the next move. He kept moving the knife back and forth from each hand. Suddenly he took a swing at Johnny, who swung the wooden slab at Jim, driving the nail into his opponent's forearm, forcing him to release the knife. Jim howled in pain and attempted to retrieve the knife. Johnny kicked it away and began punching him vigorously. He heard Jim's jaw crack from the punches so he moved to the body, where he felt his ribs give way. Jim kept begging Johnny to stop but the punching continued.

"You won't be bothering girls for a long time," Johnny yelled, delivering the final blow to Jim's crotch.

Meanwhile, Tom had the five other men spread eagle up against the side of the house while Spike gathered up the clubs and chains. They could all hear the cries coming from Jim. One of them made a break from the side of the house. Spike swung the club and hit him flush in the face, knocking out his two front teeth as he fell to the ground. Two others made an attempt to run away in the opposite direction. Tom shot a bullet into the sky.

"The next shot will be into your backs," he yelled. They both stopped and placed their hands over their heads and resumed the position against the side of the house. Spike walked over to the fallen thug and pulled him up by his hair and dragged him over to his buddies against the wall of the house.

"Man, we didn't do anything," one of the thugs pleaded.

Tom slammed his face into the side of the house.

"Put your damn hands up on the side of the building," Tom demanded. Tom kept his gun trained on the thugs.

"Spike, frisk him to see if he has any weapons," Tom said. "Keep their legs spread far apart when you go near them. If any of them try to make a break for it, fall to the ground so I can get a good shot at them."

Spike removed five switchblades from their pockets. They could hear the cries coming from their friend, Jim.

"Spike, get back there and stop Johnny before he kills that son of a bitch," Tom said.

Spike found Johnny standing over Jim who was unconscious and laying against the fence. There was blood coming out of his mouth and Spike could tell his jaw was broken. Spike wrapped his arms around Johnny tightly to restraint him.

"Take it easy Johnny," Spike said. "This guy is out cold. Tommy has the rest of the thugs up against the side of the house." He eased his grip on him, "Johnny, you cool? I'm gonna get the police."

"I'm good," Johnny said. "I'll bring this bastard by myself. Go do what you have to do."

Johnny grabbed Jim by the heels and dragged him through the alley. He then pushed the unconscious man toward the group. The men took a look at Jim's face and were shocked at the beating he took.

Tom took a closer look at Jim.

"Damn it, you nearly killed this bastard," Tom muttered.

The police sirens blasted as they entered the crime scene. The neighbors came out of their homes in their pajamas to see what was going on. The cop in charge took one look at Jim and directed his partner to call an ambulance.

"You must be Lieutenant Tom Romeo," the cop said. "What the hell happened here?"

Tom explained their initial complaint to the police and detailed what happened afterward. He told the cop that Jim and his buddies arrived at the house to attack Ann, which is when the men got involved.

The police were handcuffing the thugs standing against the wall of the house just as the ambulance pulled up.

"My God, what happened to him?" the emergency responder said. "It looks like every bone in his body is broken."

He noticed blood seeping from his crotch. He unzipped them to get a closer look and saw that his testicles were completely crushed.

"Get him on a stretcher," he said. "I'll give him a shot of morphine to ease the pain."

As Jim was placed into the ambulance Tom spoke to the police. They were told that they would have to go to the police station to discuss what happened. The cop agreed to Tom's suggestion that the gang be arrested before taken to the hospital. Jim was in such a serious condition that he needed treatment immediately. Johnny and Tom went to the station while Spike stayed behind with the women.

Tom discussed the details of the incident while Johnny remained quiet.

"These are known rapists and thugs," Tom said. "There should be a full investigation."

When Tom and Johnny got back to the bungalow a small crowd, including some newspaper reporters, had gathered. News traveled quickly of the attack on Jim and his terrorizing gang. A woman in the crowd ran up to Tom and Johnny.

"We're so glad you beat those thugs up," the woman said. "They've been harassing us for years and we've all been afraid."

Tom spoke to the media while Johnny found Ann. He took her by the hand and they walked to the beach.

"That was incredibly scary," Ann said, trembling. "I was so afraid."

"As long as you're with me," Johnny said, pulling her close. "You don't ever have to be afraid."

The remainder of the vacation went by without any further incident. Their days were filled with fun times at the beach and the weather remained perfect for the rest of their vacation. They all had deep tans and the children made many new friends. As they were packing, neighbors brought them mementos of Point Pleasant to take home with them, to show their appreciation for what Johnny and the men did.

"I'm so proud of you for what you did, John," Ann said.

"I'm happy we all had a great time," Johnny said. "And if everyone agrees, we can do this again next year."

The group agreed.

Chapter 7
Years 1956-1962

Johnny's eldest son Wayne was a gifted athlete who became involved in sports soon after Johnny moved the family to a new development in Midland Park when the Ford plant moved from Clinton to Mahwah.

Midland Park was a small suburban community in northern New Jersey about 10 miles from the Ford plant. Most of the homes were Cape Cod style but each looked different because of the added extensions. The development had no sidewalks; the neatly mowed lawns ran from the front of the homes to the paved streets. Most homes had flowered shrubs surrounding them and many had gardens in front with flowers in full bloom.

Johnny checked into the school system and was pleased to see the personal attention given to the students because of the small classes. Johnny became involved with the little league baseball team and later was instrumental in making the Babe Ruth League, for boys age 13 to 15, even more popular. He spent many hours soliciting money and securing sponsors for the league. In addition, he managed one of the teams. Johnny's primary goal was to teach each boy how to play a position. That's why he made it a rule that each boy had to play three innings regardless of his ability.

During his involvement Johnny gained respect from all the parents and players. He never yelled at any of the players when they made an error or mistake. He made it a point to correct the error through explanation or guidance. His team was in the playoffs on many occasions and won the championship on two occasions.

Wayne was big for his age when he entered the eighth grade. One day he came home to announce that he was selected by the coach to be the first string catcher on the junior varsity baseball team, even though he wasn't a high school student. He played flawless ball all season and batted over 400.

It wasn't till the end of the season that Coach Thomas learned Wayne wasn't a high school student. He allowed Wayne to finish out the season anyway. Coach Thomas even appeared before the board of education to allow them to grant Wayne a high school letter in baseball.

In addition to playing baseball, the next year Wayne made the freshman football team. His team finished the season undefeated and the varsity team still had three games to play in their regular season.

Coach Thomas came over to the Romanek's house to ask permission to play Wayne on the varsity team to close out the season. Johnny was about to agree but Ann stepped in. She felt that while Wayne had a big build, he was only thirteen years old and too young to play against seniors from other schools.

In the spring of that year, Wayne won the position of starting catcher for the varsity high school team. He was the first freshman in the county to ever be selected by a high school to start for the opening game. The local newspaper sport writers even predicted that due to Wayne's participation, Midland High School would win their division and go on to the state finals.

At the opening game, Johnny was sitting in the stands and the starting pitcher for Midland came over to him. The starting pitcher said that he was going to ask the coach to remove Wayne as a starter and replace him with the senior catcher, who was the starter the year before.

Johnny had coached the starting pitcher while he was in the Babe Ruth League and knew Wayne won the starting position because of his ability and needed the opportunity to prove himself. He asked the pitcher to try Wayne for the first inning and if he didn't live up to the coach's expectations, then ask for the senior catcher. In that inning, the pitcher struck out the first three batters. Wayne went on to play without error and hit well. The local sport writers wrote praises about his ability as a freshman, no less.

However, Wayne wasn't happy playing varsity and was constantly after Coach Thomas to allow him to play with the junior varsity league so he could play with his friends. One day the coach finally conceded when the varsity team wasn't scheduled to play. Wayne went four-for-four at the bat, with a home run, two doubles and a line drive single.

It was the first time Johnny saw his son so relaxed and acting his age by being silly as his teammates. Ann agreed and emphasized that this was why she wanted Wayne to play with boys his own age. Johnny could see that his son was at home with his teammates. However, he was a varsity-level player and a good one at that.

Ann made one request from Johnny that he honored through the years. She didn't want him to teach Wayne how to box until he was old enough to understand not to bully anyone. He spent many afternoons teaching his son how to play all sports and when she consented, he took out his old boxing gloves to teach his son the fine points of self-defense. Wayne learned fast and soon became an accomplished boxer. His high school chums came to watch him box with his father and word spread around the school about his ability. No one ever picked on him and he never bullied anyone.

* * *

On Johnny's 40th birthday, he drove up the long driveway of a white house with a large bay window and two dormers that made the house bigger. A circular paved walk extended from the driveway, across the front lawn, under the bay window and to the front door that was painted a dark maroon. Both sides of the walk had beautiful flowers and small bushes that stayed green all year long.

A white picket fence surrounded the house, primarily used to keep Duke, the Romanek family's large tri-colored collie, from roaming the neighborhood. The driveway extended through the backyard and up to the detached garage.

As Johnny got out of the car, Duke was standing up against the front gate with his paws between the pickets. He was barking furiously which is what he always did when Johnny came home.

"Hey big boy," Johnny said as he scratched the dog behind the ears.

Johnny looked around, admiring his landscape work in the yard. The wooden flower box that surrounded the concrete patio was in full bloom with multicolored flowers. The patio was sheltered with an awning that was attached to the rear of the house. The perimeter of the property had shrubs planted alongside the picket fence and the freshly mowed lawn. While scratching Duke's ears, Johnny leaned over and hugged the dog while Duke kept kissing him on the face.

"Speak," Johnny said.

Duke howled like a wolf until Johnny opened the gate to let him out. As soon as the dog got out he jumped up and placed his paws on Johnny's shoulders, trying to kiss his face. He pushed the dog away and made a dash for the front door, while Duke was nipping at his heels.

When they got to the door, Ann was standing in the doorway, wiping her hands on the apron around her waist, which was used to protect the black evening gown she was wearing that day for the special occasion. The low cut of the gown complimented her lovely figure. She wore a single strand of white pearls around her neck that enhanced her beauty.

"I was starting to get worried that someone had stopped you at the plant and that you would be late," Ann said. "The children worked so hard to make this evening perfect."

She slipped into his arms and kissed him.

"Today I parked in the salary parking lot so no one could corner me with problems that would keep me there longer," Johnny said, kissing her back. "I'm not late, am I?"

"No, for a change you're on time," she said. "Wayne's in the dining room setting up the table and Saundra cooked the entire meal and baked a chocolate cake especially for you. They worked so hard to make everything perfect."

He started to walk toward the living room but Ann shoved him toward the bathroom.

"Go wash up while I search for Frankie," Ann said. "Saundra threw him out of the dining room when she caught him taking the black olives."

Johnny sidestepped her and walked into the dining room and scooped up a hand full of black olives.

"Keep those dirty paws out of the dishes," she said.

She stood in front of him with her hands on her hips.

"Go wash up and set an example for your children, I can see where Frankie get his habits from," she said, laughing.

Wayne was just finishing setting the table and had a smile on his face while watching his mother scold his father.

"Dad, you may be the chief of the union but in this house, you're one of the peons," Wayne joked. "Mom rules with an iron fist. You see how the table is set to perfection? The minute I stopped, she was in here with her wooden spoon to make sure I go upstairs to the bathroom to wash so you better hurry so we could all get to eat."

Johnny was walking toward the bathroom when his daughter came walking out of the kitchen with outstretched arms to hug him.

"Dad, I hope you enjoy what we made," Saundra said. "Wayne took me shopping for the food, including the d'oeuvres. He paid for everything out of his savings from the newspaper route. All I did was cook."

Johnny beamed.

"I want to thank all of you for this," Johnny said. "I know that I'm going to enjoy everything."

He gathered both his children in his arms in a tight hug.

Saundra was glowing from the affection but Wayne was slightly embarrassed when his father kissed him. He shyly returned his father's embrace.

"Dad, I hope you like everything we made tonight," he said.

Wayne smiled as he glanced at his sister.

"Saundra is a pain in the neck most of the time but she worked so hard to make everything perfect," Wayne said. "But this is the last time I'll ever go shopping with her. She drove the vegetable guy crazy while she checked to see that everything was fresh and firm. Then she turned on the butcher, she had him bring out five different legs of lamb until she was satisfied. He was getting angry with her until she explained that this was a special occasion for you. We spent over three hours in the market until she was satisfied with everything we got."

Ann entered the kitchen dragging Frankie by the hand and into the bathroom. She removed her apron after she checked to make sure the table setting was perfect.

"You can start on the d'oeuvres while I make your father a gin and tonic," she said.

"Make the same for me," Wayne yelled.

"Me too," shouted Frankie who was filling his plate with black olives.

"Over my dead body," Ann said. "Your sodas are on the table."

The dinner was perfect. Johnny attempted to taste everything on the table. By the time he was done eating, he could hardly stand up from the table. He put his arms around his wife and children.

"I'll never forget this for as long as I live," he said. "The food was out of this world and the company was fabulous. I thank you all for this wonderful evening. I can't believe I'm 40-years-old today. What kind of a celebration are we going to have when mom reaches my age? It'll have to be something fabulous to out-do this affair."

Johnny thought about his son, Wayne, who had just turned seventeen. He had the fine features of his mother, his hair was dark brown with a slight wave that bunched up in front of his forehead. He was close to six feet tall, with bulging muscles from using weights daily.

He was voted by his classmates as the handsomest boy in his class and never lacked for companionship. His father taught him the fine points of each sport. He spent hours with him teaching him how to box and showed him how to move around and not take any blows to the head by bobbing and weaving. He made the varsity team as a freshman catcher. His father taught him how to catch a football with one hand with the instruction that he only use that on certain occasions, as a result he became the star of the football team in his second year as a running back and held that position until he graduated.

His sister used to drive him nuts when she brought her 12-year-old girlfriends to meet the star of Midland High School. He always scolded her for that but held tenderness toward his sister that was boundless. The newspaper always wrote about his outstanding ability in all sports.

Saundra was a 12-year-old who took the beauty from her mother's side. She loved her brother but enjoyed tormenting him with her friends. She attended the same high school as Wayne.

Frankie was a four-year-old brat according to his brother and sister but they both kept an eye on him and tried to teach him all the time. They both laughed when they saw him coming home with a bunch of flowers with the roots hanging down.

"Some day one of the neighbors is going to catch him pulling out their flowers and tell Mom to control her son," Saundra said.

Johnny recalled the day his wife summoned him to come home from work when Wayne got in trouble at school. He walked into the kitchen where he found his wife in an angry mood holding a broken spoon facing Wayne who was sitting on the chair with his hands on his head. She turned to Johnny as he walked in.

"Johnny, I want you to take your strap off and give him a beating right now," Ann said.

Johnny couldn't help but smile at his wife's reaction especially when she was angry. Her beauty was even more pronounced as she stood there angry, with her arms across her chest holding the broken wooden spoon.

"Give him a beating?" Johnny asked. "Just like that? Now tell me why he deserves this beating? So he can get angry like you?"

In all the years they were married, Johnny never raised his hands to hit the children. He always left the punishment to be doled out by his wife.

"Never mind what he did, just take your belt off and hit him," Ann demanded.

Wayne sat with his eyes glued to the floor.

"Hon, I can see you're angry and upset," Johnny said. "Why don't you tell me what he did so I can get as angry as you are right now? That way I can get the same satisfaction out of the beating that you would."

Immediately the tension in the room eased and his wife had to turn away as she started to laugh, because she knew he would never take a strap to her son. Ann regained her composure and walked into the kitchen to place the broken spoon on the table.

"John, you come home with a clear head but you don't have any idea what I have to put up with regarding your children," Ann said. "You better have a good talk with him right now. I got a call from the school secretary that he and Bobby Lacasio were caught throwing rocks at the telephone repair truck that was parked at the rear of the school. And that's not all."

Ann picked up a card from the table and handed it to him.

"Look at this report card, he went from a 'B to a D' in both English and math," Ann said. "He'll never be accepted to college with grades like this even if he were to get a scholarship for all sports. "

"Dad, let me explain to you what happened," Wayne said. "As soon as I walked into the house, mom was upset. Then she noticed the report card in my hand. After she got through looking at it, I wasn't allowed to explain what happened. She came after me with her wooden spoon and broke it over my back."

"Okay, son, tell me what happened?" Johnny said, pulling up a seat.

"Bobby and I went in back of the school during our recess break to get a bit of fresh air," Wayne said. "We started to throw stones toward the empty field but not at the truck. Then John threw a rock and it hit the rear bumper of the truck. We didn't do any damage and we went over to the driver of the truck to apologize but he was too angry to hear us out.

"The driver told the secretary that someone hit his truck with stones yesterday with rocks and damaged the side panel of his truck, which we didn't do," Wayne said. "Principal Stover came out to listen to our story and we explained it was an accident. He accepted our explanation but told the secretary to call our parents and let them do the punishment."

Wayne looked at both is parents to study their reactions.

"Ann, did the principle ask to see us?" Johnny asked.

"No, but the office made it clear that we should talk to Wayne about it and that he not to do anything like that in the future," Ann said. "The driver was angry at the boys who did the damage the other day. He wanted to be put on record that his truck was damaged. He admitted to Principal Stover that Wayne and John didn't try to run away but came over to him to apologize."

Johnny scratched his chin in thought before talking.

"Wayne, you know better than throwing rocks anywhere near school property," Johnny said. "I am proud you didn't run away and apologized. However, both your mother and I are concerned about the two classes that went from a 'B' to a 'D'. We have our heart set on you going to college. You need to bring those grades up. I'm going to ground you in all activities until both those grades are back. I know you were expected to play Glen Rock tonight but they're going to have to do without you. I'll explain to the coach that you will not be playing for the rest of the season."

Wayne knew better to protest and realized he had gotten off easy.

"Also, son, you owe your mother a new spoon," Johnny said.

"I'll get it first thing tomorrow morning," Wayne said.

That night during dinner Johnny thought about how busy Ann was with the children and their problems.

"Wayne about that report card, I'm not pleased that you went down in your grades," Johnny said. "Your mother and I intend to send you to college. You'll never get there with those grades. I'm only going to tell you this one last time, I want all your grades to improve."

Wayne knew when his father spoke softly, he was angry and it wasn't wise to interrupt.

"Son, we know you're trying hard to get an athletic scholarship but athletes are a dime a dozen," Ann said. "We want you to graduate with a degree that will get you a good job with a profession."

"Your mother is right, if you don't have the grades, no college is going to accept you," Johnny said. "No matter how good a player you are in any sport."

Johnny placed his knife and fork on his plate.

"Out of all the sport stars in college, only five percent make the pros," Johnny said. "A guy with a degree can get a job any time. We want you to be a success in life. If those grades don't go up, you'll be out of all sports. Understand, son?"

"I'm sorry, I'll buckle down and get my grades back up," Wayne said.

Wayne was true to his word and was able to get his grades up and became a star player for the Midland High School football team during his senior year. The team played flawless ball all season and were preparing to play Glen Rock for the county championship. Both teams were undefeated, with the coaches building their team around their individual stars.

Jack Ryder of Glen Rock was an outstanding halfback and most likely to be named to the New Jersey All State Team. Wayne Romanek of Midland was a big muscular halfback who was the leading scorer of the league.

The day before the big game, the Midland coach gave the team a light workout and the rest of the day off. Some of the players, including Wayne, wanted to get an edge on their opponents. So they went to Glen Rock to watch their opponents practice, hoping to see some of their plays.

Wayne was immediately recognized by a group of girls who approached the Glen Rock coach. The coach asked the Midland players to leave and directed them to walk through the hall of the high school. Although he thought that request was strange, Wayne and his other teammates did as they were told.

As they walked through the hall, Wayne was surprised to see a life-size picture of him with the words *stop him and we win* running below it. Wayne's teammates laughed at the absurdity of it all.

On their way out, the players were met by the Glen Rock principal of the school who joked with Wayne that the Glen Rock team was going to trounce Midland. Wayne laughed without saying anything. They were anxious to leave and get back to Midland.

After finally making it back to Midland, Wayne saw some of his teammates practicing. The players gathered around him and asked about their opposition.

"How did they look?" one player asked.

"They're good," Wayne said. "Their line is big and strong but they're a lot slower than our guys. But I tell you, Jack Ryder is something else, he's fast on offence and defense. But he has a habit of over running his blockers on offense. He's our biggest threat. They're coming up with some secret plays so we better be sharp for this one. But I believe in us; we have a more balanced team and we should be able to take them. Don't get me wrong, we have to play our hearts out to win this one, but I know we can."

While Wayne was talking, his girlfriend, Cathy, walked up. She linked her arm with his and whispered in his ear.

"I got a call from my friend who told me all about your escapade to her school," Cathy said. "Wayne they're geared up to get you good in Saturday's game, be careful on the field."

"They're no different than any other team, they'll be out to hit me real hard," Wayne said. "I'll play my usual game but I'm not going to be the reason we win. Every player on our team is an expert in his position. We played perfect ball all season and we're not going to blow this game Saturday."

Cathy noticed some of her friends gathering at a distance. "I'm going home with the girls," Cathy said. "Could you pick me up tonight at seven?"

Wayne nodded yes.

"I promised Ms. Gordon I would take the first shift working the refreshment stand," Cathy said. "This way we can have the rest of the evening to ourselves."

Cathy was working the refreshment stand to earn money for the senior prom. She noticed her friends trying to get her attention so she kissed Wayne goodbye and left with her friends.

* * *

Saturday morning Ann went upstairs to wake up Wayne and found him wide-awake, sitting on the end of his bed reading.

She knew what was going through his mind since he took these games so seriously.

"I didn't expect to find you awake," Ann said. "How about coming downstairs and I'll make you some breakfast? I'll cook you a batch of pancakes with sausage, your favorite."

"Mom, I'm not hungry," he said. "I couldn't sleep all night. I guess I'm all worked up over the game today. Everyone expects me to play the best game I've ever played and I don't feel well today. What happens if I don't play well and we lose?"

His mother knew the school depended on him to bring the championship to Midland High School. She sat on the bed next to him and placed her arms around her.

"Dear, it's just another game and you're a natural athlete," she said. "You'll see that everything will come together as soon as you get on the field. It's eight o'clock and you have six hours to get rid of that queasy feeling. Let's get something into your stomach and the feeling will disappear."

Ann left her son in his room, knowing she could entice him from the smell of her cooking. She was right; he came down minutes later and ate his usual big breakfast.

Johnny came into the kitchen while Wayne was digging into his food.

"I can see this guy isn't worried about the game today," Johnny said, patting Wayne's back. "Ann, that smells good. Can you make me a batch?"

Wayne looked at his mother with a relieved smile. Wayne tried hard to impress his father with his athletic ability. Over the years, Johnny spent most of his free time teaching Wayne how to play all sports. He never scolded Wayne when he'd make a mistake, he'd instead work patiently with him to correct his form or technique.

"Dear, you should be more like your son," Ann said. "Look how calm he is. I remember the day of your first election, you were up most of the night, walking the floor wondering if you would win."

"Dad, Mom is covering for me," Wayne admitted. "I was up most of the night worrying about the game. She had to coax me down for breakfast."

"Son, I guess you are a lot like me," Johnny said. "I had that same feeling before the election. The next day I was in the plant, bright and early, campaigning hard to get elected. As soon as that ball touches your hand you'll be back to normal. You'll do fine today."

He knew his son needed encouragement.

"Son, you're a good ball player and you'll have no trouble doing the right thing on the field," Johnny said. "Remember one thing, the players on the other team are going through the same thing as you, maybe even more so. What is your plan to celebrate the win?"

"If we win today, we're all going to Van Saun Park to have a cook-out," Wayne said. "If we lose, I don't know what we'd do."

"Like hell, you'll lose," Johnny said. "You guys are too good to lose this game. I've watched a lot of high school teams and never saw players work as well together as you guys. Everyone tackles, blocks and runs interference to perfection. Just play your natural game and you'll win."

"Thanks dad," Wayne said. "I'll try."

"You won't try," Johnny said. "You'll do it."

That evening the entire school turned out for the football rally. The students brought wooden boxes, discarded lumber and anything that would burn for a bonfire and placed these items in a large pile in the center of the open field.

Principal Vreeland had the football coach light the fire at eight o'clock. All the students marched around the fire carrying victory signs and singing their school song while the high school band played.

As the bonfire was being lit, Wayne saw a boy pulling on Saundra's braids and making her cry. The boy was a tenth grader and known to bully kids. Wayne ran over to him and knocked him to the ground. The bully screamed in pain and drew everyone's attention. The football players saw what happened and ran over to help. The bully just lay there as Wayne stood over him.

"Don't you ever lay a hand on my sister again," Wayne yelled. "This is only a sample of what you'll get."

The bully got up from the ground and walked away limping.

Wayne ran up to his sister.

"Saun, are you alright?" he asked.

"Yeah," she said. "Thanks big brother. Now you should go, you have a game to win."

"Nah, it's more important that my sister is ok," he said.

"I'm fine," she said. "I promise."

"I don't think he'll bother you anymore," Wayne said. He dug into his pocket and pulled out a few dollar bills.

"Get yourself something to eat and drink," Wayne said.

The stands were filled to capacity, with both sides tense but spirits high. Both schools were undefeated and confident they would win. The fans carried their pom-poms with their school colors. Because the stands were at capacity the police turned several people away from the gate. An argument erupted when some fans demanded entry. The police eventually went into the stands on both sides to make space so more fans could watch the game. They had to make room for more than 200 extra fans.

Johnny, Ann and Frankie went to the field two hours before the game and had seats on the 50-yard line. Saundra arrived at the game with her parents but left to be with her classmates. Johnny knew that he would never be able to find her once the game started.

When both teams appeared on the field, the stands erupted in applause. Both bands had a turn to play their victory song and the fans joined in singing. After introducing the players from both teams, the game was ready to begin.

Wayne wore the number 13 and was sitting on the bench while the trainer was taping up his ankles. One of the women in the stands took notice and tapped her husband on the shoulder with a gasp.

"Look, our star player is hurt and being taped up," she exclaimed. "If he doesn't play our team is going to be in trouble."

"Honey, they're taping his ankles up so that he doesn't sprain them while he's running with the ball," the husband said. "All the halfbacks in the pros do the same thing."

Ann heard the woman's remark and felt proud that the fans were concerned about her son. Johnny put his arms around her.

"Dear, they worked so hard to get this far without losing a game, they can't lose this one," Johnny said, visibly nervous.

The whistle blew to start. Midland won the coin toss and elected to receive the ball. Wayne was standing on the 20-yard line to receive the kick-off. The Glen Rock kicker sent the ball soaring so high that Wayne had to run backward to catch the ball. He ran with his back to the ball and reached up high and caught the ball with one hand, causing the Midland fans to gasp.

Although he caught the ball with ease like he did every time he caught with one hand, it gave his coach anxiety.

He tucked the ball close to his side and took off for the right side. His teammates formed a wall to protect his run. At the 50-yard line he broke into the open with only one opposing player in front of him and the goal post. Wayne tight-roped the sideline marker as Jack Ryder, the star of Glen Rock, angled him at the 20-yard line to knock him out of bounds. A sigh of relief came from the Glen Rock fans while the Midland fans came to their feet, cheering their team on to score a touchdown.

The coach took Wayne out of the game so he could catch his breath.

"Nice run," Coach Casaro said. "On the next play I want you in there. Tell Jan to call play #22. He's to fake a hand-off to Jimmy and you go around the right sideline for a pass. Got it?"

Wayne nodded as he prepared to go back in. Midland netted four yards on the first play. Coach Casaro congratulated Wayne on the sideline.

"I need a score on his play so make sure you use both hands to catch the ball," the coach said. "Don't forget #22."

"22 right side," Wayne said.

"Right, all of you know that this is a fake hand-off to Jimmy and I'll pass to Wayne on the right side," Jan said. "Okay, let's go."

Jan took the ball from the center and held the ball close to his stomach before handing off with his empty hand to Jimmy who dove into the line and was hit by most of the line backers on the opposing team. Wayne hit the opposing end with his shoulder and made a beeline down the right side of the line. Wayne outran the safety and took the pass with a leaping one-hand catch over his head and he fell into the end zone with the first score of the game.

The stands went crazy on the Midland side as fans began to cheer. The entire team, including the coach, ran to pick Wayne up in jubilation.

"That was a beautiful catch," the coach said. "But please catch with both hands so I don't have my ulcers inflamed when we throw a pass to you."

Ever since Wayne was a small boy, his father spent hours teaching him how to catch a football with one hand. He never threw the ball to the stomach, but always threw it high and wide so he had to stretch out to bring the ball in with one hand.

Johnny taught him the technique of stretching his fingers out wide and softly bringing it into his stomach. Due to this training, many times Wayne felt more confident catching the ball with one hand.

The point after the touchdown, Jimmy Grip from Midland sent the ball sailing through the center of the posts. Midland was leading 7-0. At that point in the game the opposition put all their focus on Wayne, whether he had the ball or not. When Wayne came to the sideline, he complained to the coach.

"Coach, they're hitting me whether I have the ball or not," Wayne said. "Why don't we fake the ball to me and then hand-off to either Jimmy or Roger? We could roll up yards that way."

Coach Casaro agreed and changed his game plan and used Jimmy and Roger on almost every play. At halftime Midland was ahead 24-6. During the break, coach gave the team a pep talk in the locker room. He praised the boys and explained his strategy for the second half.

"We've been scoring pretty good by faking to Wayne," Coach Casaro "At this point Glen Rock will probably change their game plan. They'll go back to playing their regular game and forget all about Wayne."

Coach addressed the quarterback next.

"Jan, on the first play, I want you to hand-off to Wayne who will go right up the middle of the line," the coach said.

He then turned to the offensive linemen.

"I want you guys to open up a hole that I could drive a Mack truck through," Coach Casaro said. "All of you have been playing championship ball. Keep up the good work."

"Wayne, on the first play, Glen Rock will be thinking that we're going to continue faking to you," Coach Casaro said. "When you get the ball, pull it tight into your stomach so they can't see it and take off. We need a lot more points to put this game on ice. They're an impressive team and you're going to see a whole new ball game the second half. It's not going to be easy to beat them, so I'll need you to dig deep. Now let's go and win!"

The team was all shouting when they left the locker room and came back onto the field.

Glen Rock received the kickoff for the start of the second half. They drove up to Midlands 20 yard before Midland's powerful linebackers stopped them. Jan huddled the team.

"Wayne, it's going to be up to you to keep us in the lead," Jan said. "I'll make sure I put the ball in the middle of your stomach. Let's go!"

Jan called the signals with a loud clear voice and at the snap of the ball, he turned and put the ball right into Wayne's stomach like he said and ran back to fake a pass play. The linemen opened up a huge hole for Wayne who ran as fast as he could and was in the open field and on his way to the opposite goal line.

Jack Ryder was considered the fastest runner in the county and he was the only one between Wayne and the goal. Jack was slightly behind Wayne who was running as fast as he could with Jack right on his tail. Coach Casaro believed that Wayne was actually a faster runner than Jack and here was the test he always looked for.

Wayne passed 40 yards with Jack right on his tail trying to catch him. Both of them were straining and giving their all. As they both were getting closer to the goal line, Wayne started to pull ahead and crossed the goal line. The Midland fans could hear the coach shouting encouragement to Wayne as he ran by.

Johnny was standing up in the stands shouting.

"Wayne, run faster!" Johnny shouted. "Beat Jack, put on the speed, I know you can do it!"

Ann was holding onto her husband, praying that her son wouldn't get hurt and that he would make the touchdown.

Wayne couldn't hear anyone but he could see the goal line ahead. He could hear the footsteps behind him and put on his most powerful thrust of speed. He ran as fast as he could while holding the ball close to his chest.

He ran so hard he felt his lungs would burst with the effort. At the 50-yard line, he pulled ahead by five yards and now it was a foot race to the goal line.

Midland fans were standing up and cheering him on and the Glen Rock fans shouted for Jack to catch him. Wayne crossed the goal line and was 10 yards ahead of Jack when he scored. Jack dropped to the turf, pounding the ground with his fists in disgust.

Coach Casaro was the first to reach Wayne, who was gasping for air. Coach picked Wayne up in a bear hug.

"I always knew that you could out run Jack," Coach Casaro said. "That run was beautiful."

The bigger players picked Wayne up on their shoulders and carried him to the sideline bench. The umpires were trying to restore order to clear the field so Midland could try for the extra point. Midland was winning 31-6.

Glen Rock settled down to play hard football and held Midland to low yardage. They resumed concentrating on Wayne again in hopes of containing him. In the third quarter, Glen Rock scored on a pass to Jack making the score 31-13. On the kick-off, the kicker hit an onside kick that was fumbled by a Midland lineman and Glen Rock recovered on Midland's 30-yard line.

Glen Rock was fired up and had Jack hitting the center of the line and after a few plays, he scored and now the score was 31-20. The Glen Rock fans came back to life and were elated. They were cheering their team onto what they thought could now be victory.

At the start of the fourth quarter Midland marched down into Glen Rock territory and the ball was stripped from Jimmy Grip and Glen Rock recovered. On the first play, Glen Rock called for their secret play. The quarterback took the snap from the center and laid the ball on the ground between the center's legs, making it a live ball and faking a hand-off to his running back.

Meanwhile, a lineman picked up the ball and ran unnoticed to the goal line and scored a touchdown. They converted the extra point and now the score was 31 to 27.

Coach Casaro was upset and called a time-out to consult with his quarterback.

"Jan, call play #22 again but to the opposite side," Coach Casaro said. "Tell Wayne I want him to run down the left side of the line and tell him to use both hands when he catches the ball. It's going to be hard for you to throw the ball from that side so tell the linemen to give you more time to throw the ball. Tell Wayne we need this score badly. Jan, get them moving. Good luck."

Jan called his team to a huddle.

"Okay guys," Jan said. "Coach is mad that Glen Rock scored three times in this half. We're going to try play #22 to the left. This is going to be a bitch, give me a little more time to get the pass off, it's a bad angle for me because I'm not used to throwing from this side."

He turned to Wayne.

"Wayne make the coach happy and use two hands when you catch the ball," Jan said. "Okay fellas, let's go!"

Wayne lined up on the right side and broke down field at the snap of the ball. He moved to the center of the field and cut sharply to the left side marker. He ran downfield, running as fast as he could. He looked over his shoulder and saw Jack right behind him as the ball came soaring through the air right on target.

He caught the ball with two hands and made a sharp break toward the sideline causing Jack to break stride and stumble. Before Jack could recover, Wayne crossed the goal line. The Midland fans went crazy. The entire bench was cleared as they gathered around Wayne to pick him up and carry him on their shoulders to the sideline. Midland took the lead at 38-27.

The spirit of the Midland team was at its highest and the Glen Rock fans were in a state of shock seeing the momentum turn around. Glen Rock tried an assortment of plays but couldn't penetrate the Midland defense. They had to kick the ball on fourth down. There were still ten minutes to play and the Glen Rock defense team began to play dirty with Wayne, hoping to put him out of the game.

One of the defensive tackles reached under Wayne's helmet and scratched his face just under his eyes. To determine who was the culprit Wayne grabbed the player's hand and held it until they all piled off of him. He saw it was Glen Rock's #86 who scratched him.

"You want to play dirty, I'll help you," Wayne said to the Glen Rock player.

Wayne removed his helmet when came to the huddle showing the deep scratches. He turned to his teammates Bob Reed and Joey DeMarco.

"Number 86 tried to poke my eyes out," he told his two teammates. "Get him up in the air so I can get a shot at him."

As soon as the ball was snapped, Wayne made a break toward #86 who was lifted up high. Wayne dove into his midsection with his helmet and shoulder pads and could hear the boy moan with pain. When the players scattered off the pile, the player was still laying on the turf unable to move. The doctor and trainers came running to the field to treat the injured man. After the examination the doctor diagnosed him with a broken rib.

"Get a stretcher to take him to the ambulance," the doctor ordered.

Wayne stood near the sidelines with his helmet off. Blood was now running down his cheeks due to the scratches.

Coach Casaro saw Wayne's face and sent in a substitution.

"Wayne go to the bench," Coach Casaro said. "I'll have the Doc patch you up."

"Coach this is the last game of the season," Wayne said. "Please let me finish the game."

"Wayne, we need you for the state championship game," Coach Casaro explained. "Glen Rock is determined to get at you at any cost. I'm sorry Wayne, I know how much you want to play but I can't take that chance. Now please go to the bench."

Wayne reluctantly went to the bench where he received a standing ovation from the Midland fans. Wayne sat among the freshmen that were suited up in their football uniforms only for show. As the game came to a close, Wayne stood up in front of the freshmen.

"Put your helmet and mouthpieces on," he ordered. "And please stay on the bench after the game is over."

As the whistle blew ending the game, Midland won 38-27. A fistfight broke out between the players so Wayne ran out to help his teammates. He threw heavy punches into one of the opposing player's midsection.

One of the Glen Rock players hit Wayne in the helmet with his fist and cried out with pain from a broken hand. The coaches, police, doctors and first aid support were all on the field trying to break up the fight. When order was restored the coaches made the teams line up and shake hands before they left the field.

When the teams returned to their side of the field, both stands applauded a game well played. The Midland band played the victory song, and Wayne and his team took in the moment that was before them. They played the hardest game they'd ever played, and they won.

Cathy broke away from the other cheerleaders and ran over to Wayne, throwing her arms around him and kissing him on the lips. The fans saw this and began calling out their names. Wayne's face turned a crimson red as he hugged Cathy.

"Wayne you were great, those cheers are for you," Cathy said. "Let's wave to them."

She took Wayne's hand in hers and waved them in the air. The fans responded with a standing ovation for the entire Midland team.

"Hold on guys, let's go in front of the Midland fans and take a bow," Wayne said. All the players, including the freshmen, walked to the 50-yard line, spread out facing the crowd and bowed. The Midland band continued to play the victory song and all the fans in the stands began singing the words until the players left the field.

"You must be very proud of our son," Ann said to Johnny. "He played beyond the expectation of everyone here. I hope they do as well in the state championship game."

"I have never been more proud of my son," Johnny said. "My heart stopped when I saw Wayne go for the ball with his two hands in the air. I'd have lost it if he dropped the ball."

As the fans were leaving, many came over to shake Johnny's hand due to his son's incredible performance. Ann, Johnny and Saundra went home while Wayne celebrated with his teammates.

Wayne entered the house at close to suppertime and his mom was ready to put steaks on the grill.

"Congratulations son," Johnny exclaimed, pulling Wayne into a bear hug. "I couldn't be more proud."

"I've got those steaks I've been saving for a special occasion," Ann said. "I'm going to make all the goodies that you like."

"Thanks mom and dad," Wayne said. "It was an incredible game and I'm so proud my team did as well as we did. Later on tonight I'm celebrating by taking Cathy to Frank's Sweet Shop for ice cream."

At that moment Saundra walked into the room.

"Wayne, a couple of my school chums are coming over tonight," she said. "They want to know if you will sign your autograph for them?"

With that she took off running toward the stairs in a fit of giggles. Wayne was right on her heels and caught her at the top of the stairs. He flung her over his shoulders.

"Mom, I'm going to dump this little girl into the garbage can," he said. "She is a smart aleck when her girlfriends are around."

Wayne finally put his sister down.

Johnny watched the scene and his heart felt warm as he observed his children interacting. Wayne reminded Johnny of himself. He knew no one would bother Saundra as long as Wayne was her brother.

"You kids make me so proud," Johnny said.

Chapter 8
Year 1940

A few days after Johnny had quit the battery plant job, he was driving through Clinton with Ann, Spike and his girlfriend Sally in the car. Johnny noticed in the rearview mirror that a car was following them. He stopped at a red light and saw two men sitting in the front seat of the car behind them but couldn't make out whom they were. He noticed one of them pointing to his car. The light changed and Johnny continued north and came to a junction of the highway but the green car wasn't in sight. He ignored the incident and turned his attention to Spike.

"Did anything change since I got fired?" Johnny asked.

"John, you never told me that you got fired," Ann said. She was relieved he wasn't going to continue working in that dangerous plant. She had always urged him to quit and get another job, explaining that the job market was opening up and work was available in a safer environment.

"I'm glad you're not there anymore," Ann said. "I didn't like the way you were looking lately. Your skin is pale and hands are always burnt from the acid. But what happened?"

"I got into an argument with the plant manager because I took a day off," Johnny said.

"Well, you getting fired didn't help us at all," Spike said. "We can't talk to anyone. They're scared stiff. The only good thing to come of it is that Curly doesn't come around in the plant since you left."

Ann was aware that Johnny's parents depended on his income.

"What are you going to do now?" she asked.

"We're going to celebrate tonight," Johnny said, pulling her closer to him.

"I'm not asking about tonight," Ann implored.

"I'm starting at the Ford plant on Monday," Johnny said.

He was pleased Ann showed concern but he didn't want her to worry.

He came to a sharp curve on the highway had to apply the brakes hard, placing both hands on the wheel. He noticed in the rearview mirror that the green car was still there. He slowed down and the car behind him did the same thing. He pulled over on the side of the highway to wait and see if the green car was still following them.

"What's wrong?" Spike asked, leaning forward toward Johnny.

Johnny got out of the car and stood at the front door just as the green car drove by. He was sure this was the same car that was following them in Clinton. He slowly walked around the car and pretended to kick at the tires. When the green car passed he got back into the driver's seat.

"I thought I had a low tire but I was wrong," he said.

They drove for miles until they came to the Rustic Cabin, a club and restaurant. He pulled into a parking lot that was near to capacity with old vintage cars and luxury cars. He drove to the far end of the lot and parked his car on the shoulder of the road. He noticed the green car appeared at the entrance, then continued north on the highway.

An elderly couple was leaving as they approached the club. The host smiled as he greeted them.

"You're in luck," he said. "I've been turning people away all evening. If it wasn't for them leaving I wouldn't have a table to seat you. Follow me."

The dining room was filled with a mixed crowd of young and old couples. They were all there to listen to Frank Sinatra, who was just becoming an idol to teenagers. Frank Sinatra had gone to the very same high school as Johnny in Hoboken, but had left before Johnny started. Johnny was still surprised by how big of a star he'd become. They followed the host to a table at the far end of the room, next to an open window.

"Would you care to order drinks before the waiter comes to take your dinner order?" the host asked.

"We'd like to order a bottle of your best champagne," Johnny said, as he helped Ann out of her jacket. "And please chill the glasses."

"The music is beautiful," said Ann. "Let's not waste it."

She took Johnny's hand and led him to the dance floor.

Most of the couples were standing in front of the bandstand listening to Sinatra sing, so they had the whole dance floor to themselves. Sinatra was singing a popular love song and Johnny drew Ann close to him.

"Ann, I don't know if you know this, but I'm madly in love with you," Johnny said.

He looked into her eyes.

"I'll be earning twice as much money now at Ford. I'd like you to be my steady girlfriend."

"Johnny, I'm in love with you too but I'm not ready to go steady with anyone," she said, blinking back tears. "We're both too young to get serious. We have so much fun together when we go out. Let's not spoil that. We'll talk about this later when we're alone."

Johnny knew Ann was just trying to protect herself so he drew her closer to him. He knew she was the girl for him. They ended their dance just as the meal arrived at their table.

The meal was perfect, the music soothing and the singing by Sinatra was sensational. They sat at the table holding hands while Spike and Sally were dancing.

The waiter placed their bill on the silver plate that Johnny picked up. He paid the bill with cash and left a substantial tip for the waiter and got up from the table. He reached over and took Ann by the hand.

"I'm stuffed," Johnny said. "Let's walk around the grounds."

He stopped by the dance floor to tell Spike they would be right back.

They walked outside into what looked like a fairyland, laden with blooming flowers. The gravel walk was lit with lights that enhanced the picturesque scene. They walked by the benches that were adjacent to the rich green lawn where many couples were sitting, enjoying the cool breeze. Through the open window, they could see other couples dancing. When they reached the end of the garden, Johnny noticed a few empty parking spots right near the entrance. He took Ann by the hand.

"Let's go get the car so we can park here and not have to walk so far when we leave the club," he said.

As they strolled toward Johnny's car they saw two men there. One was sitting on the front fender while the other was leaning against the side of the car, munching on a candy bar. The lot was dark as they approached and Johnny couldn't make out the features of the men.

"Well, if it isn't the tough guy, I hear you like to pick on old men," the man with the candy bar said.

Johnny knew that they were up to no good because his car was the only one there. He moved in quickly to hit the man leaning against the car with a sharp right cross with all his weight behind the blow. He heard a cracking noise as the man fell to the ground. He then turned to the second man sitting on the fender of his car who was completely taken by surprise.

The man jumped off the car and Johnny hit him with a volley of rights and lefts to his face and body. The man doubled up in pain as Johnny pulled him forward by his hair and threw upper cuts to the groin. The man was unconscious before he hit the ground.

Johnny grabbed Ann by the arm and ran toward the passenger seat, closing the door as soon as she was safely inside. He put the key into the ignition, started the car and sped toward the entrance of the club.

"Ann get Spike and Sally here in a hurry," Johnny shouted. "I'll keep the motor running in case they come. I'll wait here until you come back with them."

Ann disappeared into the club and reappeared in a matter of minutes. Both the girls and Spike were running. They piled into the car as Johnny gunned it toward the rear of the parking lot. No one was there but he could see a car speeding out onto the highway heading toward Clinton.

Spike leaned over his seat.

"What happened?" Spike asked. "Ann said these guys were picking a fight. Did you recognize either of them?"

"I'm not sure but one of them looked like the cop that used to come to the plant to pick up batteries for the police department," Johnny said.

His heart was racing and he was fighting to remain calm.

"I nailed into them as soon as one of them referred to me as a tough guy," Johnny said. "Did they come after me because of the Curly incident at the plant? One of them mentioned that I pick on old men."

Johnny paused a moment trying to think.

"Spike, do you still work out with Tom Romeo?"

"Yes, on Monday and Thursdays," Spike said.

"When you see him, ask him if any of his cops got beat up," Johnny said. "Be discreet."

They were silent as they drove back to Fairview. Ann leaned against the passenger door trembling, while looking out the window. She was still thinking about the fight and couldn't stop worrying. When they dropped off Sally and Spike and were alone she turned to Johnny.

"Johnny, I'm worried," Ann said. "What if they are waiting for you when you get home?"

Johnny was in deep thought and shook his head. He drove to Ann's place next.

"Dear, I'm sorry for what happened tonight," Johnny said, pulling her into his arms. "I'll stop over in the morning to see you."

"I thought we'd talk awhile," Ann said, tears in her eyes.

"I'm more shook up than I realized," he said. "I'll see you tomorrow."

Ann was surprised and blinked back tears. She was usually the one to break away first. She kissed him softly on the lips and walked away quickly up the stairs. At the door she stopped to wave but he was burning rubber in the opposite direction.

Johnny headed straight to the emergency department of the Clinton Hospital. He got out of his car and looked around to see if anyone was in the area.

He then walked to the rear entrance to look through the glass window in the door to see if the men at the club were there. He saw an old man sitting with a small boy on his lap. The child was crying while a young woman was holding a bloody white cloth on his arm. There was another old woman who was leaning her head against the chair in front of her while a young man was trying to comfort her. There was no sign of anyone in the waiting room.

Johnny was about to leave when he noticed two men walking out of the hospital toward the exit. He quickly moved away from the door and headed back to his car to avoid being seen.

He recognized one of the cops immediately as the one who frequently came to the plant. His jaw was swollen. The other cop had both eyes blackened and was limping while walking.

Johnny moved and hid behind some bushes.

"That son-of-a-bitch isn't going to get away with this," one of them said. "I've never been this caught off guard as I was tonight. Payback is tomorrow."

Their voices faded and Johnny waited until they got into their car and drove away. As they drove slowly out of the parking lot, Johnny ran to his car and followed at a safe distance behind. They drove to the opposite side of town and stopped at a small one-family home in a residential section of the town.

He watched the bigger man get out of the car slowly, holding onto the rim of the door for assistance. Johnny could see the man was still in pain from the groin injury he had given to him.

Johnny took note of the address. The other cop pulled away from the house and Johnny followed at a safe distance with his lights off.

Soon they came to a two-family house with an attached garage. Johnny parked his car on the opposite side of the road, a half block away. He then ran across a lawn to the house in a crouched position, keeping close to the bushes so he couldn't be seen. He hid behind a bush next to the garage and waited until the cop came out to close the garage.

While the cop was closing the doors, Johnny jumped him from behind. He hit the man in the right kidney with all the power he could muster. The man slumped against the garage doors as Johnny continued to hit him with strong punches to his rib cage until he could hear the ribs crack. The man fell forward flat on his face hitting the ground.

Johnny ran back to his car, leaving the thug unconscious in the driveway. He backed out his car with his lights off. As he drove home Johnny's heart was racing, but he felt satisfied that he had the power back in his corner.

The following morning, Ann walked over to Johnny's home to see if he was safe. His car was parked at the curb. She stood next to the door waiting for him to come out, as he usually did at a certain time in the morning. Johnny came bouncing down the steps and noticed Ann. He greeted her with a huge smile on his face.

"What a pleasant surprise," he said, leaning in to kiss Ann.

"Thank God you're all right," Ann said. "After you dropped me off I was so worried I walked over to your house but I couldn't find your car anywhere. I went back home and I couldn't fall asleep because I was so concerned about you. Where did you go after dropping me off?"

"I drove around for a while to clear my head," Johnny said. "Come on, let's see that pretty smile."

Johnny reached over to pinch Ann's chin.

Ann dismissed the gesture.

"I couldn't sleep a wink last night, worrying about you," she continued. "I ran into Spike while I was walking over here and he told me about some cop being beat up in his driveway last night. Did you have anything to do with that?"

Ann sat there with a look of concern on her face.

Johnny pulled Ann into his arms.

"Come on sweetheart, take that worried expression off your face," he said. "It doesn't become you. I'm starving, let's get some breakfast."

"Johnny, please don't treat me like a child," Ann said. "I'm worried and scared. You didn't answer my question about the cop."

Johnny looked away for a moment.

"Don't worry about that cop, he probably got what he deserved, they make a lot of enemies on that job," he said. "Let's go get something to eat."

Frustrated, Ann sighed and looked away. She realized this conversation was going nowhere.

She got into the car and crossed her arms across her chest. Johnny kicked on the ignition and drove the car to the diner.

He wanted to take Ann's mind off the fight from the night before. He parked in front of the diner and walked around the car to Ann. As they approached the entrance, Johnny saw Lieutenant Tom Romeo exiting.

The lieutenant extended his hand out in a greeting toward Johnny.

"How the hell are you stranger?" Lieutenant Romeo said. "I haven't seen you at the gym in months."

He glanced over at Ann who was strikingly beautiful.

"Is this the reason why you've been away?" Tom said.

He laughed when he saw Ann's face turn a few shades pink.

"I don't blame you a bit, if I had a girl as pretty as her, I'd stay away also," Tom said.

Johnny placed his arm around Ann's waist.

"Tom, this is Ann Cordone," Johnny said. "She's the main reason I've been away but I've also been tied up trying to get a union started in the battery plant where I worked before. I just got fired from that job last week so I'll have a little more time to myself. I'll probably be seeing you and the guys more often at the gym."

Johnny grabbed the lieutenant's strong shoulder.

"You look like you're keeping yourself in good shape," Johnny said.

Tom smiled at Ann as he took her hand.

"Ann, I'm pleased to meet you," Tom said. "Johnny is a good catch. A little wild at times but a level-headed man."

He turned to Johnny.

"Too bad you couldn't get them organized at the battery plant," Tom said. "You have to be a nut or hard-up to work in that hell-hole. Good to see you both."

He began to walk away but stopped and turned toward them.

"I heard something at the station about how you scared the hell out of Curly," Tom said. "Was that when he fired you?"

He paused a moment.

"Do you know one of our cops, named Russ Cooper?" Tom asked.

Johnny shook his head no as Tom continued.

"He's the wise young cop that always comes to the battery plant to pick up replacement for our cars," Tom said.

"Is there a reason that I should know this Russ guy?" Johnny asked.

"No reason," Tom said, looking Johnny squarely in the eye. "I just wanted you to know that he got beat up pretty bad last night. As a matter of fact, he was beaten up twice."

Tom had a sly smile on his face as he continued.

"He was treated at the Clinton Hospital for a broken jaw," Tom said. "Then later on that night the ambulance was called to his home to pick him up. He was severely beaten again in his driveway. I spoke to the doctor who treated him and he said that

Cooper was worked over by a professional. Cooper was always a wise guy, but I guess he took on the wrong guy last night."

Tom turned back to Ann.

"Ann it was nice meeting you," Tom said. "By the way, are you Springy's young sister?" Ann was too caught up in the conversation to answer and looked at Johnny nervously.

"Tom, why are you telling me about Russ?" Johnny asked.

"Russ is going out with Ray Curly's daughter and he's pretty tight with the family," Tom said. "There's another cop who was assaulted last night with Russ, his name is Terry Laughlin. He's got a mean streak in him. He's the kind who gives out tickets for any trivial violations. He and Russ are real tight."

Tom stopped to look down at his watch.

"I got to go," Tom said. "It was great meeting you, Ann. See ya Johnny."

After Tom walked away Johnny pulled Ann toward him. She was trembling with fright. They walked into the diner and Ann turned to Johnny with concern written all over her face.

"Johnny, he knows you're the one who beat those two up and he's trying to tell you to be careful," Ann said.

Johnny was about to answer when he noticed Spike walk into the diner.

"Spike, over here," Johnny called out.

Spike walked over with a huge smile on his face.

"Hi Ann," Spike said quickly, and then turned to Johnny.

"Did Tom tell you about that cop Russ Cooper?" Spike said. "You really did some job on him last night."

Johnny feigned innocence but Spike continued.

"You should have told me what you had in mind, we could have done a job on both of them," Spike said.

He pointed to the door.

"That was Tom Romeo talking to you and Ann outside the diner a minute ago, right?" Spike said.

"Yes, and he told us what happened to a cop named Russ and that he was going steady with Curly's daughter," Ann said. "He warned Johnny to be careful of both those cops, they're both spiteful. But Johnny is too stubborn to take heed of these warnings."

Ann was shaking her head, her eyes wide with worry.

Spike shouted to the short order cook who was in the kitchen.

"Get me three cups of coffee and three orders of ham and eggs," Spike said.

He turned to Johnny.

"This one is on me," Spike said.

He stopped talking while the cook placed the coffees on the table in front of them.

"Did Tom say how Russ is?" Spike asked.

"I'm not interested in Russ," Johnny said, sipping some coffee. "He got what he deserved. He was the one looking for trouble. Just because they're cops doesn't mean they can go around threatening people. We'll see what happens down the road."

Spike rose from his seat and pointed outside.

"Johnny, that cop is putting a ticket on your car for something," Spike said.

Johnny got up from his seat to look out the window and recognized the cop as one of the men who attacked him the night before. He rushed out of the diner with Spike and Ann at his heels. Johnny approached the officer who had his summons book open in his hand and was beginning to write. He saw Johnny approaching.

"Sir, does this car belong to you?" the cop asked.

"You know damn well it belongs to me," Johnny said. "It's the same one that you were sitting on last night at the Rustic Cabin."

Johnny had a clenched fist at his side.

"Now wait a minute," the cop said. "I don't know what you're talking about."

He pointed to the rear tire that was pressing up against the curb.

"I noticed your car was illegally parked against the curb which is a violation of the town ordinance," the cop said. "If everyone parked here like that, all the curbs in town would be broken in no time at all."

"Officer Laughlin, what ordinance were you violating when you and your partner attempted to attack me and my girlfriend last night?" Johnny asked, moving closer to the cop.

"I don't know who you are or anything about the Rustic Cabin," the cop said. "I do know that you're in violation of the town's ordinance # 32 which forbids anyone from parking on the curb."

The cop began writing up the violation in his summons book.

Johnny was annoyed especially after Lieutenant Romeo warned him about that Terry and Russ would be after him for anything. He knew he had to go on the offensive with this cop. He shouted in a loud voice so that everyone nearby could hear and see what was going on.

"Officer Laughlin, I'm not going to play games with you," Johnny said. "I was warned a few minutes ago that you and Officer Cooper would try to ticket me for any minor violation. I'm not going to take this laying down. As soon as you get through writing that ticket I expect you to come with me to the Clinton Hospital to see if Officer Cooper was treated by them after being in a fight last night."

Johnny pointed to Ann.

"My girlfriend will come along, she was a witness when you guys tried to jump me," Johnny said. "She'll have a damn good case against you two for attempting to assault a woman. That'll make news in this town, police brutality."

Officer Laughlin's face flushed with anger. A crowd began to gather to witness the argument. He knew he would be in trouble if he didn't back away from issuing the summons.

"I'll forget this violation but in the future, you be careful how you park your car," Officer Laughlin stammered.

The squad car with Lieutenant Romeo pulled up alongside the crowd.

"Officer Laughlin, what's the problem?" he asked.

"No trouble sir, just a misunderstanding on my part," Officer Laughlin said. "I'm sorry if I inconvenienced you in any way, Mr. Romanek."

"See, you knew who I was this entire time," Johnny said.

He turned to Lieutenant Romeo.

"I think Officer Laughlin and I have an understanding now," Johnny said. "I don't think we'll have any more trouble in the future. Right, Officer Laughlin?"

"There'll be no more problems in the future, Mr. Romanek," Officer Laughlin said. He closed the summons book and placed it in his pocket. Then walked slowly back to his squad car.

On Monday morning, Johnny reported to the Ford employment office along with the new men who were anxious to get to work. The employment manager called off names and the men were separated into groups so they could report to their appointed department and each assigned a task. Johnny was appointed to the paint department.

His foreman, named Smokey Joe, took his group to the general store to buy them tools and garments to perform their jobs. Johnny was given a pair of boots, a large rubber apron and a pack of fine sand paper.

After given the proper work tools, Smokey Joe took Johnny up a steel stairway to the paint department. He led them past a line stored with unfinished car bodies to be worked on until they came into the area called the duck pond. It was here where the workers had to sand paper the coat of paint to a smooth finish until it was to be sprayed for the final coat of paint.

"I want you guys to put on the boots and apron now," Smokey Joe said. "You're all going to be working here from now on. You rub the cars down with the sand paper like the other guys are doing. You gotta use the water with the sand paper because the water helps to cut the paint. The reason we sand the paint is to get the paint smooth so when we spray the finishing coat, it's nice and polished. The most important thing is to finish your job in the time allowed and make sure you don't get in the other workers' way. There's an inspector at the end of the line to make sure every job is done right. If he finds fault with your job, he'll call you down to fix it."

"Romanek, I'm assigning you to sand the front quarter panel," Smokey Joe said. "It's tricky because of the fine curves so make sure you make it smooth. Once you get the hang of the job, it'll be real easy."

Johnny found working on a moving line was the most boring job he ever had. He was forever checking and rechecking to make sure the surface was smooth and that he did it right.

The line was in perpetual motion with the cars never failing to arrive. He couldn't go to the bathroom unless another man relieved him and then he had to hurry back so the man could relieve someone else.

When the quitting bell rang, he gave a deep sigh of relief. He would be so tired he could hardly walk to the locker room to change his clothes and boots.

He slowly walked out of the locker and down the stairs to the crane way where he ran into his father who was talking with his co-workers. He slapped his son on his back.

"Hey Johnny, how do you like working at Ford?" the elder Romanek asked.

"Pop, this is the hardest job I've ever worked on," Johnny sighed. "There's no end of that moving line. It's also really boring. This job could drive a man nuts."

"The job might be boring but at least your clothes and pants aren't falling apart," Frank Romanek said. "Be patient, you'll get used to working here."

When they walked into the house, his mother had a large pot roast sitting on the table.

"Son, I made your favorite meal today," Ann said. "It's a treat to celebrate your new job and working alongside your father."

"Mom, I don't know what's worse, getting burned with acid or dying from sheer exhaustion and boredom," Johnny said, throwing his jacket on the dining room chair.

"Ford sure knows how to get the most out of a man," Johnny said. "I don't know how Pop was able to work there all the years."

"Now don't be a baby, go wash up so we can all eat," his mother said. "You worked a lot harder when you were unloading the ships. My heart ached when you worked those long hours and fell asleep at the table."

"Mom, soon as we're done eating, I'm going to take a bath and then take Ann for a ride," Johnny said.

"I thought you said that you were too tired," his mother said, serving him a heaping portion of pot roast and special homemade noodles. "You should go to bed so you can be rested for tomorrow's work."

"I won't be too late," Johnny said, anxious to eat his mother's delicious supper.

He ate quickly and changed his clothes. He couldn't bring Ann home too late.

He picked up Ann at her home and they drove into the country by a local lake to enjoy the view, but Ann could see that Johnny wasn't his normal self. He looked tired and he didn't have any of the enthusiasm that showed when he first got the job at Ford. She snuggled up close to him.

"Dear, you look so tired," she said. "The job is not what you expected is it?"

"It's very boring," he said. "At least at the battery plant, you could stop at any time to go to the bathroom or take a breather. The working conditions are about the same. They're never satisfied with your work and there's always a threat of being fired if you don't produce. With the working conditions the way they are today, everyone is afraid of being fired. Out of the four guys who were hired with me today, two of them already quit within an hour. To even go to the bathroom, it's like being back in elementary school. You have to get the foreman's permission and he gets a man to relieve you, then you have to get right back. If you had a stomach problem and walked off to relieve yourself, they'd fire you on the spot."

He sighed.

"That's enough about my job," Johnny said. He kicked on the ignition.

"The evening is young," Johnny said. "Let's take a ride over to the gym. I haven't been there in months."

"I'd like that," Ann said. "I'm curious what it's like there. You talk about it so much."

When they entered the gym, the fighters stopped and joked around with Johnny. Some welcomed him back while others asked how he was doing. All of them stared at Ann. She turned a crimson red as the "oh's" and "ah's" came.

Johnny placed his arm around her waist and introduced her to them. She was surprised to see their reaction to seeing Johnny and was pleased to see so many gather around him and ask questions.

While they were talking she noticed two fighters who were slugging it out in the ring. It was the first time that she witnessed such a fight. Their quickness and graceful movements fascinated her as they threw punches at each other. They noticed her watching and one of them threw up his hands to stop the fighting. He walked toward Ann while removing his boxing gloves and his headgear. She recognized one of the fighters as Spike.

"Please don't stop on my account," she said.

The other fighter was Lieutenant Romeo, who jumped over the ropes and came down from the ring to see Ann.

"We were just winding down and you gave us an excuse to stop," Spike said.

Spike was removing his gloves and turned to the other fighter.

"Tom, you've met Ann Cordone before," Spike said.

"It's nice to see you again, Ann," Tom said.

He looked around and spotted Johnny with a group of fighters.

"Ann, I have to talk to Johnny for a bit," Tom said. Tom walked up to Johnny and asked to chat.

"Sure thing, Tommy," Johnny said. Johnny and Tom drifted to the far corner of the gym so no one could hear them talk.

"It's good seeing you again," Tom said. "It's like old times having you around. But that's not what I want to talk about. I went to see Russ Cooper in the hospital and had a long talk with him. He admitted that he and Terry came up to the Rustic Cabin, to work you over because of the Ray Curly incident."

Tom said Russ couldn't talk because his jaw was wired shut but he wrote the whole incident down on a pad. Russ referred to the fight with Ray Curly and it was Roy's suggestion that Johnny ought to be taught a lesson. Tom said both of them underestimated Johnny completely.

"They're both rough guys and can handle themselves but they never expected you to come out punching right off the bat," Tom continued. "All Russ could remember was getting hit on the jaw and Terry helping him to get into the car. He was in a fog as Terry was burning rubber as they headed for home. They were treated at the Clinton Hospital and gave the doctor a phony story about what happened. I asked him about the working over he got in his driveway but he never saw who or what hit him. He remembered that someone hit him in the balls and he passed out from the shot. He had no idea how his ribs were broken but he suspects it was you who did that as well."

Johnny began to get angry at the accusation but Romeo placed his hand on his shoulder.

"Don't get hot just hear me out," Tom said.

"I'm sorry Tommy, go ahead," Johnny said.

"All Russ could remember was waking up in the hospital with the nurse wiping his forehead with a wet cloth," Tom said. "He didn't say it was you who worked him over but he felt it was you because you had a reason to go after him and rightfully so. Johnny, they deserved what they got. I talked to the doctor and he said that whoever worked Russ over was a professional. I saw you fight and I know your capabilities."

"Tommy, I wasn't the one who worked him over in the driveway," Johnny said. "I admit that I was the one who beat them up by the Rustic Cabin. If Ann wasn't there with me, I assure you that both of them would be in the hospital right now."

"Now, now Johnny, don't get all upset," Tom said, urging Johnny to relax. "I'm only relating what Russ told me. The reason I'm telling you all this is that I warned Russ to forget about the incident and I told him to tell Terry to do likewise. Terry is on a long weekend and when he comes back, I'll tell him the same thing."

Tom paused.

"Johnny, I'd like you to forget about the fight also," Tom said. "The only one who was the victim in this whole incident is Ann. No cop has the right to scare a girl like they did."

"I'm glad Russ admitted to the attack," Johnny said, relaxing a bit.

"Russ has to be the sorriest son-of-a-bitch around," Tom said. "I saw the expression on his face while we were talking."

They both noticed Ann walking over toward them.

"What are you talking about?" she asked with a worried expression on her face. "Is everything all right?"

"Everything is fine, hon," said Johnny.

He placed his arm around her waist to assure her not to worry. He glanced at Tom.

"Tom was telling me that Russ admitted to attacking us," Johnny said. "I told Tom that I didn't know who attacked Russ in his driveway but I feel he deserves everything he got. I don't feel any policeman has the right to intimidate any citizen for something that happened in a personal setting."

"Ann, I'm sorry it had to be a cop who scared you but they got what they deserved," Tom said. "I'm making sure that nothing like this happens again. I talked to the chief-of-police about the fight and he's going to talk to both of them. He mentioned that if any of them have any dealings with either of you they better be a thousand times on the side of the law, if not, their necks will be in a noose."

"Thanks Tom," Johnny said, patting his friend on the back. "I appreciate all that you told me."

He took Ann by the hand and waved goodbye to the other fighters in the distance.

"Let's leave so we can take a walk in the park and enjoy this pleasant weather," Johnny said.

They walked outside and Johnny noticed Spike coming out.

"Here comes Spike, I'll ask him if he wants to come along?" Johnny said to Ann.

"No John, I really want to be alone with you," she said.

She linked her arm inside his as she led him away from the gym.

"If Spike comes along, all you will talk about is the fight," Ann said. "He saw you talking to Lieutenant Romeo and he's gonna spend the whole evening asking questions."

Tom was outside too and noticed Ann pulling Johnny by the arm to get away, so he intercepted Spike and talked to him instead.

At the park couples were taking advantage of the beautiful evening by laying on the grass or sitting on blankets while listening to music from their radios.

Johnny and Ann walked along the lake until they found an empty bench to sit on. Johnny placed his arm around her neck but she pushed him away.

"Please John, this is no place to neck," Ann said. "Let's be serious. There's so much that we have to talk about."

"Okay, let's talk serious, not about the cops, not about Tommy or the gym," Johnny said. "Let's talk about us."

"Actually I want to know everything Tom told you," Ann said. "This concerns me."

"I know that you're concerned about me," Johnny said, taking her in his arms. "I love you very much. I meant what I said at the Rustic Cabin. I want to go steady with you. I loved you from the very first time I met you. We've been going out together for some time now and I'm always looking forward to being with you."

She snuggled closer to him.

"After the attack, I realized I was very much in love with you too, John," she said. "But is this the right time to start going steady? It won't be long before we're dragged into the war with Germany. Our government is now meeting with Japan to avert a war and yet we're shipping used metal over to Japan and they'll probably make weapons out of that and use it against us."

He could see tears in her eyes as she spoke. He took her in his arms, pulling her close to him.

"Hey, what's with the tears?" Johnny asked, hugging her. "President Roosevelt is no fool, he knows what he's doing. I don't see him getting us in any war right now. All our factories are going full-blast making all kinds of weapons for England and their allies. Germany can't afford to take on another front, they have their hands full fighting Russia who wants a piece of the action. Germany and Japan want to expand to get more land to feed their people and control the world. Japan already conquered a lot of land from China and as soon as the Germans get the Russians out of Poland, they'll both be satisfied and then both countries will start negotiating for peace. We're in no position to get into the war. We just started drafting men into the armed forces and it will take them years of training before we could be prepared to do anything. "

"I guess I'm a worrywart," Ann sighed, pulling away from him. "John if we were to go steady, we'd both have to save money for the future. So I gotta ask you, do you have any money in the bank?"

Johnny looked away from Ann before answering.

"No, I don't have a bank account," he said. "For the last few years, I've been the main support for my family and I was giving my whole paycheck to my mother. I had enough for myself to buy my lunch, gas for my car and enough money to take you out. Now that my father got called back to work at Ford, my family won't need much from me. And now that I'm working at Ford, I'll be making twice as much as I was in the battery plant. I'll be able to keep most of my pay from now on. I could also get a couple of fights and we'll have plenty of money."

"No John, you don't need to fight," Ann said. "I've been putting away sheets, curtains and other small things to start a home. My mother promised me that I could have the new set of dishes that she set aside a few years ago. She also said I could have her old set of silverware that she has."

He took her hands in his.

"We can't be spending money like we were," she said. "I enjoy the simple things in life, like going swimming at the lake or taking a ride in the country, having picnics. We don't have to go to nightclubs. The money we save will come in handy if and when we get married."

"Hon, I know we have to save for the future but we don't need to go crazy and not do things," he said. "If we stop doing things, you'll be bored in no time at all. We have to have our enjoyment but we'll do it conservatively. Will that be all right with you?"

He took her hand and helped her off the bench. She nodded and he hugged her tight.

"I am so lucky to have found you," Johnny said.

"Me too, John," Ann said. "I'm so lucky to know you."

Chapter 9
Year 1965

Johnny made a practice of spending an equal time walking the production lines on day and night shifts. He was politically aware that workers wanted to see members of the bargaining committee so they could air their issues.

Most committeemen used their time confined to the day shift, meeting with management on safety problems, listening to grievances, health problems and problems in general. Rocky and Lou, especially, rarely went on the night shift. They felt they did their work when they met with management on plant problems during the day. Occasionally they did go on nights when a serious problem arose.

A couple days a week, Johnny came home to have supper with his family and afterward, he would go on the night shift. One night as soon as he stepped back into the plant, he met two of the committeemen who informed him that there was a problem in the body shop. The issue was so serious that men walked off the line in protest.

"It never stops, does it?" Johnny grumbled as he walked over to the body shop.

When they got there, a mob was gathered around the front of the superintendent's office, screaming that they weren't going back to work until the problem was resolved. They were gathered around their committeeman, Burt Landers, demanding that they talk to the company because a superintendent named Roy Acuff called a black worker named Byron a motherfucker. Adding insult to injury, the superintendent referred to Byron as a "boy."

"Let's get the racist bastard out of here," some of the protesters shouted.

When they spotted Johnny, one of the black workers walked up to him.

"Johnny, we're not going back to work until you do something to that racist bastard," the man said. "Who the fuck does he think he is in referring to us as 'boy'?"

The men gathered closer to hear what Johnny would say.

Johnny raised his hand above his head to quiet them down.

"I just got here," Johnny said. "Let me talk to Bud to get all the facts."

He then went into Bud's office to discuss the incident.

Bud told Johnny that Byron was absent, but produced a doctor's note excusing his absence. As he was being assigned a new job, superintendent Acuff intervened and asked that Byron go back to the job he was at before his absence. He told him to get his ass on the job assigned to him. Byron balked at the way Superintendent Acuff was talking to him. A lot of the other workers were there listening to what happened, Bud said.

Superintendent Acuff had then shouted to another superintendent to "get this motherfucker on the job I assigned to him or he's fired."

Byron asked to be treated like a man, which is when Superintendent Acuff called him a "boy" and said "all you niggers are alike."

"You know the body shop office has windows all around and all the men outside could hear the remarks, the shouting and the action taking place in the office," Bud said. "After that all the black workers walked off their jobs and a riot started. Now we have a wild cat strike on our hands."

Johnny glanced outside the office and saw the group grew to over 100 angry men. The production lines were now all stopped. Some of the workers didn't want to get involved and stood next to their machines, silent. The foreman stayed in the office not knowing what to do. No one made any attempt to get the workers back to the production lines.

During this period the leaders of the black militants realized that they could unite the black workers within the plant especially since a black labor rep, Ed Hubot, was involved.

Manny Head, a black militant leader, shouted at the disgruntled crowd.

"Are we going to let this racist get away with this?" he asked.

The group responded with yells and screamed profanities. They began picking up items and throwing them at the production line. One pointed to a foreman nearby.

"These motherfuckers are all the same," one worker snarled.

The foreman moved into his office for protection.

"We're not going to stand for this any longer," Manny said.

He pointed to Ed, relations only black representative. Ed was still standing outside the office door with a couple of foreman watching the crowd gather.

"Look at our rep standing there," Manny shouted. "He knows we are being abused. And that's why you don't see him coming over to tell us to go back to work. We're not going back to work until superintendent Acuff is fired. We're going to get the respect we deserve."

The mob began to get unruly. Johnny realized they were not going to let go of this issue.

Johnny walked to the crowd with his hands up in the air to get their attention.

"We're not going to be able to resolve anything standing here," Johnny said. "Bud and I are going to go meet with top officials to discuss appropriate action against Superintendent Acuff."

The workers cheered.

"This will take time," Johnny said. "That means either you go home or you go back to work. I don't want anyone milling about. When we're through with our meeting, we'll let you know what happened."

Johnny felt satisfied that he had control over the situation but he had to have a meeting with the entire night shift committeemen to discuss the incident.

"This is one hot potato and it could carry over to the day shift," Johnny said. "We can't afford for that to happen. "He turned to Freddie McCoy. "This worker is from your department," Johnny said. "Fill me in on him."

Freddie told Johnny that the worker had just completed his probationary period. He had a light job assembling taillights and completed his job without complaint. He was observed meeting with Manny's people, but never got involved in civil disobedience.

"Is this a setup to get Roy fired?" asked Johnny.

"No," Freddie said, shaking his head. "The incident leading up to this work stoppage was caused by Roy."

Johnny sat there reviewing all the facts in his head.

"This is going to be one headache to put to bed," he said. "The newspapers have been playing up the unrest in the black community due to them being denied their rights in the work place. Roy has to be one dumb son-of-a-bitch or he never reads newspapers. This is one hell of a time for him to pull off something like this."

Johnny realized black workers were very touchy about being called "boy." He wasn't sure how best to approach the company on this matter.

"You said Ed refused to send the worker back to the previous job as directed by Roy?" Johnny asked.

"No," Burt said. "Looks like he wanted this situation to run its course. Maybe to hang Roy at our expense. Ed has to play it safe and not get involved in all this. He's ambitious and knows that he has to protect the company in this situation. He also knows there are no black representatives in labor relations so he's going to watch what he says since he's the only black rep there."

Johnny stood up with an idea.

"Let's get Tony Rodgers off his dead ass and force him back into the plant," Johnny said. "He'll love this situation. I want to be there when Ed tells his side of the story."

The production manager and Tony Rodgers were standing outside of labor relations with worried expressions. Ed who called them at their homes summoned them. As soon as Tony saw Johnny he warned him.

"Johnny, I hope you realize this is a wildcat strike and could cost everyone striking their jobs," Tony said.

"If anyone is going to lose their job over this, it better be Roy Acuff," Johnny seethed.

He turned to the production manager.

"You better take some drastic action against Roy for his foul mouth and blatant disrespect to workers," Johnny said. "The black workers made it crystal clear they're not going back to work until Roy is punished."

"Are they going back tomorrow?" Tony asked, rubbing his eyes out of tiredness.

"That depends on how you handle Roy," Johnny said.

Tony noticed some body shop foremen walking toward them.

"Let's go in my office to discuss this," Tony said.

"You better get in touch with Jay," Johnny said, taking a seat at the table. "It's going to take someone who has greater authority than you two."

"I can't do that," Tony said, visibly annoyed. "Jay has been in here all day. It's after eight now. Jay has made it clear to everyone that he is not to be contacted at home for plant problems. We have managers here who are capable of resolving these issues."

"I've been here all day and so have the both of you," Johnny said. "Why is Jay any different? Don't you realize that we have a plant shutdown on our hands?"

"We're big enough to handle this," Tony said.

"Well, then good," Johnny said. "For starters, fire Roy. I can go tell the men they can all go back to work then."

Johnny started to rise from his chair.

Tony's face flushed red in anger.

"Even Jay doesn't have the authority to fire a plant superintendent," Tony snarled. "That can only be done by our central office in Detroit."

"Well then you better get Jay on the phone so we can put this to bed," Johnny said. "That's unless you don't mind our workers walking off their jobs for God knows how long."

Tony reluctantly dialed Jay's private phone and put him on speaker. He explained in detail the incident that took place.

"Johnny, there's no way I could meet with you tonight until I get all the facts to review," Jay said. "I don't approve of any member of our management abusing our employees. But to rule fairly, I have to hear both side of the story."

Jay directed Tony to interview Roy, Ed and everyone else who was present during the incident. From those interviews he wanted a full written report on his desk by 7 the next morning.

"I also want Roy and all those involved in my office at the same time so I can question them," Jay said. "Later I'll hold a meeting with the union at 9 to discuss the decision. Is that agreeable with you Johnny?"

"We'll be at your office at nine sharp," Johnny said. "I urge you to review the facts thoroughly, especially with Ed. I want to warn you that the black workers are up in arms over this incident, so we must act accordingly."

After leaving the meeting Johnny and several other committeemen headed over to the union hall. Johnny knew there would be a crowd gathered to find out the decision on Roy.

They had to park their cars on the access road because the union parking lot was that full. The lights in the union hall were lit and there were members standing outside the door. Allen Dairy, a trustee, met them.

"Johnny, I opened the doors to allow members to go in but they are refusing to allow any whites into the meeting," Allen said. "They're deciding what course of action they're going to take against the company."

"Come on, let's go," Johnny said, leading the men into the hall.

They were met by a black member who stopped them.

"Sorry Johnny, this meeting only is for black members," the man said.

Johnny shoved past him and continued walking into the hall. The committeemen were pushing their way right behind Johnny. Manny was holding the microphone and getting the crowd riled up. Johnny jumped onto the stage and wrestled the microphone away.

"I just got through speaking to the plant manager and his top representatives and demanded they take disciplinary action against Superintendent Acuff immediately," Johnny said as the crowd listened. "I was assured by the plant manager that he would review all the facts in the case with everyone involved. We're scheduled to have a formal meeting with the company at nine o'clock in the morning. I made it clear that we won't allow any member of management to abuse any members of our hourly employees and that the company must be prepared to take severe disciplinary action against Superintendent Acuff. When you come to work tomorrow, stop at union hall and I'll give you the results of the meeting."

Manny Head and other leaders of the United Black Brothers began to shout in opposition.

"We're not going to accept any whitewashing on this," Manny said. "Let's stay on the street until that racist pig is fired and the company recognizes our demands for black workers' rights."

"I'm the president of the local and I'll call the shots here, not you, Manny," Johnny said. "We have a meeting at nine in the morning. You'll be given the results of the meeting and I will decide what action will be taken then. I'm asking all of you to leave the hall now. We want to close up for the night."

Johnny began pulling the microphone from the wall plug and placed it into his briefcase. Manny tried to wrestle it away from him but Johnny shoved him.

"Don't put your hands on me," Johnny said. "This mic is going to be put in my office where it belongs."

He stared directly into Manny's eyes until he saw him relent.

"Brothers, it's been a long day," Manny said to the crowd. "Let's rest up and come back tomorrow ready to fight."

Johnny directed Pete to secure the hall and told the rest of the committeemen to meet him tomorrow morning at 7.

"We're going to have quite a day tomorrow," Johnny said.

Johnny arrived at the union headquarters before seven the next morning and was surprised to see Betty sitting at her desk sharpening her pencils and ready to take notes. She normally started her day no earlier than nine. Rocky and Lou were in the office they shared, making phone calls to their supporters on the night shift inquiring about the results of the work stoppage.

Johnny knew this was an incident that Rocky and Lou would exploit to show Johnny as a poor leader. They had high hopes that Johnny would be politically damaged. They were aware the black militants and the communists in the plant would gain sympathy from the membership and attempt to gain control of the local.

The night shift was about 60 percent black and the young militants had a cause they could sink their teeth into. Most of the black workers on the day shift were older men with high seniority. They were established and most owned their own homes with costly monthly payments and their main concern was to build a better life for their family.

Like many black citizens they were concerned with equal rights for minorities but constantly ignored the young black militants who were always engaged in issues of black supremacy. The black workers on day shifts had prime jobs they were reluctant to jeopardize for the sake of the United Black Brothers.

In turn the United Black Brothers were trying to gain control of the union.

Johnny knew Rocky was looking for a reason to make Johnny look bad but he had to be strategic because he couldn't antagonize the day shift. Rocky recognized Johnny's strength was in his relationship with the night shift members and he had to find a way to pit the night and day shifts against one another, but not implicate themselves in the fight. Rocky would have to be patient and watch and exploit whatever mistakes Johnny would make.

Rocky and Lou emerged from their office when they heard Betty speaking to Johnny.

"You had a real doozy on your hands last night," Rocky said.

Lou had no love for Johnny and was more business-like and asked with a stern look on his face.

"The black movement was looking for an issue to break our backs," Lou snapped. "Looks like Roy gave them one. What time is our meeting with the company?"

"Nine o'clock," Johnny said, motioning them to follow him into the office.

Johnny filled them in on the incident and his discussion with the plant manager and Tony Rodgers. He stopped talking when the black worker's committeeman, Burt Landers, walked in. His eyes were puffed up from a lack of sleep.

"You look like hell," Johnny said. "Did you get any sleep last night?"

"I had only about an hour," Bud said. "I didn't expect to see you guys here this early. I stopped at the diner and only picked up two containers of coffee. The two of you could share one coffee and Johnny and I will share the other one."

Bud told them that several workers were still angry about the incident. They were willing to keep striking until a resolution was made. They also wanted to be in the meeting when union officials met with the company.

"That's bullshit," Lou grumbled. "We just had our union election and they had the right to run for any union office, including president." He turned to Johnny. "I guess you're right, they're going to string us up, along with the company. I agree that they have a legitimate beef with the company but it doesn't warrant shutting down the plant."

"The night shift is focused on being at that meeting," Bud said. "They are throwing all their weight behind that."

Just then Betty knocked on the door and said Tony was on the phone and was ready to meet.

"Betty, tell him that we'll be right over and it's a must that Jay also be at the meeting," Johnny said.

"Give Betty all your notes and statements that have to be typed up," Johnny said to Bud. "Betty will get them prepared for later. We won't need them at this meeting. The company is going to play on our emotions and explain that Roy is only human and made a mistake that he wants to settle with a meager apology. They'll even go as far as giving Byron a soft job on the line."

When they got to the administration building, the group consisting of Johnny, Rocky, Lou and Bud went directly to the conference room where the company's top officials were seated at a table.

Jay was at the head of the table, as usual. Marie Collins, the secretary, was seated to his right. Johnny assumed his usual seat at the top of the table, across from Jay. At all previous meetings, Johnny had never seen a secretary take notes. This made Johnny suspicious.

"If Marie is here to take notes, I expect the union be given a full copy of the proceedings," Johnny said.

"That's fine," Tony said. "We'll do that." He turned to Marie. "See that an extra set of minutes are mailed to the union office."

"I requested this meeting to review your findings about last night's confrontation where Superintendent Acuff cursed at and abused one of our black workers," Johnny said, getting directly to the point.

He glanced over at Roy who was sitting at the table with his head downcast.

"I'm glad Roy is at this meeting," Johnny said. "He should be aware of the impact of his actions on us and those black workers who walked out in protest. We want to know what management is going to do to Superintendent Acuff for this unfair treatment of one of our hourly employees?"

Jay picked up his notes to review them for a moment.

"Gentlemen, I reviewed everything with Roy and our staff," Jay said, addressing the union members. "Roy admits to using the language, not as a slur but as shop talk. Profanity is the

way of life in the auto industry; we use it all the time. It's agreed
that this was not a good choice of words by Roy. In the heat of the
moment, the words just came out. We agree that Roy should be
taken off the night shift for the time being. We haven't made a
decision as to where he'll be placed. The mostly likely spot would
be on the day shift in the body shop. He's an expert in that
department."

Johnny was disappointed and didn't hide it.

"Mr. Cannon, I don't think you realize the seriousness of
the situation caused by Superintendent Acuff," Johnny said. "I
was present at the meeting with the United Black Brothers that
took place at our union hall. I had to force my way into the hall.
The United Black Brothers wouldn't allow any white members
into their meeting. Everyone there was up in arms over the
abusive and racist language used by Superintendent Acuff. Right
now the company is on trial for all the misdeeds it's committed
over the years."

Johnny paused for a moment before continuing.

"Transferring Roy is not the answer," he said. "Until a
final decision is reached, I suggest that he not be allowed in the
plant. He must be discharged or transferred to another assembly
plant. Under no circumstances should you allow him to work here.
This situation is a live grenade ready to explode."

Johnny looked toward his committee members and they all
nodded their heads in agreement.

"Johnny, you were my committeeman when I first started
to work at Ford and you know me fairly well," Roy pleaded. "I
admit that I got a terrible temper and say things that I'm sorry for
later. I promise all of you that I'll go to the worker personally and
apologize."

"Roy, those remarks you made last night were completely
uncalled for," Johnny said. "And to make things worse, you
angered a black representative of the company by saying all
blacks were alike. The black workers all heard what you said. I
can't see us resolving this through a simple apology. You went
too far this time."

Johnny turned to Jay.

"The only solution is for Superintendent Acuff to be
terminated," Johnny said. "It's as simple as that. This afternoon
there will be a mass meeting at our union hall demanding to know
what action the company is taking against Superintendent Acuff

and what action the company is going to take against the workers that walked off their job in protest. What shall I tell them?"

"Johnny, you know the decision you're requesting has to come out of Detroit central staff," Jay said, visibly exasperated. "I can assure that Roy won't be in the plant for the remainder of the week or Monday. By that time, I'm sure that most of the night shift will be cooled down. We will then transfer Roy off the night shift to another department other than the body shop. And as for what action the company will take against the workers who walked off their jobs, that will be reviewed by our labor relation staff."

Jay turned to Tony.

"Tony get your people on that immediately," Jay said. "See if there was any damage done and get back to the union on what action will be taken, if any. Johnny, you're aware that since there's a loss of production, we have to send that to Detroit through a full written report and what action was taken to correct the situation."

"Thanks Mr. Cannon," Johnny said. "But that's not the answer we are looking for. We're going to have about 500 workers packed into the union hall. I'll tell them that Superintendent Acuff will be out on disciplinary action for a few days. But I don't know what their reaction will be to that. They are already striking and I'm not sure I can prevent them from striking if we don't hold a strong line on this issue."

"Johnny, you can tell the members that the company took disciplinary action against Superintendent Acuff," Rocky said. "I'm sure that they'll be satisfied."

Johnny knew Rocky was attempting to show the company that he was in complete support of Johnny's position.

"Rocky, I wish I had your confidence," Johnny said. "Let's go to the union hall and see their reaction."

"Hold on a minute," Jay said. "I'd rather you not say the company put Superintendent Acuff out on disciplinary leave. You can say that Superintendent Acuff won't be at the plant for a few days and they'll understand that we took appropriate action against him. This is our internal affair and not to be shared with your union members."

The meeting closed with Johnny acknowledging the company's position. Johnny and other union officials headed to the union hall next.

Bummy Harris and a group of black supporters stopped Johnny. Bummy knew Johnny needed all the help he could get from the black community.

"Johnny we're here as your soldiers," Bummy said. "We have a lot of members who'll follow your lead but in case any trouble starts, we'll be on your side."

"I appreciate that Bummy," Johnny said. "I need most of you by the exits and a couple near me at the podium. Bummy, I need you to be at the rear of the hall."

They entered the hall that was standing room only. Every chair was occupied; men were standing in the aisles and along the walls. Johnny and his band of supporters had to fight their way up to the stage. Three militant leaders were standing at attention with their arms folded across their chests. They were dressed in blue denim jackets, pants that matched and fatigue hats on their heads.

When Johnny stationed himself in front of the microphone, the black leaders raised their right hand up in the air with their fists clenched, the black power salute. The hall became silent as everyone waited to hear the report.

"Last night I told you that I would report on what action the company would take against Superintendent Acuff," Johnny began. "What's important is that this is a union problem and I'd like to make sure that there's no one in the hall who isn't a member of our union. I see some men in the rear who are not members. I'm requesting that they leave immediately."

No one moved. Some members stood to look at some white men in denim at the rear of the hall. Bummy made his way through the crowd toward the interlopers.

"Bummy please ask the men in the blue denim to produce their union membership cards," Johnny said. "If they don't have a union card, please escort them out of the hall."

Everyone in the hall stood up to watch the proceedings.

"They're O.K. Johnny," Manny Head hollered. "They belong to our black caucus and I invited them to this meeting."

A calm settled over the meeting. Johnny ignored Manny, whom he felt was simply stirring up trouble.

"Bummy, like I said, if they don't have a local union card, escort them out of the hall," Johnny said. "We don't need outsiders involved with our union problems."

Bummy was near the white militants as one of them started to shout.

"Man, get on with the meeting," he yelled. "We're all here to see that justice be granted to our black brothers."

"Let's see your union card or leave," Bummy threatened.

One of them had a heavy red beard and weighed close to 300 pounds. He moved to the front of the white militants.

"Man, be on your way," he sneered. "We're here to see that justice is done for our black brothers."

Bummy was on the man in a flash. He grabbed the man's arm and locked it behind his back. When he applied pressure, the man screamed in pain while Bummy shoved him toward the exit as the crowd opened a passageway for him to leave. He pushed the man violently through the doorway, up the marble steps and smashed his face through the double glass doors. Bummy sent the man sprawling to the concrete, scraping his nose and chin.

The militant was up in a flash and charged Bummy. He didn't realize that he was up against a professional prizefighter and an expert street fighter. Bummy hit the charging man with a solid right hand to the chin that sent him flying backward. As the militant was trying to regain his balance, Bummy was on him again and hit the man with a hard right chop to the chin and knocking him out before he fell to the ground.

Bummy returned to the hall and walked over to the remaining white militants.

"Brothers, are you going to leave peacefully or do I have to do to you what I just did to your friend?" he asked.

The group saw what he did to their comrade and left in a hurry.

There was a moment of brief frenzy as some of the black militants attempted to intercede on behalf of their white militant supporters, but Manny motioned to them to return to the hall.

Johnny rapped his gavel on the speakers stand to get the meeting back in order.

"Everyone knows why we're here," Johnny said. "So I'm not going to belabor this meeting by going over all the facts. We just came out of the meeting with the plant manager and his labor relation staff. At the meeting we demanded that Superintendent Acuff be fired."

Noise erupted in the hall with everyone cheering and shouting. Johnny rapped the gavel to bring everyone back to order.

"The company wouldn't agree to our demands," Johnny said, as some in the crowd began booing. "Mr. Cannon tried to make excuses for Superintendent Acuff's language, referring to it as simply shop talk. But we wouldn't buy that. We insisted that disciplinary action be taken against Superintendent Acuff. The company was reluctant to admit that he did anything that serious to warrant permanent dismissal. They did agree that the language he used was improper and uncalled for and they would see that management would not tolerate any such language again. They instructed Superintendent Acuff to personally apologize but we still demanded that disciplinary action be taken against him. Mr. Cannon assured us that Superintendent Acuff would be out of the plant for the rest of the week and also absent Monday of next week. He will not be working on the night shift and will be transferred to another department on the day shift."

The black militant leaders standing in front of the podium raised their clenched fist up in the air and mayhem broke loose in the hall.

"We aren't working until Roy is fired and they acknowledge our demands," they yelled.

Johnny tried to restore order but they ignored him. He looked at Rocky to see if Rocky wanted to say anything, but he shook his head. It was clear to Johnny that Rocky didn't want to get his hands dirty with this mess.

"I want to resolve this dispute as much as you do," Johnny yelled to the unruly crowd.

Everyone ignored him until they realized he was about to leave. The members stopped their shouting and came back to order to allow Johnny to speak.

"I told Mr. Cannon that I didn't think transferring Superintendent Acuff to another department wouldn't do any good," Johnny said. "Again I told him the only solution to this problem was that they fire him."

The crowd interrupted him with cheers. Johnny held his hand up and they quieted.

"Mr. Cannon knows this is a hot potato and agreed to convey our demands to the central staff in Detroit," Johnny said. "Detroit staff are the only ones who are authorized to fire a superintendent. We will be meeting with the company when they get their answer from them."

"What are they going to do to those of us who walked out of the plant yesterday?" a member asked. "We're not going back into that plant to face discipline for fighting for our rights."

"Labor relation is going to investigate all the facts and review the damage that might have been incurred during the work stoppage," Johnny said. "They have to send a written report of their investigation. I'm pretty sure there won't be any hearings if we go back to work tonight."

The militants raised their clenched fists up in the air to get everyone incited. They weren't going to allow the members go back to work. They had the momentum going their way and weren't going to let up.

"Justice now, work later!" they shouted.

Johnny made an attempted to stop it. He knew that he had come to some kind of agreement with the United Black Brothers. He nodded to the leaders to put their clenched fist down, they complied but let him know that they were in full control of the meeting and had the black workers supporting.

Johnny realized that the workers weren't going back to work at the plant that night. He thought another approach might work.

"We're only spinning our wheels here," Johnny said. "You are not going to accept anything I say. I suggest you select two members to come back to the meeting with the company and express your feelings. Maybe directly from you the company might get a better picture of your demands."

This caused a stir within the crowd.

"We support that," Manny said. "Let's send Leon Saint and Willie Barnes, they know what our demands are."

Johnny knew he was close to a resolution. This would buy him some time to work out a long-term solution.

After Johnny left the hall he went to his office to call Tony. He explained what had just happened with the black workers and the militant leaders and how they only calmed down when a special meeting including their involvement was suggested. Tony had no choice but to agree. Jay had made it clear that he was focused on getting the night shift to resume work as soon as possible. It was costing the company a huge drain on their profits when they were shut down.

Tony and Ed, the labor relation representative, were anxiously waiting for them outside the conference room. The company was using Ed as part of its effort to persuade the blacks that the company was taking their demands seriously. Johnny introduced the black representatives to company officials. Johnny was pleased that Ed was there.

"Ed, I'm glad the company finally realized how important it was that you be at this meeting," Johnny said. "You understand where we're coming from and maybe you can speak to them."

Company officials explained that they were unable to run the night shift due to heavy absenteeism, particularly in the body shop where most of the jobs required skilled workers like welders, metal finishers, door fitters and solder torch man. The normal pool of men were laborers and too few were skilled workers. Normal workers couldn't replace these jobs.

"By our head count the entire body shop is at the union hall," Tony said. "We had to send all the other departments home after six minutes. That's all we'll be paying them for. I instructed the foreman to advise them that the body shop workers sent them home due to a strike. I hope Johnny told you that Superintendent Acuff is not working in the plant and won't be until a decision is made in Detroit."

"Mr. Rodgers, Johnny explained all of this at our membership meeting," Willie Barnes said. "We have a very serious situation on our hands. A superintendent degrades one of our black brothers and the company is trying to whitewash the situation. If any of our hourly workers did that, they'd be fired right on the spot."

"That's not correct, we did do something immediately," Tony snapped. "Superintendent Acuff is not in the plant and won't be back until appropriate action is determined."

Tony looked directly at Johnny.

"Didn't you tell your members that we're not going to put Superintendent Acuff back in the night shift body shop and instead we're transferring him to the opposite shift in another department?" Tony asked.

"Mr. Rodgers we're well aware of your position," said Leon. "But placing Superintendent Acuff on vacation for a few days isn't our concept of disciplinary action. What he did was inexcusable to the black community, yet you're minimizing this serious situation. There are many changes all over the country and people must open their eyes to these changing times. Tempers are building up in the black communities and there are a lot of outsiders coming in to help these changes come about. Management must use more discretion in regard to this problem. When I see a member of management abuse another member, black or white, I'm disturbed and uncomfortable. The country is in the midst of a civil rights revolution and there will be more trouble ahead unless there are changes."

"We want to work in harmony with one another but not as second class citizens," Willie added. "If management were to change their ways, things would be better for everyone. The workers at union hall are waiting for concrete action by management in regard to the black issue. I'm not talking for myself but for members of the union who are not going to go back unless the company assures them that they're serious in their thinking."

The black representatives explained that all black workers were at a tipping point. They wouldn't go back to work under the same conditions, period. They also took notice of the lack of blacks in management positions. The only black person in labor relations was Ed. There were no blacks in the employment or administrative offices.

"Before I give you our position, how will you convey our thoughts to the black community?" Tony asked cautiously.

He realized the black representatives weren't going to be easily swayed.

"We'll communicate by word of mouth and bulletins," said Leon, shrugging his shoulders dismissively.

"The company has done a great deal over the years to correct abuses in the plant," Tony said. "Our methods aren't always right but we are interested in our supervisors treating the hourly employees fairly. Superintendent Acuff, up until this point, has always been a fair man. Nothing was going right for him yesterday. High absenteeism and replacement workers who weren't familiar with body shop operations. Then to top it off, Byron was assigned to the body shop but he is a chassis man, Let's look at Byron, he just completed his probationary period by a couple days and was loaned to the body shop because of the high absenteeism and we needed him to work there. He is just an assembler in chassis with no assignment. I guess that's what ticked Roy off. He was wrong but desperate to get his department going and Byron worked for him the day before. Then he came in with a doctor's note for being absent. Superintendent Acuff knew that he performed the job the day before when he was told Byron didn't want to work there anymore that got under his skin and blew his top."

"Mr. Rodgers, we want cohesiveness between workers and management," Leon interrupted. "I know everything I need to know about the incident. You're beating around the bush and not giving us answers. We know the company is going to give Superintendent Acuff a few days off but he'll be paid for that time."

"This is not true," Tony interjected. "Many times we take disciplinary action against members of management which we don't advertise. I assure you that Superintendent Acuff will be punished. But I'm not at liberty to tell you what action we will take."

"Mr. Rodgers, I realize that a lot of us use the word motherfucker but when a high-ranking member of management uses that term and further humiliates the worker by referring to his as 'boy', that's an expression that everyone knows is taboo," Leon said. "Also, can you declare clemency to the workers who walked out due to this incident?"

"I understand your concern," Tony said.

He told black workers that the company would be reviewing footage of the strike to observe which employees were turning on picketers, kicking in car doors and assaulting them.

"We will never tolerate that sort of action taken against our employees," Tony said.

"We aren't talking about that," Willie interrupted. "We feel the number one issue is the attitude of management toward blacks in the plant and what measures are going to be taken to correct this."

Tony motioned for Ed to turn on the movie projector that was set up on the conference table.

"This is the film we're showing to members of management on how we want them to treat minorities at the plant," Tony said.

The film was an hour long and portrayed the company's positive actions toward the black community. The black representatives agreed that the film showed a welcome change in management's attitude.

"I hope you'll convey to the membership that the company is aware of the changes in the black community and we're in the process of changing our ways and attitude toward the needs of our black workers," Tony said.

"We'll relate what we saw and what you said to the membership," said Willie Barnes.

Willie turned toward Ed Hubot with his eyes flashing in anger.

"Ed, you're the only black representative in labor relations here at Ford," Willie said. "You haven't contributed anything at this meeting but running the movie projector. Have you spoken about the way you were treated by Superintendent Acuff? He called you a black bastard and made reference that we're all alike. What role are you playing in this scenario? Are you doing anything to help the black community?"

Ed was embarrassed and wasn't sure how to answer. Johnny interjected.

"We've been sitting here listening for the last hour-and-a-half but so far no concrete answers," Johnny said. "Before we go back Tony, I want you to tell us what you're going to do to Superintendent Acuff? Don't double-talk us. You wanted to know how the blacks feel. I think Leon and Willie gave you a picture of what we're up against."

"Johnny, you know our position," Tony said. "We told you that Roy will be out of the plant until our central staff makes a ruling. It's strictly up to them. We're asking that the workers go back to their jobs and nothing is going to happen until we review all the films and tapes of the picketing. After that we'll meet with your committee to render our decision. Right now we met your demands. Roy is out of the plant so there's no reason why the workers can't go back to work."

"We did what you asked and also we outlined changes that we'll be taking toward minorities," Tony said. Leon and Willie nodded their heads but uttered no words. They got up from their chairs and shook hands with Tony and his representatives and left the room.

After the meeting everyone left for the union hall. It was agreed that the two black representatives would report to members without any of the union representatives present. The bargaining committee reported to Johnny's office where they could hear the full discussion between Leon and Willie to black members. There was booing and shouting as the two related the facts of the meeting. It was clear the black workers were not accepting the company's proposal.

"That blows your theory that the blacks would accept the company's proposal," Johnny said to Rocky. "The United Black Brothers got them all steamed up and now they'd like to take over the union if we let them. There are a lot of rational black workers at the meeting and even they are listening to the black militants. It's the black movement that's sweeping the country. We're going to have to do a lot of thinking on how we're going to get them back to work on the night shift."

"You're right Johnny," Rocky said. "I'm not sure what else we can do. I'm going to make a few calls and get a drink. I'll be right back."

Rocky headed for his office to call Marie to take her out to dinner.

"I can't," she replied.

She was in the middle of typing a full report of the wildcat strike and was frustrated by the assignment.

"Mr. Rodgers told me the report has to be completed by tonight," Marie said. "The report is so big and I'll be here until late."

She hesitated a moment to hold back the sobs.

"I'm so angry," she said. "I have to stay here while Mr. Rodgers goes out Geraldine. She came into the office, all bubbly and happy and convinced him to take her out to the grand opening of the new Holiday Inn Lounge on Route 17. I get stuck doing this and she gets to have a good time. That's not fair."

Rocky thought a moment.

"Is that the new Pirate's Cove in Rochelle Park?" he asked.

"Yes," she said. "I'd love to see his wife walk in on them while they're there. That won't happen, I heard him tell his wife that he had to work late because of the walk-out by the workers."

Rocky hung up the phone and walked back to Johnny's office with a grin on his face. He entered the office and could hear the shouting from the meeting hall.

"By the sound of the meeting, it looks like they're not going back to work," Rocky said. "We might as well go downstairs and hear what they decided. I can see it's a lost cause."

The bargaining committee had to push their way through the crowded hall to get to the podium. The hall quieted down when Johnny got to the microphone. He stood there a moment to observe the crowd's reaction, but saw none.

"Before I make any remarks, I want to know whether the company's proposal is acceptable," he said.

Every man began to boo and chanted, "justice, no white wash!"

Johnny raised his hand up in the air to get them to quiet down but to no avail. They continued shouting until the black leaders who were standing in front of the podium opened their clenched fists. The hall got quiet and Johnny continued.

"I'm not going to belabor this any longer than necessary," Johnny said. "When we left the meeting with the company, the officials assured us that Superintendent Acuff wouldn't be in the plant until this incident is put to bed to the satisfaction of the union. No matter what anyone says to the contrary, this is disciplinary action taken against him."

The boos began again and Johnny raised his hands to hush the crowd.

"Yet here we are still on the street demanding further action," Johnny said. "I'll tell you loud and clear that the company is not going to meet the United Black Brother's demand for job preference or have the company place the blacks into managerial positions."

The crowd began getting restless and Johnny was afraid he was losing their attention. He raised his voice.

"A final decision has not been made in regard to Roy," Johnny said, getting the attention of the crowd again. "That will come from Detroit. When that comes, we'll inform you immediately."

He paused before continuing with the next part of the speech.

"I have to warn you, it's only going to be a matter of time that the company is going to take action against our members who are still striking," Johnny said. "When that happens, the Roy incident will be pushed into the background. You won your fight against Roy in getting him disciplined. Don't lose it because the black militants want to be recognized as your leaders. If they want to be leaders of the union all they have to do is get elected to the job. That's all I have to say."

The black militants raised their clenched fist above their heads and the crowd grew loud with shouts and boos. Johnny knew that there was no way to convince them to go back to work. He calmly walked off the podium and pushed his way through the crowd. Some tried to restrain him but he pushed them aside.

Johnny walked toward George Plassard who was standing by the doorway observing the reactions by the membership.

"They'll be leaving shortly when they have no one to shout at," Johnny said to George. "Would you do me a favor and lock up the hall when they leave?"

George nodded his head as Rocky ran up to them.

"Johnny, how about stopping by the Holiday Inn for a drink before we go home?" Rocky asked. "We can talk about our future strategy without anyone interrupting us."

"Sure, is that the new place they opened up on Route 17?" Johnny asked.

Ann wasn't expecting him to get home until late and he was interested in what Rocky had to say. Rocky always had a secret agenda when he wanted to talk to him alone.

"Yeah, you interested?" Rocky asked.

"Sure, I'll follow you in my car," Johnny said. "I could use a drink after this meeting." They headed to the Pirate's Cove.

Chapter 10
Years 1940-1942

Although Johnny worked hard at the Ford plant, he couldn't concentrate on his job. No matter how hard he tried, he was called down the line to repair mistakes he made. After a month of chasing the never-ending line, he knew this wasn't the kind of job that he was going to do for the rest of his life. The next time he got called by the inspector, he informed him that he was quitting at the end of the week.

The inspector was a grouchy old man named Bob Vonderhaden who had been working at Ford for the last 25 years and demanded each job to be done to perfection. None of the workers liked him and were always arguing with him. Hours after Johnny had told Bob he was quitting, he felt a tap on the shoulder. Bob gave him some good news.

"Kid, you've been doing a better job than most of the old-timers," Bob said. "Smokey Joe told me that he had to get rid of one man today from the department. After lunch, take your boots and apron to the general store and then report to the employment office for a reassignment. I don't know where they'll place you but it won't be in the paint department."

Johnny was finally happy and the morning went by quickly. After lunch, he was reassigned to a newly created job in the truck division. In fact the reassignment felt like starting to work in a new plant. He was taught to assemble the body from scratch. First step was the two-by-ten wood studs that were ten feet long, and had to be assembled on a steel structure for the floor of the truck. Then he had to bolt down the boards to the steel structure with an automatic air gun.

He soon learned every operation that afternoon and enjoyed working there. He was so engrossed in his new job that

his fellow workers had to tell him it was quitting time. He waited
for his father after work and told him about his new job.

"Son, I'm glad you got a job that you like," his father said.
"My foreman told me that Ford got a big order from the
government building trucks for the Army because of the war. If
you learn the job well, they'll probably keep you there for a long
time. How come they transferred you to this new job?"

"I told the paint inspector that I was going to quit at the
end of the week," Johnny said. "I guess he took a liking to me and
had me transferred instead. This job isn't boring and you're
required to assemble the whole job and the best part is that it's not
on a moving line. We do our work on a stationary jig. This means
I can go to the bathroom without looking for a foreman's
permission whenever I need to."

"I'm glad you didn't need to quit," his father said.
"There's going to be a lot of work here for a long time. The talk is
that they're going to turn this plant into a defense plant for the
government."

"Pop, you worked here for a long time before you got laid
off," Johnny said. "Did you ever hear anything about a union
coming to Ford? Some of the workers in my department said they
heard that the union won their court case in Detroit and that the
company has to recognize the union as the agent for all workers.
They said they think the company will have to recognize the union
all over the country but I'm wondering if this is only a rumor."

"It's not a rumor, they heard right," the elder Romanek
said. "The court upheld the findings by the National Labor
Relations Board. They made the company bring back all the
workers that were fired in Detroit when they joined the union. The
company had to pay them all the time they lost while they were
out of jobs. Besides that, the state ruled that the company must
post on every bulletin board in the country giving the workers the
right to vote on whether they want a union to represent them or
not. In Detroit, they voted 95 percent for the union. That union is
affiliated with the coal miners union headed by John L. Lewis.
Now that that union is recognized in Detroit, the company will
have to recognize the union here."

"How come you didn't tell me before that the union was
fighting to get into the Ford plants?" Johnny asked. "You know
that I tried to start a union while I was working at the battery
plant."

"You were only working there six months and you didn't have any idea what a man has to go through to start a union," his father said. "Another thing, if anyone would try to start a union or show any interest in a union they get fired and branded a troublemaker. The workers want to have an old-timer here to represent the union because they know what the workers went through while they were working here and how bad the company treated the workers over the years. Another thing is you have to be working here over a year to qualify to run for any union position. You go back to school and learn all about union contracts and then run for a union job."

"Pop, how did they go about trying to start a union in Detroit?" Johnny asked. "When I tried to start a union the workers were afraid to listen, let alone do something about getting something started." He was deeply interested in workers rights and how the union went about protecting those rights.

"Son, it's a long story," Frank Romanek said. "There were a few union leaders that elected to take on Ford because they were considered the worst company regarding workers' rights and the company hated the union with a passion."

Frank proceeded to tell Johnny the story about the owner of Ford. Henry Ford hired a former boxer and ex-Navy sailor, named Harry Bennett, as his bodyguard and later put him in charge of hiring men to work in the Ford plants. To make sure the workers wouldn't get a union in the plant, he hired security guards that were ex-convicts, boxers, wrestlers and cops that were fired from the police force for brutality against strikers.

Back in 1937 there were only a couple of union organizers. One was Walter Reuther and the other, Richard Frankenstein who tried to pass out union literature at the plant gates. They had about 50 union people with them, including women. In order to get to the company's gate they had to walk over a bridge to get there. While walking on the overpass, they were assaulted by company goons carrying clubs who brutally worked them over. They kicked the union people, hit them with clubs and bloodied them all up. They didn't care if the attacked men or women, they all got beat up. Newspaper reporters were there and took pictures of the Ford security guards beating the people who were assembled there protesting peacefully.

"All Reuther and the union sympathizers proved was that they got beat up by company goons," Johnny said. "How come they couldn't get Ford organized after all that publicity?"

His father began to smile because his son had no idea what a union had to go through to become established.

"The reason they couldn't get organized was because Ford went through the courts and tied the union up for years before they could get a decision," Frank Romanek said. "Before that at a General Motors plant, organizers had a different strategy and had the workers sit down at their jobs, chaining themselves to their machines so the company couldn't use them."

Frank told his son that security guards tried beating the workers up but couldn't move them. The guards had to be careful because reporters were taking pictures and published them in the newspapers. The police were forced to come into the plants so the guards wouldn't kill the chained workers. The rest of the workers were picketing outside the plant and handed the striking workers food through open windows. About ten days later, the company gave in. They negotiated with the union for a vote to see if the workers wanted a union to represent them. In the General Motors case the union won but Ford was able to stop the workers to organize through court action.

"How do you think they'll go in trying to get a union here?" Johnny asked.

"I was talking to Harvey Smithers today," the elder Romanek said. "He told me he received a telegram from Walter Reuther and that the courts ruled in favor of unions being recognized in all Ford plants in the U.S."

"Who is Harvey Smithers?" Johnny asked.

"Harvey Smithers as the person who tried to start a union at our plant about five years ago," the elder Romanek said. "While we were picketing the plant, Frank was thrown in jail."

The elder Romanek told his son the entire story about the incident. The local cops hit the rest of the picketers on the legs to keep moving and not to stray out of the line. At the same time picketers were on top of the hill and began rolling big boulders down to crash into the police cars. When the picketers near the cops saw the rocks were damaging the police cars, the picketers scattered because the police started going after them with clubs. The next day they fired Harvey who was the leader of the strike along with five other workers. When the strikers lost their leader, they all went back to work the next day.

"I should have asked you about the union before," Johnny said. "You know an awful lot. I thought I knew a lot about a union because I met with union organizers in Jersey City when I tried to get a union started at the battery plant. Let's keep talking about this. I have many more questions."

"I know you do, son," Frank Romanek said. "But today, let's not keep your mother waiting any longer."

His mother opened the door when she heard voices.

"What kept you so long?" his mother said, hugging and kissing them both. "I have supper on the table and it's getting cold."

"We were talking about the fight we had years ago when we wanted to get a union in Ford," Frank said.

His mother's expression changed entirely.

"Son, please don't start any trouble at the Ford plant," his mother said. "That company isn't anything like the battery plant. Let your father tell you how they beat the people up with clubs and put them in the hospital."

Frank placed his lunch box into the cupboard while Johnny went by the kitchen sink to wash up before sitting down to eat. When they sat to eat supper, Johnny wouldn't stop asking his father about his involvement trying to get a union started at Ford.

"Pop, tell me about the union leaders and what they did," Johnny said in between bites of food.

"I really don't know much about them except that the Reuthers brothers worked all over Europe and Russia," the elder Romanek said. "Later on they got jobs at General Motors as tool makers and that's where they started the sit-down strike. Even the cops were afraid to break up the strike because it was something new and they didn't know what to do, they weren't sure of their rights."

His father told him that the working conditions were always bad and the security guards put the fear of God into all the workers. The workers really had to earn every penny they were given. The guards were so terrible that if a worker was caught smoking in the latrines, a guard would retrieve the cigarette with the shit all over it to prove the worker was smoking and had him fired on the spot.

"That's how powerful the guards were here at Clinton," Frank Romanek said. "It was like a prison. I have to say I'll be relieved when we get a union in here."

"You're always too tired to talk but today you're talking so much about unions and their leaders," his mother said. "Your father is trying to eat before his meal gets cold."

"Mom, I never knew that pop knew so much about the unions and their leaders," Johnny said, shoving food in his mouth.

"That's the trouble with you young people, you think you know it all," his mother said. "You think old people like me and your father just sit at home and do nothing. You should talk to your father more often and you'll be smarter for it."

He smiled at his mother and took another heaping spoonful of food onto his plate.

"Mom, you're right," he said. "By the way I got a new job at the plant today and it's great. I'll tell you about it tomorrow. I'm going to pick up Ann to celebrate my liberation from the moving line."

"You just got home, you've been out late every night this week," his mother said. "Pretty soon you're going to get sick from all this lack of sleep."

Johnny kissed his mom on the cheek and walked out the door.

"He never listens, all he thinks about is his girlfriend," she said to Frank Romanek.

The following morning, Johnny and his father entered the plant parking lot. They saw a large group of workers milling around the plant gate. They crossed over the pedestrian bridge and saw large banners strung across the cyclone fence that read: "Elect Harvey Smithers for President of local 3001 and His Entire Slate."

While they were going through the plant gate they were handed a bulletin by the union organizers. It listed the details of a meeting, where it was being held, the agenda and information about a union election. Johnny couldn't contain his excitement.

"Pop, I know I can't run for office but I'm going to be at that meeting real early," Johnny said. "I want to sit in the front row so I can hear everything. We'll be the first to sign up."

"Come on son, or we'll be late for work," Frank said. They observed on both sides banners hanging from the rafters, urging the members to vote for Harvey. While walking down the crane way, the elder Romanek turned to his son.

"It looks like Harvey will win this election and he deserves it," Frank said. "He was the only one who stuck his neck out years ago and he knows all about the union."

They then came to the truck department and saw Harvey talking to a group of workers. He was explaining how the union was established and the procedures of the upcoming election. When he was finished talking the elder Romanek approached him.

"Harvey, I want you to meet my son, John," Frank Romanek said. "He started here six months ago and he works in the new truck department."

Harvey shook hands with Johnny.

"Your father is quite the man and is respected by everyone," Harvey said. "He helped me picket the plant a few years back. I got fired then and your father got laid off when he refused to pay kickback money to the bosses. We both have an interest in seeing the union succeed here. The number one issue here is seniority rights and changing the company rules."

One of the workers overheard and cried out.

"Bullshit, the company is still going to shove it up our asses until it hurts," the worker said. "The union is not going to be able to change the company's ways and rules. If we do anything wrong we'll be thrown out on the street."

"You're wrong," Harvey Smithers said. "That's all been changed in General Motors since the union got there. Their contract gives them seniority rights and if the company wants to lay anyone off out of seniority, they'll be paid all that time off through the grievance procedure. Another plus is that the company has to post all job promotions on a bulletin board so the workers in the plant can bid for the job. Then the union sits down with the company representative to select the highest seniority man who qualifies for the job."

The worker was still skeptical.

"We all have to pay to get a decent job in this place," he said. "You got stars in your eyes if you think the company bosses are going to give us all of this. Look at Romanek. He was on the street for four years because he wouldn't pay kick-backs."

"That'll never happen again," Harvey said. "I assure you of that."

The warning whistle blew, alerting the workers that they had five minutes to get to their jobs. Johnny ran to his which was just off the crane way. He thought back to the time he tried to organize the workers at the battery plant, here it seemed like it was being handed to them on a silver platter. Despite this many workers were suspicious that it wouldn't work. He remembered when he first started to work his father forced him to go back to school nights to get his high school diploma. He was bitter at the time but realized the wisdom of his parents and was now grateful. He knew he could be just like those uneducated workers who were always skeptical and afraid.

He pictured a president of a union as a two-fisted fighter who was ready to take the company on through force to win an agreement. Somehow Harvey Smithers didn't look the part. He came across as a very intelligent man with a deep understanding of the workers needs but didn't give the impression that he could and would go toe-to-toe with the company. But Johnny knew deep in his heart that the union depended on men like Smithers who would fight the company to get good written agreements.

It was known that the company hired the best lawyers to write their contracts to protect their rights and restrict the workers gains to a minimum. Johnny realized that he would have to go back to school to further his education if he wanted to be effective as a union official.

The meeting on Saturday morning was filled to capacity with workers interested about how the union was going to effect them. President Warren presided over the meeting and explained in full detail how the union would represent them. He spoke for hours and detailed how Harvey helped the union cause in Clinton.

When Harvey Smithers was nominated he received a standing ovation. There were many names nominated for the president position but they all declined in favor of Harvey Smithers. Most of the workers were only interested in Smithers' slate of candidates and they were elected in a landslide. Local 3001 UAW union at the Clinton Assembly Plant was born.

* * *

On December 7, 1941, Johnny was driving his brand new Ford two-door sport coupe down the boulevard with Ann snuggled close to him. They were returning from a movie and listening to the radio. The music was interrupted by a news bulletin.

"We interrupt this program with news that Pearl Harbor had just been attacked by the Japanese Air Force and inflicted heavy damage to the United States Pacific fleet that was anchored in Hawaii."

The report mentioned heavy casualties to sailors onboard ships and to civilians on the island. The White House announced that President Roosevelt would address the full Congress following the attack. The speech would be delivered on the radio for the everyone to hear.

"We believe that the President will declare war on Japan," the news bulletin concluded.

Many cars pulled off the road to listen to the news. Ann moved closer to Johnny with tears forming in her eyes.

"What are we going to do now?" she asked.

"The President doesn't have any choice but to declare war on Japan," Johnny said.

He took her in his arms to comfort her.

The tears were rolling down her cheeks now.

"John, what's going to happen to us?" she asked. "What if you have to go fight the war? I always said that I wasn't ready to get married but now it's different."

Johnny thought a moment as he continued hugging her. He released her from his embrace and wiped her tears away.

"What I can do is make you my wife," he said. "This weekend we will make it official and get married by the Justice of the Peace."

"John, we can't do that," Ann said.

"Why not?" Johnny asked.

"All my life, I dreamed of a church wedding," Ann said. "Let's do it right and get married in the Italian church."

"I hope you realize that both our parents will try to talk us out of getting married with the war going on," Johnny said. "They'll tell us to wait until the war is over."

"I know, but let's talk to them," Ann said. "Maybe they'll understand."

At this point Johnny and Ann had been going steady for three years and were already engaged.

"Before we go to see our parents, let's go to the courthouse and get a marriage license, just so we don't get talked into changing our minds," Johnny said.

Johnny was afraid because he knew he'd be drafted into the Army and didn't know how long he'd be away. The following day, Johnny and Ann went to the courthouse to get the marriage license. At the courthouse Johnny ran into his friend, Jessie Prisco. He told him their plan of getting married. Jessie knew a county judge who could marry them immediately. Ann hesitated but Johnny told him to go ahead and ask.

"What have we got to lose?" Johnny asked Ann.

"I guess you're right," she said.

Jessie had his phone number and called him. The judge agreed to marry them and asked for them to bring a marriage certificate, evidence of a blood test and two witnesses. Ann asked her sister, Nancy, to be a witness and Jessie served as the other. After the judge performed the ceremony he asked the couple if they wanted to make an announcement in the newspaper.

"No, we want to keep this secret," Johnny said.

In the car drive home Ann turned to Johnny.

"I still want to get married in the Catholic Church," she said.

"Soon as we can, we'll go see your father and mother to tell them that we're going to get married in the Italian church in town," Johnny promised. "We won't tell them we are already married."

That evening they both went to see Ann's parents. Both her parents were sitting in the living room listening to the radio. Ann was holding Johnny by the hand as they approached her father. Johnny was nervous and realized Ann was too because her hand was trembling. He squeezed her hand to assure her that everything would be all right.

"Mr. Cordone, Ann and I would like to talk to you for a moment," Johnny said.

Her father got up from the large couch against the wall and turned the radio off.

"Come sit down, what's on your mind?" Mr. Cordone said.

They both sat facing her father, while her mother continued knitting.

"Mr. Cordone, we came to ask you to give us your blessing because Ann and I are going to get married in the Italian church in three weeks," Johnny said.

Ann's father was stunned. It was disrespectful for Johnny to not ask permission and to instead tell him he was marrying his daughter.

"I won't give you permission to marry Ann," Mr. Cordone said.

"We didn't ask for your permission, we asked for your blessing," Johnny said, squeezing Ann's hand.

Mr. Cordone's face flushed with anger.

"I'm the head of this household and I am the only one who decides when any of my children will get married," Mr. Cordone said.

He stood up, then turned and left the room, slamming the door behind him.

Ann's mother abandoned her knitting to hug her daughter.

"I'm so happy for you," her mother said. "Don't mind your father, he'll change his mind."

"Mama, we love each other so much and Papa knows that we're engaged and have been going out steady for years," Ann said. "Why is he so angry?"

Ann's brother Charlie entered the living room and asked why everyone was upset.

"Father became angry when John and Ann said that they were going to get married in the Catholic Church," Ann's mother said. "He said he wouldn't give Ann permission to get married."

Charlie just shook his head.

"You know, Papa thinks he's the boss and he made all of us to wait until he said it was okay," Charlie said. "He made Louie and Millie wait four years before he gave permission."

While Ann was being consoled, Johnny motioned for Charlie to meet him in the kitchen.

"If your father refuses to walk Ann down the aisle, will you walk her down?" Johnny said, whispering. "We're planning on getting married in three weeks. "

"I'll walk her down the aisle," Charlie said, nodding. "I know my father made me wait before I could get married." He paused. "I can't believe Ann is standing up to him. She was always his favorite."

"Charlie, make sure this conversation stays between us," Johnny said. "Please don't repeat what I'm about to say."

"Sure Johnny, what's going on?" Charlie asked.

"Ann and I are already married," Johnny said. "We eloped last week."

"That was the smartest thing you ever did," Charlie said. "I'm sure Ann would have listened to our father and you'd be up a creek."

"I understand your father being worried that I'll be entering the Army and that something could happen while I'm away, but he said no right off the bat," Johnny said. "We both knew he wouldn't give us permission, that's why we eloped."

"That's my old man, he'll never change," Charlie said. "When is the church wedding?"

"We're planning on getting married in three weeks, January 25," replied Johnny.

"You took your first physical last week," Charlie said. "When do you think you'll go into active service?"

"I'll probably be told after I take my final physical," Johnny said. "They usually give us a week's notice before we're called for the final physical. Then they give us about a week's notice about the date I'll be inducted into the Army."

Johnny and Charley went back to the living room where Ann was still crying.

"What are we going to do now?" Ann asked Johnny.

Johnny turned to Ann's mother.

"Mama, we'll go see Father Paul at the Lady of Grace Church," Johnny said. "I'm sure he'll waive the reading of the bans so that we'll be able to get married on January 25, especially when I tell him I have to go into the Army. Now I have to go tell my parents about our wedding arrangements."

Before Johnny left Ann, she expressed concern.

"What will your parents say when you spring this on them?" Ann asked.

"I won't have trouble with that," Johnny said, kissing her. "They both knew I had every intention of marrying you when the time came. I've got to go, I'll let you know how it goes."

Johnny drove home and took the steps two at a time, bolting through the kitchen door. When he saw his mother, she was standing in the middle of the kitchen with tears running down her face.

"Mom, what's wrong?" Johnny asked, hugging his mom.

"Son what's going to happen to you when you enlist?" she asked. "I'm so afraid of what could happen to you."

"Come on Mom, everything is going to work out," Johnny said. "We're the most powerful country in the world. We'll kick those Japanese asses in a year. You watch and see."

"Son, why don't you go to that aircraft company to work and get a defense job?" his mom asked. "They don't want young boys like you. You could be more help by making airplanes to bomb those sneaky Japanese."

"Come on mom," Johnny said. "I'm a grown man and you'd be ashamed of me if I didn't fulfill my duty as an American."

He looked around the room.

"Where's Dad? We have to sit down and talk," Johnny said.

"Son, I'm in the living room listening to the news," his father called from the other room.

When Johnny entered, his father's eyes were glued to the floor while the radio was blaring in the corner.

"It looks like the Japanese destroyed our whole fleet," he said. "I don't know how we're going to protect ourselves with no Navy. Come on, son, sit down and listen."

He motioned toward the sofa.

"Pop, I told Mom that I was going to join the Army," Johnny said. "They'll be needing every able body they can get."

"I knew you would do that," his father said. "They will need every able body. But your mother will be sick with fear if you enlist."

The elder Romanek looked toward the kitchen and asked his wife for a couple of cold beers. When she appeared with a tray of beer bottles, tears were streaming down her face.

"Now Mama," the elder Romanek said, hugging his wife close. "Our son has to do what he think is right. He wants to serve his country and he knows they need him."

But Johnny's mom wouldn't stop crying. He then saw his father turn away and start to sob. He had never seen his father cry. The elder Romanek wiped away his tears and went over to adjust the radio.

While both his parents composed themselves, they all listened to the news bulletin on the latest regarding the war. Johnny allowed himself to relax while thinking about just how to tell his parents about Ann.

When the news bulletin ended his father turned off the radio. Johnny knew he had to tell them now.

"Ann and I are getting married in three weeks," Johnny blurted out.

He leaned forward in his chair to gauge their reactions. Both were taken by surprise.

"Son, aren't you rushing things?" the elder Romanek asked, clasping his hands together. "The Catholic Church must read the banns for three weeks before the wedding and we have to have time to invite our relatives. I know that they would like to see you and Ann get married."

"Pop, that will be taken care of," Johnny said. "I'll meet with Father Paul and I'm sure he'll agree to waive the reading of the banns because of the war since I'll have to go into the Army. They'll announce our coming marriage this Sunday and the following Sunday. When we get married, we're going to only have a small reception at Ann's house. We're only going to invite close relatives and friends."

His father's expression relaxed as he realized his son had thought a lot of this through. But Johnny's mother still had concerns.

"You're going into the Army any day now," his mother said. "What about Ann? Where will she stay? What will she do?"

"Ann will continue to live with her parents and she's going to keep working until I get back from the war," Johnny said.

"What did her parents say about all this?" the elder Romanek asked. "Aren't they worried about you going into the service and being away from her?"

Johnny hesitated before answering.

"We didn't tell them yet," he said. "You're the first ones I talked to about the wedding."

"Son, have you both thought this through carefully?" his father asked. "How do you both feel about you going into the Army? God forbid if something happens to you while in combat. Then there's a possibility that she could become pregnant, who's going to take care of the baby?"

"We talked about all these things," Johnny said. "And we're still going to get married regardless of who objects."

He stood up with the intent of ending the discussion.

His father sighed in resignation.

"I see you both made your minds up," he said. "So it's probably best that your mother and I support you. Let's make the arrangements for the wedding and the reception. I can pay a portion of the cost. I'll contact our relatives. It's short notice but I'm sure most of them will come."

Ann and Charlie were close as siblings. She was his favorite sister because she was always there for him. She always babysat her nephew and treated him like her own. Charlie knew how much it meant to Ann to get married in the Catholic Church.

The day after Johnny told his parents about the upcoming wedding, he and Ann met with Charlie.

"Papa will never change," Charlie said. "He's stubborn and he always wants to be the boss but most of the time he's wrong. He knew for years that you and John were going to get married. But for whatever reason he wants his way so he is probably not going to walk you down the aisle."

Ann cried as he said this.

"But I will be there for you," Charlie said. "I'm the eldest in the family and it will look proper for me to walk you down the aisle. It's all going to work out. Just you see."

He shook hands with Johnny in congratulations.

"We'll have to make arrangements for the reception," Charlie said.

"I did all of that before we came to see your father," Johnny said. "We also met with Father Paul. I ordered a wedding cake from the bakery and the deli will handle the sandwiches. My father is handling all the drinks. All we need is permission to use this house since my parent's home is too small."

"I'll talk to Mama," Charlie said. "My father may have control over family affairs but when it comes to the house, my mother is the boss and I know she'll give you permission."

Ann ran upstairs to get her mother. In a matter of minutes, Ann and her mother came walking into the living room. Her mother hugged and embraced Johnny. She was speaking in Italian, but from her expressions and motions Johnny knew she approved and granted permission to use the house. For the first time since they began talking about the wedding, Ann smiled.

"Johnny you're lucky you've got my mother on your side," Charlie joked. "She just was saying in Italian that she is so pleased you and Ann are getting married and she wishes you the best married life. She can't change my father's mind but she'll make sure the reception will take place here."

Three weeks later, Johnny and Ann got married in the Catholic Church. Ann looked stunning in a form-fitting white wedding gown that showed off her gorgeous figure. The train of the gown was trailing behind her as her sister Nancy, the maid-of-honor, carried it in her hands.

Charlie walked Ann down the aisle on his arm and was smiling at everyone as they passed the altar. When they got there, Charlie handed her off to Johnny, who took her by the arm as they approached Father Paul to perform the wedding ceremony.

Jessie was standing at Johnny's side as the best man and Nancy was on the other side next to Ann. When the ceremony was over, Johnny kissed the bride and they walked down the aisle and into a limousine.

The limo headed to Ann's parents' house for a reception for a select few family and friends. Although Ann's father was nowhere in sight, none of the guests questioned his absence. Ann's mother had a radiant smile on her face and Johnny's parents also were joyful. Johnny had paid for the sandwiches and wedding cake from his own savings and Frank Romanek contributed funds for liquor and beer.

"Even though my father isn't here, this was my dream day," Ann said to her new husband.

"Hon, I'm so happy to see you with a smile on your face," Johnny said.

After the last guests left, Johnny and Ann were eager to spend some time alone. They went to the rooming house where they had access to a kitchen and a private bedroom. Johnny put his arms around his wife.

"This is our first night as husband and wife," he said.

Ann was blushing at the thought of being his wife, she was no more just a girlfriend. She was a virgin and didn't know what to expect next. Johnny also had only one girlfriend and never had been with any women and he wasn't sure how to start.

For a while they just stood there looking at each other nervously. Then he began to kiss her gently. She responded to his kisses and they both fell onto the bed with their arms wrapped around each other. Johnny was patient and gentle with Ann, realizing she was nervous and had never been touched this way. He removed her dress until she was just in her bra and panties, and then after a while removed the undergarments. He noticed Ann was feeling more comfortable. When they were both naked Ann started to giggle, which got Johnny to laugh too.

"I've known you for so long and I can't believe we are now married," Ann said, kissing him.

"I feel the same way," Johnny said, kissing her back. He remembered that Ann might bleed so he stopped kissing her to get a towel for the bed.

"What's that for?" she asked.

"The blood," he said. When he noticed her look of alarm he reassured her. "I promise to be gentle with you, always."

That night she felt him inside her for the first time. It hurt, but it also felt good to be that close to Johnny. She bled a little on the towel.

"Did I hurt you?" Johnny asked.

"Not really," Ann said. "How did it feel for you?"

"It felt amazing," he said, kissing her.

After they dressed, Johnny asked Ann if she was hungry.

"I am starving actually," she said. "I just wasn't thinking about food really." She chuckled.

"There's a new restaurant in the area," Johnny said, pulling on his clothes. "I heard the food is excellent. Want to try it out?"

"Sure, sounds good," Ann said.

To celebrate their wedding they both ordered Italian Wedding soup to start and shared entrees.

He got spaghetti carbonara and she ordered pasta fagioli. They finished off their meals by sharing ricotta cheesecake.

As they walked out of the restaurant holding hands, Johnny asked if Ann was tired. She shook her head no so he suggested they go to the movies. "Gone With the Wind" was playing.

Ann enjoyed the movie and thought it was the perfect ending to her wedding day.

"This is the most beautiful time of my life," Johnny said. "I can't imagine a more perfect day."

"I'm so glad we eloped," Ann said. "If not I might have listened to my father like Millie did. I love you so much and I'm so glad to be married to you."

That night they went to sleep embracing each other.

Two weeks later, Johnny was called to take his final physical for the Army and was informed that he would be enlisted on March 4. Ann and Johnny would only have one more week together. When March 4 arrived, Army personnel picked up Johnny at the courthouse. Ann stood outside with tears in her eyes and waved as the truck pulled away. Johnny was driven to Camp Dix which was about 16 miles from Trenton, where he was going to do basic training.

The next morning at 6 a.m. Johnny heard the music for roll call. As he struggled to wake up he heard the sergeant call his name.

"I'm Romanek," Johnny said, standing up and stepping forward.

"Your wife is here to see you," the sergeant said.

When Johnny saw Ann he asked her if everything was ok.

"I just wanted to see where you were and where you were going for basic training," Ann said.

"Please don't worry about me," Johnny said, hugging her. "Just take care of yourself and we'll be together in no time."

While Johnny was serving stateside Ann visited as much as she could. During one visit he made a wrong turn on the way to the train station where he was picking up Ann. He was pulled over and given a ticket for the violation.

"I have to turn this over to the captain," Sergeant MacDonald said. "Be careful, he's a stickler for discipline."

"We just got Private Haberman out of jail and now you show up with this?" the captain shouted. He was walking back and forth behind his deck while Johnny stood there saluting and standing at attention.

"At ease," he said. He turned to Sergeant MacDonald.

"He's a good soldier," the captain said. "So how do I discipline him?"

"Sir, I'll discipline him," said Sergeant MacDonald.

Sergeant MacDonald had a lot of respect for Johnny because he knew he always sent the majority of his check home to his wife while keeping enough to cover the occasional beer and a movie. He also played a lot of sports with Johnny and enjoyed his competitive spirit. He also had witnessed Johnny sparring in the gym. One day an infantry soldier had challenged Johnny and went at him hard. Johnny was at the gym working out solely for exercise when the soldier had approached him.

Johnny had reluctantly agreed to spar him. When the bell rang, his opponent came out swinging furiously. Johnny covered up to ward off the blows and tried to move away but the fighter kept trying to knock him out. Johnny then went into a fighter's crouch, blocked the fighter's swing and made a move to expose his head. Johnny then threw a left hook with all his power behind it. The man was driven back into the ropes of the ring with his head unprotected. Johnny moved in with hard left and rights to his head, staggering the man. He then followed up with a final body blow to the solar plexus. The soldier fell to the floor unconscious.

Sergeant MacDonald witnessed the entire incident. As Johnny sat on his stool removing his gloves, Sergeant MacDonald approached him.

"Johnny that guy is a professional," the sergeant said. "He really thought he was going to knock you out."

"I didn't come to the gym to fight," Johnny said. "All I'm looking for is exercise. I didn't intend to hurt the guy, all I did was protect myself."

Sergeant MacDonald remembered this incident while in the captain's office.

"Johnny, go back to the barracks," the sergeant said. "I'll deal with you later."

"Sergeant, I know I did wrong in getting the ticket but my wife came in today," Johnny said.

The sergeant had a smile on his face.

"I know you got the ticket when you went to pick her up at the train station," the sergeant said. "Don't worry. I'll have your pass ready when you leave."

For the next month, Ann and Johnny had a grand time. When Johnny wasn't on Army duty, he and Ann explored the town and made love. Sergeant MacDonald took a liking to Ann, and asked that she help fix up the day room, to give it a "woman's touch."

It wasn't until a month later that Johnny was punished for making that wrong turn. The division was transferred to Augusta, Georgia. Ann, who was then pregnant, followed. While she was shopping in town, she ran into a childhood friend named Alice, who was now a first lieutenant in the Air Force. Ann invited Alice back to her place to freshen up. While Ann was showering,

Johnny walked into his room and was startled to see a woman hiding behind a newspaper.

Johnny thought he walked into the wrong room. He walked out, which is when Ann emerged from the shower clad in a bathrobe.

"I see you met Alice," Ann said.

Johnny and her both went back into the room where Alice was now standing, dressed in an Air Force uniform. She extended her hand toward Johnny.

"I'm Alice Sorone," she said. "Ann and I were childhood friends while we were in the same class back in grammar school. I'm sorry I startled you. Ann told me all about you."

Johnny noticed Alice's rank of lieutenant.

"Is this proper or should I salute?" Johnny said, unsure.

"No formalities here," Alice said. "It's a pleasure to meet you. Ann told me you worked at Ford. You must know my brother, Mark, he works at Ford also."

"I do know Mark," Johnny said. "He's been there a long time and is popular with all the workers."

Johnny looked at Ann then back at Alice.

"How did you and Ann run into each other?"

"We were both shopping," Ann said. "I was so surprised to see her, we hugged right there in the store."

"It's hard being stationed so far from your friends," Alice said. "I'm glad I'll have you to spend time with. You will both have to meet my boyfriend. He's a sergeant in the Air Force. We keep that hush-hush since the military frowns upon officers and enlisted going out together. But now that I've found my maid-of-honor we're going to make it official."

Alice hugged Ann, smiling.

"They're going to elope like we did," Ann said.

"Well congratulations are in order," Johnny said.

Alice glanced at her watch.

"I have to get back to the base," Alice said. "Now that I know where you're staying, I'll be here a lot to see you, just like old times."

"I'm having a great time meeting the soldiers' wives but running into an old friend like Alice was so refreshing," said Ann, after Alice left. "We had so much fun discussing our childhood. Nothing beats the connection you have to old friends."

After Johnny and Ann grabbed dinner they went to watch a movie on the base. "Fiddler on the Roof" was great fun and Ann laughed a lot. After they went back to their room and made love, Johnny set the alarm for 5 a.m. so he'd be on time for roll call.

After being in Augusta for a month, money was getting tight so Ann had to return home. Johnny and Ann stopped to say goodbye to Sergeant MacDonald, who was sad to see Ann go. The sergeant asked Johnny to look at the bulletin after coming back to drop off Ann.

Dropping Ann off was more difficult than usual. Tears ran down her cheeks and Johnny's throat was lodged with pressure as he held back his own. He sobbed when the train pulled out and then slowly made his way back to base.

Johnny went straight to the bulletin board and saw the weekly duties posted. He was posted for a Friday overnight shift. His Saturday shift was no better. He would be cleaning the mess hall and helping the mess sergeant prepare food. Sunday was Guard Duty, consisting of 24 hours, with two hours of guard duty, then four hours off. He had the same assignment 8 weeks in a row. Johnny knew this was punishment for the ticket he got.

After noticing Johnny's assignment, Lieutenant Wade Haslip went to see Sergeant MacDonald.

"What the hell did Romanek do to deserve this?" Lieutenant Haslip asked.

"Did Romanek come to you and complain?" Sergeant MacDonald asked.

"No, he's in my platoon and he's a good soldier," Lieutenant Haslip asked. "What the hell did he do to deserve this?"

"Go see Romanek," Sergeant MacDonald said.

But Lieutenant Haslip knew he wouldn't get any answer from Johnny. He went to the barracks and saw Johnny in a card game with some of the soldiers from his platoon. He walked over to the game and whispered into Johnny's ear to ask him to come outside. He took all eight weekly assignments out of his pocket and showed them to Johnny.

"What the hell did you do to deserve all this discipline?" Lieutenant Haslip asked.

Johnny looked at the papers and looked at Lieutenant Haslip.

"This was my own doing," Johnny said. "I appreciate you being concerned but don't worry about me."

Lieutenant Haslip sighed.

"I don't know what you did but I can see you're not going to tell me," he said.

He shrugged his shoulders and walked away.

Johnny couldn't tell him that he got a ticket in town more than a month ago. And that the sergeant had given him a free pass every day while Ann was here. Johnny knew he had gotten off easy.

Chapter 11
Year 1965

The Pirate's Cove parking lot was full to capacity, so they parked on the lawn outside the inn. They headed for the bar where they spotted two vacant seats. Rocky and Johnny ordered their usual. Rocky kept looking around.

"You ok buddy?" Johnny asked him, putting his hand on his shoulder.

"Yeah," Rocky said, continuing to look distracted.

He then spotted Tony Rodgers sitting at a table nearby with Geraldine who was leaning all over him. Rocky motioned with his head and Johnny turned around.

"That's Tony over there with that good-looking broad from the admin office," Rocky chuckled.

"Well I'll be dammed," Johnny said. "Here we are up to our necks in alligator and that bastard has pussy on his mind."

"You know that stiff prick has no conscience," Rocky said, gulping down his drink and motioning to the bartender for another. "I wouldn't mind banging her myself. She's built like a brick house. She's the one who wiggles her ass when she walks by in the hallway. Why don't we stick around to see if he rents a room to get some nookie?"

"That son of a bitch should get his ass kicked for cheating on his wife," Johnny said. "I was told his wife is easy on the eyes as well. I guess with all the troubles we have at the plant, he's using this as a good time to sneak out on her."

Unlike Rocky, Johnny wasn't interested in Tony's personal life and didn't believe in blackmailing anyone. Rocky, however, was a different breed. He had a vicious streak in him and wanted to have something to hold over Tony's head. Rocky was aware that Tony was using him in his feud with Johnny to get what he needed at the plant. This would be Rocky's insurance for the future. Johnny got up from the bar.

"With that guy around, this isn't a good place to talk about anything," Johnny said. "Let's continue our conversation another day. I'm going to head home. Thanks for the drink."

"I'm gonna stick around," Rocky said. "I see some friends at the other end of the bar."

But Rocky kept his eyes glued on Tony and Geraldine. Johnny shook his head as he walked out. He knew Rocky was up to no good but this wasn't his problem. He had bigger issues to deal with at the plant.

When Johnny left, Rocky positioned himself in front of the large mirror set up behind the bar so he could watch them. In a short time he noticed that they got up to go to the lobby desk to register for a room. Rocky followed them, then stopped at the news stand, pretending to leaf through a magazine while he was waiting for them to pass by on their way to the elevator. As they were passing, Rocky accidently bumped into them.

"Oh, so sorry, sir," Rocky said. "I was so consumed by what I was reading that I didn't see you come by."

Rocky looked into Tony's flushed and surprised face. "
Oh, Tony, I didn't recognize you," Rocky said.
He turned to the beautiful brunette to his side.
"Hi Gerry," Rocky said. "Strange running into you here."
Tony stood still, speechless.

"I had some work that had to be done and I thought it was better doing it here rather than at the plant where we are constantly being interrupted," Tony stammered.

"I know how that is," Rocky said with a smile. "Look, you two take care. I'll see you at the plant tomorrow."

Rocky winked at Gerry and left.

Geraldine took Tony by the hand and they walked to the elevator. Tony was in a daze. He couldn't understand how Rocky left the membership meeting that fast. The only thing that he could surmise was that he left early and let Johnny deal with the members by himself. He knew Rocky wasn't the type to get his hands dirty getting too involved with the crisis. One thing was for sure, Tony was afraid of being seen by someone from the union. Gerry picked up on this and reached over to kiss him.

"Honey, I'll soon have you forgetting all your problems," she said, nuzzling his neck. "Don't worry about Rocky, he's no angel when it comes to women. It's just a coincidence that he's here."

The elevator door opened and she linked her arm into his and walked to their room.

Tony wasn't so sure about Rocky; that was the problem. He glanced around the hall as he placed the key into the door. Gerry tried to kiss him, but he pushed her away.

"Not until we are in the room," Tony snapped.

Gerry reeled back, tears forming in her large doe eyes that were framed with luscious eyelashes.

"I can't afford to get caught going out with you," Tony said. "Mr. Cannon is a close friend of my wife's father who is a vice president with Ford. If he ever found out that I was taking you out and sneaking behind his daughter, it would be the end of my job."

He turned to look at Gerry, who looked sympathetic and like she understood.

Tony's hand was trembling as he tried to insert the key into the lock. Finally the door opened and as soon they entered the room, Gerry placed her arms around Tony's neck, kissing him and pushing her body into his. Immediately she felt his body respond to hers.

"Now you're being your old self again," she murmured.

She reached to open his fly and gently pulled him toward the bed. He took off his shirt as she pleasured him. Although he was enjoying his time with Gerry, he couldn't take his mind off of running into Rocky.

"Hon, was there anyone else with Rocky when he was at the bar?" Tony asked, stroking her head.

Gerry stopped and looked him, wiping her mouth.

"He was with that other man who always comes to your office, the one you hate so much," Gerry said.

Tony pushed her away.

"Why didn't you tell me this before?" he shouted.

"Honey, what's wrong?" Gerry said. "I thought we were having a good time?"

She sat on the bed completely confused as he zipped up his pants. He then pulled her off the bed and dragged her out of the room. What if Johnny saw him there with Geraldine? Would he say something if they were in a meeting with Jay Cannon?

"I'm sorry, Gerry," Tony said when they got to the elevator. "We need to get out of here now. I didn't mean to yell at you, but Johnny is the one guy who could ruin this for the both of us. I can't afford to be caught in a compromising position. Johnny knows that I can't stand him and that I was doing everything to make him look bad. He'll use whatever ammunition he can to take me down."

As they rushed out of the elevator into the lobby, Gerry noticed Rocky sitting at the bar. He lifted his drink to salute her.

"Honey, I can't take a chance of getting caught here with you," Tony said, looking around before he kissed her on the cheek. "I'll make this up to you the next time we go out. But right now I have to head back to the plant before someone decides to call my wife."

Gerry nodded her head, blinking back tears. Tony quickly headed for his car parked in the lot.

Gerry wiped away her tears and sat in the parked car. She started to feel very angry and felt Tony was making a big deal. Instead of going home she returned to the lounge to get another drink. Rocky was sitting nearby and ordered a scotch on the rocks. He tapped the stool next to him.

"Gerry, I got you a drink," he said. "You look upset. Why don't you join me?"

As soon as her drink came, Gerry started gulping it down. Rocky ordered another.

"Slow down, sweetie," Rocky said, amused.

"Tony is scared shitless that you'll blow the whistle on him," she blurted out. "He's afraid he's going to lose his job."

She took small, rapid sips of her drink.

"Gerry, I'd never do that," Rocky said, putting his arm around her shoulder.

He noticed how good she smelled and he immediately got excited.

"I told him that but he panicked when I mentioned that the president of your union was sitting at the bar with you," she said. "He cancelled our entire plans for tonight."

She began sobbing.

"Let's go somewhere where we can be alone," Rocky said. "You're upset and I don't want people staring."

"I still have the key from our room," Gerry said, a slow smile spreading across her face. "Let's not waste it."

As soon as they entered the room, he called room service and ordered a bottle of scotch and a bucket of ice. Gerry lay across the bed with a sad look on her face. When the bottle arrived Rocky poured a generous amount in a glass and handed it to her. She took several big gulps and Rocky sat down next to her. He placed his arm around her and pulled her close to him.

"Gerry, we'll stay here a while until you regain your composure," Rocky said, stroking her hair. Gerry was even more stunning up close.

She gulped down her drink and stood up to place the empty glass on the dresser. She then walked back to the bed and sat down next to Rocky. He began brushing away her tears and gently kissed her cheek. He then kissed the rest of her face, eventually kissing her on the mouth.

"I can't do this," Gerry said, pushing him away.

"Do what?" Rocky said. "It's just a kiss. Am I making you feel better at least?"

Gerry nodded. Rocky leaned toward her slowly, kissing her on the mouth, then the neck. He could feel Gerry relax and began unbuttoning her blouse. She was a curvy girl, on the buxom side, but her body was well proportioned and shapely. Her dark hair fell loosely around her shoulders as he pushed her backward on the bed. Rocky was on top of Gerry, feeling her under him, kissing her face and lips. He reached under her skirt to touch in between her legs. She finally stopped resisting him.

He unzipped his pants and pushed her face down. She started pleasuring him immediately. After a few minutes he pushed her onto her back and opened her legs wide. He entered her slowly and he heard her sigh with pleasure. She wrapped her legs around his hips and her body softened underneath him.

"Keep relaxing and move slowly with me," he said as he kissed her hard on the mouth.

Rocky could feel Gerry get very excited to he started to move faster, feeling her deeper and deeper. She began moaning with pleasure. The thrill was so great she began to scream. They came at the exact time and the both released each other as they lay in a pile of sweat.

"What have I done?" Gerry cried.

"Well, do you feel better?" Rocky asked, as Gerry pulled on her clothes.

Gerry didn't say anything. Problem was, Rocky was just getting started.

* * *

The United Black Brothers and the white militant allies were out in full force trying to shut down the day shift to get the company to acquiesce to their demands. They stood on the highway, waving their placards denouncing the company and urging the members to go to the union hall for a meeting and to listen to their demands.

The members were well aware of their problem and knew that the local union leadership was not supportive of the demonstration, so they ignored the protest and drove into the parking lot to go to work.

Johnny was there long before the day shift started and parked his car on the overpass leading into the plant where he could study the response of the day shift workers toward the demonstrators. He saw a young white militant banging on the car doors of the workers going into the plant. They weren't paying any attention to the militant's demands so he started kicking into the side of the car and damaging it.

Two black workers jumped out of the car and went after the white militant but were restrained by some of the black workers who were standing nearby. The driver of the car came out with a lug wrench and cracked it over the white militant's head.

The driver, a black worker, then waved to his buddies to get in the car and they drove into the plant parking lot leaving the injured white militant lying there with his head bleeding. The black demonstrators ran over to assist their fallen comrade. This ended the demonstration and the whole day shift went to work.

The militants were unsuccessful at preventing the cars from entering the plant, so one of them pulled his late model Corvette into the entrance of the access road to block it and created a traffic jam on the main highway. Other militants noticed the effect of the blockage and did likewise but never saw the police parked at the end of the road with tow trucks. The police moved in immediately with the trucks to tow the illegally parked vehicles and attached them first to the Corvette and towed them away. The drivers of the remaining cars tried to get in them to drive away and avoid the tow truck but were shoved by the police who wanted to teach the demonstrators a lesson.

The drivers were well aware of the heavy fines imposed for blocking the main highway plus the cost of towing and parking costs while their cars were in the county parking lot while waiting for the court order. They were mainly concerned by the length of time the court held their vehicle, this added to a lot of extra fines.

The United Black Brothers were successful in getting some of the younger black workers to join them but many of them were new and in probationary periods on their jobs. Many of the senior blacks were set in their ways and were beholden to the union who helped them over the years. The senior blacks were dedicated to the union and believed it would resolve this problem to their satisfaction. The day shift only experienced the normal amount of absenteeism and production continued without interruption. The black militants and their newfound supporters drove over to the union parking lot to meet and wait until the union headquarters opened so they could use the hall.

Betty was the first one to arrive at the union hall. She sat in her car a moment and realized that the demonstrators were waiting for someone to open the hall. She knew this was unwise since the union leadership was against the wildcat. She drove to a nearby diner to collect her thoughts and noticed Johnny Romanek driving into the lot. He invited her to have breakfast while he explained what happened.

"You nearly ran into a donnybrook," Johnny said. "I didn't expect you for another hour."

"I know," Betty replied. "I purposely came in early to type the report for your meeting with the company this morning."

"Betty here's some cash," Johnny said as he handed her some money. "Take the day off and call the other girls and tell them to do the same, with pay of course. The cash is for you and the girls to have breakfast. I'll call you this afternoon if I need you, but I doubt I will."

Johnny left for his scheduled 9 a.m. meeting with the company representatives. When he got there, he met Rocky and Lou waiting outside Tony Rodgers' office. They walked into Tony's outer office where Marie Collins was busy typing. She stopped when she saw Johnny.

"Is he in?" Johnny asked.

"Yes Mr. Romanek," Marie said. "He's expecting you."

She buzzed Tony's inner office and heard his reply to send them in.

Johnny walked in and saw the pained expression on Tony's face. At first he assumed Tony was worried about the demonstrators but noticed an anxious look aimed at Rocky who was ignoring him. Johnny knew that something must have happened at the Holiday Inn when he left. Johnny didn't have the time or energy to worry about that, so shrugged it off and threw his briefcase on the conference table.

"Tony the night shift didn't buy your explanation yesterday," Johnny said. "They were out in full force this morning."

"I was out there with my labor reps," Tony said. "Marie handed me this set of demands that the black militants dropped off on her desk this morning."

Tony pushed over the set of demands so the men could view them.

"They list everything from being placed on management jobs to negotiating with the company without the union being there," Tony continued.

Rocky and Lou leaned over so they could read the demands.

"This is pretty heavy stuff," Johnny said. "What's this Tuesday deadline they're referring to? And going into phase 2?"

"The only thing is our formal meeting our staff has with the Detroit representatives," Tony said. "As far as phase 2 goes, I imagine they'll have some kind of demonstration to impress Sid McMann and Ken Bannon."

He hesitated for a moment before speaking again.

"You guys were at their meeting, did they refer to a deadline?" Tony said.

"No, I laid out the facts to them but they weren't buying anything," Johnny said. "Their main concern was what the company was going to do about Superintendent Acuff and what happens to them when this is over."

Tony was deeply concerned for two reasons. The plant manager wanted the night shift to go back with no concessions regarding the Roy incident and he had a major problem on his hands because of his date with Geraldine. He was afraid Johnny would bring it up when they had a meeting with Jay Cannon there. Tony kept trying to make eye contact with Rocky who continued reading and looking at his notes. Rocky had no intention of letting

Tony off the hook. He was going to use the Geraldine information in case he needed something.

"Johnny did they keep you guys long at the meeting?" Tony asked.

"No, not too long," Johnny replied. "Leon Saint and Willie Barnes made their report while we went to my office. We could hear everything from there. Their report was a farce. They had no intention of buying anything you said at our meeting. When they were through with our meeting, we went down to their larger meeting to address them. That only took a few moments. I laid the facts before them but they all began booing. I took the microphone and left. The leaders tried to stop us but we had to shove our way out. They were pissed but we were beating a dead horse."

Lou Sargent knew that Tony was in a bind.

"After you guys left, I stayed behind with George Plassard," Lou said. "Manny Head steamed up the members by calling us company stooges and demanded that they shut the plant down until justice is served. He's real serious about those demands he gave you."

Lou stopped for a moment to light up a cigarette.

"He urged the members to come out in full force today but only a handful showed up," Lou said, taking a drag. "This isn't over by a long shot."

Tony made a feeble attempt to explain why the plant manager wasn't at the meeting. He said Jay was on the phone with the central staff trying to come up with a solution to the problem that they could live with. Johnny knew Tony had no power to act and was only doing a beg job with the union. Johnny knew it was his time to leave so he picked up his briefcase from the table.

"I have to go to the union hall to draft up a bulletin urging the members to go back to work," Johnny said to Rocky and Lou. "Soon as I get it done, we'll go over it to make necessary changes to satisfy the executive board and the committeemen before we all sign it. Call me at the hall if anything comes up."

Rocky left Tony's office to talk with Marie. He heard Tony call his name.

"Rocky, can I see you for a moment?" Tony asked.

Rocky whispered to Marie before heading back to Tony's office. Tony was as white as a sheet and thoroughly shaken up.

"Did Johnny say anything to you about our being at the Holiday Inn last night?" Tony asked.

"Hell no," Rocky said. "I didn't mention anything about my bumping into you. Why, did he mention anything to you?"

"No," Tony said, mildly relieved. "I'm only asking because Geraldine mentioned that she saw you and Johnny at the bar having a drink while we were eating. While you were there at the bar did he see us there?"

Tony was worried about being on a date while the plant was shut down and if that would affect his job.

"He never mentioned anything to me about last night," Rocky said. "What are you worried about? I wouldn't open my mouth about anything like that. Just forget about last night. I don't remember a thing."

Rocky shook Tony's hand and left. He went to find Marie but she wasn't at her desk so he walked up the stairs to the coffee area. She was waiting alone with a cup of coffee in her hand.

"I see your boss allows you to have a coffee break," Rocky said in a loud voice.

She smiled as she pushed a strand of hair from her face.

"Yes and I enjoy some of the fruits from the union's hard-fought benefits," Marie said. "Unfortunately, all my tasks are waiting for me when I go back to work."

Rocky smiled as he led her away from the office girls who were milling around the coffee machine. He explained his encounter with Tony and Geraldine but obviously left out what he did later. Marie began to giggle.

"So that's why he came back so early?" she said.

She looked around so no one could hear their conversation.

"As soon as he walked in, he asked me to call his wife," she whispered. "In a few minutes she called back. I guess that was to convince her that he was still at the plant. He stayed with me until 10 p.m. while I typed the entire report and then we both left."

She began giggling again and placed her hand over her mouth.

"I'd have given a million dollars to see their expression when you bumped into them," Marie whispered. "I'll bet it didn't faze Gerry one bit."

Rocky nodded and waited to see if Marie could give him any more insider information on what was going on. She finished her coffee and threw her empty cup into the waste bucket while he tried to press her for more information.

"I hear Gerry always boasts about going out with Tony?" Rocky asked.

Marie just nodded since she was paranoid other staff would overhear.

"I have to go back to my typing," she said. "I have loads of work to get through."

He walked with her downstairs and suggested they go out to dinner that evening. She agreed with a smile spreading across her face and then hurried back to the office.

Johnny returned to the union hall and saw Pat Fager having a conversation with George Plassard. Johnny showed them the demands from the United Black Brothers. They took their time reading the demands. Pat then moved closer to Johnny and whispered that he needed to speak to him in private.

They entered Johnny's office and sat on the sofa. Pat had a concerned expression on his face.

"Don Byrne and his caucus is having a meeting today," Pat said. "They are going to try to pin the wildcat on you and say it was because you are inexperienced as a president. They're revving up the whites, saying that you're letting the blacks run the union and the only ones trying to keep control of the union is Rocky and Lou. On the night shift, they're telling the whites that you agreed to let the blacks get the promotional job regardless of seniority. They're also having their black supporters on the night shift tell the blacks that you're afraid to force the company to fire Roy and the only reason that Roy is out of the plant is because Rocky and Lou forced the company to place him on the street until Detroit settles this."

Pat took a pause to lean toward Johnny and continued talking.

"They're hitting you from all sides," Pat said. "They even have the company saying that you're afraid to tell the workers to go back to work even though Roy isn't working in the plant since the incident happened. Rocky and Lou are telling the members what they want to hear and are distorting the facts to make you look weak and bad in the eyes of the members. We have to go on the offensive and cut the balls of those two."

Johnny was blindsided even though he knew Rocky and Lou were out to get him.

"I know they're clobbering me," Johnny said. "Were you able to find out if Rocky's going to go to their meeting?"

"My sister told me Marie is going out with Rocky tonight," Pat said. "She's head over heels in love with that prick. I'll bet any kind of money that he's getting all kinds of information from her on things she hears in Tony's office. Rocky is our biggest problem. We have to get him out of the equation. He's cutting you up with some of our caucus members. He's telling them that you lost your balls when you let the black militants dictate their demands to you. After this demonstration is over, we're going to have to take those two down. Don isn't saying anything real bad about you but he's been fixated on the fact that when Roy was put out of the plant, you should have told the night shift to go back to work. He's harping on the fact that you don't have the experience to deal with this kind of action by the blacks."

"Pat, we will have a meeting with the international union, our executive board and all the committeemen and bargaining committee," Johnny said. "We'll construct a bulletin that will pull no punches with the black militants, their hippie friends and the demonstrators. I'll make sure everyone signs the bulletin. I'll show the members that we're all united in our thinking and there will be no passing the buck."

"Another thing my sister told me is that Rocky told Marie that he would be the next president of the local union," Pat said. "She hinted that Tony is having his labor reps tell the foreman that you're not living up to your responsibilities with the membership. Tony hates you with a passion and will do everything to make sure you don't get re-elected as president in the next election."

Johnny leaned his head back on the rear of the sofa and closed his eyes to take in everything that Pat was saying. As Pat was talking Johnny felt a net was closing around him from all sides.

"I never realized as president that you could get hit from so many sides all at once," Johnny said. "I finally clipped George Plassard's wings by slashing his hours down to forty hours a week, no overtime. That stopped him from blasting me on union expenditures. Maybe I'll do the same with Lou."

"You better start with Rocky first," Pat said. "He needs more money than any one of them because of his extra activities with his girlfriends and Marie."

"No," Johnny said, shaking his head firmly. "Rocky has money coming in from other activities so cutting him down won't have any effect. Lou needs money to support his family and to keep his followers drinking at the local bars. Rocky's not too smart. He'll make a mistake and I'll be all over him."

Johnny then sat there with his eyes closed, thinking about his next move.

In the meantime, Rocky and Lou were meeting to discuss the caucus meeting Don Byrne's group was holding that evening. Lou was trying to convince Rocky to attend, especially since they decided to support Don as president of the union in the next election. At the caucus meeting they were going to prepare the narrative to place the entire blame on Johnny for the wildcat strike.

The night shift was restless after being on strike for four days with no pay and 90 percent of the workers coming in and being sent home because of the high absenteeism in the body shop by the black militants in skilled operations. The day shift was starting to get worried that the wildcat would shift over to the day shift for the bullshit the black militants were demanding. Don's followers knew that the night shift was enjoying the excitement in the beginning but now it was costing them money and no relief in sight. They intended to characterize Johnny as gutless and afraid to take a position.

Johnny made a lot of inroads with the membership and now it was their time to take him down, Lou said. Lou explained that Rocky was sorely needed at the meeting to show them leadership.

Rocky's ego wanted to attend but he didn't want to pass up his date with Marie. She was too important as his continuous source of information to take out Tony.

"Lou, you knew I had this date with Marie and I got tickets to a Broadway show," Rocky explained. "I'll go along with whatever the caucus decides but I'm pissed that you guys selected me to head the group but didn't tell me that you were planning the meeting tonight. You're now telling me something that was planned a week ago."

Rocky was annoyed at being considered an afterthought. He should be the one calling the shots. More important, he didn't want Johnny on his back this early in the game. The election was a year away and he knew Johnny wouldn't take shit laying down. Rocky's philosophy was to pull the underhand strategy just prior to the election so the opposition couldn't get back at him in time. He didn't want to give his opponent time to counter his moves and offset his chance of winning.

Lou understood Rocky's predicament and his taking offense at not being informed properly.

"The reason we called this meeting so quickly was because we feel the night shift will be back to work on Monday," Lou said. "Once that bulletin comes out with all our names on it, the blacks who aren't members of the Black Brothers will come back to work because if they don't they could lose their job. There will only be a handful of workers that'll continue to stay out. We want to get due credit that we got the workers back to work and blame Johnny for everything that went wrong."

Lou knew he was beating a dead horse by trying to persuade Rocky.

"Have a good time with Marie," Lou said. "I'll call you at your home and let you know what the caucus decided."

Lou drove over to the bar where Don's caucus meeting was being held. As he walked into the dark bar he heard Don call out.

"Lou, over here," Don said. "Where's Rocky?"

The men moved into a booth to make room for Lou.

"Rocky had a previous appointment which he couldn't miss," Lou said. "I told you guys that we should have had him at the first meeting when we decided to meet today. He's pissed and rightfully so but he said that he would go along with whatever we decide."

Don was sipping a beer as Lou spoke.

"You're right, but time was of the essence," Don said. "In order to be effective, we have to hit Johnny while the iron is still hot. Look how he hit me on the night shift versus day shift issue during our election, his timing was perfect. It eventually cost me my election."

Earl Johnson, a strong supporter of Rocky spoke up.

"Rocky has every right to be pissed for not being told of this meeting," Earl said. "I'll tell you a little bit about his strategy.

He doesn't like to rush into things without a lot of planning. He's been very successful and won every election that he was in by a landslide, including the last one. I realize that the caucus wants to hit Johnny right away. But Rocky's strategy is that you give a lot of time to retaliate. Whatever we do has to be underground. We have to knock Johnny's brains out and at the same time make it look like we're cooperating with the president of the union."

"I agree with this line of strategy," George said, who was quiet until now. "Look how I attacked him on the spending of union funds? That son-of-a-bitch in turn took away all my extra jobs. And when I ran short of money I had to ask him to take my vacation in lieu of pay. He had the audacity to tell me to straighten out and he'd reinstate my overtime. He's a mean bastard when you take him on so you guys better be careful regarding what you do. I'm for going underground and using our caucus members in spreading the shit. We can't have the membership sympathizing with him."

Earl put up his hand to be recognized by Don who was still the unofficial leader of the group.

"For the last year, our group has been rapping him on every sensitive issue in the plant," Earl said. "We could do some job on him with this issue in the eyes of the membership. Monday's meeting with the region is the key. We got to suck him into agreeing that the blacks were justified in walking out. Then the whites will eat him up alive. But we have to be careful how we go about it. Johnny's a smart politician and he came from the body shop which is loaded with blacks and he knows their needs. We better convince him to make the wrong move."

"Earl is right," Don said. "There's no way Johnny can come out of this looking good. If he goes against the blacks, they'll hate him. If he goes with them, the whites will conclude that he sold them down the river. I can't be at that meeting, but Rocky, Lou and George will be."

Don turned to Lou.

"Make sure you fill Rocky in on what we discussed and I'm sure we'll come up with something," Don said. "We have to play it by ear."

Everyone was in agreement.

"Let's get everyone in the main room so we can start the caucus," Don said.

They summoned all the caucus members in the hall behind the bar and started the meeting.

Jay Cannon set up the meeting with his top management staff to discuss the course of action to resolve the wildcat strike and set the tempo for the formal meeting with the executive vice president of industrial labor relations.

Jay was concerned that if Tony did his job properly, this could have been avoided. The previous month Tony and Ed Hubot, the black labor relations representative, attended a conference dealing with the black movement that was sweeping the country. They spent a week attending classes showing films and literature which explained the direction the company had to take in order to have peace in the working area. Tony didn't think it was a problem at the plant but Ed kept urging Tony to hold classes with the supervisors and upgrade the qualified blacks into management positions but Tony ignored all those suggestions.

After the Roy incident Tony contacted other Ford assembly plants to see if they instructed their supervisors to follow what the classes taught but none of the other plants did anything. After the Roy incident all plants started to take heed and were following what the classes dictated. Tony explained this all to Jay, who realized he really couldn't fault Tony because he never took an interest in the black movement.

Jay was looking for some inside information that could help to resolve the situation at the plant.

"Ed, I'd like to hear any suggestions on what we could do to resolve the Roy affair?" Jay said. "You have a handle on what's going on within the black movement around the country."

Ed was in a peculiar position. He felt disrespected by Roy during the confrontation and wanted to be vindicated in the eyes of the black community, but at the same time, he was interested in getting one of the promotions that he knew was promised to one of the blacks at the plant. He had to be careful in what he said and still be able to meet needs of the black constituents he was representing.

"Mr. Cannon, I participated in a meeting held in Newark with the leaders of the black community," Ed said. "They expressed their dissatisfaction regarding the lack of interest from whites toward black workers in politics and the work place. They're banding together to be a more powerful force and to be recognized at last."

"In our plant there is a need to place blacks in key positions within all departments," Ed continued. "We have many blacks working here with a good education who should be given consideration. The black force here at the plant numbers 35 percent, yet we only have three percent of black workers in supervisory positions. The imbalance is definitely there. Look at your office staff in the administration building and labor relations, I'm the only black working there. I'm not being critical but you did ask me for my opinion."

"I appreciate your candid opinion so go on," Jay said.

"I've been going over the records which is part of my job, and I saw that we have many blacks with some college education who are working on the line," Ed said. "They can't get ahead because the union contract bases promotions on seniority when jobs are posted. The salary staff is not based on a union contract so we can promote and not be in any violation. Over the last few days, blacks have been visiting me at my home and asked what I was doing to resolve this problem."

"I had to tell them my hands were tied but I sympathized with their concerns," Ed continued. "Otto Brodwick, who is one of the leaders of the black movement, wants this protest to stop. When we reviewed the footage of the demonstration, Otto wasn't one of the leaders provoking the workers to stay out. My informants tell me he's the most vocal speaker at their rally and is seriously looking for a solution to get the men back to work, but at the same time he wants to protect those who are fighting for basic human rights. He made it clear that there cannot be any recourse for those fighting for justice and Roy must be removed from the plant. He spoke freely about this to me, knowing that I would carry this information back to management."

Jay was looking at a means of settling the issue by getting the night shift back. The car they were making in the plant was one of Ford's best sellers and Detroit's concern was that this issue could carry over to the day shift.

"Otto hinted that he had no problem with the company transferring Roy to another assembly plant," Ed said. "The bitterness from our workers is the result of how blacks are being treated all over the country and Roy was the straw that broke the camel's back. Otto is asking for the company to impose only a light sentence on the black leaders who caused the walk out, and ensure the rest of the workers face no punishment. They only protested to correct the injustice against them. Otto emphasized that the whole country is looking at us to see what we would do to correct the situation. This issue is beyond Clinton. He talked about Martin Luther King, Jr.'s approach to resolve this without any violence and in a peaceful manner. The other militant leaders don't share Otto's views and instead would like to shut down the whole plant. My opinion is that Roy should be transferred to another assembly plant. The company keeps insisting that language he used was no more than shop talk but referring to Byron as a boy is taboo. Then he attacked me in a racist manner when I tried to resolve the situation. The blacks that are on the street and those working on the day shift should be handled with kid gloves during this critical period. A wrong move on our part could create a riot. Sir, it's your decision on how this problem should be handled. Please don't think that I condone this action by the black militants but they have the support of blacks throughout the country."

Jay was very concerned.

"Thanks Ed, you put it on the line as clear as anyone could and I appreciate what you told us," Jay said. "That's all for now. Tony and I will discuss this further. One more thing, Sid McMann will be here on Tuesday and we'll have to lay this out for him. He's going to be the deciding factor in what's going to happen with Roy."

He paused before continuing to talk.

"Ed, I want you to be here to tell him what you told us," Jay said. "He'll probably ask you a lot of questions. Think about what you're going to say over the weekend."

Ed understood that his answers must set the right tone if he ever intended to get ahead in Clinton.

Chapter 12
Years 1944-1945

There were rumors the 26th Infantry Division would be leaving the states to join the forces in combat. A month later on June 26, 1944, Johnny's division was ordered to go overseas to join the 3rd Army, under General George S. Patton's command.

Johnny had his bag and all his field equipment on the street outside his barracks ready to be picked up. The trucks would then move to the train station and then the ships waiting for them at New York Harbor.

While the soldiers were assembled on the street waiting, the Red Cross sent a request to the company commander that Johnny be given a pass to visit his wife and newborn son. Johnny wasn't aware that Ann had given birth to their son, Wayne. Instead of being granted a pass, the captain assigned to military police to stand guard over him. Johnny was told he would only be able to see his son when he returned from combat. On the train he saw the hospital where she had just given birth. To make sure she knew he was thinking of her, Johnny sent Ann a dozen roses.

The 26th Infantry Division joined Patton's Third Army at the battle of Saint-Lô, in France. While there, Patton famously said to the British Commander: "Get your boy scouts out of the way, we're coming through."

The 26th was paired with the 4th Tank Division, who drove through France blowing away the German forces and soldiers. They were very effective in destroying the enemy forces and tanks. While the tank division pulverized the enemies, the foot soldiers fought hand-to-hand against German soldiers, killing many while others surrendered. General Patton blew right past Paris, pushing the German forces into retreat until they had reached Fort Metz, which was on the border of the German fortifications.

The Germans had captured one of France's forts during the invasion and used it to fire on American troops. The walls were deeply fortified, being four feet in depth with 50-caliber machine guns used on the Americans. Some American foot soldiers were able to creep up close to the walls of the fort and pushed grenades under the barrels of the machine guns. When the first grenade exploded inside, American troops continued pushing grenades into all the openings until the guns stopped firing. The Allied Forces broke into the fort where they found all the German soldiers dead.

Patton's tanks then moved forward through Germany, finding resistance constantly but eventually making the German forces retreat. While moving forward through the forests and fields, many of the enemy forces either retreated or were captured. The German tanks and armored vehicles retreated rather than being captured.

The trucks from Johnny's company were assigned to drive the infantry soldiers to dispose of the German and American bodies that were left behind. The trucks were driving during the night under blackout conditions with only small lights on to avoid being spotted by the enemy. These lights were the size of pin needles and provided little to no visibility. Throughout the war, Johnny drove in blackout conditions with no problem. But during one incident while driving through the German forest with soldiers on board he lost sight of the blackout lights in the vehicle ahead of him. He slowed down looking frantically for the lights ahead when the sergeant sitting in front with him shouted.

"There are the lights going left," he hollered.

Johnny immediately yanked the steering wheel left and the truck slipped into a ditch, dumping the soldiers onboard. Luckily none of the soldiers were injured except for Johnny, who had banged his head on the windshield. He had a deep cut above his eyebrow that began to bleed severely. He was able to stop the bleeding by applying pressure with his handkerchief. Meanwhile the captain was notified and he sent a maintenance crew to pull the truck out the ditch.

An officer approached Johnny and pointed at his jeep.

"Corporal, you're not driving this truck," the officer said. "Let's get you into my jeep and over to the medical tent to treat your injury."

"Sir, this is my truck," Johnny said, refusing to leave. "I can drive."

The officer shook his head and pointed to his jeep. Johnny realized he wasn't going to win this fight so he walked toward the jeep. He first checked on the troops from the truck and was relieved to know that everyone was okay.

After being sewn up by a doctor Johnny went over to a jeep that was to take him back to his unit.

A few weeks later Johnny was on guard duty in Luxemburg. It was 2 o'clock in the morning when Johnny saw a jeep drive up with a flag with three stars on the front fender. Johnny gave them a rifle salute and asked for the password. When the man replied with the right number, Johnny stepped back and recognized General Patton. He returned his salute and allowed them to pass through. A corporal on duty with him named Ben Hardy said it looked like they would be pulling out tomorrow.

"Patton doesn't visit anyone at 2 in the morning unless it's something important," Ben said.

That morning the company was assembled on the road and was informed that their division was being assigned to Belgium to help the 101 Airborne Division that was surrounded by German forces. The division dropped further back than intended and were now surrounded by Germans.

The Airborne Division, also known as the "Screaming Eagles" were the elite soldiers in the Army who had set up fortifications to resist the enemy's attack. They were able to drive back the enemy and inflict heavy casualties, forcing the Germans to pull back. The Germans had thought this would be a routine operation but then they realized the Airborne Division was a superior force. The American commander set up a defense that the Germans couldn't master. Every move they made against the Americans was opposed and the Germans lost a lot of their soldiers in their attack. The German leaders discussed many new ways to attack but couldn't come up with one idea on how to dislodge the Americans.

Meanwhile the 26th Infantry division commanding general assigned trucks to carry soldiers into Belgium to liberate the

Airborne troops who were dropped off in a designated area. Those Airborne troops were in position to attack the Germans.

American trucks moved to park in a safe area to be ready to move troops to a new position when necessary. The captain had the drivers in one place so they could be utilized when needed. The drivers broke off to pass the time, some played cards while others stood around talking. Johnny went to his sergeant and said he was going to wait in the truck.

"Don't drift off," the sergeant warned. "Be ready if we have to move out."

Johnny climbed into the driver's seat of the truck. He then reached into his pocket and pulled out pictures that Ann had sent him. They were pictures of Wayne that Johnny had only before skimmed through. This was the first time he was able to see what his newborn son looked like. Tears formed in his eyes as he looked at a picture of Ann peering at Wayne in his crib. He then heard a knock on the window. Lefty Demers was looking at him with wide eyes. He rolled down the window.

"You better get back to where the drivers are assembled and pray that you don't get hit by any of the incoming shells," Lefty said. "The Germans don't know where we are and are checker boarding their shells hoping to destroy all the equipment in the area."

"Thanks, Lefty," Johnny said, stuffing the pictures back into his pocket.

The Germans continued the bombing and the shells were coming close. The Germans were hoping to destroy all the American trucks and troops. They didn't know where the soldiers were. There really was no safe place. The bombs came as close as a hundred yards away and the order came that all trucks leave the area and move away from the bombing.

There was snow on the ground and the roads were icy. The trucks had to move out fast since the bombs were landing nearby. While they were leaving, a lot of trucks were skidding around on the ice. After moving a few miles, one of the trucks skidded off the road and into a snow pile in the middle of a field. The convoy kept going and no one stopped to help. Johnny was toward the end of the convoy. He saw the stranded driver climb out of the truck, pushing his way through the deep snow. He was covered with the falling snow and was struggling toward the road. Johnny stopped to help, discovering that the stranded driver was his buddy, Ben Hardy. Ben was only carrying his bedroll.

"You dumb fuck, where's your rifle?" Johnny asked. "Get your ass back and get it."

Ben gave Johnny a look that made Johnny realize he hadn't been thinking straight. Ben then dropped his bedroll and hurried back to the truck to get his rifle. He had to dig the snow away from the door and reached in to get the rifle out of the carrier. He tried to hurry because the convoy was gone and out of sight. He joined Johnny in the truck with his bedroll and rifle. Johnny drove for miles until they came to what looked like a dead-end. Johnny got out to see which way the convoy went. The road was covered with snow and there were no marks in the road.

"I'm going to flip a coin," Ben said. "If it falls on heads, we'll go right or otherwise, go left."

Johnny ignored him and kept walking and looking for some signs in the snow. He walked about a hundred yards and saw a skid mark on the right of the road where the driver almost ran off the road.

"You're correct, we'll take the road to the right," Johnny said.

They drove for miles before they came upon the convoy. The captain came over to them.

"Good job, corporal," he said. "We were alerted that one truck went off the road and into a snow pile but we didn't know if anyone stopped to pick up the stranded driver."

He held out his hand to shake Johnny's.

"You never know how anyone will act in a crisis," the captain said. "Thanks again soldier."

He headed to where the truck drivers were standing and began giving them orders.

Known as the Battle of the Bulge, this German offensive was hard fought with heavy deaths and injuries on both sides. The German soldiers who were facing Americans began climbing out of their foxholes with their hands up over their heads to surrender. The trucks were ordered to go back to where the fighting ended. American troops had their rifles pointed at the enemy as the enemy soldiers were ordered to get into trucks to be driven to a prison compound.

The Germans on the other side of the surrounded Airborne troops retreated with their tanks and trucks, knowing they were defeated. General Patton called all commanders to a meeting to plan their next move. He knew he achieved a huge victory and wanted to go after the retreating Germans while they were on the run and fragmented. He moved all his forces to strike before the Germans could get themselves in order. He moved his tank and foot soldiers back into Germany, taking over villages one after the other. There was no stopping General Patton.

While the Allied Forces were deep inside Germany, the captain sent for Johnny. When Johnny entered, he stopped in front of Captain Ardita, saluted and stood at attention. Captain Ardita returned the salute.

"I have a mission for you," the captain said. "We're running short of medical supplies. I want you and private first class Jim Covey to go to Fort Metz to pick up medical supplies from the depot there."

He handed Johnny a large list of supplies and a map.

"Yes, captain," Johnny said.

He took both items and went to his truck with Jim. When he got into his truck he studied the map. He decided to take the autobahn to Fort Metz, which would save them several hours. Jim agreed to Johnny's plan because he knew the corporal was a good at reading maps and made sense.

Johnny took the road to the super German highway that ran through the forest. They were driving for miles until they came to a large white house. Johnny slowed down to watch the house and saw German soldiers coming out the front door. He jammed on the brakes and cut across the entrance road and sharply left, knocking down the picket fence. He stepped on the gas and took off back the way they came. Jim was looking back at the house.

"Those soldiers scrambled back into the house, probably to get their rifles," Jim said. "We better get out of here real fast or they'll have someone after us. I think we surprised them, let's hope that they don't have any fast vehicles."

Johnny was pushing all the way down on the gas. After about ten miles, they were stopped by a platoon of American soldiers who had rifles pointed at them. A lieutenant came over with his side arm pointed at them.

"Get out of the truck with your hands up," he commanded.

Johnny and Jim did as they were instructed.

"Sir, we're American soldiers," Johnny said.

"Bullshit, you're coming from the German area," the lieutenant said. "Turn around and place your hands on the side of the truck and keep them there while we question you." The lieutenant kicked Johnny's feet apart while he was holding the side of the truck.

"Sir, we're with the 26th Division and I'm Corporal John Romanek from the 26th Quarter Master Company," Johnny said.

"You say you're American, where did you live in the United States?" asked the lieutenant.

"I lived in Fairview New Jersey," Johnny replied.

"Yeah, name New York baseball teams," he asked.

"New York Yankees, New York Giants and Brooklyn Dodgers," Johnny said. "Look lieutenant, I got a trip ticket that I was given to follow when I left my company. Can I can get the trip ticket I received when I left my unit?"

The lieutenant nodded. "Okay but don't try anything funny," he said. "I have my gun in the center of your back." Johnny slowly opened the truck door and leaned in to get the trip ticket and the map. He handed it to the lieutenant, who stepped back to peruse the items while still pointing the gun at Johnny. He studied the papers Johnny gave him. Then he walked to the front of the truck and saw the inscriptions saying 26th Q.M. He was satisfied and told them they could put their hands down.

"Why are you coming from the German side?" the lieutenant asked.

"I thought I could take a shortcut by taking the autobahn," Johnny said, pointing at the map. "It would save us hours."

"You're a smart ass who doesn't follow orders," the lieutenant said. "Well how did that go? You run into anyone? You were driving really fast when we stopped you."

"About ten miles up the road there's a large white house where we saw some German troops," Johnny said. "When you get there, you'll see where we made a quick turn and knocked down the picket fence."

The lieutenant handed the documents back to Johnny. "You better follow the route they gave you," he said. "Carry on." Johnny saluted the lieutenant, who returned the gesture.

Johnny and Jim both got into the truck and went back to follow the designated route. The rest of the trip occurred without incident and it took them the rest of the day to get to Fort Metz. It was dark by the time they arrived and they had to hunt around to find a place to sleep. An officer in charge of the medical depot set them up in a warehouse with cots to sleep on.

The next day they ate at the mess hall and then went to the medical depot to pick up supplies. They loaded the truck and were on their way out when a soldier walked up to them.

"Are you from the 26th Division?" he asked.

"Yes," Johnny said, puzzled that a soldier would recognize his division.

"Could I go back with you?" the soldier asked. "I'm from 26th Headquarters Company. My name is Private Edward Cooper."

"We have room in back of the truck," Johnny said. "You'll have to sit on boxes and it's a long way back."

Just as Johnny was getting into the truck, another soldier came up to him.

"I'm Lieutenant Jeff Kelly and I've been reassigned to the 26th Infantry Division," the soldier said. He showed his assignment papers to Johnny and continued to talk. "While I was being treated the doctor told me that you were from the 26th and pointed you out. He also told me that you finished here and were going back. I hope you have room for me."

After glancing at his papers Johnny nodded his head. "That's fine with me," Johnny said. He turned to Jim, telling him he would have to sit in back with the private since the lieutenant was riding with them.

"Also, I want you to keep an eye on him so he doesn't try to open any of the boxes," Johnny said. "He has me worried because he's so far away from our division."

It was a longer trip back because the division base moved deeper into Germany as the Americans advanced. At a halfway point they stopped at a military police post and were set up in a warehouse to sleep on cots. While the three of them were laying on their cots, Edward shared his story.

"I got separated from my unit," Edward said. "I was with the company headquarters and then we ran into trouble in Fort Metz. The commander assigned me to guard an Infantry Guard Post with a rifle. I never had any real training with a rifle. All the while I've been in the army, I never carried a rifle. This assignment scared the shit out of me and I took off. Now I want to go back to rejoin our company headquarters and resume my job."

None of them knew what to say and eventually fell asleep. The next morning they had breakfast and took off to return to the 26th Division base. It took a few more hours and soon as they got there, the lieutenant reported to division headquarters along with Edward. Meanwhile Johnny and Jim drove the truck to another location and unloaded them. While Johnny was talking to Captain Ardita, he saw military police handcuffing Edward and taking him away. Johnny never found out anything more about Edward.

* * *

Hollywood stars attended a Christmas party for troops to liven their spirits. Johnny's company was assigned to a large warehouse outside of Luxembourg. The stars who came to entertain them included Mickey Rooney and Bobby Breen. Mr. Rooney was the headliner and soldiers asked him personal questions but he ignored them and instead made jokes about the women he married and his movies with Judy Garland.

Bobby Breen sang a lot of popular songs using Frank Sinatra's style. Hearing this, Johnny approached him.

"Why are you imitating Frank Sinatra when you had the most beautiful voice as a young singer," Johnny asked the singer. "Now you don't sound at all like yourself." Bobby took the comment in good stride, smiling and shrugging his shoulders.

As the party was winding down, Sergeant MacDonald came over to Johnny with an assignment.

"Johnny, you and five drivers are assigned to go over to the field depot to bring field artillery shells to the 105th Battalion," Sergeant MacDonald said.

Johnny went to the trucks that were parked in front of the building and saw the five drivers standing there. Johnny knew that they were all drunk from all the liquor he had seen them consume.

Johnny was driving the lead truck and the other trucks followed. The snow came down heavily causing the roads to be slippery and wet. As Johnny was looking in his rearview mirror he noticed one of the men skidding. He had lost control of the truck and it landed in a huge snow pile. The truck landed in a huge embankment on the side of the road, enveloping the truck in snow, making it impossible to extricate it.

Thinking fast, Johnny instructed the driver of that truck to get into one of the other trucks and they continued to their destination. When they got to the depot, Johnny gathered the drivers.

"We're going to add additional shells to our trucks to make up for the missing fifth truck," Johnny said. "I want to make sure you pile the shells tight so they won't move."

No one questioned his authority and the trucks were all fully loaded. The officer in charge was pleased with how the drivers worked together to assure that the truck was loaded properly. Johnny led the convoy on the slippery road in a slow and safe manner.

When they got to their final destination, Johnny went over to the officer in charge.

"Sir were you satisfied with how we accomplished this assignment?" he asked.

The officer nodded.

"I certainly am," he said. "I'm glad you were in charge. We even brought more shells than we had ordered."

"Sir, could I ask you for a favor?" Johnny asked.

"What did you have in mind?" the officer asked.

"Sir, we had a party before we were assigned to this mission with a lot of hard drinks," Johnny said. "No one was aware that soon after we'd have to go out on a mission. The truck that went off the road, would you report it as an accident?"

"Done," the officer said. "I can see why they put you in charge. I want you to know that I appreciated what you guys did. That accident was beyond your control." The officer put out his hand for Johnny to shake it and Johnny saluted the officer.

In the year 1945, the Q.M. Company was stationed in Linz, Austria. It was a lovely summer day and the war with Germany was in its final stage with Germany surrendering to the allied forces.

The soldiers were all sitting in a warehouse that was assigned to them as their sleeping quarters. They just received an Army newspaper announcing that the U.S. Air Forces dropped an atom bomb on a large city in Japan, Hiroshima killing over fifty thousand people. They described the bomb's power as one with the might to wipe out a whole city. An atom bomb the size of a golf ball would demolish a large building completely.

Japan was pulverized and realized they underestimated the military might of the United States. A week later the U.S. Air Force dropped a second bomb on the city of Nagasaki, killing almost everyone there. Those that lived were so badly injured or crippled for life, that the leaders of Japan immediately asked for a meeting with the United States Army Forces Command to surrender. They knew they were defeated and had no weapons compared to the U.S.

The U.S. President, Harry Truman, knew the power of the bomb and didn't hesitate to use it. While he knew the bomb would kill many people, he also knew it would end World War II, ultimately saving more lives than the atom bombs killed. He named General Douglas MacArthur to head the negotiators where the peace treaty was signed.

The signing of the peace treaty saved the 26th Division from going overseas to fight in Japan. The division had just completed all the medical physicals of the troops that were to be deported to the Far East. Johnny and the rest of the drivers couldn't believe that this happened, they were overjoyed and began hugging each other. Johnny pointed at the newspaper exclaiming, " I can't believe this, now I can go home and see my wife and my newborn son."

Johnny sat there in shock as he envisioned going back home to be with his wife and the son whom he had never even seen. He went over to his buddies and asked them to go on a walk to work out their emotions.

They walked toward the train station in Linz. They were walking along the path adjacent to the railroad tracks. A high steel picket fence separated the path from the tracks so no one would accidently walk too close as a train was approaching. One side of the path was surrounded with full blooming flowers. On the opposite side of the fence, one could see the railroad station which was picturesque and neatly kept in its original state. For the first time in a long time the men walked and enjoyed the beautiful scenery.

"How about it," Johnny said. "Let's go in town. I heard there's a little bar at the other end of the railroad station. I was told that the beer isn't half bad. Let's try it out."

"The beer they make now, tastes like piss," said Ben Hardy, a teetotaler. "I'd just as soon have a cup of tea or coffee. Linz was known for its beer before the war. But now they don't have the ingredients to make it right."

As they were strolling down the path, Johnny noticed a little boy dressed in a typical Austrian suit with a pointed skullcap and a bright red feather attached to the band on the hat. He wore cobbled shoes with knee-high stockings and couldn't be more than two years old. He could see from the distance that something excited the little boy as he pulled away from his mother's hand. He was running as fast as his legs could go down the path toward the soldiers. Johnny laughed and pointed to the little boy.

"Look at that little guy run, he's faster than his mother," Johnny said. He looked around to see what attracted the youngster but there was no one behind them. "Do either of you know him?" Johnny turned to look at his fellow soldiers.

"How the hell would any of us know him," Marty Coelhelo chuckled. "We all just got here last night."

Johnny felt in his pockets to see if he had any gum or candy which he usually carried for such an occasion. The little boy kept running ahead of his mother with outstretched hands and made a beeline for Johnny, who was in the center of the group. Johnny knew the boy was mistaking him for someone else, but he went with it. Johnny went down on one knee to catch the boy as he continuing running. The boy clasped his arms around Johnny's neck and began speaking in Austrian. Johnny moved by this exchange and his thoughts went immediately to the son he had never met. He tossed the little boy in the air and brought him down into his arms to receive more hugs.

Johnny looked at the boy and smiled. He reached into his pocket for a package of chewing gum and a pack of hard candy.

"Would you like this?" Johnny asked. The little boy's face lit up like a street lamp and he nodded his head. The boy reached for the candy and gum and then held them close to his chest, careful not to lose them.

By the time the young mother reached them, she had a shy smile on her face, realizing her son was in no danger. Her son was busy ripping the paper off the candy and showed it to his mother. She reached over and took the candy from her son. She then took her son's hand and looked at Johnny.

"He mistake you for another American," the mother said.

"He's a sweet little boy," Johnny said. "What's his name?"

The boy squirmed to get back into Johnny's arms. Johnny squatted down to pick up the boy as his mother continued to stare at Johnny.

"His name is Hans," she said.

"Do either of you have any more candy or gum?" Johnny asked his comrades. They searched in their pockets and gave Johnny all they had.

"Johnny, you sure you haven't been here before?" Marty asked. "This little guy looks like a long-lost relative."

The young boy began to remove the wrappers from the candy and gum before Johnny took them away and handed them to his mother.

"Save them for another day," Johnny said. He paused before he asked the next question. "Do I look like someone he knows?"

"Yes," the woman said. "I have an American friend who looks a lot like you. My husband was an Austrian soldier but he was killed in battle." The woman looked away, nervous suddenly.

"I'm sorry to hear that," Johnny said. He hugged the little boy again and reluctantly handed him back to his mother.

"Thank you for this," Johnny said. "I have a son who is a year and six months old but I have never met him or held him in my arms. Goodbye and I wish you and Hans a good future."

The mother nodded her head with a smile and pulled her son away, who waved at Johnny and continued to eat the candy.

Johnny and the two men continued walking.

"Let's go to that small pub," Ben Hardy said. "Funny how that little boy picked out Johnny to run to. Him being married and with a little son and all. I'll bet that little kid made you feel ten feet high? Did he remind you of your own son?"

Johnny was considered by the whole outfit as a tough and fearless leader. Yet as tough as he was, he couldn't overcome the emotion he felt from the interaction with the boy. He swallowed hard before responding.

"I'll meet my boy soon enough," he said. "Let's get that drink. I could use one now."

That evening when they returned to their sleeping quarters, Sergeant MacDonald was sitting on Johnny's bunk, waiting for them to return. He told them that orders came from division headquarters that their unit was on the list to be disbanded from service. Trucks would be in front of the company headquarters at 6 a.m., which would transfer them to the 30th Tank Corporation. Everyone with 98 points was allowed to go home. The points were computed by giving soldiers one point for every month in service, an additional point for every month served overseas, five points for each major battle and extra points for soldiers who were married and had children. The soldiers were stunned by the pleasant news.

"Serge, how many guys from our outfit are going?"
Johnny asked Sergeant MacDonald. His company was established
before the United States entered World War II. The 26th Division
was an old National Guard unit and just about everyone had to
have a lot of high points.

"The first wave includes you three, with 36 from here
going tomorrow," Sergeant MacDonald said. "In a week, we'll
send out another three dozen. I want to wish you all the best of
luck and bon voyage home. It was a pleasure serving with all of
you." He turned to shake Johnny's hand.

"You are a damn good soldier," Sergeant MacDonald said.
"We had a lot of good times together. So long Johnny, it was good
knowing you." He then pulled Johnny into a bear hug.

As soon as Sergeant MacDonald was gone, Ben and Marty
wrapped their arms around Johnny and began jumping up and
down with joy. The friends then broke apart to pack their gear.

As Johnny began putting all his gear into his barracks bag
he picked up a picture of Ann and Wayne. The tears of joy came
rushing to his eyes at the thought of going home. His mind flashed
to the little boy at the train station in Linz and he wondered how
his son would react when he saw him for the first time.

It took Johnny and the other disbanded soldiers two days
to get to Camp Lucky Stroke, a military installation where troops
assembled to get their final physical examination before heading
back to the United States. They were given shots for debarkation
and received psychological instructions on how to transition back
to civilian life. They would remain there for three weeks before
leaving for LeHavre, France, the port of debarkation. Most of the
time waiting was spent playing cards, softball or other forms of
relaxation.

Ben Hardy was a professional gambler before he came into
the service. He wanted to get into high-stakes card games. He
walked over to Johnny who was laying on his cot reading a novel.

"Let's go to the next tent," Ben said, closing the book
Johnny was reading. "I was told they have a good poker game
there every day. I'd like to make some good spending money
before we head back to the States."

"Fine," Johnny said. "But I'm only going to put in 200
bucks. I need enough money to spend on my family when I get
home." He was a good gambler and had won quite a bit of money.

But Johnny knew out here they would run into professional gamblers that made a living off the soldiers going home.

They entered the tent where every bunk had a game going. At one of the games there were two seats open. Johnny inquired if it was an open game.

"The game is open poker, no limit," a man shuffling cards said. "Jacks or better to open."

Johnny took out his money and placed it in front of him on the bunk. The game went back and forth with Johnny soon ahead of the game by a few hundred dollars. A new player arrived and asked if he could get into the game. He looked like a hick out of the backwoods. His hands were big and he looked clumsy when he dealt the cards.

Johnny was the first to receive a card. Johnny was dealt three kings and opened with 20 bucks. Everyone stayed in. The dealer was holding his cards tightly and passing them out slowly. He seemed confused as he looked at the players.

"I'll call and raise the pot by another twenty," he said. The dealer pulled his cards closer to his chest, not looking at anyone except at his cards. Everyone continued to stay in. Johnny tried to study the guy who raised the pot but he had a blank expression on his face and gave away nothing.

Johnny took two cards and the rest of the players stayed in except Ben Hardy, who folded his cards and threw them into the center of the bunk. The dealer with his clumsy fingers slowly held each card as he discarded three and threw them into the center of the bunk. When the dealer's turn came to draw, he held the card in a strange way, squeezing each one tight then laying each individual one down in front of him one-by-one.

Johnny was shocked how a man could raise a pot when taking three cards, this must be some real hick who didn't know how to play poker. Johnny was the opener.

"I'll bet 20 bucks," Johnny said. The rest of the players stayed in and when it came to the dealer, he was still squeezing his cards, looking at them a long time with a blank expression on his face.

"I'll call and raise you another 20," the dealer said. Johnny looked at his cards and didn't draw any help to his hand. He studied the dealer who drew three cards and was now studying his hand. The dealer waited to see if Johnny would raise him again, he had a blank expression all the while.

Johnny thought back at Ben's warning, to beware of professionals. He could see that the dealer was still holding the cards close to his chest and was sneaking looks at them, Johnny wasn't sure if the guy was a hick or a pro. Johnny thought it best that he play his hand.

"I'll see the raiser and raise another 20," the dealer said. The dealer was still holding his hand close to his chest and continued to hold that blank expression. After he heard Johnny raise, he opened his cards to look at them again, then shook his head as if he was uncertain.

"I'll raise you again," the dealer said. Most of the other players folded and Johnny was confused, wondering if the guy was a poor player.

"I'll raise you another 20," Johnny said. The dealer squeezed his cards again and opened up his hand to get a better look. It took him a while to make up his mind. "I'll raise you another 20." Johnny now was sure that he had been suckered and called. The dealer slowly placed his cards on the bunk single file showing that he had a flush of hearts. Johnny showed his openers, which were a pair of kings, but didn't reveal the rest of his cards.

"You win," Johnny mumbled. Johnny knew he was suckered. The dealer picked up the money and placed it in front of him. Johnny looked over at Ben Hardy who showcased a big smile indicating that he realized Johnny had been played.

Johnny knew all the players in the game were semi-professional and he would have to adjust his way of playing. He was a competent gambler who had gambled quite a bit before entering the service. Throughout the game, Johnny was ahead and was holding his own. When the hick started to deal again, Johnny let the cards lay on the bunk in front of him. He slowly picked up each card and glanced at what he had but never took his eyes off the dealer. When the dealer was through giving each player their cards, Johnny waited until he placed the rest of the cards in the deck. Then he picked up his cards and noticed that he got three queens. He closed his cards and laid them in front of him on the bunk.

"I'll be 20 to open," Johnny said.

All the players called. Ben Hardy tried to read Johnny's expression. The bet came to the dealer who was still squeezing his cards and holding them close to his chest. He looked Johnny square in the eyes.

"I'll call and raise you another 20," the dealer said.

Johnny picked up his cards to look at them but continued to look at the dealer. He closed his cards and placed them in front of him.

"I'll call the raiser and raise the pot 80 dollars," Johnny said.

The rest of the players stayed in except Ben who knew that Johnny had the cards. He discarded his cards into the center of the bunk while focusing his attention on the dealer. The dealer made sure that everyone put money in the pot. He took another look at his cards and with no expression at all, raised the stakes even higher.

"I'll see the bet and raise it by another 200 dollars," the dealer said.

Johnny never bat an eyelash as he allowed his cards to lay in front of him.

"I'll see the raiser and bet another 200 dollars," Johnny said. The other players stayed in the bet and it came to the dealer who was still squeezing his cards and looking at them hard. He shook his head.

"I'll see the raiser and bet another 400 dollars," the dealer said.

"I'll see the raiser and raise the pot another 500 dollars," Johnny replied without taking his eyes off the dealer.

All the other players dropped out since it was too expensive for them except the dealer.

"I'll call," the dealer said. He picked up the cards. "How many cards?" the dealer asked Johnny.

"I'll take two," Johnny said.

"Aren't you going to discard?" asked the dealer.

Johnny never took his eyes off of the dealer's hands.

"I'll discard when you take your cards, I won't touch my cards until you finish your deal."

The dealer just shrugged his shoulders.

"The dealer will take three cards," the dealer said. All the players were surprised and confused. They watched the dealer who in the same manner squeezed his top three cards that he placed in front of him. He picked up his cards with the same clumsiness and squeezed the cards tight while holding them close to his chest. The dealer was aware that all eyes were watching him. The dealer glanced at his cards.

"You win," the dealer said. With a surprising motion, he discarded his cards into the center of the deck without the usual clumsiness.

Johnny carefully picked the two cards from the bottom of his cards to show that he had two queens as openers and never looked at the two cards that were dealt to him on his draw. He pulled the money from the center of the bunk and piled it neatly in front of him.

"Gentlemen, I had an enjoyable afternoon," Johnny said. "Thank you." He picked up the money which totaled over 2,000 dollars and put it in his pocket as he left the game.

He walked to the P.X. military store where he knew his buddy Marty would be at this hour. When he got there, Marty asked how he made out.

"I was lucky that I didn't go for my lungs," Johnny said, shaking his head. "I made a few thousand dollars. The guy that I thought was a hick was a damn good professional gambler. I hope Ben doesn't get taken by that guy."

A few hours later Ben came walking in with a huge smile on his face. He called out to the bartender. "Let's have a couple beers here," Ben said. "I thought I'd find you guys here."

"How did you make out with that hick in the game?" Johnny asked, opening a bottle of beer.

"I had the guy pegged right from the start," Ben said. "You had to get burned before you wised up." Ben sipped his beer while eyeing Johnny with a sly smile on his face. "You had a pair of balls on that last hand you played, that hick had the cards stacked before he dealt them out. The only reason you won was that you forced all the other players out of the game and all the attention was centered on him. He couldn't afford to pull any kind of move. Did you notice how he discarded the cards that last game? He did it like the pro that he is. A guy like him only wants to win a couple hundred each game and he'll lose a couple bucks when he's in a game with the same players. He knew that you were onto him and was relieved when you left the game."

Johnny left the group and went to the post office to send most of his winnings home to Ann. He kept 600 dollars for expenses and other card games. Then he headed back to his tent to do some reading and relax.

They sailed out of *Port* of *Le Havre*, France on a Liberty ship. While onboard Ben, who didn't do well in the card games, came over to Johnny.

"Johnny, I need to borrow that 600 dollars," Ben said. "I want to gamble with the sailors and need money when we hit the States."

Johnny shook his head no. "Ben, I need that money when I get home to buy things for Ann and Wayne," Johnny said.

Ben insisted. "You know I'm good for the money," Ben said. Johnny reluctantly gave him the 600. He knew Ben was telling the truth, he would take the sailors in any gambling game. Ben came back about three hours later and handed him back the 600 dollars.

"I made 3,000 dollars," Ben beamed.

The Liberty ship took ten days to reach New York. It was the most beautiful image for the soldiers who were standing on one side of the ship and caught sight of the Statue of Liberty. There were tears in their eyes when it struck them that they all made it home still alive.

The ship sailed up the Hudson River until it came to dock at Camp Shank. The Red Cross nurses who handed each of them a bottle of milk and fresh donuts met them. They all climbed onto the buses that were there to transfer them to their assigned barracks. Johnny walked into the barracks and dropped his barracks bags on the first empty cot available and made a dash for the telephones that were set up for the soldiers. He dialed information and explained to the operator that he just got back from the war and had landed in Camp Shank but was not in contact with his wife for more than two months. He told her that in the last letter from his wife she was hunting for an apartment where they could live when he got home. He told her that she mentioned Bergen County and she always had a telephone. The operator was very understanding and she said it might take a few minutes while she searched for the number.

"Soldier, I think you're in luck," the operator said. "Please deposit forty cents." He deposited the money and he could hear the phone ringing. Although it seemed like eternity, the phone only rang three times. His heart skipped a beat when he heard his wife's voice.

"Hi hon, we just landed at Camp Shank which is just up the Hudson River off of Route 9," he said quickly.

He could hear a gasp on the other end of the phone. "John, is that really you?" Ann asked.

He was so excited that the words could hardly come out of his mouth.

"Ann, it's so good to hear your voice again," Johnny said. "How are you? How is our little son? I missed you both so very much. I can't wait to see you both."

"We're doing well," Ann said. "Wait until you see your son. He's so handsome and smart. He's grown so tall, it's hard to believe he's already a year and a half old. You're going to love him so much."

She turned away from the phone and called out to Wayne.

"Wayne come over to say hello to your daddy," Ann said in the background.

Johnny could hear the patter of little feet running in the background and then a tiny voice came over the phone.

"Daddy?" the voice said. Jonny lost his composure and felt the tears running down the side of his cheeks.

"Hello son," Johnny sobbed. "I love you so much."

"What did you say to him?" Ann said as she got back on the phone. "He's kissing the phone so much."

"I just told him that I love him," Johnny said, as he wiped the tears from his cheeks. "You mean to say that he understood what I said? He has to be a real smart boy. Ann I didn't have the time to tell you that I love you very much and I missed you so much. Honey, could you get someone to drive you here to pick me up?" He gave her directions to get to Camp Shank.

"Josh Proctor is home on leave," Ann said. "I'm sure he'll take me. Hold on a second dear, Wayne has my big wooden spoon and he's banging them against the pots and pans. Let me hang up so I can come and meet you."

"Honey, I'll meet you at the front gate," Johnny said. "We're in quarantine so I'll have to sneak out of camp."

"Honey, you won't get in trouble, will you?" she asked.

"No dear, I'll be waiting at the front gate when you get there," Johnny said. "Kiss Wayne for me. I can't wait to kiss my son myself. " He then headed back to his barracks to figure out how he could get out of camp without getting caught.

He put on his Eisenhower jacket and started walking toward the main gate and was stopped by the military policeman who was walking up and down in front of all the barracks of the soldiers who were confined to quarters. The military policeman told Johnny that his barracks was confined to quarters and no one could leave until the medics checked out the unit.

"I'm just going to the P.X. for a couple beers and some shaving supplies," Johnny said.

"Soldier, in order to go anywhere from these barracks, you have to have a pass from your company commander," the military policeman said. "I doubt he'll give you on. I'm sorry but I can't let you go."

Johnny nodded his head in agreement. "I'm lost, which way is the main gate?" Johnny asked.

"Straight out past the P.X., there's a couple military police patrolling the barracks and some at the gate," the military policeman said. He paused before adding: "I wouldn't try it if I were you. You'd never make it."

Johnny walked back to his barracks and went out the rear exit and strolled by the big fence with barbed wire strung along the top. He noticed a path running along the fence on the outside. He observed how long it took for the military policeman to pass his barracks and how long it took him to come back again. He knew then that he wouldn't have any trouble getting out of the camp.

He returned to the barracks and saw his buddies unpacking their bags. He walked over to them.

"Marty, I'm going to leave here in a few minutes to go see my wife and son," Johnny said. "Would you stand by my bunk in case they pull a surprise inspection?"

"You must be some kind of a nut to try this," Marty snickered. "We waited a year and a half to get home so don't blow your mustering date by being thrown into the guard house for going A.W.O.L."

"Johnny, I'm going with you," said Ben Hardy. "I want to see the city while I'm here. I was told they won't give passes while we're stationed here. We'll only be given passes when we're at our home base. My closest camp is Fort Devens in Massachusetts. But I'll be damned if I'm gonna survive the war, get all the way back to the States, and then be chained up like some dog."

"I'll cover for both of you while you're gone," Marty said. But I think both of you are fools."

Ben looked around and saw Jim Covey. "I'll get Covey to cover for me." He walked over to Jim to explain the situation and came back to join Johnny.

They walked to the rear of the barracks in their formal Eisenhower jackets and headed for the fence. Johnny looked around the area to see if any military police could see them.

He picked a spot of the fence which couldn't be seen unless someone walked back there. He had a heavy towel with him which he draped over the barbwire fence. He took one more look around and was sure no one could see them.

"Ben, we got to do this real fast," Johnny said. Then he scrambled up the fence, digging his fingers into the web and pushing himself up on the towel. Thankfully the soldiers had learned a similar exercise while in basic training. Ben followed in the same way and when he landed on the ground Johnny gave him his next order.

"Let's move but we've got to go fast but real quiet," Johnny whispered. They ran along the path in back of the fence leading to the front entrance of the camp. In back of the path was a wooded area which protected them from being seen. As they were running, they couldn't see much of the camp due to the shrubbery planted close to the fence. They came up to the road in front of the camp and could see the entrance about a hundred feet ahead. Across the road was a wooded area. They looked up and down the road to see if there were any military police stationed in front of the entrance, seeing none, Johnny pointed to the woods away from the gate and they walked back about 50 feet to make sure no one could see them.

They crossed the street, entered the wooded area and started to make their way toward the main entrance but walked behind trees, making sure that they couldn't be seen by the military police at the entrance. When they were about 30 feet from the entrance, Johnny stopped.

"We'll stay here out of sight and wait," Johnny said. "I don't know how long that'll be. It might be to the end of the night but I'm sure Ann will find someone to drive her here. Let's sit down and watch for a car that comes in very slow."

In a short time they saw a car just crawling along as if it were lost. Johnny could see that the driver's window was down. Johnny watched very closely.

"Ben, I think that's our car," Johnny said. He moved out of the woods. "Ann, is that you?" Johnny asked.

"John, it's us," Ann called out very softly.

Johnny waved to Ben and they ran to the car. Ben jumped into the back while Johnny jumped into the front, next to Ann.

"Hi, Josh," Johnny said. "That's Ben Hardy in the back, he wanted to come along, we'll drop him off at the George Washington Bridge so he can get a bus to the city."

Johnny was so excited he could hardly contain his excitement. He pulled Ann close to him and kissed her on the lips and held her in his arms for quite a while. "Josh, thanks for bringing Ann."

Josh just smiled as he drove the car the car.

"Like old times before with you," Josh said. "I'll have you home in about 20 minutes. Where can I drop you off, Ben?"

"At any bus stop that will take me to New York City," Ben said.

Ann rented a house just a block away from the George Washington Bridge. When they got there, Ben stopped the car on the over pass where there was a stairway going to the bus stop in front of the bridge.

"Ben, take the stairway down going to the highway to the lower level, that's the bus stop that takes you into the city to the Port Authority bus terminal where you can ride the subway to wherever you want to go in the city," Josh said.

Ben leaned into the car to thank Johnny. Johnny thought of something.

"Ben, you have 5 grand on you," Johnny said. "You don't want to be carrying that into the city. Keep 300 and give me the rest for safekeeping."

Ben rummaged in his things for an envelope. He pulled out three crisp 100-dollar bills and handed the envelope to Johnny.

"Good thinking, Johnny," Ben said. "Ann, it was good seeing you again. Thanks for the ride, Josh. I appreciate it."

"Ben before you go another bit of advice," Johnny said. "When you get to the city put a hundred dollars in your stocking, not the shoe, just in case you get held up. That will ensure that you will be able to get back to the base. New York is rough place and there are a lot of pickpockets here and they're good at their trade."

"Johnny, I'm a big boy and I've been around," Ben smiled. "Don't worry about me. I'll do just fine. You forgot that Boston is a big city." Ben saluted them and then dashed off.

Josh drove two blocks from the bridge to the small house that Ann rented in Fort Lee. Josh stopped to let them out.

"Johnny, I'll pick you up at five in the morning so you can make reveille," Josh said. "You'll have to sneak back into camp the same way you got out. The guards at the gate check everyone for their passes who comes in. They're strict as hell."

"Thanks so much Josh," Johnny said. "I'll be awake at 4 a.m. and ready to go by 5." Josh waved to Ann as he left.

Chapter 13
Year 1965

Local 906 committee scheduled a meeting with Ken Bannon, a director at Ford, regarding the wildcat strike. Johnny was charged with giving a blow-by-blow description of the strike and what led up to it. Ken and the others realized they had a serious problem to deal with and needed help from the international union to diffuse the situation.

The meeting took place with the top union officials and company officials from Detroit along with the local union committee. The union requested that Otto Brodwick, a United Black Brothers leader who worked in the plant, be allowed to attend the meeting. Otto was there to express the viewpoint of the black workers. Otto assured Ed Hubot, labor relations only black representative, that he would do everything possible to put the demonstration to bed if the union came up with a reasonable agreement. He in turn would report to the picketing members with an honest evaluation of the result.

"I'd like to open this meeting by stating the fact that the union did not shut down the plant on the night shift nor are they in any way responsible for any demonstration that occurred last week or this week," Ken said. "There is a policy in our handbook that details how we manage a strike and we will never hesitate to take that course of action if needed."

"Ken we got the tiger by the tail with this one," Johnny said. "A lot of blacks are uptight about this and want Roy fired on account of his verbal abuse against one of the black workers. The day shift isn't gung-ho about this but they do want to see that justice is served. We have a black worker on the day shift who actually pulled a worker out of his car to prevent him from going to work. He's a big powerful guy who really scares the shit out of the workers. The strange thing about him is that when it was time to go to work, he left the strikers and reported on time to his job in the paint department. I made a point to ask him why he was stopping workers from going to work but he himself wasn't striking. His answer was that he didn't want to get fired."

Ken shook his head in disbelief as Johnny reached into his briefcase to extract a stack of bulletins that he passed to all that were in the room.

"I constructed this bulletin telling the membership that we're not going to be dictated by a few militants and their hippy friends whose only intent is to shut down the plant operations," Johnny said. "It's a strong bulletin condemning their actions while urging the members to cross the unauthorized wildcat and come into work. I also included the point that Roy is not coming back to the plant."

Ken put his eyeglasses on to read through the bulletin carefully.

"I'm glad you included that last sentence, that's why I called you last night," Ken said. "I flew in with Sid on the same flight where he committed to that but he gave me no details. That should satisfy the members and get them back to work."

"I don't think we should refer to the members being led by the hippies, yuppies and the black militants," Lou Sargent interjected. "I think we should give credit to the members for demonstrating for a just cause."

Johnny just smiled as he recognized Lou's approach to undermine him.

"Why would you want to ease up on the unauthorized strike?" Johnny asked.

"Hell, let the company realize we're not going to tolerate them abusing our members," Lou said.

"I feel very strongly that the black members were misled, especially when we came to them and explained that Roy was suspended," Johnny said. "As long as you feel strong about this point, let's put this bulletin out and we'll add your comment on the bottom which will be signed by you. Is that fair enough for the rest of the committee?"

All the committee nodded their heads in agreement, including Rocky. Lou, however, became flustered.

"That would single me out as being in favor of their actions," Lou said.

"I'm not in favor of the view that you're expressing," Johnny said. "I think it's only fair that you have the right to express your views if you don't agree with ours. My intent is to get the membership back to work and see that justice is served."

Johnny looked Lou directly in the eye. Lou was eyeing everyone around the room searching for support, but everyone had their eyes down reading the bulletin, including Rocky and George.

"Lou, why don't you write up your statement and attach it to our bulletin," Johnny said.

Lou turned red when he saw that no one was coming to his aid.

"I'll go along with whatever the committee decides," Lou mumbled.

Lou knew the rest of the men were afraid of Johnny's motives. They discussed the bulletin and made only minor changes. Then they discussed their approach to the meeting with the company that was going to take place that afternoon. Later that day the bulletin was handed out to the day shift departing and the night shift entering.

The workers applauded the union's firm stand and the militants still picketing were confused. They saw the night shift read the bulletin and left to go into the plant to work. Some night shift workers who intended to continue the picket came over to the union hall to see that the doors were bolted shut with chains draped around the door handles. On the inside of the doors was the bulletin posted for everyone to see. The militants couldn't tear down the bulletin unless they broke the glass doors.

Many members who read the bulletin headed to their cars that were parked in the lot. This led the black militants to try to prevent them from leaving the parking lot by standing in front of their cars. This infuriated the members who were annoyed by outside groups that didn't work in the plant, telling them to stay out. Some of the workers got out of their cars and physically attacked the student protesters who tried to stop them from leaving.

In spite of the bulletin, many of the night shift workers remained out but the company was able to get some day shift workers who were willing to work a double shift to break up the unauthorized wildcat strike.

Johnny detailed how he had gone into the plant, walking up and down the line jobs talking to members. He told them that he wouldn't allow some dissident group to shut the plant down. The members commended him for his firm stance against the black militants. He spent the entire night explaining that the union was every member, not just a select few.

Ken shared about a meeting he attended a year ago about the problems in Clinton. Unfortunately there was a double set of standards; one for management and another for hourly workers.

"Our report from the region and the local union show little has been done to correct the inequities," Ken said. "The company must change their attitude and management of the hourly workers. When an hourly worker becomes abusive toward management, the company immediately summons that person to labor relations where he is subject to discipline for that infraction. In contrast, if a member of management were to do the same thing, the company tells us that they'll take care of the person in their own way but usually nothing comes of it."

"That's not true," Sid interrupted. "We didn't tell you what we did to Roy but it was visible to the union. He hasn't been back to work since the incident occurred."

"That may be true," Ken said, taking a drink of water. "Some of your foremen are half-decent people but there are many who are not. This is why we're here today. Many of our members are on the street because of the abuse by a member of management. I feel that management has the responsibility to tell the union what action the company is going to take against Mr. Acuff."

Sid McMann was Ford's vice president of labor relations and the spokesman for the company. He took offense at what Ken was saying.

"Ken, what happened here was wrong," Sid said. "We take our obligation toward the hourly workers very seriously at all times. Over the past year, we corrected many supervisors who the union complained about. Maybe not as many as the union would like, but every violation was investigated and when we found an error on the part of management, action was taken. This was done either by demotion, transfer or the supervisor just disappeared from the scene. We feel that discipline on members of management is strictly our business and not for public knowledge."

Sid looked toward the company representatives, who nodded their heads in agreement.

"Given the times we are living in now, I want to make sure the company has all of our workers' interests in mind," Johnny said. "We can't have one standard for one type of employee and then another. That is exactly the inequity our union opposes."

"We set a higher degree of standards toward our salaried employees than we do toward the hourly employees," Sid said. "Most of our supervisors came up from the ranks where they have showed the ability to lead. We also expect that union officials show a greater degree of restraint when a crisis occurs. Here at Clinton, they did."

Sid paused to let attendees really hear that last statement.

"When members of management break the rules, we don't go through the same disciplinary actions as we do toward the hourly worker," Sid said. "If it's serious we let him go."

Ken showed his annoyance by interrupting.

"Sid, this is all well and good to hear but I assure you that your strategy didn't work," Ken said. "The reason we're here today is that your superintendent abused one of our members and yet you're failing to tell us what you're going to do with him."

"Ken, actually I did tell you that Roy won't be working here," Sid said. "What we do to him is our strictly our business and it's of no concern to the union."

Otto sat through the whole meeting, not saying a word before turning to Ken and asking if he could comment. Ken said he would be pleased to hear his thoughts.

"Mr. McMann, we're pleased to hear that Mr. Acuff is not returning to the plant," Otto said to Sid. "That is a positive approach by the company. However, I was told by two of our union members who participated in the strike that they received registered letters notifying them that they were fired. Is that true?"

Sid looked at Tony who pushed a sheet of paper toward him.

"Yes, we did let go of two employees by mail," Tony said. "We were satisfied with our investigation and upon that, the discharges are final. The others involved with the unauthorized wildcat strike are being held in abeyance until we review all the footage and we'll make our decision afterward. We will deal individually with each employee based on their record and the contract."

"Tony, could you give me the names of the two who were discharged?" Otto asked.

"Their names are Wilton Hatter and Manny Head," Tony said.

Ken then asked the members to take a recess.

"Sid, I'd like to talk to the committee in private for a little bit," Ken said. "We'll talk in the hallway and be right back."

The union delegation left the conference room and invited Otto along while the company delegation remained in the conference room.

They walked to the far end of the hallway out of earshot.

"Where do we go from here?" Ken asked Otto and Johnny. "We presented all the facts and got an answer that Roy was fired."

"I think it's best that Otto answer this question," Johnny said. "Otto, what do you think?"

Otto felt uneasy because the meeting did bring some resolution but not everything the black workers asked for. He shifted from one foot to the other, unsure of his response.

"What about the guys who were fired and the others that might get fired because of the walkout?" Otto said. "The company was responsible for what occurred and no one should be disciplined."

"So if the workers are not fired, will this completely resolve our complaint?" Ken asked.

"Yes, I believe so," Otto said.

Ken realized Otto was afraid to face his people even though some positive developments came from the meeting.

"Otto, ever since the inception of the union, the company had the right to take disciplinary action against any one who was responsible for shutting the plant down illegally," Ken said. "I can't answer what action the company will take, but we'll use every legal means to protect them."

"While I realized the company has the right to take action, so do workers whose rights have been violated," Johnny said. "That is what this meeting is all about."

"What if we were able to set up a committee headed by the civil rights chairman, Howard Eikers and James Cook from the region," Ken continued. "They would work as a team with the company's black representatives and look into the abuses by management. They would then make suggestions based on their findings. "

"I don't think the company will buy this but it sure sounds good to me," Otto said.

"Let's go back into the meeting and bring this suggestion up," Ken said.

"No harm in trying," Johnny said.

Ken was confident his idea would break up the wildcat strike. They entered the room and resumed their respective seats.

"We submitted a number of problems and we're asking for corrective action to resolve this situation," Ken said. "You tell us that you're working to get better working relations with the hourly employees but we need more than just talk. Nationwide we are having problems in the auto plants but nothing like we have here. We formulated a plan that we would like to launch, but we need your help and support. Our plan consists of four men who will review all the grievances in the plant, particularly observing foremen who are constantly viewed as being abusive to our hourly members. Our two members will be Howard Eikers and James Cook. They'll have free access to go into any department to interview the workers on the job and listen to their complaints."

Sid showed immediate hesitation about this plan. He turned to Tony, who was nodding his head in agreement.

"We've never done anything like this before," Sid stammered. "Especially allowing two international representatives roaming our plant unescorted. We will agree to Howard and Jim but they'll have to abide by our company rules while at the plant. I also want our representatives there. This should not be seen as a joint committee but as a separate team trying to find where the friction lies. The suggestion is a good one and we're in agreement and hopefully this should ease the tension in the plant. It's not going to be easy but we'll try to correct the problems. It's a good start."

Otto voiced his concern about the two terminated employees and the discipline that might ensue for those who were taking part in the strike.

"It's a legitimate question," Ken added.

"Discipline isn't anything new for UAW," Sid said. "We will review the facts and act fairly on them. So far, the only action taken was against the two spearheads of the wildcat."

"We're aware of that but we want you to realize that this action was provoked by a member of management," Ken said. "This should be taken in consideration when you weigh the facts. You have footage of men on the picket lines but how could you determine that they were all participating in the wildcat? Maybe they were passing by to go into the plant or going by to talk to the men on the picket line. Just being there doesn't mean they were participating in the strike."

"We're aware of that," Sid said. "That's why we are now concentrating on the leaders of the strike. Your own leaflet refers to this as an unauthorized strike."

"Our leadership put this bulletin out to get the workers back to work and you better not use the bulletin to strengthen your case against the innocent picketers," Ken roared.

"We have no intention of doing that," Sid said.

"This demonstration was started to protest the company and the black militants lumped the union into it," Ken snarled. "Our members were hurt bad with many on the night shift coming into work, then sent home without pay. You have to take all of those facts into consideration."

"We will use discretion when investigating the incident," Sid said. "We will also consider having a hearing for all those who were fired, to hear their side of the story. We will probably conduct hearings on the picketers when we review the facts."

"Even though your people were responsible for the incident, you intend to have hearings?" Ken said.

"I read the bulletins put out by the United Black Brothers but saw no purpose to them," Sid said. "The facts are clear. There was picketing by employees and non-employees who stopped the cars and caused many to turn away from the plant and thus causing us to lose four days of production on the night shift. Those leaders will have to be dealt with. There is a long established rule dealing with penalties for this kind of action. We can never condone a wildcat strike. We have to do something about it."

Otto realized he was looking for the impossible.

"It was better that this action took place outside the plant and not inside," Otto said. "Our main concern was to prevent a riot from erupting, we were successful there. I urge you not to take discipline against those innocent men who were seeking justice and you have to take into consideration that there were no injuries and no destruction of company property. Look at it as an action for a cause."

"We'll take a good look at this and take your request under consideration," Sid said. "Our guys will be in the plant by

Thursday to review everything and interview the workers. How about your guys?"

"Our team will also be here by Thursday and will remain as long as it takes to clear this matter up based on all the complaints they receive," Ken said.

"Our first order of business is for our committee is to go over to the union hall to tell the union members that the strike is over," Johnny said.

Johnny turned to Otto and Ken and asked them to come to the union hall to talk to members.

"I know that there will be many questions asked," Johnny said. "Otto can give them an honest account of what transpired at the meeting."

Outside the hall many union members were standing in groups in front of the headquarters, others were outside by the river that flowed behind the hall and some were in their cars. Seeing the union officials, they all quickly gathered around to hear the results.

"We'll be meeting with the company during the week to resolve all the cases that are still pending," Johnny began.

"Man, you sold us down the river," Manny Head hollered. "Wilton and I were fired and we don't know what's going to happen to the rest of us."

Otto raised his hands up to get their attention and calm the men down.

"Look, we just left the meeting and the union did a damn good job," Otto said. "Roy is fired and they agreed to hear the discharge cases in hearings before the end of the month. I'm sure that the company isn't going to fire anyone else. The company is only interested in getting the men back to work."

Some members were shaking their heads in disagreement while others waved their arms in disgust. However most of the group was satisfied and walked away. Otto was focused on persuading those who were critical of these developments.

"I was there and saw how Ken Bannon had the company eating out of his hand," Otto said. "I never thought that he could get the company to agree to allow two committees of black representatives from both sides to review our complaints, but he did. We won our fight and we'll win when they see how the company treated us in the past. Let's all go back to work and see for ourselves the benefits of the strike."

Most returned back to work except a few of the diehard militants. That evening the company's operations was back to normal. Labor relations went to each department to get the names of the workers who didn't show up to work and sent them a letter instructing them to come back to work or be terminated after missing five shifts. Those men who were absent had their jobs manned by day shift workers who volunteered to work the double shift and production flowed smoothly for the rest of the shift. The following evening the night shift was back to normal.

During the week, the bargaining committee met with the company to set up a procedure for hearing the discharge cases. For the rest of the employees that participated in the wildcat, the company agreed to give them a paper discipline with no time off and no loss of pay.

The human relations committee was very effective as they roamed the plant and the cafeteria to investigate the complaints. Black workers on both shifts were satisfied that the union did get them the necessary resolution and brought harmony back to the plant.

Chapter 14
Years 1945-1954

Johnny walked toward the house with his arms around Ann's waist. It was an old, broken-down house that seen better days but he was just so happy to be with Ann.

Johnny knew that his first task now that he was back was to find a decent apartment to rent. He realized that with the amount of G.I.s getting out of the service, apartments were going to be scarce. He was glad Ann didn't want to live with her parents and instead they got their own apartment.

A teenage girl who was babysitting their son met them at the door.

"Welcome home Mr. Romanek," she said, holding out her hand for a shake. She turned to Ann.

"Wayne couldn't stay awake so I put him to sleep in his crib," she said.

Johnny walked quickly to the bedroom while Ann continued to talk to the babysitter. He took a first look at his son who had rolled himself into a ball and looked so small as he slept in the center of his crib. He saw the long blond hair which reached the top of his shoulders and his face which was the spitting image of Ann. The tears began to roll down Johnny's cheeks as he kept watching his son.

Ann came into the room. She leaned into the crib to pick Wayne up, but the baby kept pulling himself back into the crib to sleep. She kissed him gently while he continued to squeeze his eyes shut.

"Wayne honey, I have someone here who wants to say hello to you," Ann whispered. Wayne began to open his eyes and rubbed them awake with the small knuckles of his hand.

"John put your hat on when he looks at you," Ann said.

Johnny quickly put his hat on and turned toward his son. The baby's face broke out in a smile.

"Daddy!" he said.

Johnny gathered his son in his arms.

"Wayne, you're so big," Johnny said, tears flowing down his cheeks. "How did you get so big when daddy was gone? I got something for you."

Johnny took out a pair of wooden shoes that he had a cobbler in Austria make to fit his tiny feet.

Wayne took the shoes and immediately started to put them in his mouth. Ann took them away and gently took the baby from Johnny and placed him back in the crib.

"Honey, you go back to sleep," Ann said. "Daddy is home again and this time to stay forever."

Ann then started to cry. Johnny pulled her into his arms and kissed her.

"That's right, Ann, I'm here to stay," he whispered.

They walked out of the room toward the kitchen to let Wayne sleep. In the kitchen Ann made Wayne a fresh pot of coffee and told Johnny she got some fresh meat from the A&P.

"I haven't had a hamburger since I left the States," Johnny said. "That'll be a treat for me."

He took her in his arms to kiss her but he felt her pulling away. He realized she was feeling shy after his being away for so long. He held her away from him at arm's length.

"Hon, you're a little scared of me, aren't you?" Johnny asked. She gave him a look that answered his question.

"I've been away a long time and we'll have to get used to each other again," Johnny said. "Whenever you're ready, I'll be waiting."

"I've been waiting forever for you to come home and now that you are, it feels strange that you're here," Ann said. "All these years, I had do everything for myself. Every now and again my mother or Nancy would help me with Wayne but I wanted him all to myself. It'll be different with you being back home. I know that Wayne is going to adore you. He needs his father to guide him in everything he has to learn about in life. My parents and sisters showered him with love but he needs you. Wait until you see all the things he can do, you'll be surprised."

She brushed the tears from her cheeks and started preparing the food. After she began preparing his meal Ann took

Johnny's and seated him at the table. The only furniture in the room was Wayne's highchair and four chairs. They were brand new; she must have bought the set when she moved into the house. Ann went back to the stove to finish the hamburgers. Then she sat down next to him at the table.

"Let's eat and then we'll talk, you must be starving," she said.

She placed a plate with a steaming hamburger in front of him.

After eating, they went into the living room. They cuddled up on the sofa and he held her close.

"It was such a surprised to hear Wayne call me daddy," Johnny said. "How did you teach him that?"

"Every day when I fed Wayne his food, I put your picture next to his highchair and pretended to feed you first," Ann said. "I would do this every time I gave Wayne food. He came to know your face and would reach for your picture with his dirty little hands."

She picked up the framed picture to show Johnny all the little fingerprints on it.

"I really didn't know how he would react when he saw you for the first time," Ann said. "And I wasn't sure he would recognize you without the hat. He's such a smart boy. He knew who you were immediately."

He held her all night long on the sofa talking until they heard a knock at the door. They didn't realize how fast the time flew. Johnny looked at the clock in the living room. Five minutes to 5 a.m.

"I can't believe I have to say goodbye to you now," Johnny murmured.

"But this time it won't be for long," Ann said.

Johnny opened the door and Josh walked in to tell them it was time to go back to camp. Johnny got up and walked into the bedroom to have another look at his sleeping son. He kissed and embraced his wife.

Johnny's mind was taken over with images of his beautiful wife and son. He was anxious to be back with them and was happy he made the decision to leave camp to see them. Josh dropped him off just before the main gate so the guards wouldn't spot him. He backtracked his way through the woods until he came to the towel over the fence.

He headed back to his barracks and was just in time to make reveille. The sergeant looked at him all dressed up.

"Soldier, get out of those dress clothes and put on your fatigues," the sergeant said. "You'll be going on a hike with the rest of us."

The sergeant heard some muffled laughter and wondered why but didn't press the issue.

After the sergeant left the soldiers loosened up. As Johnny entered the barracks, Marty spotted him and came over.

"I see you made it back all right," Marty said. "Wait till you see Ben, he's a mess."

Johnny spotted Ben when he came out of the bathroom. Johnny was shocked at what he saw. Ben's face was swollen to twice the normal size.

"What the hell happened?" Johnny asked.

"I went to Harlem to get laid and I picked up a good looking broad," Ben said, wincing as he pressed a towel into his face. "She led me to her apartment through an alley. I was feeling great next to this good-looking American chick. That's all I remember. Someone hit me across the head with a crowbar. When I came to, they took my wallet and all the money I had in my pocket. They even removed my shoes. The only thing I did was right was taking your advice and putting some money in my socks. I had a hundred dollars in there so all they got from me was about 60 in cash. When I came to, I headed right back to camp."

"Oh man," Johnny said. "I guess Boston is no match for the mean streets of New York, eh? Good thing I kept the rest of your money."

Johnny handed Ben the envelope with the remainder of the cash. Ben took the money out of the envelope and put it into the money belt he was wearing around his waist.

They were ready to leave for the mess hall when the sergeant called the barracks to attention.

They all came to attention as the company commander came by to inspect the troops. Ben was standing right next to Johnny when the commander saw Ben.

The commander stopped and leaned closer to Ben's face.

"What happened to you soldier and how did your face get banged up?" the commander asked.

"I did it, sir," Johnny said before Ben could answer.

The commander turned to Johnny with an annoyed expression on his face.

"I didn't ask you soldier," the commander said. "Speak only when spoken to."

The commander turned back to Ben.

"Tell me how this happened," the commander said.

"Sir, I had a couple bottles of Cognac that we were saving to celebrate our getting back to the States alive," Ben said. "I had one too many drinks and got drunk. I bet Johnny he couldn't knock me off my feet with one punch. He refused to hit me so I called him names. He hauled off and hit me clean across the room. I asked for it, sir."

"Did you pay off the bet?" the commander asked.

"No, sir, he refused to take the money," Ben said.

The commander sighed and looked at Johnny and Ben and back again.

"We'll forget about this incident," the commander said, to both Ben and Johnny's relief. "I respect both of you for telling the truth and not making up a story."

After walking by each soldier, the commander spoke to his sergeant. Both then left the barracks.

"Thanks Johnny," Ben said, shortly after the men were alone. "That was quick thinking. I would have blabbed my mouth about Harlem and gotten both of us in trouble."

The soldiers all walked to the mess hall for their breakfast before departing for their homes.

* * *

Johnny walked up the unpaved driveway with his duffle bag slung over his shoulder, heading toward the small three-room white house that his wife rented. During the time that Johnny served in the war, Ann lived with her parents. All she owned was the bedroom set and Wayne's crib.

Johnny had to be careful where he stepped because of the deep ridges in the ground leading right up to the front door. He stopped before entering the house to look around. This was the first time he saw the house and grounds in the daytime. The yard was cluttered with old tires, the swing was broken and rusty, and the garbage can was upside down with the contents pulled apart, probably by some hungry raccoon or fox. There were two white ducks pecking at the ground.

He trotted up the three steps to the front door which was partially open and he could see that the inside of the house was immaculately clean, with everything in place. Ann was fortunate to get cast-off furniture from both parents and friends. She did a wonderful job restoring the pieces. The house looked warm and comfortable.

"Stop that, you're getting me all wet," Johnny heard Ann say from the other room.

Wayne was screaming with laughter as Johnny tiptoed into the bathroom. Ann was struggling as the baby kept splashing water all around during his bath. His little hands were moving rapid fire, splashing the water in all directions. Johnny stood there a moment enjoying the scene. He stepped up quietly behind his wife and placed his hands over her eyes. She let out a scream in fright and wrestled herself away. She had her right hand in a clenched fist ready to strike until she saw her husband standing with a startled expression on his face.

"I didn't expect you to come home until tonight," Ann said. "You frightened me."

"I'm sorry sweetheart," Johnny said, pulling her into his arms. "I wanted to surprise you, instead I frightened you half to death."

He moved her away to look into her eyes.

"I was lucky to get a ride from another soldier who was coming my way," Johnny said. "He dropped me off right at the house."

Johnny was standing with his back to the tub when his son sent a stream of water at him. He jumped to get out of the way but it was too late. His pants were drenched with water.

Ann chuckled as she reached for a towel.

"Welcome home," Ann said. "You ain't seen nothing yet."

Ann took Wayne out of the tub and wrapped him in a towel, still laughing as she placed her son on the kitchen table.

"John, he's all boy," she said, rubbing the water off of Wayne. "You're going to love him. He's so smart."

Johnny ruffled through his duffle bag to get a clean pair of pants. Wayne reached for an open box of baby powder which he threw, squarely landing on his father's clean pants.

"You better get into the bedroom to change before something else happens," Ann said.

Johnny came back with a change of clothes while Ann had Wayne sitting in his highchair and was ready to feed him.

"It's time for his lunch," Ann said. "Would you like to feed him?"

"I better watch to see how you do it," Johnny laughed. "I don't have another pair of clean pants."

Johnny watched as Ann deftly was able to maneuver around Wayne's moving arms as she fed him. She laughed and tickled him while she told him a fairy tale. Wayne sat there wide-eyed, listening to the story while gulping down his food. Johnny sat there, taking in the entire moment. It felt unreal to him that he was home with his wife and son. He felt so much love for Ann in that moment.

"Hon, I can't believe you got by on so little," Johnny said.

He reached into his pocket for his wallet.

"I want you to buy what you need most with this money," Johnny said. "My Army pay was 300 dollars and I won more than two-thousand in a card game."

Ann's eyes widened.

"I'm just so happy you came back to us safe and sound," Ann said, hugging Johnny.

Johnny told her they also needed to get a car, preferably a cheap, used one. He had already spoken to her brother on the phone about it.

While he was talking, he saw his wife open up the kitchen window and saw a box attached to the windowsill. She reached into it and took out some cold cuts and a bottle of milk. She smiled at his bewildered expression.

"This is our refrigerator," Ann said. "It does the same job except in extreme cold weather."

She started making their lunch when the phone rang. She answered before handing the phone to Johnny.

"How you doing Charlie?" Johnny asked Ann's brother.

Charlie told Johnny about a 1932 Chevy that he was selling for 30 bucks.

"It needs a lot of work but it still runs," Charlie said.

Johnny knew that it almost impossible to buy a half-decent car, especially since the auto companies didn't make cars during the war. He placed his hand over the phone to talk to Ann.

"Hon, your brother found an old car that we could buy," he said. "I'm going to take it." She nodded her head in agreement.

"Charlie can you bring the car down?" Johnny said. "We'll take it."

"We'll be at your place in fifteen minutes," Charlie said. "That's if the heap makes it."

Ann smiled as she took 30 dollars out of her pocketbook and handed it to her husband.

"That's awful cheap for a car," Ann said. "But we'll see when it gets here. Too bad I had to sell our car. It was like new but I needed the money when Wayne was born."

"Hon, I know you struggled," Johnny said. "Plus you got more money for it than I paid for it, so it was worth it. This junk that we'll get will help us to go to stores to buy food and visit our parents and to go to work every day."

In a short while Charlie was at the door with a smile on his face.

"Well, we made it without a breakdown," Charlie said. His friend, Anthony, who was selling the car, joined him.

"It needs a lot of work but it'll get you around," Anthony said. "Let's have a look."

Ann picked up her son as they walked outside to see the car.

The body of the car was in one piece with no rust showing anywhere. The windows were intact, but the doors were held closed by a clothesline rope tied to the center post. The roof was made of wood with vinyl over it and the vinyl had holes in it. Also, the tires were bald. Johnny walked around the car to inspect it and looked under the car to see if it had any leaks, seeing none.

"Would you start it up please," Johnny asked.

Anthony stepped on the starter and the car roared to life. It was noisy but not that bad. Johnny walked around the car again and was satisfied that the car was in good working condition.

"Hon, what do you think?" Johnny said. "I think we should take it."

"I'm game if you are," Ann said. "It's quite a let down from the car we had during the war. And you're going to have to do a lot of work on it before I let you take Wayne in it."

Ann knew Johnny was handy around cars.

"Anthony you just sold your car," Johnny said, slapping the roof. "Here is the 30 dollars."

"Johnny the car runs pretty good but you're going to have to put on a new set of brakes and you can see that the roof leaks," Anthony said. "The hardware store can sell you a set of rubber patches that works in the short term, I did that before. And you see that the tires are bald, you'll have to buy a new set. Outside of that, the car will get you around just fine."

Johnny nodded.

"Thanks for your honesty," Johnny said, grabbing the keys. "Come on, jump in, I'll drive you back to the city."

"You better not take that chance," Anthony said. "The license plates expired a while back. We took a risk in driving here and we were lucky the police didn't catch us. We'll both take a bus back home."

"You guys aren't going home until you taste the apple pie I just baked," Ann said.

"Ann, thanks but we can't stay," Charlie said. "We're on the night shift and if we stay we'd be late for work. Another time."

Charlie kissed Ann goodbye and shook Johnny's hand.

"That's the bus, we have to get going," Anthony said.

The bus was coming down the street and they both ran to the corner to get on.

Johnny immediately began to work on the car. First he put the car up on cinder blocks. Then he walked into town to go to the auto store to pick up a set of new brakes. While he was in town, he also went to get the car license plates and registration.

As soon as he got home, with the parts in hand, he went right to work to replace the brakes. It didn't take him long and when he was through, he took the car off the blocks and went into the house to get his wife and son.

"I put new brakes on and I got the license plates for the car," Johnny said. "Let's take a short ride to the A&P store to buy the food that you need for the week and we'll come right back. The store is only a mile away so we can see how it rides. We won't use the car again until I fix it all up. What do you say?"

"John, all I'll agree to is to the store and directly back," Ann said. "I'll sit in front with Wayne on my lap. We'll shop and come right home."

Johnny opened the car door and tied the door shut with rope. He noticed Ann's eyes were wide with alarm as he went around to the driver's seat. She had Wayne securely in her lap, her hands clasped together.

At the store Johnny noticed Ann was stressed and quickly shopped, anxious to get home. He put his arm around her shoulders.

"Nothing is going to happen as long as I'm here," he said. "I promise you I will fix that car and it will be as good as new."

"Thanks John," Ann said, relaxing. "I'm nervous about riding in that car but I know we will be ok as long as you are with us."

She gave a sigh of relief when they reached home.

"Thank God, we made it," she said.

Johnny came around to the front of the car and untied her door.

"See that wasn't bad," Johnny said. "At least we know that this car will run. I'll fix everything before we go out again."

He took Wayne from her lap and held him close. As he held his son and watched his wife get out of the car, he felt an overwhelming sense of gratitude that he was now here with his family. He realized what he missed during the war and felt elated at being with them now.

The following week, Johnny had the car fully repaired and ready to run. He placed his son in the back seat and his wife sat in the passenger seat. As Johnny backed out of the driveway they heard Wayne's piercing scream. Johnny looked in the rearview mirror and could see his son hanging on the back door that had flown open. Johnny stopped the car and Wayne tumbled to the ground. Ann rushed out of the car to grab Wayne. Amazingly Wayne wasn't hurt. Instead he giggled and said "more."

Johnny was shaken up by the fact that his son could have been killed due to his carelessness and Ann held her son while sobbing. Johnny walked around the car to secure the back doors with the rope again, making sure the rope was securely tied. Ann returned to the front seat with Wayne in her arms.

"Thank God it happened when it did," Ann said. "If that door flew open when we were on the highway, Wayne would have been killed. From now on, he's going to be in my lap every time we go out in this car."

* * *

Johnny reported to work at Ford and was one of the first returning veterans. Production on the lines started at a slow pace due to the re-learning process that all the workers had to go through when they converted back to making cars on the moving line. There was unrest throughout the manufacturing industry with unions demanding higher pay because wages had been frozen during the war years while the prices of food and commodities were going up.

The unions also were demanding safer working conditions because the companies were using old and antiquated machinery that was very dangerous. Within a month, the steel industry went on strike, forcing Johnny to be laid off and to apply for unemployment. The strike would go on for months and Johnny was unable to support his family on unemployment and he had very little savings in the bank.

He got in touch with Josh Proctor's father, Paul, who worked for the AFL labor union and asked if he could connect him with a construction job. Paul Proctor had him placed on a job immediately in a construction job at a paper container plant in Clinton.

On Johnny's first day he reported to the foreman of the construction gang. He introduced himself and told the foreman Paul had suggested he come to the office.

The foreman, named Mike Ruddick, was a big ruddy man who weighed about 250 pounds without an ounce of fat on him. His complexion was rugged from constantly working outdoors and he stood six feet, three inches. He sized Johnny up for a moment.

"You're the ex-G.I. that Paul spoke about," Mike said. "You look strong enough to handle the job. Did you do any laboring job before?"

"Yes," Johnny said. "I do just about anything."

A cement truck was in front of the building with the truck unloading cement directly into a wheelbarrow that the laborer pushed up on planks that were set on top of the stairs going to the second floor.

"Take that to be loaded with cement from the truck," Mike said, pointing to the wheelbarrow. "You push the wheelbarrow up on those planks to the second floor. There will be workers there to show you where to dump the load."

Johnny had never pushed a wheelbarrow filled with wet cement. As he was pushing the load up on the plank, the load shifted and the wheelbarrow toppled to the ground spilling the cement all over. Mike ran over to the dropped load to see if Johnny was alright. Johnny picked himself up with an embarrassed look on his face.

"I'm glad you didn't get hurt," Mike said. "Come with me. I'll place you on a job that I know you can do."

He took him inside the building where bricklayers were in the process of placing a large window ledge onto a layer of finished bricks. Mike addressed the mason in charge.

"This is John Romanek who will be helping you today," Mike said. He pointed to a pole that had what looked like half a box attached to it, called a hod carrier.

"You use this hod carrier to bring up bricks and cement whenever the bricklayers call for it," Mike said. "Just be careful when you carry a load and don't lean backward when you're going up the ladder or you'll topple off and get seriously hurt."

"Mike, I'm sorry about that incident before with me losing that load of cement," Johnny said. "I thought I could handle the job."

Mike laughed and slapped him on the back.

"Don't worry about it," Mike said. "You'll do alright as soon as you get the hang of the job. Good luck."

The bricklayers were using a level to make sure the window ledge was perfectly balanced. The construction crew had other work to do before they needed Johnny so one of them asked Johnny to go across the street to the diner to get some bacon and egg sandwiches and coffee. Johnny begrudgingly went to get the sandwiches for the crew and himself.

When he came back the crew all ate together and that's when he felt a sense of connection with them. From that point on Johnny had no trouble with the job. He worked hard and never complained when he was assigned a tough job.

Many returning veterans who also worked at the site complained about the rough jobs. When Paul Proctor came to the site, he always stopped a moment to talk to Johnny to see how he was doing. The workers noticed this and also saw that Johnny wasn't singled out for any light jobs. He was treated like all the other workers and they respected him for that. When the construction job was complete, the laborers asked Johnny if he would come with them to the next assigned construction job to become their union shop steward.

One evening Johnny received a telegram from Ford to report to work on the following Monday. After supper, he told his wife about the workers asking him to stay on the next construction job as their union shop steward. He had the telegram from Ford in his hand and was concerned about what to do.

"Hon, I really don't know what to do," he said. "The work isn't bad in either job and the pay per hour is the same."

"Dear, that's your decision to make," Ann said. "You worked both jobs. Which one are you most comfortable with?"

"When I think about it, I think I would be better off at Ford," Johnny said. "The strikes are over and the public is needing new cars. I like the outside cement work but I can't afford to be out of work every time it rains or when we have a real cold spell and can't pour the cement because it freezes. We need every penny I earn to buy all the essentials. Look around, it looks like we need everything. You haven't bought a new dress since I came home from service. I've been lucky so far with the work. There's a good chance that Ford will be working on an overtime schedule to make up for the lost production due to the strikes. It's a risk, but I think one that will pay off."

Johnny was right and after returning to Ford, he was able to earn his wages plus overtime. Ann started to buy the accessories they needed. They still had the old car that took them all over without any major breakdowns.

One day while driving up the hill after work, Johnny saw a co-worker walking up the hill.

"Carl, I'm going toward borough hall," Johnny said. "If you need a lift, jump in."

"Swell but how do I get in?" Carl asked, chuckling.

"Wise guy," Johnny said. "I'll help you get in."

Johnny laughed as he reached over to loosen the rope for Carl to get in.

"I live just on top of the hill," Carl said.

He nervously held the rope to secure the door closed the entire car ride. They rode a short distance before Carl pointed to a small white house on the corner.

"That's my place," Carl said. "You can let me out here. Thanks for the ride, that hill is a bitch to walk up after a day's work."

The following morning, Johnny walked into the cafeteria to get a bite to eat and a cup of coffee. He overheard Carl telling the other men about the old piece of junk that Johnny was driving. Johnny's annoyance grew as he heard the men and Carl laughing.

"Is it true that you have to tie the doors down with a rope to keep them shut and you have to put your feet outside the car to stop it?" one of the men asked Johnny.

"You heard right," Johnny said, smiling. "It's an old car but it does get me around."

That evening it was raining very hard and Johnny noticed Carl walking up the hill, getting drenched. Carl saw Johnny coming and waved him down. Johnny stopped and lowered the window as Carl came running toward the car.

"Carl, I heard you make quite a joke about me having me having a junk of a car," Johnny said. "I wouldn't want to be responsible if you got hurt. I picked you up yesterday as a Good Samaritan but then you turned around and made fun of me. So yeah, not picking you up tonight buddy, you're shit out of luck."

Johnny then put his car in gear and sped away, leaving Carl standing in the pouring rain.

* * *

Johnny wasn't content simply remaining an assembler at Ford. One day after work, he went to visit the Department of Veterans Affairs to inquire about the G.I. Bill. He inquired about going to college to further his education and get a better job. That evening during supper he told Ann about his idea.

"I'm not getting anywhere working without a formal education," Johnny explained. "I could go part time in the evenings and the government will pay for my tuition, my books and any supplies that I need for my courses."

"That's great, maybe I can also get a job to help out," Ann replied.

She was well aware of her husband's desire to get ahead.

"I wanted to go full-time but all the government will give me is about a hundred dollars a month, we can't live on that," Johnny said.

"I think you should," Ann said. "I could go to work to make up the difference."

"No, hon," Johnny said. "You're needed at home to take care of Wayne."

It was decided that Johnny would go to school at night and continue working full-time during the day.

They had no night courses at Stevens Institute of Technology in Hoboken but Johnny found out that Brooklyn Collegiate and Polytechnic Institute had night courses. He would commute by bus and subway. For three years, Johnny spent every spare moment after work studying. Soon he realized he was neglecting his wife and family so he tried to study during working hours.

He perfected a tool that increased his time to work his job, and allowed him time to study a half-minute on every job. In between jobs, he read his schoolbooks and was able to study three hours every day.

One day a young engineer came to Johnny and told him he was going to do a time study, which meant he was going to measure how long it took Johnny to complete a task. He asked Johnny to first explain the steps of the task and then was going to time him.

Johnny was so annoyed that he walked to the open window next to the moving line and threw the tool he had made out the window. He knew the company just wanted to add more work to his plate. Then he went back to his toolbox to get the company paddle for the operation, which added time to the job.

During Johnny's explanation of the sequences of his operation, three jobs went by which Johnny didn't complete. The young engineer inquired about the missed operations.

"I can only do one thing at a time," Johnny explained. "You took me off to the side to ask about my operation, the missed jobs are your responsibility."

Johnny checked his watch before he started his operation to make sure that the job was done exactly in the time allowed by the speed of the line, which took a minute and a half for every job. The engineer stayed with him for four hours and Johnny completed his operation in the same time as the assembly line allowed for the operation.

After lunch, the manager of engineering and the young engineer approached Johnny.

"Mr. Romanek, we timed you quite a few times last week and your figures show that you could complete your operation in about a half a minute," the manager said. "I'd like to time how long it takes you to do the job."

Johnny shrugged his shoulders and started the task. He took the allotted time to complete his operation and moved to the next job. The manager looked at his figures and saw that he finished the operation in the specified time allowed for the operation.

"I see you're not using the same tool as you did last week," the supervisor said. "Will you use that tool while I take your time study?"

Before Johnny could answer, the young engineer told the supervisor that Johnny had thrown the tool out the window.

"I'll use any tool that the company provides," Johnny said. "You run the plant. Just give me the tool you're talking about and I'll use it."

The supervisor went over to the foreman in charge of line operations.

"Mr. Harris, I think Romanek is pulling a fast one on us," the supervisor said. "We timed him from behind the racks yesterday and he was able to do his operation in a half minute. At that time he was using a different tool and did a perfect job, now he's using a wooden paddle, which takes a longer time. The way he's doing the job, he uses more lead. Can you give me the tool he was using before?"

The foreman was on Johnny's side. In his mind Johnny was doing his job to perfection and he saved the company a lot of money by using a lot less lead.

"Sir, we don't have any other tool except the wooden paddle," Mr. Michaels said. "Look at all the other workers doing Johnny's task, they all use the same tool. Johnny was experimenting with a new tool that he invented and it does do the job better. But you'll have to ask him for it. It belongs to him."

The supervisor realized that he had made a mistake in acting so hastily. He approached Johnny to apologize.

"Mr. Romanek, I wasn't aware that the tool you were using was an invention of yours," the supervisor said. "I'd like to look at it, and if we use it in other Ford plants, you could get a lot of money."

Johnny was still annoyed by the sneaky way that they timed his operation, which was a violation of the union contract. All employees must be notified when there was going to be a timed study of their operation.

"You guys must be nuts to think that I would show you my tool," Johnny said. "I know that you would then double my work load on my operation. I'm just going to use this antiquated tool that forces me to use more lead in the operation."

That evening he told his wife about the confrontation. It was then that Johnny decided to run for the committeeman job in his district.

"Those time study guys are sneaky and do things in violation of the union contract," Johnny said. "I've always been interested in the rights of workers, so I want to run for a union position in this coming election."

He took a small booklet out of his pocket and showed it to his wife.

"I picked up this union contract at union hall so I could study it," Johnny said. "Knowing the contract isn't going to be a problem but getting campaigning will be. I'm confined to a moving line most of the day and the only free time I have is when I go on relief. That's just for 15 minutes twice a day."

Johnny started to think about ways to use time during the day to campaign.

"I also have a half hour of lunch so I can talk to the workers in the cafeteria or in the department while they are eating," Johnny said. "I've got to think of a new approach to get elected. I'm going to write a bulletin explaining why I'm the best man for the job. No one running for committeeman ever did that. Running for that job means I'm going to meet workers and talk to them to show them I'm the right man for the job."

"What about all the engineering courses you're taking at the college for the last three years?" Ann asked. "Is that all going to go down the drain?"

"No, I'll be able to use that knowledge to protect the workers I represent," Johnny said.

He went on to explain that he had taken courses on time study and knew how to read the study properly and pick out the flaws in their report. Most of the problems in the body shop were because the work operation was so tight and at times the work couldn't be done properly in the time allowed. That's where the union comes in to take a grievance of the operation to get the job load corrected.

Ann listened to her husband patiently.

"You've always been interested in worker's rights," Ann said. "If that's what you want to do, then do it."

They sat together night after night going over the contents of the bulletin. Many times she would question the reasons for placing things in the bulletin. She pointed out flaws including his criticism of the present committeeman who was spending too much time in certain departments. He listened as she explained that all workers wanted their union representative to spend time with them. Her reasoning was that he needed all the departments on his side. Write only what is constructive for the members, she said.

When they were satisfied that the bulletin brought out all his good points, they took it to a union printing shop to have it finalized. Then Johnny spent every available moment explaining his views to members.

The day before election, he handed out his bulletin in his district and also to the maintenance shop that was part of that district. The timing was perfect; his opposition had no time to give their views. Also, most of the members liked his views and the fact that he had a formal education.

While Johnny won his first election for a union position in a landslide, he was put to the test on his first day as a union representative. Along with the body shop, he represented the maintenance department. It was his responsibility to see that skilled tradesmen shared overtime equally in their respective trades. When he visited the maintenance department, the clerk was typing up the overtime list. When the clerk was through, he handed Johnny the list of workers that were assigned to work the Saturday overtime shifts.

Johnny looked over the list and went to the overtime chart hung on the bulletin board. He examined it with the list of workers coming in on the weekend. He went back into the office to chat with the clerk.

"This list doesn't coincide with the overtime chart posted in the shop," Johnny said. "I see that you have the men listed to work with the highest overtime on the chart and the men with the lowest not coming in."

He handed the list back to the clerk.

"I'll make up the list of workers who will be coming in over the weekend," Johnny said.

Then he went back to the overtime chart. He had the number of skilled tradesmen who were needed to perform the work. Johnny wrote the names of the lowest men in overtime in each trade to be scheduled to work and handed the list to the clerk.

"Here's the list of workers who'll be coming in to work this weekend," Johnny said. Then he crumbled the list the clerk had given him and threw it into the wastebasket by the clerk's desk.

"From now on, give me the number of workers you need in each trade and I'll supply the workers necessary," Johnny said.

"Some of the workers you picked are not capable of performing the jobs scheduled," the clerk stammered.

"Bullshit, they're all skilled workers or they wouldn't be working here," Johnny said, pointing to the list. "Let's stick to the rules and not play favorites."

Artie Bach, superintendent of maintenance, heard the conversation and came out of his office.

"We know the qualified skill tradesmen who can do certain jobs," Artie said. "When we take out broken parts of the production line we have to be sure that it works when we get the job done or we'll all be out of a job."

"Mr. Bach, I'm aware of your needs but we've got to play by the rules," Johnny said. "If there is any man on my list and he is not qualified to do the job, all that needs to happen is one of you come and tell me. Then I'll replace him with the next man on the chart."

Johnny began walking away but paused, informing the superintendent that he would be by tomorrow to see how the tradesmen performed.

When Johnny left Mr. Bach showed his anger and turned to his foreman who had observed the confrontation.

"He's a bitch of a committeeman," Mr. Bach said. "If one of those men on the list can't do the job, I want him disciplined and sent home. I'm not going to be forced to work with unqualified men."

"Art, do we go at it alone with his list or do we bring in the men that we know can do the job?" one of the foreman asked.

"No, let's stay with the list and play it by ear," Mr. Bach said. "Just make sure we don't get stuck on any job."

Mr. Bach stomped out in anger.

The next day Johnny came into work bright and early to see how the jobs were progressing. He went from job to job and was pleased to see that all the tasks were being performed and moving along smoothly. At the end of the shift, he walked into Mr. Bach's office as he was finishing up on his report.

"How did it go today?" Johnny asked.

Mr. Bach knew that every job was locked up and completed to perfection. Despite his initial hesitation, Mr. Bach was pleased with the outcome.

"Very well," Mr. Bach said. "We buttoned up every job and we will be able to get production started with no trouble."

"I'm glad to hear that," Johnny said. "I was told by everyone that we have the most qualified and skilled group. From now on, you let me know how many skilled men you need on weekends and I'll supply the manpower. I'm sure that we're going to get along just fine."

Chapter 15
Year 1965

It was a Saturday morning. Johnny and Ann were getting ready to go to the big union meeting in San Diego, where all the representatives of Ford from the United States and Canada would be in attendance.

Ann was flustered as she tried to get all the things she needed into her suitcase and Wayne was helping his mother close the overstuffed luggage. He was sitting on top of it to get it closed.

"Mom, you have enough clothes to last you a month," Wayne chuckled. "Why so much?"

"I don't have any idea what kind of clothes I'll have to wear or what kind of hotel we'll be staying at," Ann said. "If the weather is warm like I've been told, I'm bringing my swim clothing. In case there is a formal event I've packed a gown. Your father has attended many conferences like this and when I asked him what the other wives wore he told me that he never paid attention to what they wore. So I'm pretty much making a wild guess here."

She began laughing as she watched Wayne struggle with her suitcase. He finally was able to close the suitcase, with Ann breathing a sigh of relief.

"We're going to be gone for a week and I'm leaving you in charge of taking care of Saundra and Frankie," Ann said. "Please be a good older brother to them."

Saundra came walking into the room carrying her mother's dress which had just come back from the cleaners.

"Mom, I'm not a little girl anymore," Saundra said, overhearing her mother's conversation with Wayne. "I'm thirteen and I can take care of myself. Just go with Dad and have a good time and don't worry about me. I know how to cook and keep the house clean. Also, I was hoping it would be alright to go over to Aunt Millie's for the weekend to swim in their pool."

Wayne stood there with a smile on his face as he watched his mother take the clean dresses from Saundra. He wondered if she was going to try to stuff them into her suitcase, but instead she placed them into her husband's carry-on. This was the first time she was going to be away from her children.

"Mom, I'll drive you to the airport and on our way back, I'll drive Saun and Frankie over to Aunt Millie's house," Wayne said. "We're all having dinner there on Sunday and after that I'll be home every evening."

Ann looked around the room to see if there was anything she forgot and continued.

"I want both of you to remember to close the doors when you go out and check to make sure they are locked every night when you go to bed," Ann said.

"Mom if a robber ever came to this house to see what we got, he'd probably leave a donation for us," Wayne said, laughing. "Don't worry Mom, we'll do just fine. I'll make sure everything is A-OK while you and dad are gone."

Wayne struggled to pick up his mother's suitcase which was incredibly heavy. He dragged it down the stairs and brought it to the car where his father was placing everything in the trunk.

"Dad, Mom was worried that someone would break into the house and steal our belongings," Wayne said, chuckling. "I think she put everything valuable in this suitcase. She packed enough to last her a year."

Johnny smiled at his son and picked up the suitcase.

"She packed a load, that's right," Johnny said. "She took enough to change her outfit three times a day. But you know your mom; she has to be sure she has the proper attire for every occasion. This is the first time I've had the opportunity to take her to a decent place. While I'm in meetings in the morning, mom can go out with the other women and see the town and do some shopping. In the evening, I'll take her to some nightclub and see some good shows."

Johnny stopped talking and made sure the car was adequately packed.

"Your sister thinks she's a grown-up, but she's still just a little girl," Johnny said. "See to it that nothing happens to her. Are you staying overnight at Aunt Millie's?"

"No Dad, I'm going to Jay's birthday tonight," Wayne said. "I mentioned the party to you and mom a few weeks ago."

"Son, just be careful at the party," Johnny said. "Will there be drinking there? I don't want you to get mixed up in that."

"Dad, Jay's parents are very religious and the strongest drink we'll get there is fruit juice," Johnny said. "His mother has been baking all week long. All the guys are excited about getting plenty of home-cooked food. Some of them are bringing over their musical instruments. But that's about it. By midnight everything is over. Jay's parents are religious and go to church on Sunday."

Wayne drove his parents to the airport and watched his mom in the rearview, as she wiped away tears. Saundra and Frankie were sitting next to her.

"Mom, everything will be fine," Wayne said. "I promise, ok?"

"I've just never left you all alone before," Ann sobbed.

"There is a first time for everything, hon," Johnny said. "I trust Wayne, he's grown into a fine young man."

Johnny reached toward the back seat to take his wife's hand and she stopped crying.

"Mom, we'll be fine," Saundra said, reaching over to hug her mom.

At the airport Johnny walked toward the airline counter and saw Lou standing there waiting for a seat assignment.

"Good morning Lou," Johnny said, patting him on the back. "You met Ann before."

He then introduced Lou to Wayne and Saundra while young Frankie was running around the airport departure area.

"Where's Rocky?" Johnny asked.

Lou took his ticket from the agent.

"Rocky called me last night and told me that something came up and he had to make an arrangement for another flight," Lou said. "He'll be at the meeting on Tuesday morning. He also said while he was out there that he would be staying with relatives."

"Hmm, interesting," Johnny said, scratching his chin.

"Lou, is your wife coming with you?" Ann asked.

"No, Shelly couldn't come," Lou said. "Her work schedule wouldn't allow for it."

Ann was disappointed since she thought she would be spending time with Shelly, whom she knew the best out of all the wives.

Delegates from other UAW groups spotted Johnny and came over to greet him. Jack Regan, President of the Trenton Assembly Plant, came over with his wife.

"Hello Johnny," Jack said. "So this is the Mrs. Romanek I've heard so much about. I heard she was very beautiful. I can see that they weren't wrong."

Jack took Ann's hand and kissed it.

Ann turned to Jack's wife, Molly, and introduced herself.

"I'm so glad there will be another person I can spend my days with," Ann said to Molly.

"I agree," Molly said. "I was so mad at Jack because he wouldn't tell me anything about the other wives. I thought I would be all alone."

Wayne, Frankie and Saundra got ready to leave as the time to board drew near.

"Wayne, you take good care of your brother and sister," Johnny said.

Ann hugged them all close and gave them kisses on the forehead.

"Be safe and I'll call you every day," she said.

Johnny, Ann, Lou and Molly all started walking to the departing gate.

Ann and Molly began making plans of what to do during the day.

"This is the first time I've attended a conference with John," Ann said.

"Me too," Molly said. "Jack usually goes to these things alone."

The flight to San Diego was smooth and upon landing, all of the UAW delegates went to the Hilton Hotel where the meeting was taking place.

Next to the hotel was a large golf course and a swimming pool located next to the hotel. Johnny requested that their room be on the top floor with a view of the pool. The room had a large king size bed with walls paneled in mahogany and matching furniture. The far wall was encased with glass sliding doors that opened to a balcony overlooking the Pacific Ocean.

Ann opened the sliding doors to view the breath-taking scenery. Leading outside the hotel was a small wooden bridge that went over a rippling brook that led to a rustic path and an assortment of blooming flowers on both sides of the path. The end of the path led to artificial waterfalls emptying into a fish pool made up of jagged rocks and dark green plants.

Ann leaned over the rail of the balcony in the opposite direction and saw that the brook emptied into a large lake that bordered the hotel on the other side.

"John, the view is amazing," Ann said. "Come and look. It's unbelievable that they could make the grounds so beautiful. It must be so beautiful in the evening when they put the lights on in the center of the waterfalls. Let's get out our bathing suits and go for a swim."

"Hon, I'm glad you like it," Johnny said. "This is the first time we've been alone in a long time."

They grabbed their bathing suits and headed to the pool, where they met many of the delegates and their wives.

Meanwhile, Rocky was still at the airport waiting to depart. Marie walked into the airport lobby with her parents. She spotted Rocky reading a newspaper donning a black velvet jacket, white pants and matching shoes. He looked so handsome, she thought.

Marie's parents walked her to the counter to make sure she was checked-in.

"Dear, are your girlfriends going to be on this flight?" her father asked.

"No," she lied. "They they're flying out of Kennedy Airport. We're all meeting in San Diego. Let's go over to the news stand to get something to read."

"I doubt you'll have time to read," her father said. "Hurry up, they just announced that they're boarding your flight."

Her dad paid for the magazines and candy. She hugged and kissed both her parents as she stood in the line to board. Rocky was still reading his newspaper.

"Honey, do you have your ticket and boarding pass ready?" her father asked nervously.

"Yes, I have everything," Marie said. "You and mom can go, I don't want you to get stuck in traffic."

"Ok, have a good time, dear," her father said. "Call us the moment you land so we don't worry. Also, be careful when you're at the hotel, make sure you lock your door with the safety chain that's there. Thieves prey on unescorted young girls. You listen to me and be careful."

Her mother hugged her with tears in her eyes. This was the first time their daughter was going away on a vacation without them.

"Please be careful," her mother said.

Marie returned her mother's hug and kissed her father on his cheek. She felt guilty lying to them and felt a lump in her throat as she watched them walk away. Her sadness turned to excitement when she boarded the plane and saw Rocky standing by their seats.

He hugged and kissed her on the lips. Then he placed her carry-on bag in the compartment above.

"You look so handsome," she said. "I was tempted to run over to you when we entered the airport lobby but I tried my best not to look at you. My parents think I'm going with my girlfriends."

"Did Tony say anything about your vacation coming up at the same time as our council meeting?" Rocky asked.

Marie sat in her seat and fastened her safety belt.

"No one gave my vacation a thought," Marie said. "I told my girlfriend Wendy that I was going with you to San Diego with you."

As Rocky took his seat he became visibly upset.

"Now why would you do that?" he asked.

"I had to tell someone," Marie explained. "I told my parents that I was going to California with some of my girlfriends from the office. Wendy agreed to say if she was questioned, she would say she came along with me on vacation."

"Ok," he said. "I guess that's fine."

He relaxed a little.

The take off was smooth and the hostess came by with complimentary drinks. After dinner, Marie pulled out brochures from San Diego showing places of interest. She was excited to show him all the sights. He caught her excitement and also was looking forward to getting to know the city. Marie dozed on Rocky's shoulder and it felt like mere moments had passed before they landed in San Diego.

They took a taxi to the Holiday Inn that was on the beach facing the Pacific Ocean. As they entered the lobby, Rocky asked Marie if she wanted a room up high with a view.

"Let's get a room up high facing the ocean," Marie said. "It's so beautiful here."

They got a room on the top floor with a balcony overlooking the ocean. The room had a king size bed in the center of the room and a large colored TV with a combination radio that was playing some soft music.

Marie took Rocky by the hand and led him to the sliding door leading to the balcony. They could see for miles in three directions. She pulled him close and felt the breeze move through her hair.

"Look at the sailboats and ships moving in the ocean," she said. "It must be wonderful to live this sort of life all the time. I'm glad I came with you."

They decided to head down to the beach to swim in the Pacific Ocean.

"Tonight we'll go to Anton's which is known worldwide for their exotic sea food and steaks," Rocky said.

They swam and played on the beach the whole afternoon and in the evening, he dressed in a dark suit and she put on a low-cut evening gown. They went to Anton's for dinner then went to a nightclub where they danced till well after midnight.

As soon as they got back to their room, Rocky ordered champagne packed in ice. Marie disappeared into the bedroom where she changed into a sheer white nightgown and matching negligee.

"Honey I've got the champagne," Rocky said. "Come out and enjoy it while it's cold."

Marie finally came out and Rocky's eyes lit up. Marie looked beautiful with the moon shining through the big window behind her. He turned the radio to soft music and took her into his arms. He led her to the sofa and poured the champagne into the fine glasses.

"Marie, here's to us," Rocky said. "I hope we always stay as happy as we are tonight."

"I'll drink to that," Marie said. She placed her drink on the end table as he took her into his arms and they began dancing. He started to kiss her and she returned the kisses.

He picked her up and carried her to the bed and gently placed her in the center. He removed his robe and placed it on the bed beside her. He knew that this was the first time she had ever been with a man and he wanted to make her feel safe. They fell asleep in one another's arms after making love.

"I was frightened but you were incredibly gentle with me," Marie murmured.

"Dear, it was my pleasure," Rocky said.

* * *

The day after everyone arrived, the meeting representing all Ford plants in United States and Canada was called to order. The meeting room was set up in a classroom arrangement with Chairman Daniels and his two officers facing the delegates. There were tablets and pencils on the table for them to take notes if necessary.

Immediately after roll call, the chairman called on Johnny to give them a report on the wildcat strike. To Johnny's dismay, one of the other delegates passed out newspaper clippings capturing the protests with images of police on the overpasses with rifles and shotguns poised to help keep order.

Johnny walked to the microphone that was set up in the center of the aisle to address the delegates.

"Tony, we had quite a number of workers protesting but it was contained to the night shift and there was absolutely no violence," Johnny said. "The newspaper blew the affair out of proportion."

He explained in full detail the incident that led to the wildcat strike and the events that followed. He praised Ken Bannon and his staff for their outstanding work coming up with a solution that ended the strike.

"The best thing that came out of this was the change in the foremen's attitude toward our workers," Johnny said. "As for Superintendent Acuff, the company assigned him to another position outside of the plant."

Johnny felt the union and the members in attendance were satisfied by the report.

"We sat in over 300 hearings dealing with the demonstration and ultimately the company handed out only paper disciplines with no loss of pay," Johnny continued. "Finally, there are two discharge cases that will be heard by the umpire when I get back next week. We lost a lot of probationary members that participated in the wildcat and wouldn't listen to the union. But I feel we have a good chance of winning the rest of the cases before the umpire because of the outstanding job done by the international union."

The delegates were pleased with his explanation and hands started shooting up.

"Johnny in your opinion, do you think it would be wise for the rest of our union to ask for such a committee in all of the plants?" one of the delegates asked.

"If you don't have a problem now I wouldn't advise you to open a Pandora's box," Johnny said. "I would suggest that when you meet with the company, get them to institute the program that we instituted here in Clinton. They have the sensitivity training films that you should show to your foremen to make them aware of plight of black workers in America. Headquarters in Detroit has films that explain the sensitivity of the black community and how management should approach their problems. I'm sure Ken and his staff can help you implement this program."

He paused and scanned the room before continuing.

"This demonstration opened my eyes to the needs of black workers and their right to have black representatives in the union," Johnny said. "Look around the room and we can count the black workers on one hand. Take our plant in Clinton for example, we have over 3,500 workers there and we only have one black committeeman. We have a few blacks on our executive board but there is the need to have more black representation on the shop floor. The incident at the Clinton plant has indicated to me a larger trend moving around the country. If we want peace in our plants, we better get together with the blacks to elect some that we can train to be part of the union. In the next few years we're going to see that the black population in auto plants will reach over 50 percent because whites don't like working on a moving line. Of the new hires, the largest percent of those who quit are white workers who feel bored about working on a moving line and feel they can get a better job elsewhere. Our black workers stay because of the high rate of pay and benefits that are second to none. As the quota goes up, we will do better if we have qualified blacks represent the people or we're all going to be losers."

"Are you saying that we should drop our white representatives to achieve equality?" a delegate from the deep South asked.

"No," Johnny answered, shaking his head. "In all your plants, you know your needs. All I'm saying is that you better take a good hard look at what is in front of you. In the next election, I'm going to have a black man run for a key position so I don't run into the same problems we had at Clinton. Barring any questions, this concludes my report."

The delegates applauded. Chairman Daniels restored order and asked members to focus.

"We still have a lot of business to conduct," he said. "The most important is the election of officers to Sub Council #2. I'm not seeking re-election. I feel we take a coffee break so our delegates can have the opportunity to nominate their candidates for office and then we'll conduct the election. After the coffee break we will accept nominations for president, vice-president and financial secretary. We'll reconvene in 15 minutes."

During the break many delegates gathered around Johnny. One of the delegates asked if he would be interested in running for president of the sub council. Johnny shook his head.

"No, I have my own re-election coming up next year and I couldn't do justice to both jobs," Johnny said. "Being president of the council is a very important job and time-consuming. I have to establish a firm base at my own local before I take on other assignments."

Some of the delegates then asked whom he preferred for the positions.

"My wife joined me on this trip and I plan to enjoy the sights and have a good time with her," Johnny said. "I'll review the candidates but I don't intend to campaign for anyone. I heard that Albert Henry is running for vice-president. He's well qualified and if he runs for that position, I'll probably support him. Outside of him, I don't know about anyone else."

During the coffee break, the delegate from Texas came over to Johnny.

"Johnny, I was drinking last night with some of the guys and I heard Lou Sargent blasting off about you," the delegate said. "He blames you for the black uprising and made it clear that Don Byrne's caucus was going to support Rocky Durango for president in opposition to you. I know that Rocky ran with you at the last election. A word of warning, watch your back with those two. Most of the delegates are supportive of you and your ideas."

"Thanks for the warning," Johnny said, irritated that this issue was constantly flaring up. "Rocky and I were in the same caucus for years and I know that he'd sell his soul to become president. Fortunately I am one step ahead of him. Thanks for the information, I see Tony is ready to call the meeting to order."

* * *

Ann ran across the parking lot with her hands full of towels, blankets and sunscreen lotion to counter the hot sun. All the wives were already by the car dressed in shorts with their bathing suits underneath. Molly Regan couldn't help but laugh at Ann's attire.

"Ann, you look cute in those tight blue jeans and your husband's football jersey," Molly said. "When you have a figure like her, anything looks good."

Ann took the car keys from her bag and opened the trunk of the car so the ladies could put in all their belongings.

"The shirt is kinda big but what the heck," Ann said. "We're only going to the ocean to swim. Where would you girls like to go?"

"One of the delegates said the Holiday Inn is right on the beach," Molly said. "There's a restaurant and restrooms right on the beach and by the pool."

"It's settled then, Holiday Inn it is," Ann said.

As soon as Ann pulled into the parking lot, the ladies scrambled to the beach. They placed their blankets on the sand and peeled off their outer garments. They ran to the water and dipped their toes to test the temperature of the ocean. Eventually every single one of them got in and enjoyed immersing themselves in the water. Ann was the first one to get out and head to the blanket. She picked up her towel and began wiping herself down and soon all the other ladies followed and came out of the water. They were completely exhausted and laid on the blankets shaking sand off and wiping the water away.

Ann sat there drying her hair when a very pretty blond girl approached them.

"You ladies are having a ball out here," she said. "Are you with some convention?"

"Kind of," Ann said, shielding her eyes from the sun and squinting. "Our husbands are having a meeting here. We tagged along and are enjoying the sights of San Diego while our

husbands are busy with work. What about you? Are you alone?
By the way, my name is Ann."

Ann stood up to shake her hand.

"I'm Marie Collins," the lady said. "Nice to meet you."

"Why don't you join us on the blanket?" Ann said.

Marie nodded and took up a spot on the blankets. Ann
liked her right away and noticed her beauty and shapely figure.

"My husband is also here for a business meeting and I'm
on my own trying to get a sun tan," Marie said. "It would be a
shame to come all the way out here and go home without a tan."

The other ladies walked over to Ann and Marie.

"Ann we're going over to the refreshment stand to get
something to eat and drink, we're starved after all the running
around," Molly said. "Should we get you ladies something or do
you want to join us?"

"We'll join you," Ann said. "This will give us a chance to
get out of the sun."

"Thanks Ann but I'm going to catch some rays on the
blanket," Marie said. "I had a heavy breakfast and I'm not
hungry."

Ann got up and ran to join the girls at the stand. She was
back shortly carrying a bag with a hamburger and two Cokes.

"You might work up an appetite as you lay in the sun,"
Ann said.

She handed Marie the bag and the coke.

"That's so sweet of you," Marie said. "On second though
I'm now a tad hungry."

"Where are you from?" Ann asked.

"I'm from New Jersey," Marie said, chewing her
hamburger.

"So am I," Ann said. "The other ladies are from all over
the country."

"It's funny meeting you all the way in California when
we're from the same state," Marie said. "Do you work back
home? What do you do?"

"No I'm just a plain old housewife with three children to
take of every day," Ann said. "This is the first time I've been
away from my children since our marriage."

Marie brushed a chunk of hair from her forehead.

"Did you get a babysitter to mind the children?"

Ann laughed and rubbed the sand off of her legs.

"Heavens no, my oldest Wayne is graduating high school," Ann said. "My daughter, Saundra, is thirteen and my youngest, Frankie, is five."

"My goodness, you look so young," Marie said. "It's hard to believe that you have grown children. How do you keep such a lovely figure and look so young?"

"I guess maintaining the household, running after the children and walking our big collie every morning and afternoon," Ann said. "Do you work?"

"Yes, I'm a secretary and I love my job," Marie said. "This trip is like a second honeymoon for my husband and me. How long are you staying in California?"

"My husband's council meeting will probably end by Friday," Ann said. "We're not sure if we will stay any longer. I miss the children already, so if it was up to me, we'd fly back Saturday."

Marie became nervous at Ann's mentioning of the council meeting. She wondered if it was the same meeting that Rocky was attending. She had better be careful before she revealed too much more of herself.

"What hotel are you staying at?" Marie asked.

"The Hilton," Ann replied. "It's the same hotel where the meeting is taking place."

Marie was convinced that all of the ladies husband's were at the same meeting. In her nervousness Marie began to choke on her Coke. Ann began hitting her on her back.

"Are you ok?" Ann asked. "Marie, can you breathe?"

"I'm ok," Marie said, as soon as she caught her breath.

She looked at her watch. Rocky would join her any minute on the beach and she wanted to intercept him at the lobby.

"Girls, I have to run," Marie said. "I expect my husband any moment now and he'll be wondering where I'm at. Ann, it was nice meeting you. Maybe we'll run into each other again."

Marie hugged Ann quickly and gave a slight wave to the rest of the wives. She scrambled to her feet and hurried off the beach.

Soon after Ann and the other wives returned to their hotel rooms. Ann was writing postcards to her family and friends when Johnny returned.

"How did the meeting go?" Ann asked.

Johnny threw his briefcase on the bed and removed his jacket.

"The meeting turned out fine," Johnny said, loosening his tie. "Some of the delegates asked me to run for the presidency but I told them that my beautiful wife joined me and we were enjoying our second honeymoon."

"Did you really say that?" Ann asked, as Johnny pulled him toward her. "They'll think we are spending all our time in bed."

"I'm going to take a shower and then let's go to that Chinese restaurant that we saw in the center of the town," Johnny said. "Some of the locals said the food is good there and the price is reasonable."

"Sounds great," Ann said. "I showered after the beach so I'll just change into a dress."

Johnny was driving along the main street near the beach heading downtown. The windows were down and Ann was enjoying the ocean breeze. She was staring out the window when someone caught her eye.

"John, isn't that Rocky walking out of the Holiday Inn?" Ann asked. She noticed a beautiful blonde on his arm.

Johnny slowed down to get a better look.

"I'll be damned, that's Marie Collins, Tony's secretary," Johnny said. "I knew he was taking her out but I didn't think he would go this far."

As they neared the couple, Ann recognized the woman from the beach.

"Oh that poor girl," Ann said. "I met her at the beach this morning with the other wives. She's a lovely girl but I noticed she suddenly got nervous toward the end when I mentioned that we were staying at the Hilton. Now I understand why."

Johnny shook his head in disgust.

"Rocky is not an honorable man," Johnny said. "He's using her to get information from Tony's office. I knew that she had a crush on him but Rocky is not the marrying kind and has no intention of going steady with her. She comes from a good Catholic family and they'd be devastated if they knew what was going on. I hope she knows what she's doing. If I know Rocky, he'll have her in bed the entire time they are here."

"What a shame to take a girl clean across the country just to have an affair," Ann said. "I've seen him with lots of ladies but she's the prettiest one I ever saw him with. What would happen if we approached them now?"

"Marie would have a heart attack but Rocky would just gloat," Johnny said. "She's in her early 20's and has been working at the plant for three years. When Rocky pursues a girl, he goes first class. I didn't tell you earlier but when Tom Romeo came to see me at the union office, he told me that Rocky runs the bookie and numbers racket in Clinton. He's the man behind the scenes, so he's got a lot of extra cash. All the years I've known him and I never knew that."

Johnny and Ann cruised past Rocky and Marie, instead of stopping to chat with them.

After a fabulous dinner, they returned to the hotel to join the delegates in the hospitality room. The place was busy and everyone seemed to be talking at the same time.

The president of the Chicago plant came over to Johnny and Ann immediately.

"Johnny, I thought that you were going to campaign in this election?" he asked.

"My wife and I just walked in," Johnny said. "You're the first person I'm talking to. What do you mean?"

"Lou Sargent has been talking to the delegates, telling them you're supporting Chico Cheverez for the presidency," he said.

Ann saw the fierce anger flash on her husband's face.

"Lou Sargent doesn't ever speak for who I'm going to support," Johnny snapped. "I don't believe Chico would do the council any good. I've never heard him talk about anything concerning the assembly plants problems. The international is committed to him because of the popularity of Cesar Chevez. At this time I'm not sure who to support."

Ann could see the adrenaline flowing and the gleam in Johnny's eyes was fiery when he was talking.

"Dear, I'm going over to the bar to get a drink," Ann said. "I know you've got some networking to do so I'll leave you to it."

Ann caught Molly Regan's eye and headed over to her.

"I see Johnny is finally getting involved with the election," Molly said. "My husband is talking to him at the bar."

Johnny ordered a gin and tonic for himself and headed over to join the group of presidents who were discussing the candidates.

"Hi Johnny, we heard Lou was speculating which candidate you are supporting but it's not Chico after all," one of the presidents said. "Who are you going with now?"

"We all know the international is committed to Chico and is campaigning like hell to get him elected," Johnny said. "Phil Denardo is a pretty decent guy and thinks a lot like us. Let's call him over to see if he's serious about running. If he is willing, let's support him."

Johnny noticed Phil talking to his delegates across the room.

"Phil, come over and join us," Johnny said, waving his hand.

Phil walked over with a group of his delegates.

"Phil, are you going to run?" Johnny asked.

A worried expression passed over Phil's face.

"I'd like to run but I only have token support," Phil said. "The international wants Chico and a lot of delegates are reluctant to go against them because they are beholden to them for all the favors they did over the years."

"Phil if you are serious about running, we have four of the biggest locals supporting you and your own local," Johnny said, putting his arm around Phil's shoulders. "Now let's go to work and give them hell."

That evening Johnny and some of his comrades campaigned hard for Phil even though most of the delegates wouldn't give public support. The delegates were supporting Chico even though they realized he would be a weak leader who could be controlled.

The delegates wanted time to weigh the advantages of their vote. While the campaigning was going on, a fight broke out between the international representative, Jim Berger and a Michigan delegate, Peter Reilly. Jim threw a punch at Peter and nearly missed Ann who was walking by to freshen up her drink. Johnny dashed across the room to go after Jim. As several men restrained Johnny, Jim approached Ann and apologized.

"Mrs. Romanek, I'm so sorry, I didn't see you walking by," Jim said. "Are you all right?"

Ann was jarred but fine.

"Thanks for your concern," Ann said. "You just missed me. I guess you guys take your elections very seriously."

Ann noticed Johnny at the corner of her eye.

"Dear, I'm ok," Ann said. "I just walked by at the wrong place, wrong time.

Jim looked over at Johnny.

"Johnny I apologized to your wife," Jim said. "I never saw her coming when I threw the punch. Thank God, I missed. I'm sorry about the incident but you should have heard the names that guy called me. Again Johnny, I'm sorry."

"I got hot when I saw the blow nearly hit my wife but these things happen," Johnny said. "Let's forget about it."

Ann noticed Johnny heading her way so ordered him his usual, a gin and tonic.

"Take this to cool you off," Ann said. "You look like you need it."

"Are you ok?" Johnny asked, sipping his drink.

"I'm fine," Ann said. "Looks like campaigning is getting serious around here, but I wasn't hurt, don't worry, honey."

The following morning the first thing on the agenda was the election of officers. The voting between Phil and Chico was in a dead heat until the last local from New Jersey was called to vote. Johnny leaned over to the delegate next to him.

"Phil needs two votes from this local to win the election," Johnny said. "Jack Regan is committed to us but I don't know about the other delegates."

Jack stood up to vote with a silence falling over the room as he walked to the microphone.

"I cast my vote for Phil Denardo," Jack said.

A group of delegates began applauding his vote but then Jack raised his hand.

"My other delegate want to cast their own vote," Jack said.

The attention centered on the two remaining delegates and on how they would vote. The first delegate got up and walked slowly toward the microphone, the crowd silent.

"I cast my vote to Chico," the delegate said.

An applause erupted from some of the delegates.

The vote was in a dead heat again and the council was buzzing with excitement as they waited for the last delegate to cast his deciding vote.

Kevin Richards the vice-president of his local stood up slowly, adding tension to the crowd. He walked up to the microphone.

"I cast my vote for the next president of Sub Council #2 to be," he paused. "Chico Cheverez."

Many of the delegates and the international union representatives stood up to applaud their win over the dissident group.

"Chico, I'd like to congratulate you on behalf of the council," Chairman Daniels said. "I'd like the newly elected officers to come to the podium to assume your positions."

Chico assumed the chair and called the meeting together. Billy Miken, the international representative who was assigned to the council from Detroit came over to Johnny's table and sat next to him.

"I need some answers to take back to Ken," Billy said. "You announced to the council before the election of officers that you weren't going to get involved with the election and then you made a complete turn-around and almost had our candidate defeated. Ken is very close to you and he's going to ask me why you changed your mind.

Johnny looked at Billy for a moment before explaining.

"Billy, you're entitled to an explanation," Johnny said. "I did say I was going to remain neutral. But when I got to the hospitality event, I that Lou Sargent was telling the delegates whom I was supporting. That son-of-a-bitch will never talk for me, not now, not ever. He told the delegates that I was supporting Chico. Just so you know, I never told anyone whom I was going to support. I have nothing against Chico but I was pissed at what Lou said so I got involved so that the delegates know that no one, least of all Lou, talks for me. Tell Ken I'm not anti-international. A lot of the delegates here feel that Chico will be a weak leader and will be a puppet to the international union. We all know his desire is to be put on the international staff. In all the meetings I attended, I never heard him talk in favor of any assembly plant issues. We have a lot of problems in the assembly plant that you are not aware of that we need to correct in the next contract, especially the work standards on the moving line. That's a killer to the workers on the line. Ken is aware of all of these issues. He was a past president of a large assembly plant and knows the conditions there. He was a past negotiator on the contract and was well qualified when he was put on the United Auto Workers staff."

"You're in a tough spot," Billy said. "Thanks for the honesty."

Chapter 16
Year 1965

A s soon as Johnny made it back from the conference, he had his hands full. First, he and Betty Morrow worked on the third-stage grievances to be heard by the umpire, including the discharges cases and the disciplinary cases that were a result of the wildcat strike.

It was Johnny's responsibility to write the statement of facts showing that the company was unjust in their disciplinary action against the workers. He read past umpire's decisions from several years ago and knew how to steer his defense according to the United Auto Workers and Ford agreement.

His suit jacket was draped over the back of his chair, his tie loosened and his sleeves rolled up. Betty sat in a chair directly in front of his desk with her steno pad on her lap. They worked from early morning and through their lunch break.

Johnny then received a phone call from Pat Fager who revealed that there was a confrontation between Lou Sargent and Superintendent Roger Hansen on the chassis line. Pat was vague with the details because he wasn't there when it happened. Pat had heard from workers on the line that Rocky and Lou were coming over to tell Johnny about the incident.

Johnny's face was withdrawn while listening to Pat. He just got out of a major confrontation and now they were dumping another one on him. He thanked Pat for the information and concluded his work with Betty. He filled her in about the phone call and instructed her to usher the men in when they came.

The moment Betty got to her desk, in walked Rocky and Lou. They stated that it was important that they see Johnny at once. Betty walked them to the door and knocked softly and entered his room. Johnny looked up from his paperwork and motioned for Betty to leave. Rocky sat on the chair in front of the desk while Lou remained standing. Lou lifted his shirt up to expose the left side of his rib cage, which had turned black and blue and was surrounded by a red inflammation.

"Roger Hansen gave me a shot in the ribs when I tried to stop him from working," Lou said, pointing to his ribs.

Johnny leaned back in his chair expecting the worst.

"Lou, I need you to start from the beginning," Johnny said. "By the looks of your ribs, he gave you quite a shot."

"Rocky and I were walking down 'B' aisle when one of the workers told us that Roger was performing an hourly job," Lou said. "I noticed him trying to pull apart a unit that was jammed together, rather than calling the maintenance department to do the work. I tried to stop him but he told me to go fuck myself, so I stepped in between him and the unit. That's when he hit me with his elbow to the ribs and continued unjamming the units. He caught me unexpectedly and I was doubled up with pain. He cleared the jam and left before I could catch my breath."

"Lou, that's a pretty bad bang," Johnny said. "Did you go to the medical department to get treated?"

"No," Lou said. "How could I? We came right over to the hall after it happened. I wanted you to be filled in on what happened immediately. While coming over here I told Rocky that we should put out a bulletin telling the members what happened. We can't let Roger get away with this."

Johnny knew that Lou was baiting him to take the company on. He was prepared for this.

"Lou, I want you to go on record that Roger struck you in the presence of Rocky and the men on the line," Johnny said. "Now go over to the medics to get treated and put up a fuss that you should go to the hospital to get an X-ray. Have the medics write up a report on what led up to the blow and how Roger struck you. Meanwhile, Rocky and I will go over to labor relations to demand that they fire Roger. If they don't, we have a load of grievances that are in the policy book on work standards, health and safety and we can use that to shut the plant down legally to pressure the company to take action against him."

Johnny could tell that he surprised both Rocky and Lou. They weren't expecting him to take such action.

"Lou, I'm not going to let a member of management hit one of my bargaining reps and get away with it," Johnny said.

"You said you wanted to put out a bulletin to the membership, explaining what happened. That's a good idea. Make sure I see it before you put it out."

Johnny and Rocky drove over to the administration building to meet with Tony while Lou went to the medical department to get treated. When they entered, Marie was typing then stopped to place a cover over her notes.

"What can I help you with?" Marie asked.

"We're here to see Tony," Johnny said. "It's urgent."

She dialed the inner office and told them to go right in. Johnny walked in first and sat at the conference table next to Tony.

"Tony we had a serious incident happen about a half hour ago when Lou attempted to stop Roger from working an hourly function," Johnny said. "Roger hit him in the rib cage, causing considerable damage to Lou's body."

"Whoa, whoa, whoa," Tony said. "You come in here, unannounced and you dump this on me? Slow down and please take it from the top."

Johnny hesitated before talking again.

"There was an incident between Lou and Superintendent Hansen," Johnny said. "Superintendent Hansen was performing an hourly job meant for a maintenance worker. When Lou told him this and tried to stop him, Superintendent Hansen elbowed him hard in the ribs, causing considerable damage."

Tony nodded as he listened.

"Are you sure that wasn't an accident?" Tony asked.

"No," Rocky said. "Roger told Lou to go 'fuck himself' so he was clearly angry and intended to cause Lou harm."

"Where is Lou right now?" Tony asked.

"Lou would've been here but he had to go to the medics to be treated," Johnny said.

"Ok, so Roger called me a few hours ago telling me about the jammed units on the line but he never mentioned any run-in with Lou," Tony said.

"Rather than me giving you a version of what happened, why don't we let Rocky fill you in?" Johnny said. "He was there when this happened."

Rocky was annoyed at being put on the spot. It made it look like he was lodging the complaint rather than Johnny. He wanted to keep a good rapport with Tony and didn't want to say anything that would to disrupt that.

"I actually wasn't there when the incident happened," Rocky said. "I was up the line talking to one of the workers when I heard a lot of shouting. I know basically everything that Johnny knows. It was Johnny's idea to send Lou to the medical department."

This time Johnny was annoyed. He was sick of Rocky acting like a little boy and punting matters back to him.

"Johnny we could have settled this without anything going on record," Tony said. "Now I'm afraid this could cause another strike."

"Your instructions to your supervisors was that if any hourly worker strikes a member of management, he was to go to the medical department immediately to go record that he was assaulted," Johnny snapped. "There's a good chance that Lou may have a broken rib from the severe blow. This is another thing Lou wants to put in the bulletin to the membership."

"Are you looking for another wildcat strike?" Tony asked.

"No Tony, we're not going to have any wildcat," Johnny said. "But we will have a problem on our hands if this matter isn't dealt with appropriately. That's the reason for this meeting. I want Roger removed from his job immediately. He's not going to hit a member of my bargaining committee and get away with it."

Johnny noticed Rocky gesturing slightly with his hand, indicating to Tony that this wasn't his idea. Johnny was annoyed at Rocky's ambivalence.

Tony was upset as he shuffled his papers on his desk. He kept looking at Rocky for support, but Rocky wouldn't make eye contact.

"We're not going to take Roger off his job," Tony fumed. "You got rid of Roy but you're not going to pull the same shit on Superintendent Hansen. I heard his side of the story and everything you are telling me is from second-hand sources. He was doing his job preventing the units from being damaged. It's hard for me to believe that Lou got hit out of malice. Roger has a good reputation and has been around too long and never laid a hand on anyone."

Johnny was pissed. He knew there was no sense continuing a conversation with Tony.

"Come on Rocky, let's get out of here," Johnny said. "We're wasting our time. This guy still takes the position that management can never do anything wrong."

Johnny picked up his briefcase to leave before making one last statement.

"We have enough grievances to shut the plant down legally," Johnny threatened. "We have a membership meeting this Saturday so I'll add to the agenda that we'll be requesting a strike authorization to remove Superintendent Roger Hansen from the plant for assaulting Lou Sargent."

Rocky followed him into the hallway and grabbed Johnny's shoulder.

"You know that you can't strike the plant over this issue," Rocky said.

"First of all, get your hands off me," Johnny said, shaking his arm loose. "Secondly, the hell I can't. I'll make our demands so high on the strike issues that they'll never be able to meet them unless Roger goes. We'll look like pussies if we ever let the company get away with this."

Tony made a beeline to the plant manager's office while Johnny and Rocky returned to the union hall. They found Lou waiting in Johnny's office with the bulletin that he constructed. The bulletin stated the facts with a passionate plea that the members take immediate action against the plant even if it meant a strike. Johnny read the bulletin several times and called Betty into his office.

"I want this bulletin go out under Lou Sargent's signature as a first-hand report by him," Johnny ordered. "It's a good bulletin that should rally the membership around him."

Lou's supporters between shifts handed the bulletin. Johnny also called a meeting with close caucus members.

"This is the first break we've gotten since the election to get both Lou and Rocky in a bind, like they have been doing to me," Johnny said. "I want a firsthand report on the response from the membership to the bulletin and on what Lou is advocating. I don't want any guesswork. Talk to the members to rile them up so they come to the membership meeting in force. I'll make sure Lou and Rocky give a first hand report on the issue and what they did to resolve it."

"Johnny, won't it look funny that we're not out there handing out the bulletin?" Burt Landers asked. He was the main committeeman on the night shift.

"No, it won't," Johnny said. "I don't want any of our caucus members advocating strike action when Rocky and Lou didn't have the balls to take the company on. Our only recourse was to walk off the line and they knew that and they didn't do it. I want this sticking out like a sore thumb when Rocky and Lou are asking the members to resolve something that they should have done in the first place."

That evening at home, Johnny got a call from Burt saying that the night shift was up in arms about the bulletin. Their complaint was that they just lost a week's pay over the wildcat and now Lou was asking them to protest again. One of their concerns was that Johnny's signature wasn't on the bulletin. Since he's the president and not Lou, they felt his signature should have been on it.

"This was strictly Lou's idea and how he wanted to handle the incident," Johnny said.

"The night shift is upset that Lou and Rocky didn't have the balls to walk the men out when Lou got hit," Burt said. "Johnny, you gotta come into the plant to talk to these guys."

"Sure, Burt," Johnny said. "Thanks for relaying all of this information to me. I'll have a meeting with the night shift tomorrow. I'll have a full report and decide how to resolve this issue."

As Johnny hung up the phone, he realized that no one wanted a strike, especially because it was the year the UAW contract was coming up for the three Detroit auto plants and a strike might affect the demands in the contracts.

Ann heard most of the conversation with Burt.

"John, be careful how you handle this," she warned. "You're the president of the local and the membership is looking to you for leadership. When a member loses money, they blame the leadership."

"Hon, both these guys have been blasting me undercover for everything that went wrong," Johnny said. "This time I intend to keep the pressure on them but I won't let it come to a strike. I'll make sure that they withdraw their complaint and they'll have to live with the settlement. If they want to play hardball, I'm all for it."

That Saturday morning the union hall was packed to capacity, with members standing in the aisle, along the wall and in the vestibule waiting to hear why a strike vote was added to the agenda. Johnny called the meeting to order and immediately a member called for a point of special privilege, which allows a member to interrupt the agenda of a meeting to make an urgent statement or motion.

"Mr. Chairman, I make a motion to suspend the regular order of business and get to the reason why a strike vote was called," the member said. "We just got back from a wildcat strike. We're pissed because this means our jobs are going to be affected again."

The motion was passed and Johnny spoke briefly on what led up to the strike vote. Rather than go in depth on the details, Johnny called on Lou to fill in the details. Lou was nervous when he stepped up to the microphone. He saw that the membership was out in full force and totally against any strike. He told the same story he told Johnny about the incident. A member jumped up and interrupted.

"Lou, when Superintendent Hansen hit you, what did you do about it?" the member asked.

"I was doubled up in pain," Lou said. "Before I could do anything about it, Roger ran away. It took me a while to get my breath back. That's when Rocky came over to help me."

"Mr. Chairman, our vice-president, Mr. Rocky Durango, was there when it happened," another member said. "We'd like to know what he did about it when he saw Lou doubled with pain after Superintendent Hansen hit him."

Johnny looked toward Rocky who was sitting uneasily on the platform next to Johnny. He knew he was put on the spot and this was a make or break question. He also knew he could do nothing to avoid the question. He stepped up to the microphone and saw he was facing Johnny's supporters with hostility in their faces.

"I wasn't really there when Lou got hit," Rocky said. "I was up the line talking to someone else when I heard the shouting. I rushed down to Lou and saw Roger quickly running away. I wasn't aware of what happened until Lou got his breath back and filled me in."

"Come on Rocky, you've been around a long time," another member said. "Why didn't you walk the guys off the line when you found out that Superintendent Hansen belted Lou? On the night shift, we got rid of Roy and for verbally assaulting a worker. Lou is one of our union bargaining reps. Didn't you think it was important enough to walk out the members since the company was in violation?"

That question caused an eruption in the hall. Everyone was up on their feet, shouting and demanding answers. Rocky's hands were shaking and he knew this was the same crowd that Johnny had difficulty managing. Rocky and Lou had accused Johnny of not having the balls to stand up to this crowd. This was more serious, a union official was hit by management and all the union did was write a bulletin calling for a strike to solve the problem.

"It happened so fast that before I realized Lou was hit, the bell rang sending the chassis line to lunch," Rocky said. "Everyone took off to the cafeteria."

Members from Johnny's caucus stood up to applaud.

"Saved by the bell!" one member yelled. The others responded in hoots and claps.

"If the bell didn't ring, I'd of got him!" another yelled. Laughter broke out throughout the hall and others cheered.

Johnny grabbed the microphone away from Rocky.

"This isn't a laughing matter," Johnny roared. "I wasn't there but I'm telling you that as long as I'm president of this local, I'm not going to allow any member of management hit any member of the union and get away with it. Especially a union representative."

He paused for a moment to allow the members to quiet down.

"Rocky and I met with the company and I told them without a doubt, I want Roger Hansen fired," Johnny said. The members stood up and cheered.

"Tony Rodgers gave us the same bullshit, giving us that line that he was going to investigate the incident," Johnny said. "I told him that if Roger isn't fired, I'd call for a strike authorization. We have enough grievances in the system to strike the plant legally and no jobs would be placed in jeopardy. I'll make sure nothing is settled unless Roger is out of the plant for good."

"We won't get paid while we're out on strike but Rocky and Lou will?" a member shouted. "That's bullshit!"

Johnny restored order by raising his hands and gesturing the crowd to be calm.

"None of us will be paid by the company, including me," Johnny said. "The only ones who'll be paid by our union are the union secretaries. They'll be doing more work than anyone while we're on strike. If we're forced out, the international union will pay for our medical and life insurance, plus a weekly subsistence based on our dependents.

Bill Bradley, a staunch supporter of Johnny's, asked to be recognized.

"Mr. Chairman, I'm all for preserving the dignity of the union, but I don't think this is the right time to go out on strike," Bill said. "Our national contract comes up in a few months and we'll probably have to go on strike then to get all the demands that we're asking for. If the union did like we did in the Roy affair, we wouldn't be here today and Roger would be out on the street. I'm ashamed to say that our union officials didn't have the guts to take the company on. I'm going to vote in favor of the strike authorization but with regret."

A hush came over the hall after Bill voiced his opinion.

"Bill, I can appreciate your feelings but I wasn't there when it happened," Johnny said. Then he took a moment before turning to the crowd.

"Are you ready to vote?" Johnny asked.

The vote was unanimous in favor of strike authorization. Johnny banged his gavel for their attention.

"I want to thank the membership for their support and together we'll see that justice will be served," Johnny said. "This strike authorization means you're giving me the right to take a strike vote in the event that we don't resolve the issues to our satisfaction. I assure you that I won't abuse this privilege. I'll only call for a strike vote after we've exhausted all contractual provisions to settle the issues. Now I'll accept a motion to adjourn."

The members all left the hall with the exception of Johnny's caucus. They gathered in Johnny's office to discuss their future plans.

There were 20 caucus members crowded in Johnny's office. Absent were Lou and Rocky. They sat on chairs, on the cabinets and others on the floor. Pat Fager opened the discussion.

"Johnny, I was pacing the floor during the meeting," Pat said. "I heard consensus that none of our members are in favor of going on strike. They liked what Bill said. Right now these guys hate Lou and Rocky with a passion. We have to make sure that feeling doesn't bleed over to us. If you allow us to go out on the street, we'll all be dead ducks. They're saying you had no choice but to take a strike vote but you have the power to settle the issues without a strike. We have to keep the pressure on both of those bastards and keep reminding the membership that they're responsible for us being in this position. Just be careful that we don't get labeled with them."

"Rocky saying that he didn't do anything because of the bell ringing was about the dumbest thing he could say," Burt Landers said. "He'll never be able to live that down. Our guys picked up on that beautifully by claiming he was 'saved by the bell.' When we get back to the plant, we'll spread that idea so the whole night shift will catch on, too."

Johnny was aware of the discontent among the membership and realized he had his job cut out for him. He leaned back in his chair.

"All of you did a good job at the meeting," Johnny said. "My biggest task is to get Rocky to withdraw his complaint against Roger so we don't strike. Once he does, I'll get all the grievances settled to our satisfaction."

Johnny then dismissed the meeting of his close comrades, feeling confident he had Rocky and Lou just where he wanted them.

The following week, Paul Larsen, the international regional representative, walked the plant with Johnny to review the operations that were noted as unsafe. The first job they reviewed involved a 63-year-old worker who had to climb up three feet to get onto the chain-driven line and then climb into the rear trunk of the car, carrying an air gun, an adapter and bolts that attached the body of the car to the frame of the unit. He had to squat down under the rear seat to insert the bolts and secure them to the frame. The back of his coveralls was soaked with perspiration as he rushed to complete the operation.

Tony Rodgers and the company engineer, Stephen Petro from Detroit also came to review the jobs at the same time.

"Mr. Petro, the problem with this job is that the operator is just too old for this type of work," Johnny said. "The committeeman in this district has met with the foreman a number of times to get this operator changed to a different job. The foreman told him he couldn't find a donkey on the dayshift that could do this job."

Stephen nodded his head in agreement.

"I gotta agree," Stephen said, turning to Tony. "This guy is old enough to retire. He shouldn't be working this labor job all day."

Stephen opened up his file to observe the time it took for that same job to be done by a young night shift worker.

"They have a young man on the same job and he works much faster," Stephen said. "This guy has 27 years of seniority, he should be placed on an off-line operation. He looks like he's in shape to work anywhere."

"There's a tug driver's job open in the freight department," Johnny said. "This worker drives his own car so I know he has a license."

The operator just finished the job and was getting out of his unit.

"How good a driver are you?" Johnny asked.

"I've been driving over forty years," the man said. "Why?"

"We're going to try to get you off this job and move you into the freight department as a tug driver," Johnny said.

"That's great, this job is getting to be rough lately," the operator said, wiping his brow.

"We could resolve this grievance if the operator is transferred to the freight department on the tug job," Johnny said to the men.

Tony was annoyed by the suggestion and wouldn't show that Johnny outsmarted him. He nodded his head and called the foreman over.

"Get your utility man on Rob's job," Tony said. "We're transferring him to the freight department. Put the new man that we just hired as his replacement."

As they were walking to review the next job, Paul Larsen remarked that the incident didn't take long to resolve.

"Please don't take that as an indication of how things run around here," Johnny said. "Tony has been terrible to work with. But as long as there is a strike threat hanging over their heads, they'll give."

Before they walked 10 feet down the aisle, a worker stopped them to complain.

"Johnny, I saw someone go up the panel control box to speed up the line," the worker said. "Our committeeman wasn't with him. I'd appreciate it if you would check the line speed, to see that it's correct. I'm having a tough time doing my operation, since that guy went up there."

Johnny took out his watch and timed the speed of the line and was annoyed when he saw that the line was going faster than the agreed line speed. He called the foreman over and instructed him to get the time study man to slow the line down to the agreed line speed. In a matter of minutes, a time study engineer came over and corrected the speed of the line to the agreed line speed.

"Were you the one who sped the line up a half hour ago?" Johnny asked the foreman.

"No," the foreman said. "I hate to name names, but I don't want the wrong person accused. Pete Reynolds sped it up. I happened to be in the office when you called and I came right over. The line was a little fast but I got it right on the money now."

"Thanks, would you tell Pete that he's never to go in the panel control box without a committeeman present," Johnny said. "I'm in a meeting with your boss and I'm going to blow my top on what Pete did. That's a big no-no."

"I'll relay your message," the foreman said.

Johnny walked over to Paul who was talking to some of the workers.

"Paul, I'm sorry about the hold up," Johnny said. "Now we'll have to hustle through the rest of the jobs or we'll be late to the meeting."

"While you were timing the line speed, a group of workers expressed their dissatisfaction with the strike vote being called," Paul said. "They're saying this isn't the right time to call for a strike. Shades of the past from my old plant. There's never a right time to call a strike when you're going to lose money to prove your point. They're pissed off at Rocky and Lou, so don't do anything in haste. You're a good building chairman, so be careful how you handle yourself in this meeting."

He stopped in the aisle with a confused expression on his face.

"Why aren't Rocky and Lou out here with us?" Paul asked. "They're the key to this whole affair."

"They're afraid to face the membership," Johnny said. "This wasn't part of their plan when they first lodged their complaint against Roger. They figured that I wouldn't do anything about it. Then they would go behind the tier racks to tell the members that I didn't have the balls to take the company on. Now they got the tiger by the tail and don't know what to do about it."

Paul didn't want to get involved in an internal union fight. He knew that Rocky and Lou have been responsible in dividing the union to make Johnny look bad but now the attitude of the members changed to Johnny's favor. Paul's concern was to get the strike issues settled to the union's satisfaction.

The meeting began promptly in the company's conference room. Stephen Petro showed without a doubt that he was in control of the company's part.

"Tony and I reviewed all the protested jobs and we're prepared to make adjustments on many of them," Stephen said. "Some of the jobs, the employees doing a bad job at."

He shook his head in disgust.

"One of the guys was moving so slow that I thought that he wasn't going to catch up to the line," Stephen said. "That's uncalled for. We don't intend to make any adjustment on that job. Other jobs we looked at were well within the cycle of the operation. We think the standard there is fair. The bulk of the protested standard jobs, we're going to make adjustments to them."

"Johnny we saw the old-timer who was transferred to the freight department," Tony said. "He gave us a big wave as he drove by."

"See Tony, we both feel good about that move," Johnny said. "The foreman should have shown some compassion to that worker a long time ago."

Stephen separated the grievances into two separate stacks.

"I'd like to hold off on the health and safety grievances until we have the plant engineer in here with us," Stephen said. He's aware of the issues and he could explain how he's going to correct them. Let's start off with the standard grievances one-by-one."

Johnny took the standard grievances from his briefcase and placed then in front of him.

"Paul, included in this package is one dealing with the assault by one of the manager's on one of our union officials,"

Johnny said. "I doubt we'll be able to resolve any of these until Superintendent Hansen is fired or taken out of the plant."

"You know I can't be a party to this," Paul interrupted. "The strike issues are the only ones that we'll be discussing. The assault on Mr. Sargent will have to be dealt with separately and not part of this meeting."

"I'm aware of that but I want everyone to know that our demands will be very high until Roger is fired," Johnny said. "If we stay focused and positive I'm sure we can settle all the grievances today."

Lou was nervously shuffling the papers in front of him. He turned to Johnny.

"Paul is right," Lou said. "Let's take the cases one at a time to see if we can settle them. I'm sure we can work this out."

"I'd like to caucus with the union committee for a few minutes," Johnny said, standing up.

The committee gathered in the far end of the hall so they couldn't be overheard.

"Last week you came over to the union hall full of piss and vinegar demanding that we take action against Roger," Johnny fumed at Lou. "I supported you. I even allowed you to put out a bulletin condemning Roger's action and rallying the membership around you, even to the extent of a strike. I promised members that I'd get rid of Roger and I'm determined to do it. The only way we can do this is to shut the plant down legally. It's up to the company to shit or get off the pot. Now are you with me or against me?"

"Johnny, you know that I can't be any party to what you're proposing," Paul said.

"I know, we'll deal separately with the local representatives prior to settling any of the strike issues," Johnny said. "Paul, you won't be part of that meeting. We'll take our stand there with Tony and his committee. I had to make my demands clear to Stephen Petro and I expect him to put the pressure on Tony who hasn't got the balls to fire Roger. This incident is a lot more serious than the Roy affair. We'll look like pussies if we let them get away with hitting a union official and not doing something about it."

Lou didn't respond, he was staring down at the floor.

"You guys dropped this in my lap and I expect you two to back me up," Johnny said.

"Johnny you're not going to put me in a position where I'm to blame if the plant goes on strike," Rocky said. "If they offer us a fair settlement, I'm going to vote in favor of it. I'll take that stand in front of the membership."

Rocky realized he was in a Catch-22 situation.

Lou felt nervous about how this whole situation had panned out. This wasn't the way he planned it.

"I feel the same way as Rocky," Lou said. "This wasn't what I asked for when I came to your office."

"You're the one who demanded we do something," Johnny said. "You're the one who wrote the bulletin advocating strike action. Both of you guys didn't have the balls to do the right thing when Roger acted out, so you figured you would drop this hot potato in my lap. Now I'm going to do something about it. The members expect us to take the company on to preserve our leadership role. I'm determined to do that. I need your support. Now, let's stay unified in front of management."

"Johnny if these cases come to the fourth stage, they're in my jurisdiction to settle," Paul said. "At this meeting we all have an equal vote, so remember this; I won't let these cases lead to a wildcat strike. Then we'd all be in deep shit, including the international union. I'll give you every opportunity to get Roger disciplined but no strike. I promise you, I'll review every settlement very closely before I recommend any strike action to the membership."

Paul then turned to Rocky and Lou.

"Do you agree?" Paul asked. They both nodded their heads in agreement. The men returned to the conference room to address the others.

"I'm sorry it took so long, there were issues that had to be aired out," Paul said. "I want to discuss the cases we'd like to move on and when we're done, I'd like the local union committee and the local management to meet to settle the grievance regarding Roger Hansen. After the meeting, we'll come back to discuss a settlement. Is that agreeable with you, Stephen?"

"That's a favorable approach," Stephen Petro said.

"I don't intend to meet with the local committee on the Roger Hansen case as part of the strike issues," Tony said. "I'll meet with the local committee after we settle the strike issues." Johnny could tell that Tony was indicating that he wouldn't be pushed into disciplining a member of management.

"Tony, I'm in charge here," Stephen said. "After we conclude this meeting, you and your staff will meet with the local union to resolve all outstanding issues. We're building the premiere car in the nation and none of us can afford to shut down production. We're aware that your membership is dead-set against any strike. I'm sure the local union committee will take that into consideration when they meet."

"I know that you were there with Lou when he was allegedly hit by Roger," Tony said to Rocky. "You can't compare Roger Hansen to Roy Acuff because the night shift went on a wildcat strike. We both lost in that one. Two guys were fired and you lost a lot of probationary men. The night shift lost a week of work with no pay and are hungry for the buck."

Tony turned toward Johnny.

"I'm not being disrespectful toward you," Tony said. "I realize you're the president of the union and you have an obligation to protect your union committee. Rocky and Lou went at it the wrong way. If they came to me first, we wouldn't be in this position today. Paul and Joe want these grievances settled but I can't dump Roger Hansen in with the strike cases. It's against the contract and I'd be out of a job when this is over."

Tony looked toward Rocky who was averting his eyes.

"You have an election soon and a strike would negate your chances of winning," Tony said.

"I appreciate your concern for our welfare," Johnny said. "But right now I'm the president of this local and I want Roger fired."

Johnny then turned to Rocky.

"You have more than me to lose in this settlement," Johnny said. "What do you think should be done to Superintendent Hansen?"

"I feel the same way as you," Rocky said. "Something should be done about Superintendent Hansen."

Rocky turned to Tony before continuing.

"We could have pushed for a strike of the plant when Roger Hansen hit Lou but we didn't," Rocky said. "We went through the normal channels of the grievance procedure. I'm not going to ask that Superintendent Hansen be fired but he must be punished. At the very least give him time off and transfer him to another department."

"Lou, what do you want?" Johnny asked.

Lou was nervous and felt embarrassed. He wanted Roger Hansen to be disciplined but he knows a strike at the plant would kill him politically.

"I feel the same way as you, Rocky," Lou said. "Something has to be done about Superintendent Hansen. I approve of Rocky's suggestion. It's a good one. I could live with that."

"Lou, I know that you're embarrassed by this affair and I know you're in a challenging situation," Tony said. "Don't get me wrong, I can't picture you getting hit and not doing anything about it."

Lou became angry at the idea that he was lying but Tony put his hand up.

"Lou, let me finish," Tony said. "I'm not referring to you as a liar. I just have a gut feeling that you had something else in mind, but when the bell rang, you changed your mind. There were only a handful of workers there who saw this happen when the bell rang."

"Bullshit," Lou snarled.

"Let me finish," Tony said. "I know for a fact that you and Roger used to be buddies and hang out at Lord's Bar before he took the management job. As a foreman, he gave you everything you asked for when you came to him with a problem. I'd like to see both of you go back to that strong relationship. What do you say, let's sign this agreement and get back to work."

Johnny knew Tony's appealing to Lou and Rocky would impact Johnny negatively. He would be seen as being weak if Superintendent Hansen wasn't disciplined. Johnny picked up the grievances and placed them back into his briefcase.

"We're wasting our time here," Johnny said. "Tony you better get it through your head, I want Roger fired. He's not going to hit one of my union reps and get away with it."

Lou was flushed with embarrassment and just wanted the meeting to be over.

"We feel that something has to be done regarding Superintendent Hansen," Lou said. "Why don't we break for lunch so Tony can meet with Stephen to work it out."

"Let's get Paul since he's the only one that can resolve this," Johnny said. He picked up his briefcase and headed for the door.

"Tony, we'll be back in two hours," Johnny said. "I hope you can come back with some answers."

"Where are we going to eat?" Rocky asked.

"Club 17 is close and we'll be served in a hurry," Johnny said. "Why don't you give Betty a call to get us a reservation?"

Rocky walked into Tony's office where Marie was busy typing the strike settlement agreement. He noticed through the open doorway that Paul Larsen was giving someone the okay on the agreement.

"Marie, I'm calling the union office," Rocky said.

She nodded her head and continued typing. He leaned over close to her so no one could hear and whispered.

"Is that Stephen in there with Paul Larsen?" Rocky asked.

"Yes," she whispered back, looking around to see if anyone was close by.

"I won't be able to see you tonight," she added. "This agreement will take hours to complete."

He nodded his head and called Betty, asking her to secure them a lunch reservation. After he hung up the phone he turned to Marie.

"Marie, please tell Mr. Larsen that we're ready to go to lunch," Rocky said.

Paul emerged soon after and he and Rocky left for lunch. Rocky walked with Paul to the parking lot where they met up with Johnny. Johnny suggested they all ride in his car. Paul reiterated his position that he wasn't going to get involved in taking sides with their internal union dispute. On the car ride to the restaurant neither of the men spoke of the union issues. The restaurant host met them at the door and addressed Johnny.

"Mr. Romanek," he said. "Your secretary mentioned that you're pressed for time, so I took the liberty of placing you at the far end of the room so you won't be interrupted. The waitress will take your orders immediately."

The men all ordered the same thing, turkey club sandwiches with fries and tomato soup. They also ordered a round of beers.

When the waitress left, Lou turned to Johnny.

"Johnny, I went along with you in that meeting, but I want to make clear that I don't intend to strike the plant if Roger isn't fired," Lou said.

"I feel the same way," added Rocky. He turned to Paul for his opinion. "Paul, what are your thoughts?" Rocky wanted support from the international union.

"I think we got a hell of an agreement and we should sign it," Paul said. "I'll back you guys up all the way in order to get Roger disciplined."

Johnny waited until the waitress finished putting the drinks in front of them. When she left, he turned to the men.

"I see you guys got your minds made up," Johnny said. "The company is giving us a good settlement because we have them over a barrel. If we stick to our guns, the company will have to fire Roger. Stephen Petro isn't going to allow them to shut the plant down since the public is invested in this car. Under no uncertain terms will I sign this settlement unless he's fired. Paul, let's protect the dignity of this union."

After lunch at the restaurant the men returned to resume the meeting. When Johnny entered the conference room, the company representatives were seated and drinking coffee. A quick exchange occurred between Paul and Stephen indicating that an agreement could be made. When everyone was seated, Stephen spoke.

"We decided that Roger won't be in the plant for the rest of the week," Stephen said. "To satisfy the union he will be transferred to another department. This should suffice and please the union and membership. What do you say?"

"We could put out a bulletin that Roger was disciplined for a week," Lou said. He wanted the company to know that he would settle without a strike.

"I'd urge you not to do that," Tony said. "All I said was that Roger wouldn't be in the plant for the rest of the week. The members could read between the lines that Roger got time off. So let it go at that."

Tony wanted to protect Roger from humiliation from the rank-and-file members. He knew how the workers could jeer management that stepped out of line.

"We got a settlement," Paul said. "Have your secretary type up the agreement and we'll sign it at a formal meeting tomorrow."

"Paul, I hope you're not including me in this," Johnny asserted. "My position has been clear from start. I won't allow a member of management to hit a union official without being fired.

The company always took the position that when an hourly worker hit a member of management the penalty was discharge. Why are we changing that policy when it's the other way around? Giving Roger a week off with pay is a vacation. It's a reward. I'm not signing anything unless he's fired."

"Johnny, I know how you feel but Rocky and Lou agreed to settle," Paul said. "Lou was the one who got hit and he's willing to let this go. Why don't you sign to make this unanimous when we present this to the membership?"

Paul was determined to get past this issue.

Johnny shook his head and picked up his briefcase, leaving the room.

"The agreement is binding if the majority of the committee sign," Rocky said. "I'm sure we could get the membership to approve this settlement."

"Rocky, you've been buddies with him for years," Stephen said about Johnny. "Why don't you try convincing him to sign the agreement before tomorrow's meeting?"

Stephen knew how important it was to have Johnny's signature on the agreement. Without his signature the union could override the agreement.

Rocky knew Johnny better than anyone and he knew that once Johnny made up his mind about something, there was no changing it. He also knew that Johnny was aware that Rocky and Lou had been bad-mouthing him for months. Rocky knew he had no sway with Johnny. But he told Stephen he would try to talk to his friend.

The membership meeting was called on a Saturday during a time that there was no production scheduled, so all the members could attend. Every seat in the hall was occupied, the aisles had members standing in them and there were members standing ten deep in the parking lot wanting to hear what the union was going to do.

Johnny anticipated the crowd so arranged for loud speakers on the outside of the building so everyone could hear what transpired during the meeting. Many came because they didn't want to go on strike. Others came to see the position that the union would take when a member of management hit one of their union representatives. There were others who wanted to see the union leadership fight amongst themselves.

Johnny opened the meeting and outlined the tentative strike agreement. He gave his reasons why he would not sign the agreement. He took a firm position that the union would be showing a sign of weakness if they didn't fire Roger.

The members began to rally behind Johnny before Paul Larsen requested to speak. He outlined that the agreement was a fair one and that the union members were the victors. He explained that the international union could not participate in the strike issues involving Roger Hansen because of the national contract. The members understood his position and applauded.

Lou Sargent spoke after Paul, explaining that he was satisfied that Roger Hansen had been punished appropriately and the strike issue was settled in favor of the union. Rocky stood up immediately and concurred with Lou's position. The members were now favoring the settlement and were anxious to vote. Johnny again spoke passionately for the members to turn down the settlement. He stood firm that he wanted Roger to be fired. The tide began to turn again as the members began to hoot and holler in favor of the union taking a firm position against the company and to take a strike vote.

Paul saw the members rallying behind Johnny. He felt that a secret ballot vote would allow the members to sober up and vote against any strike action. His goal was to not lose a paycheck. He ordered the trustees of the union to hand out paper ballots to every member in the hall and in the parking lot. He explained to the members that this was a secret ballot vote. All everyone had to do was mark "yes" if they wanted a strike or "no" if they were against it.

The members in the hall were the first to vote. They placed their ballot into a large sealed cardboard box that was set up in front. Then the members who were in the parking lot came into the hall and cast their votes. Most of the members cheered Johnny's position and gave a victory salute. Their gestures indicated that they were in agreement with Johnny's stance.

It took hours for the committee to count the votes. The members lingered outside the union hall, some went by the river to scale rocks into it. Others went to the bars close by to drink. After hours of waiting the final count came in. The final vote was 83 percent in favor of accepting the agreement.

There was sigh of relief at the outcome and members drifted out of the hall and parking lot satisfied by the result of the vote. Many expressed their dissatisfaction with Rocky and Lou who they believe took a gutless position. Paul was satisfied with the result. He knew what the outcome would be in a secret ballot. He also knew that Johnny came out of this a winner.

Rocky and Lou realized that most of the members were disappointed in them, so they left the building after the results were announced to avoid being questioned or embarrassed by their stance. They stood on the side of the building near a small group of supporters. Johnny remained inside for some time talking and answering questions. Despite the results, he realized he had won in this incident. The membership had all agreed with his stance, but felt a strike at this time wasn't appropriate. He left the hall feeling ten feet tall.

Chapter 17
Year 1965

When Johnny walked into union headquarters, Betty Morrow broke into a smile, waving a large manila envelope in the air. She had a pencil stuck in her hair, her eyeglasses propped above her forehead and papers strewn all over the top of her desk. She handed him the envelope.

"I think we finally got the decision on the demonstration," she said.

"This should be interesting," Johnny said, taking the envelope from her. He cut open the envelope and extracted the memorandum.

"Betty, I got the feeling that he'll give us a good decision because of the Civil Rights Movement taking storm in the U.S."

Johnny walked toward his office while reading the decision and stopped.

"Betty, we have both Manny and Wilton's phone numbers in our files," Johnny said. "Would you please give them a call and let them know that I would like to see them as soon as possible?"

Betty retreated to her office where Johnny heard her rustling through files and dialing the phone. She reappeared in his office minutes later.

"I contacted both Wilton Hatter and Manny Head," Betty said. "They said they would be here within an hour. They asked about the decision but I told them you would give them the results when they got here. They both were anxious to know the results so I guess they'll be rushing to get here."

Johnny was feeling uneasy about what the men's reaction would be when they found out they were both reinstated, but with no back pay.

"Betty, call the diner to order sweets buns and some coffee," Johnny said. "They'll have something to do with their mouths besides screaming at me. They are going to say the whiteys sold them down the river."

"I'm sure you won't have any trouble handling them," Betty said. "You did just fine during the demonstration. I'm sure they're both aware that by shutting the plant down, there would be some repercussions."

Johnny took his jacket off and placed it on the back of his chair. He sat down and began re-reading the decision while loosening his tie and the top button of his shirt. He re-read many paragraphs to get a clear understanding of why the umpire granted their cases but with no back pay. He was interrupted with a soft knock on the door.

"Mr. Hatter and Mr. Hand are here to see you," Betty said, opening the door.

Johnny saw the men standing outside the door. Both were dressed in matching blue denim pants and a jacket with similar peaked hats. Wilton was six feet tall, clean-shaven with a slight hook to his nose. He was very muscular with not a trace of fat. He stood erect outside the door with a knapsack strung across his back. His dark eyes were blazing. He must have known that the news was not all good.

Manny was a very straightforward type of person. He was five feet seven inches tall, and very thin with a large black beard and sparse hair. He was carrying a brown leather case that was strung around his shoulder with a long strap.

"Please come in and sit down," Johnny said.

Johnny picked up the decision from the desk and handed each of them a copy.

"This ruling came in this morning and I've been going over it for the past hour," Johnny said. "You have both been reinstated with full benefits and full seniority. Blue Cross and Blue Shield will pay any outstanding medical bills that were incurred during your termination in full. You'll both be required to take a physical by the medical department to return to work and you can return today."

Manny took his knapsack off his shoulder and threw it on the sofa. Wilton sat down next to him to read. Manny went directly to the last paragraph and became irate.

"This decision is bullshit," Manny said. "That fucker ruled in our favor but didn't give us any back pay. There's no way we could be wrong when the fucking company fired Acuff for what he did. They admitted that we were right when we shut the plant down."

Johnny ignored his outburst and buzzed Betty to come into the office. When she entered he asked her to make two copies of the decision so Wilton and Manny could have their own copy.

"Sure," Betty said. "Also, the man from the diner is here with the coffee and sweet buns. I'll make these copies while you eat."

Betty returned with a tray of buns and three containers of coffee.

"Read the decision in its entirety and you can see that the umpire never thought that you were right in shutting the plant down," Johnny explained. "His position actually was that the company dragged its feet too long before they took the position to remove Acuff from the plant. The umpire highlighted the flaws in the company's position especially when they refused to bring Ed Hubot in to testify. The reasons he gave for bringing you two back had to do with the civil rights movement sweeping the country."

Johnny picked up the memorandum and flipped a few pages to a specific paragraph.

"Here he ruled on the paper penalties that were handed out by the company," Johnny said. "The umpire held that the company was justified in terminating the probationary men who were on a trial period with the company."

"Were there any whites involved with probationary discharges?" Manny asked.

"I have to get back to you on that," Johnny said. "But I think the answer is no."

"This is bullshit," Manny repeated.

"It's the best they can do," Wilton muttered.

"I don't intend to go back to work until I'm paid for all the time we lost while we were on the street," Manny said. "I want you to come into the plant with me and go to labor relations and demand that they pay us for all time lost."

"That opinion is binding to all the parties and I'm not going to spend my time blowing smoke rings," Johnny said. "I already made arrangements for you to take your physical."

"Johnny, I can't go back to work for another two weeks," Wilton said. "I started a project for the city of Newark. I'm committed to get it done."

"I'll get you the two week extension but you'll have to take the physical today," Johnny said.

"I'll take the physical but then I'm heading straight to my lawyer and labor board to sue," Manny said. "As long as you don't have the balls to see Tony Rodgers, I'll handle this myself. I intend to get paid for my time off."

"You do what you have to," Johnny said. "All I can do is contact Mr. Rodgers to get you the two week extension. Now, I have a lot of work to do, so why don't you guys go over to the company to handle your business."

After the men left Johnny completed the necessary paperwork. He then called Tony's office.

"Tony, I sent Wilton Hatter and Manny Head to take their physicals," Johnny said. "Wilton needs a two week extension before he comes back."

Tony was sitting behind his desk with a big cigar in his mouth and his feet propped up on his desk.

"Johnny these guys are not going to fight the company," Tony said. "I had the employment department type up the two week extension for both of them."

"I don't understand?" Johnny said.

"Manny already came into my office with the same line," Tony said. "When I showed him the report showing evidence that he was working for the Free Press in Newark, he just laughed. He was making 100 dollars a week, which is a lot more than he was earning here. When I confronted him he said you can't blame a man for trying. I feel that we saw the last of Manny He has a degree in journalism from NYU and I hear that he's working toward a master's degree."

"I knew he was going to college but I wasn't aware he already had a degree," Johnny said. "But I wouldn't sell those two short. Both are dedicated black militants and they're up to their old tricks again. We are lucky the blacks picked Otto to lead the movement and not Manny."

Tony sat back in his chair and leaned against the wall deep in thought.

"Johnny you have to admit that you came out of that demonstration looking really good," Tony said. "My labor representatives told me that both black and white workers think you took a good position when you formed the good will committee."

Tony paused to gather his thoughts before making the next point.

"I know we are meeting on new local agreements shortly," Tony said. "I hope you will take it easy on the company with your demands. When are you going to send us a copy of them?"

Johnny cleared his throat.

"Betty is in the process of typing them up now," he said. "You'll get them at the end of the week. I heard that you intend to propose to try to take away something from the existing local agreements."

Johnny paused before continuing.

"Listen, don't waste your time in submitting the demands to us," Johnny said. "We don't intend to take any backward steps in these negotiations. We have ten major demands and the main one is to install air conditioning at the plant."

"You have got to be out of your mind," Tony snapped. "First, we can't afford it and second is that we'd be recirculating the carbon monoxide through the system. Everyone would get sick!"

Tony paused before telling Johnny to hold on because another call was coming in. In a few minutes he was back on the line.

"That was Detroit," Tony said. "They asked if we submitted the local agreement demands. I told them you said you would submit them by the end of the week."

While Johnny was on the phone with Tony, Pat Fager and the entire night committee were standing by Betty's desk waiting to speak with Johnny. When he concluded his conversation with Tony, Pat was buzzed into his office.

They all walked in and sat on the sofa. Burt Landers was the spokesman, and he spoke first.

"Johnny, we all had a vote and agreed that Freddie McCoy should be the night plant committeeman," Burt said.

"Are you nuts?" asked Johnny, shaking his head in bewilderment.

"We understand he doesn't belong to our caucus," Burt said. "But he's the most qualified committeeman on nights. He used to be the chairman at the Chester plant before they shut the plant down. Since his transfer to Clinton, he's really played it straight with us. He's the only committeeman who didn't play politics during the demonstration and he supports you. We've been working on him for months to join our caucus. He's knowledgeable on the contract and could be an asset for us at the bargaining table. He assured us that he would play it straight with you all the way, not like Rocky who went behind your back and stabbed you."

"I hope you guys know what you're doing," Johnny said, rubbing his eyes. "He's beholden to Lou Sargent for getting him elected as committeeman."

Johnny paused as a new idea came to him.

"Burt, you've been a committeeman for years, why don't you take the job?" Johnny said. "I'd feel a lot more comfortable with you at my side, than Freddie. I already have thorns in my side with Rocky and Lou. I need a strong allies on my team."

"Freddie has more on the ball than I do," Burt explained. "He's been guiding us on nights and the only time we had to call you was when we had the wildcat strike. He knows how to handle the company and we have faith in him."

"Freddie's a drunk," Johnny said. "When I came on the night shift, he was sauced to the gills. I need a guy at the table who has his wits about him at all times. I admit he knows the contract but I need someone who's going to back me up on our local demands. Freddie has everything to lose there. He represents car delivery, which is known as the ideal department. It's lily-white and has the most overtime opportunities. Everyone in the plant wants to work there."

"Johnny, I was there when the committee gave him the chairmanship and he took a position that he was in favor of the promotional agreement and that we honor seniority rights," Pat said. "He said they had a similar agreement in the Chester plant which the members loved. Although I'm not a committeeman, I was there when he made that statement. I feel the same as the committee, that he'd back you all the way. Freddie is disillusioned with Rocky. After the Roger Hansen affair, there's a good chance Freddie will break away from them entirely."

"I'll go along with you, but I don't have the best feeling about this," Johnny said. "The decision to appoint a night shift plant committeeman is up to me. What about Mike Ferrera, didn't he want the job?"

"We asked Mike before we selected Freddie but he said that being on the midnight shift would cause a problem," Pat said. "His shift ends at 8:30 in the morning and most of the meetings with the company usually start at 11 a.m. He'd never get any sleep. He also cast his vote for Freddie."

When the meeting broke up, Johnny and the committeemen went into the plant. While walking down 'A' aisle someone behind the racks started shouting "boo!" at the union members. They ran toward the booing and they saw a fight happening behind the racks. They came up to a young man who was punching another worker. Johnny ran over to break up the fight.

"Mr. Romanek, this prick was hiding behind the rack booing you and he's done this before," Tommy Wright said, catching his breath. "We didn't catch him until now. He's nothing but a company stooge. Our foreman is always writing us up for any minor infraction but this bum can get away with anything. He's not a union man."

Moody Sullivan didn't deny that he was the culprit behind the booing. Tommy was standing close with clenched fists, ready to keep fighting. Johnny knew Lou Sargent was the type to do things undercover. Johnny realized that Lou was behind this mischief and got Moody to harass Johnny.

Tommy Wright felt indebted to Johnny since Johnny secured him the job at the plant. Moody was bleeding around his right eye and Johnny told him to go to the medics to get treated. Moody was embarrassed when he saw so many workers had witnessed the confrontation. They were all looking at him in disgust before returning to their jobs.

"Tommy do you still fight professionally?" Johnny asked Tommy.

"No, I quit a year ago," Tommy said. "My wife was upset with me coming home all the time all banged up. I wasn't a real contender and I wasn't making enough money in any of the fights I got. I took a lot of beatings but I wasn't too good so it wasn't worth it to me. Another thing that made me quit is that my wife is expecting a baby. I need a steady income and medical coverage when the baby comes."

"That sounds like the right choice for you and your family," Johnny said, patting Tommy's shoulder.

As they were approaching the chassis line they could hear Freddie McCoy's booming voice cursing out a foreman. Freddie was a man in his sixties, who wore glasses and was forty pounds overweight. He was highly respected by his constituents and feared by the foreman because of his wide knowledge of the contract. He knew every angle of the book on how to protect his workers and he did just that. Freddie had a very bad temper, especially when he was drunk, and never hesitated to take a swing at anyone who disagreed with him. Johnny smiled at the stories he heard and was amused by Freddie, who told the men stories about how many men wouldn't fight him for fear that they would kill him or give him a heart attack.

"Mac, let's go over to the coffee machine so we can talk," Johnny said to Freddie. There were empty chairs and a table nearby. Pat bought coffee for everyone as they sat down to talk.

"Freddie, you're aware that the night committeemen selected you as the night plant committeeman," Johnny said. "I want you to know that I'm not too keen on the assignment because you're not from our caucus. All my guys feel comfortable with you and said that you wouldn't play politics with the job so I'm going to along with them. Are you interested in the job?"

"They are absolutely right," Freddie said. "You won't be sorry. I like your ideas for the coming contract and the local agreements. I'll make you the same promise I made to the committeemen. I'll back you up 100 percent at the bargaining table and I won't play politics with the job."

"We could use your knowledge at the table," Johnny admitted. "Lou and Rocky have been tough on me in the last year and they didn't offer a single suggestion for our local agreement. They're hoping I fall flat on my ass but I assure you that that won't happen. As soon as this contract is settled, we'll be going into our own elections. I'd like you to come into our caucus. We could offer you a lot more than the Rocky caucus. I believe your ideas of unionism are parallel to ours."

"Johnny, I don't want to lead you astray," Freddie said. "I'm beholden to Lou for getting me elected to his old committeeman job in the chassis department. Without his help, I wouldn't have made it. However, I'm not a Rocky Durango fan and I don't approve of his sneaky union bullshit. I guarantee you that I won't play politics since it will involve the welfare of our union members."

"I appreciate your frankness and I hope after you see how I operate that you'll change your mind regarding your loyalty to Lou," Johnny said. "Just keep an open mind and I'm sure we'll make a good team at the bargaining table."

Johnny shook hands with Freddie and left. Johnny left the group but didn't get far. A utility worker approached Johnny with a worried look on his face.

"The company is holding T.J. O'Leary and Leo Florio in the trim office on charges that they sabotaged the line," the worker said. "The superintendent called labor relations to fire both of them."

Johnny knew both members intimately and refused to believe either of them would do any damage to company property. A utility worker told him the men were both in the office with Superintendent Mallero waiting for labor relations to come.

"Thanks," Johnny said. "I better get up there and sort this situation out."

When Johnny got to the office, he saw both men with bowed heads and worried expressions on their faces. Superintendent Mallero stared at the both with an angry look. Mallero's office was built above the five assembly lines so he could observe every section of his department. A large lighted board was placed in the center of the station which had all the lines broken by numbers. When a number lit up, he knew exactly where the stoppage was. Each foreman was responsible for his section and it was his job to see that the production flowed smoothly or the foreman had to answer to him.

Superintendent Mallero looked up when Johnny came into his office.

"I'm glad you were here in the plant tonight," Superintendent Mallero said. "For the last two weeks someone was jamming line two and three, causing damage to the units and stopping the line, causing us to lose production. We had a security guard hiding in a freight car next to those two lines with a clear view of those lines. He observed Leo Florio and T.J. O'Leary coming across those lines at 6 p.m. and they shoved the back end of the unit cross wise to cause it to jam, shutting the line down. It took us six maintenance men to pull the body out of the chain drive and get the unit back on the line. We lost fifteen minutes of production. Labor relations are on their way up. I called for the committeeman to represent them."

"I'd like to see both of you outside to hear your version of what happened," Johnny said.

Johnny told Superintendent Mallero that they would be outside his office and for the committeemen to join them when they got there. Outside with the two men, Johnny walked to the far end of the platform for privacy.

"Tell me what happened," Johnny said, leaning against the steel railing. "I want the truth. The way Superintendent Mallero is talking, he caught you both red-handed. If you tell me the truth, no bullshit, I can defend you."

"Johnny, a guy had just come to relieve me of my job and I was walking behind the unit on my way to the bathroom with Leo right behind me," T.J. said. "Just as I got to the middle of the unit, the body of the car lurched to the side and right at me. I put my hand up against the car so I wouldn't get hurt. I don't have any idea how the unit moved so fast, I figured Leo did it because he was right behind me. When I saw the unit was going to jam into the chain drive, I ran away so I wouldn't be blamed for it. I didn't see anyone around so I headed up to the coffee machine to get a cup of coffee and to eat my sandwich. A few minutes later Superintendent Mallero and a security guard came over to me and accused me of being the one who pushed the body sideways into the chain drive, causing the body to jam. Superintendent Mallero told me that as soon as I finished my break I was to go to his office for a hearing. Johnny, you know me a long time and in all those years, I have never gotten into any trouble in the plant. I would never sabotage anything in the plant. What do I have to gain if I jammed the line? I swear to you, I didn't do what he's accusing me of."

"Is that all that happened?" Johnny asked.

"I swear to you, that's all that happened with me," T.J. said. "I didn't stay to see if the unit got jammed into the chain drive. I went to the coffee machine."

"Leo, tell me what you saw and don't leave anything out," Johnny asked Leo Florio.

Leo was a man in his fifties and spoke in broken English. He became immediately nervous and had a difficult time explaining himself.

"Mr. Romanek, I was walking behind T.J. when the body of a car came flying at me," Leo said. "I grabbed the back of the car to stop from hitting me and I saw T.J. running away. I figured

I better get away from here before the company blames me for this. I went to the bathroom instead of staying there. When I was coming out of the bathroom a guard was standing at the bottom of the stairs. He asked me my name and my badge number. I asked him why and he told me that he saw me and another guy push the job around and jam it."

Leo became flustered and his face turned red from anger.

"I got real mad at the guard and I called him a fucking liar," Leo said. "I told him that I didn't jam the job. Then the guard asked me why didn't I stop to straighten the body so it wouldn't jam the line. Johnny, I swear to you, I had to piss so badly. That's all I was doing. The guard told me he was watching me from a freight car and saw me push the body into the chain drive. He then told me to go to the trim office for a hearing. I told him to fuck himself because I didn't do anything wrong and then I went back to work. He followed me and came back with Superintendent Mallero, telling me that I had to go to a hearing with labor relations. So now I'm here."

Leo worked himself up to the point where Johnny put his hand on his shoulder to calm him.

"Leo, just stay calm and finish telling me what happened," Johnny said.

"Johnny, I'd never do anything to the company," Leo said. "They pay me good money and I need this job real bad. I don't call out ever, I come to work every day and I do a good job. I come to work even if I'm sick so why would I pull shit like jamming up the line? I swear to you on my mother's grave that I didn't jam the job. Maybe I should have tried to stop the jam but I really had to take a piss real bad. There was no man to relieve me of my job. If I had stayed, the company would bring me in for a hearing for leaving my station."

Johnny was certain that both men were telling the truth. They weren't the type to sabotage a job. What he couldn't understand was how they were both there and weren't able to explain how the job got twisted around. Johnny noticed Franklin Todd with labor relations, coming up the stairs.

"Labor relations is here, so let's go in and see what they charge you with," Johnny said.

Franklin went over to the desk and placed his pad down while pulling up a chair next to Superintendent Mallero to sit down. He motioned toward a chair for Johnny to sit on.

"Johnny, I'd like to hear the cases individually," Franklin said. "Let's talk to Mr. O'Leary first. Mr. Florio, would you please wait outside until we're done in here with Mr. O'Leary?"

Franklin motioned for T.J. to be seated. He then addressed Superintendent Mallero.

"Let's hear the charges and why we're conducting this hearing," Franklin said.

"Charley, I have you in here for deliberately sabotaging the line and making us lose production," Superintendent Mallero said.

T.J. immediately became furious and jumped from his chair, approaching Superintendent Mallero.

"That's a damn lie," T.J. said. "I never sabotaged any line."

Franklin Todd and Johnny stood up to restrain T.J. and calm him down before they continued.

"Mr. O'Leary, we'll have no more outbursts while I conduct this hearing," Franklin Todd said. "We'll listen to both sides of the story. If you have any questions or disagreements, hold them until you get a chance to explain."

He turned to Superintendent Joe Mallero.

"The same goes for you," Franklin said. Superintendent Mallero just nodded his head.

T.J. became nervous as he realized the seriousness of the charges.

"Johnny, I don't know what's going on," T.J. said. "I'm not going to take the rap for something I didn't do."

"T.J., we'll get to the bottom of this," Johnny said. "Let Joe give the company's version of what happened. Then we'll tell our version of the story."

Johnny realized T.J. was in a bad predicament since he was innocent but still in fear about losing his job. T.J.'s face was deadly white with fear.

Superintendent Mallero resumed his statement and related all the facts leading to the hearing.

"Franklin, if we find Mr. O'Leary guilty, I recommend that he be fired," Superintendent Mallero said.

"Joe, let's not jump to conclusions," Johnny said. "Hear our part of the story."

"Johnny, I'll make sure that Mr. O'Leary gets a fair hearing," Franklin said. "We're not here to get anyone innocently punished. We're here to get to the bottom of this incident. We can't afford to be losing production and not doing something about it. Mr. O'Leary, please continue with your side of the story."

"It's like I told Johnny outside," T.J. said. He outlined everything he had already told Johnny. After he was finished he addressed Superintendent Mallero.

"Joe, you know I'm a relief man in my section and I get more breaks than anyone, so why would I jeopardize my job by sabotaging the line?" T.J. said. "I swear to all of you that I didn't push that unit."

"I agree that you had nothing to gain by gapping the line," Superintendent Mallero asked. "What puzzles me is why did you run away?"

"Joe, I was on my break and I figured someone was fooling around," T.J. said. "At that time, I thought that Leo Florio did it but now I'm sure he didn't. I know that I should have stopped to prevent the jam but I didn't. That's the only mistake I made and I'm sorry for that."

"I've heard enough," Franklin said, throwing up his hand. "T.J. would you please tell Mr. Florio to come in."

Leo came in and occupied the chair that T.J. had just vacated. Superintendent Mallero repeated the same charges and this time Leo went into a rage, rising from his chair and going after the superintendent.

"I know you're the superintendent but you're not going to lie and try to blame me for something I didn't do," Leo snarled.

Johnny had a hold of his arm and dragged him back into his chair.

"Leo, take it easy," Johnny said. "Joe, you can see by both of their strong reactions that they didn't have anything to do with the sabotage."

"Johnny, I don't see nothing," Superintendent Mallero said. "I'd be going through the same act if I were caught. All I know is that both these guys were next to the job that was jammed. I'd like to hear what Leo has to say."

Leo repeated the same story that T.J. did.

"Joe, I'm sorry I lost my temper," Leo said. "You've known me a long time, did I ever do anything wrong that required you to bring me into your office?"

"No, but maybe this is the first time you got caught," replied Joe.

"Leo, why didn't you go to the office when the guard told you to?" Franklin asked.

"I couldn't," Leo said. "When I left my job to take a leak, I wasn't on relief. I had to get back quickly so I wouldn't miss my operation."

He looked toward Johnny.

"You know the company tells us to take orders from the foreman," Leo explained. "I wasn't running away from the scene, I was running back to my job. Joe, I came right to your office when you told me to. I wasn't trying to hide because I didn't do anything wrong."

"Leo you're not in here for that," Joe said. "You're in here for something more serious."

"We've heard enough to judge this case," Franklin said. "Joe and I are going to discuss this case and we'll make our decision."

"I've known both these guys for many years and I feel they're telling the truth," Johnny said. "Can you give me an hour to get to the bottom of this? If I can prove they weren't responsible for the jamming, would you drop the charges?"

"Fine, but I don't want either of them to leave the area," Joe said.

"That's fair enough," Johnny said. "I'll see to it that the sabotage will be stopped."

Johnny left the room and headed to the start of Line #3. He called all the workers together.

"Look men, I don't know who's jamming the line but it has to stop," Johnny said. "The company has Leo Florio and T.J. O'Leary in on charges of sabotaging the line and are about to fire them for something that they didn't do. I want you to tell me who's doing it. I assure you that nothing will be done to the guy that did it. But I can't let them fire two union guys who are innocent.

A utility man in the area and a leader in the section stepped forward.

"Johnny, it's the hippy who is jamming the line," the man said. "He's the guy who sits in the bottom of the stock rack by the crossover line and when the unit comes up, he braces his back against the steel support and places his foot on the skid under the unit and gives it a shove to make it go sideways which jams the line. Then he crawls out of the rack and back to his operation. The reason no one ever knew it was him was because the time study engineer arrives just before the lunch hour is over and he goes to the panel board and raises the line speed to make up for any loss of production. That's the only way we could even the speed out."

"Why is the hippy jeopardizing his job over this?" Johnny asked. "If he's protesting the way things are done around here, we have a grievance procedure to correct any wrong-doing by the company. I'll make sure the company engineers won't speed up the line anymore. I'll also make sure your committeeman will be informed and he'll be there at lunch time to check the line speed every day."

"I'm going to bring Superintendent Mallero and labor relations to the line and walk them through the same way T.J. and Tom did," Johnny said, addressing the utility man. "I want you to demonstrate the jamming of the unit just like you saw. I'll explain that you had nothing to do with the jamming but you're willing to show them how it was done. My main concern is to see to it that both of our union brothers don't get fired."

Johnny returned to the trim office to explain what he found out. He asked them to go with him to see how it was done. He told them the utility man was cooperating and saw the entire incident take place and wanted to see that justice was done.

As they approached the line, they observed the security guard in the area. Johnny asked him to take the same position in the freight car where he observed the incident. The guard looked toward Superintendent Mallero for guidance and nodded his head. The security guard resumed his position in the freight car.

The utility man positioned himself in the stock rack. Johnny instructed Superintendent Mallero and Franklin Todd to walk the same way Leo and T.J. did. They both assumed the same position requested. Johnny gave the utility man the signal to kick the unit, which then went flying right at them. Quickly they both put their hands up on the unit to prevent injury. Johnny and the men ran to the unit to straighten it before it jammed into the chain drive. Johnny called the guard out and asked him if that was the same way it happened before.

"Mr. Mallero and Mr. Todd did it the same way as the other two did," the guard said.

Johnny was relieved at the guard's statement.

"Thanks very much, Johnny," Superintendent Mallero said, shaking his head. "Looks like I was wrong in accusing those two of sabotage but they were wrong in running away. I gave Johnny my word that if he proved me wrong, I'd drop the charges. I'm going to send them back to their jobs and pay them for all the lost time I had them in here for the hearing. Now tell me, who's the bastard who caused the jamming?"

"Joe, you know me better than that," Johnny said. "I assure you that it will never happen again. I'm going to talk to him personally. Joe, thanks for keeping your word."

Johnny shook hands with the men then walked over to where the hippie was working.

"I'll make sure the committeeman checks the line speed every day right after the lunch break," Johnny said. "I will go after the time standard man's ass for tampering with the line speed without the committeeman present. If you see anyone going to the panel box without the committeeman there, give me a call and I'll be over to correct it. It's not worth sacrificing your job to correct a misdemeanor by a time standard man. T.J. and Leo were lucky I was around tonight. But if you do it again, I'm not sure I can help you out."

The hippie broke into a small smile, indicating that he recognized his complaint was being honored. He shook hands with Johnny and thanked him.

Johnny looked down at his watch, realizing Ann would be very upset at him for not coming home to supper with his family when he promised her he'd be on time. He walked quickly through the plant to quickly exit.

As he was just about to exit, a member called out.

"Johnny, can I see you for a moment?" the member asked. "I just walked into the medic department to be treated, but the nurse refused to treat me and called me an animal."

Johnny was confused as he looked at the man. The man had a dirty rag covering his hand and was bleeding. The nurses on the night were professionals and there was never any complaint about their willingness to treat the workers. He could see that there was no end that night to the problems in the plant.

"Come on," Johnny sighed. "Let's go in and get you treated."

Johnny went over to the nurse that the worker pointed out.

"Margaret, why wouldn't you treat him?" Johnny asked. "He was sent by his foreman for an injury to his hand. You see it, it's bleeding quite badly."

"We're not working in some kind of a back alley," the nurse said. "Look at his T-shirt. Men like him have no respect for women working in this plant."

For the first time Johnny noticed the man's shirt which included a graphic image and text. Johnny shook his head in disbelief as he realized what bothered Margaret. Johnny walked over to the man.

"Come on, turn that shirt inside out," Johnny said. "You know better than that. I'm sure you wouldn't wear that T-shirt in front of your mother, so don't wear it in here. We now have women working in the plant."

The man looked mortified.

"I didn't mean to offend anyone," he mumbled.

"Just change your shirt," Johnny said.

He put the shirt inside out and shook hands with Johnny, thanking him. Hours after he had promised Ann, he finally made it home.

"Look who finally got home," Ann said as soon as she saw her husband. "What's your excuse this time? We ate a cold supper over five hours ago. You've heard of that little invention called a telephone, right? Or is it that Ford wouldn't allow you to use their phone?"

Johnny walked over to his wife to kiss her but she turned her cheek to him.

"You wouldn't believe me if I told you what I went through," Johnny said.

He sat down at the kitchen table as Ann took out the steaming hot plate from the oven and placed it in front of him.

"Try me," she said.

As Johnny ate, he gave Ann a run down of his day. Her eyes softened as she listened to all of the issues he had to handle.

"I'm so sorry I was late," Johnny said. "And thank you so much for making this delicious dinner and being my wife."

"I know you are under a lot of pressure at work," Ann said. "We are just so happy to have you around and home for dinner."

"I will try my best to join you more often," Johnny promised.

Chapter 18
Year 1965

On a Tuesday evening Johnny picked up Pat Fager and Otto Brodwick and drove over to the Governor Clinton Hotel in New York City. They entered the meeting hall just as Charles Kerrigan, Regional Director of 9A, called the meeting to order. There were over 100 delegates sitting in the hall facing the large table that was elevated on a two-foot platform. The microphone was directly in front of Charles.

"You know why we're here," Charles said. "We need to get a number of blacks to march with Martin Luther King Jr. in Montgomery, Alabama. This isn't going to be a picnic. Many of us may get hurt by the Southerners who won't appreciate us going down there to change their ways. It's not going to be an easy job to get the South to accept the Civil Rights Act. But it's the law they are going to have to accept it. We have to start somewhere, why not there? I'm sure Governor Wallace will tell us he doesn't appreciate us going down to his state to fight for the rights of the black man. I want to warn you that those who go, might get banged up. At this time I'd like to open the floor for suggestions."

Johnny raised his hand to be recognized, Charles pointed with his gavel and nodded for him to speak.

"Charles, I've been giving Dr. King's march a lot of thought," Johnny said. "I feel we shouldn't send any blacks. To impress the Southerners, we should send all white leaders on this march. The south isn't going to be impressed with the blacks but when the whites are marching for the Civil Rights Act, it's a different ball game. We must show the whole country that we're behind this movement. I'm going to be the first one to volunteer to participate in this march."

The delegates stood up to applaud Johnny's idea.

Sam Martin, a white man standing six feet tall with a rugged face and a hooked nose stood up.

"I want to personally applaud Johnny's suggestion," Sam said. "It does my heart good to hear a man speak out for the black man's cause. I've been doing it for years. You got to understand that my local consists of 80 percent black workers. I know what these people go through every day. It's about time the white man understands the black man is a human being and must be treated equally. I'd like to follow up on Johnny's suggestion, I make a motion that each local send at least two white members."

The motion was seconded.

"It's up to us to get behind the movement to make it a success," Sam said. "If we have a strong show of strength, the south will look upon this march as a meaningful change in America. What's in our favor is that Dr. King wants to do this with no violence. His Washington march was a terrific success and televised throughout the country. The news commentators noted that there were few whites participating. We need to have more whites there to make it meaningful." He was applauded as he sat down.

"I never thought that you thought so deeply about civil rights," Otto said to Johnny. "Now, don't get me wrong, you're the best president I ever worked under but I never thought you gave our movement much thought. Look at you; you wear a pinstriped suit, a button-down collar on your white shirt and a distinct bearing of the establishment around you. When you go on the march, you better dress down and have that 'don't give a damn attitude' about you."

"See you're wrong again, when I go on that march, I'll be wearing the same kind of clothes I always wear," Johnny said. "I want them to know that the establishment is behind the movement and to give black men the equality they deserve. My dress has nothing to do with the way I feel. Since I got elected, did you ever see me dressing differently than I am now? You have to dress the part to get respect from the membership and management."

"I'd like to be the other member to go on the march with you," Pat whispered. "It's a worthy cause and I'd like to be part of it."

Johnny nodded his head as he jotted down the time and date of the march on his pad. He raised his hand to be recognized.

"Charles, I'd like to know how we're going to go to Alabama," Johnny asked. "By train, plane or bus. I have to report to my executive board to get the authorization to pay for the trip."

Charles Kerrigan turned the meeting over to the international representative who was handling the affair. The representative explained that they agreed to lease a plane that would take them down to the march. They would leave from LaGuardia Airport and meet at Delta Hangar at 4 a.m.

Once they reached Alabama they would assemble outside of Montgomery in a large field and then march through the center of town and up to the capitol building. The dignitaries would speak from the steps of the capitol building at 11 a.m. until well into the afternoon. After the speeches, there would be shuttles to transport the delegates to the airport. The flight back to New York was scheduled for 8 p.m. They were encouraged to stay in groups and not to wander around the city. The representative reminded them that there were a lot of hotheads in town who would love to get them alone so he urged them all to get on the busses right after the speeches concluded. The sooner they got to the airport the sooner they could leave. For those who missed the bus, he urged them to go back by taxi.

When the meeting broke up, Sam approached Johnny.

"I'm taking my vice president, named Al Diamond, along," Sam said. "He's black and said no matter what the region decided, he was going on that march. My financial secretary is white and he also volunteered to go. I'll meet you at the Delta hangar next Tuesday and we'll talk some more."

Johnny then walked over to Herb Whiting who was an international representative who was organizing the trip. Johnny confirmed that he and Pat would be needing plane reservations.

"Gotcha Johnny, thanks for your support for this movement," Herb said. "I'll see you next Tuesday at LaGuardia. I'll mail you the complete details as soon as I get your check to cover the plane cost. There will be a map enclosed with directions to the Delta hangar."

On the way back to New Jersey, Otto was impressed with the meeting.

"More of our black brothers should see what's going on," Otto said. "They would see that the UAW means business. This is my first union meeting and they completely changed my mind about the union."

"Otto, nothing comes easy in life," Johnny said. "Look how big business fought for years to keep the workers down and refused to recognize the union. They had the police breaking our heads even though as taxpayers we were paying their salaries. The fight was hard and bloody but we're here to stay. The black community is going to go through the same fight for civil rights."

"Johnny, I have to be honest, I attended many black meetings where they discussed you as a white racist and as a shrewd talker," Otto said. "I wish our black brothers could have heard you tonight. I'm going to tell them what you did and I hope to be able to change their minds and thinking."

"Thank you, Otto," Johnny said. "Any word on how the plant's been?"

"I heard Freddie has been in the plant trying to rally members to bring him back as a committeeman but no one is listening to him," Otto said. "Bryan Dill is doing a good job and won the respect of the members. The only one knocking him is Allen Dairy. He checks Bryan's time card every day to see how much he is getting paid. Bryan was a repairman and when the shift goes down, he puts on his coveralls and goes to work in the repair shop for 12 hours like the rest of the workers. I heard through the grapevine that Allen is going to bring this up at a departmental meeting."

Johnny was surprised that the opposition would bring that up, especially since Bryan Dill is black and they would do everything to capture the black vote in the plant.

"The contract gives Bryan the right to work all overtime hours as long as he performs the work," Johnny said. "I want my committeemen to work because as long as he's there, the foremen won't do the hourly work. What's Allen's gripe, he works every Saturday and the twelve hour daily?"

"Johnny, Allen is beholden to Freddie for giving him the inspector's job without any promotional posting before you became president," Otto said. "He's pissed off at you for forcing him to retire."

"Allen never came to me about working overtime," Johnny said.

"Allen got a hold of Lou Sargent who came to the department to see Bryan about working overtime," Otto said. "Bryan is a fast learner, when Lou approached him to bring Allen in every Saturday, Bryan called all the car delivery inspectors to

gather around to listen to his request. Bryan wouldn't approve
Lou's request for Allen to work overtime. All hell broke loose and
Lou Sargent had to leave. Later in the evening, Rocky had the
same overtime request and when Bryan again refused, Rocky
blew his top. Bryan suggested that Rocky go over to all the car
delivery inspectors to tell them that he overruled Bryan by
bringing Allen in every Saturday. Rocky didn't dare and told
Bryan to go fuck himself and walked out of the department."

"Rocky did a smart thing by walking away," Johnny said.
"Allen has no special right to work overtime because he's on the
board of directors. I'm glad Bryan stood his ground. He's going to
be a good committeeman."

"Watch out for Allen," Otto said. "He's been knocking
you ever since you got elected."

"Allen's a hungry son of bitch for money," Johnny said.
"He's got to remember that he has the least amount of seniority in
the inspector's classification to remain in that department."

Johnny dropped both of them off in the union parking lot
and headed home.

He walked into his house where his wife was curled up on
the living room sofa with a book in her lap. Wayne was in the
kitchen doing his homework. She closed the book and placed it on
the living room table.

"How did the meeting go?" she asked.

"Pretty good," Johnny said, taking off his jacket and
putting his briefcase down. "The region is chartering a plane to fly
down to Alabama in support of the march for civil rights. We're
flying down next week."

"What does this march have to do with your union
business?" Ann asked.

Johnny was reluctant to tell his wife that it was his idea to
send white delegates to the march.

"Someone has to help them get equality, so why not it be
us?" he said.

Johnny sat down next to his wife on the sofa.

"There's nothing to worry about," Johnny said. "This is
going to be a peaceful march by Dr. King."

"Peaceful just like that bus ride they took through the
south?" Ann asked. "The T.V. showed them getting their heads
bashed-in with baseball bats."

She was frustrated and got up from the sofa. Johnny tried to put his arms around her but she pushed him away.

"We're just going to march at the tail end of the Selma march," Johnny said. "It'll begin from the outskirts of Montgomery, through the main streets where all the businesses are located, and up to the capitol building. What could happen in the center of town with the television cameras on us?"

Johnny stood up and placed his arms around her shoulders to console her.

"How can you say that?" she asked. "The politicians and the police are more vicious than the people. Take that restaurant owner who stood in front of his restaurant with a shotgun and threatened to kill any black man who tried to go in. That same man is running for governor and he's going to get elected because of that stance. The Southerners feel the same as he does."

Ann knew her husband was doing the right thing, but she was afraid for his safety.

"Why do you have to always be the person who leads everything?" Ann asked. " Ford has a greater responsibility to civil rights. Are they sending anyone on the march?"

Despite her protestations, she knew in her heart that there was no way to change Johnny's mind once it was set.

"Dear, you know better than to ask that question," Johnny said. "Ford's only interest is in making profits."

Wayne had stopped doing his homework and was listening to their conversation for the last few minutes. He then walked into the living room and joined.

"Dad, I'd like to go on that march with you," Wayne said. "I'd get a better education there, than I could get from the books in school."

Ann looked at her husband and then back at her son. She struggled to calm herself down before speaking.

"Wayne, you get back to your books," she said. "Not only is this march dangerous for your father, the last thing I need is to have my son going on some march when he really needs to be working harder at school. Now go to your room and finish your homework."

Ann then turned to her husband.

"You've put some strange ideas into your son's head," Ann said. "He thinks that the job you have is some kind of an adventure. That's why I want him to become a professional, so it can take him out of the rat race."

"Your mother is right," Johnny said. "A union official doesn't make much money. The better salary is with the big business. You better hit the books and focus on college."

Wayne shrugged and left the room.

"He really has no idea what you are getting yourself into," Ann sighed.

"Hon, I promise I will be safe," Johnny said.

"You owe that to me and your family," Ann said, kissing him. "Please come back safe."

* * *

The alarm went off at 1:30 a.m. Johnny quickly reached over to shut it off to prevent waking Ann. He showered and dressed quietly. Then he tiptoed out of the house. He drove to union headquarters to pick up Pat Fager. When Johnny pulled up, Pat was standing in the parking lot next to his car. Pat opened the passenger door to get in and suggested they stop at the diner for some breakfast. Johnny knew they would have little time to talk before boarding the plane and argued against stopping for food. He wanted to talk to the delegates about what they were going to do in Alabama and if they had any more information from the international union.

"We've got a lot of important business to discuss," Johnny said. "I'm sure they are going to have at least coffee and breakfast buns on the plane."

Pat nodded his head in agreement. In a short time they pulled into a large parking lot that was adjacent to the Delta hangar. The lot was full of cars.

"Looks like we're the last ones to get here," Pat said. He noticed the pioneer lunch truck parked by the building. "Let's go over and get a cup of coffee and sandwiches for everyone."

They walked over to Sam and his delegates who were standing in a group. A huge black man approached them. He was over six feet eight inches tall and weighed more than 300 pounds of hard muscle. He extended his hand and introduced himself as Al Diamond, Sam's vice president.

"A lot of guys gave lip service but no action," Al said. "You're an exception in my book."

"Sam always referred to you as a big man in the labor union," Johnny said, shaking Al's hand and smiling. "I can see he meant that in more ways than one."

"Johnny, Governor Wallace is bringing out the National Guard to be posted in areas along the march to prevent violence erupting," Sam said. "He's concerned about the KKK and other radical groups that might try to attack us. We'll stay close together so we can help each other if any violence breaks out."

Sam handed out coffee and muffins to the men.

"I doubt we'll have any trouble," Johnny said. "There are too many well influential people marching with us and the T.V. cameras will be rolling. The announcer on the radio said Governor Wallace gave the state workers the day off with instructions that they stay away from the march. I agree that we stay close together. The radicals who are stubborn in their ways might try for any excuse to make an example of us."

Johnny pointed into the hanger at an old plane.

"Is that the old prop job that's going to be taking us down?" Johnny asked.

"Yes," Sam said. "It's an old plane but it's a lot safer than some of the jets. I never heard of any of the prop planes crashing. I was talking to the pilot before you guys got here and he told me that this plane is in top condition. The inside is a little beaten up but outside of that it's in perfect shape."

"I picked a doozy of a plane for my first flight," Pat said. "I hope that it's in good shape like Sam said. I'd like to get there in one piece."

"Come on, they're starting to board," Al said, as he waved to the group. Someone then caught Al's eye.

"Look, there's A. Phillip Randolph, the head of the railroad steward's union," Al said. "Let's go over to say hello."

"Johnny, save us a couple of seats so we can sit together," said Sam.

Sam and some of his group headed over to greet Asa Philip, who was a prominent black labor and civil rights leader.

Pat entered the plane ahead of Johnny and saved a few seats in the front rows for Johnny and Sam Martin's group. Johnny suggested Pat take the window seat while placing his jacket in the compartment above their seat.

"Maybe it's better that I not see anything on the ground," Pat said. "Do you think this heap can get off the ground?"

Johnny noticed Pat's nervousness.

"Come on, you'll enjoy the flight," Johnny said. "This DC8 usually flies at six thousand feet and you'll get an ideal view of the countryside. In comparison the jets fly at thirty thousand feet and you get very little view."

Sam and Al came down to their seats as the stewardess walked down the aisle. She made a safety check to ensure everyone had his or her seatbelts fastened.

The plane had a safe takeoff and Pat promptly fell asleep for the duration of the flight. They arrived after a three-and-a-half hour flight to Montgomery. It was a small but neatly kept airport with flowers blooming around the perimeter of the building. They debarked the plane down a portable staircase, proceeded through the building and directly to the outside roadway.

There were five small school buses to take them to the marching grounds. The police were casually standing next to the building, talking among themselves as they waited for the delegates to board the buses to go to Montgomery. They showed no interest in the marchers but were close at hand if there were any disruptions.

When the buses were about to depart, the police drove in front and in back of the buses, escorting the buses through the black section of town. There were many black families sitting on their porches or outside observing the marchers go by. They waved small flags and signs encouraging the marchers on. Johnny noticed the people quickly put down the signs as the police came driving by.

The delegates then arrived at St. Jude Educational Institute's athletic field. It had rained the night before and the field was a sea of mud. There were thousands of marchers waiting patiently in the mud for the last leg of the march from Selma to get under way. As the delegates dismounted from the busses they were met by young men and women playing guitars and singing solidarity songs including, "We Shall Overcome." Behind the singers were young girls carrying large thermoses of coffee that they offered to the marchers. No one paid any heed to the mud as they walked directly in the center of the field.

Martin Gerber and the UAW international representatives who were already there with banners and placards met Johnny and other union and labor officials. The march began promptly at 9 a.m. It was led by a one-legged veteran from Michigan who started singing but was interrupted by a group of black marchers who began a rally call and response with the question "what do you want?" and the answer "freedom!" A group of youths marched alongside and near the curbs singing and chanting as they waved cheerleading batons. Johnny and the other delegates walked with the black activists.

"Join us in our fight for equality," Johnny called out to observers.

One old man came forward with a cane using it to steady himself.

"God bless you for what you're doing," he said to Johnny. "After the march, you will all go home and we'll be back to the same level of harassment. We all pray for your success. Maybe some day we'll all be able to live side-by-side in harmony. Thank you and God bless all of you."

The old man limped back to his porch and sat down waving his handkerchief and periodically used it to wipe away tears.

Along the route Alabama National Guardsmen were stationed in full battle gear with their rifles held across their chest in port arms. Their assignment was to see that the marchers weren't attacked. The marchers headed to the small business district where they first came across a mob of angry whites. Johnny immediately saw the hatred in their eyes.

"White nigger lovers!" one shouted. "Why don't you come over here so we can talk some sense into you!"

Some were holding baseball bats and gesturing with them in a threatening manner. The marchers were then showered with plastic bags filled with urine and excrement which angry whites threw from the windows of the high buildings.

"Here's a little gift for you nigger lovers!" they yelled.

The marchers now numbered over 50,000 from all over the country. They could see large banners hanging across the buildings with the words "NIGGER LOVERS" scrawled. Another banner had an image of Dr. Martin Luther King, Jr. banners with a sickle along side the words, "Here's a dues paying member of the Communist Party. An enemy of the United States."

Johnny and the other marchers tried their best to ignore the banners, the booing and the harassment from the observers. They all were focused on dodging the flying plastic bags full of waste. Finally they came to the capitol building, where they could see the police stationed in each window of the buildings with binoculars and cameras, taking pictures of the marchers.

The police were constantly pointing out some participant of the march, possibly looking for local people. Their interest was in instilling the fear of God into the demonstrators who were locals, but they had no success. The police were aware that television cameras were broadcasting marchers and the police action to the entire country. The more pictures the police took the louder marchers sang, "we shall overcome!"

Dr. Martin Luther King, Jr. gave a speech during the march, speaking about his dream for equality for all races. At his side stood union leaders, politicians, religious leaders, and many dignitaries. While speaking, Dr. King lifted a part of a petition that had been signed by millions of black people supporting their right to vote, which he was going to present to Alabama Governor Wallace after the march. Many of the dignitaries spoke in favor of the Act. They all promised to do everything in the power to make the Act a reality, with justice and freedom for all.

At the conclusion of the speeches, the crowd started to disperse.

"Let's go down the street to get a cold beer," Johnny said to Pat. "After standing in the heat for five hours, I'm thirsty."

"Do you think it's safe?" Pat asked.

"Sure, this is the United States," Johnny said. "No one is going to bother us. Come on, let's go."

Johnny wasn't worried about their safety.

They left the demonstration and walked to a bar. After entering the bar, the men moved over to let them in. Johnny ordered Pat and himself two beers. Soon after, one of the men noticed the mud on their shoes and heard the Yankee accents.

"Looks like we have a couple nigger lovers among us," a man shouted.

The men near Johnny and Pat then dispersed, leaving the two alone.

"Let's get the hell out of here before they lynch us," Pat whispered in fear.

"Pat take it easy," Johnny said, gulping his beer. "They're not going to bother us. Take your time drinking your beer. Make it look like we have all the time in the world."

The group of men began to talk to one another.

"We ought to kick someone's ass for coming down here to cause trouble," one of them said.

"Look at their shoes, they sure must be white trash to wallow in the mud like pigs," another added.

"Let's get the fuck out of here," Johnny said to Pat, loud enough for everyone to hear. "I don't think we're welcome."

He took the last of his drink and gulped it down and began to leave.

As they were leaving, one of the men spit on the floor. The bartender picked up their empty glasses and threw them against the concrete wall.

"We don't want anyone to get the clap of the mouth from these black-loving cocksuckers," the bartender said.

Johnny and Pat kept their heads down and walked out of the bar. As they hit the sidewalk they heard a voice call Johnny's name.

"Hey Johnny get in here before someone knocks your brains out," Sam yelled from a cab.

Johnny and Pat quickly climbed into the cab just as a group of men came dashing out of the bar with clubs in their hands.

"Let's get the hell out of here!" Sam yelled. The cab driver burned rubber as he headed to the airport. Some of the group hit the side of the cab with their bats while the rest of them threw their bats at the departing cab.

"That was a dumb fucking thing to do," Sam lectured. "You guys could have been killed."

Sam was annoyed because the men had agreed on the plane that they wouldn't do anything foolish while they were in Montgomery.

"Sam, you're right," Johnny said. "We were standing in that sun for a long time and I think my brain wasn't functioning well. I didn't think anyone would try to hurt us in broad daylight."

Johnny felt foolish and guilty for dragging Pat into a dangerous situation.

In a matter of minutes they were at the airport. All the delegates were accounted for and they were ready to leave. Then an announcement came over the loud speaker announcing that there would be a delay due to heavy air traffic. Johnny told Sam and the group that he would take them out to dinner on his dime.

They went to a restaurant nearby and sat at a table waiting to be served. The waitress came over to inform them that the restaurant was closed for the night. Johnny pointed to the sign that indicated the hours of operation were until 9 p.m.

"It's only 6 p.m.," Johnny said.

"I'm just following orders of my manager," the waitress said, shrugging her shoulders. "If you gentlemen want something to eat, we have a vending machine with hot coffee and sandwiches."

Johnny thanked her and turned to the group.

"Listen, they don't appreciate us being here," Johnny said. "I don't know about you, but I'm starving. Come on I got a pocket full of change. Let's eat what they got."

While eating, an announcement came over the radio that A. Phillip Randolph had a heart attack and was being transferred to a hospital. After finishing dinner the group returned to the airport but didn't get clearance to leave until 2 a.m.

After landing in New York, they were walking with a young priest who had a portable radio. An announcement came on air that a young Michigan housewife named Viola Liuzzo was killed while driving a young black man to safety. Viola was gunned down by KKK members in a deserted road between Selma and Montgomery. The Klansmen thought they had also killed the black passenger, Leroy Moton, but he lay motionless as they checked both bodies. Viola was killed instantly.

"What a shame that people who were fulfilling a worthy cause, were killed," Sam said. "Only an animal would take the lives of human beings doing good for the world."

Pat was shook up by the announcement.

"We could have gotten killed back at that bar," Pat said, shaking.

Johnny placed his arms around Pat's shoulder.

"Pat, don't you realize only a coward kills when there's no one around?" Johnny said. "The men at the bar were pissed because we came to the South to try to change their ways but they're not killers. They were angry but not vicious."

"Then why do you think they came out after us with baseball bats in their hands?" Pat said, annoyed. "They wanted to teach us batting practice?"

"No Pat, they wanted to frighten us," Johnny said. "We were in the bar for quite a while and the entire time and all they did was curse at us. If they wanted to, they could have attacked us in the bar but they didn't. The people who killed that housewife were low-down cowards, not the typical Southerner. What we did yesterday was tolerated by most of them. Only a handful of men showed their anger and resentment." He noticed Pat loosening up a little.

"You worry too much," Johnny chuckled. "Let's go home. I'm bushed and I'd like to get a little sleep."

Chapter 19
Year 1966

Rocky Durango was leaning against the railing on the upper level of the administration building sipping a cup of coffee.

He noticed Pat Fager standing on the other side talking to an attractive young lady. He attempted to get closer so he could hear their conversation but Pat noticed him. He cut their conversation short and quickly left. The beautiful blonde discarded her empty coffee cup into the trash container. She turned abruptly without casting a glance in Rocky's direction and entered the accounting office.

He couldn't see where the blonde went but suddenly he noticed Geraldine talking to one of the supervisors. His pulse raced when he saw Geraldine stoop down to retrieve a pencil she dropped. He was a distance away but could clearly see she wasn't wearing a bra. While still having her conversation, Geraldine winked as she noticed him looking at her.

Marie Collins came hurrying up the marble staircase and was out of breath when she got to the landing. She came over and took the coffee container from Rocky's hand and began to take a sip.

"Hello to you too," Rocky said.

"I'm sorry but I needed that," Marie said. "I'm sorry I'm late but Tony had me tying up some communications to Detroit that have to be sent out this afternoon."

Rocky nodded his head and walked over to the coffee dispenser to get her another cup of coffee. He was still distracted by the blonde who was talking to Pat. He looked in the direction of the accounting office but instead he caught Geraldine's eye as she stuck her tongue out at him in a joking manner. He ignored Geraldine and turned back to Marie.

"Marie, Pat was talking to some blonde," Rocky said. "It looks like she works in the accounting office, do you know who she is?"

"There are over 40 girls working in that office," Marie said. "Do you want to point her out to me?"

"No, that's not necessary," Rocky said. "I'm just curious. She seemed very friendly with him. Pat is the recording secretary of the union. He's a staunch supporter of Johnny and I am just wondering if she is the one passing information over to him."

"What was she wearing?" Marie asked.

"She has blonde hair and was wearing a white knit sweater, a red and green plaid skirt and a rhinestone choker around her neck," Rocky said. "The only reason I'm asking is because I want to know who all of Johnny's connections are, especially on the management side."

"My girlfriend Wendy works there," Marie said. "Maybe she can give me the name."

Marie left to enter the office. He noticed that Geraldine stopped her to say something. Marie then walked out of his sight toward Wendy's desk. As soon as Marie saw what Wendy was wearing, she realized that Rocky had been talking about her. Wendy looked up and saw the startled expression on Marie's face.

"Marie, you look like you saw a ghost," Wendy said. "Are you all right?"

"Uh, yeah, sorry," Marie said. "I just had something on my mind. I didn't know it showed."

"Want to talk about it?" Wendy asked.

"No, no, I'm all right," Marie said. "It was really nothing."

She brushed the hair away from her face and sat down on the edge of Wendy's desk.

"I came up here to grab a cup of coffee and thought I'd drop in to see you," Marie said. "How about we grab lunch at that cute place that just opened up?"

"Sure," Wendy said. "That would be great," Wendy said. "I have to finish up some assignments. I can meet you there at noon."

She could tell Marie had something worrying her, but she didn't pry.

"Noon sharp," Marie said.

Marie walked away from Wendy's office and toward Rocky. He was still in the coffee area talking to Geraldine, who was standing a little too close to him. As Marie approached, Geraldine left. She wiggled her hips seductively and looked over her shoulder at Rocky. Marie rolled her eyes and ignored her.

"That girl that you asked about is Wendy Reilly," Marie said. "She's my closest friend in the office. She wouldn't divulge any information to Johnny. In fact, she knows all about us. She was the one who covered up for me when we went to San Diego."

Rocky was nervous. He knew Johnny was getting his information from a reliable source. Rocky didn't want to upset Marie by asking her to spy on her friend, but he had no choice.

"Listen, I get that she's your friend," Rocky said. "But when you're with her, just casually ask her about Pat Fager. Let me know how she reacts to that question. I've got a lot of eyes on me and I need to be one step ahead of Johnny."

Rocky saw Marie's face start to scowl so he looked around. Noticing no one, he leaned toward her and kissed her on the lips softly.

"Hon, I have to go now or I'll be late for my meeting," Rocky said. "I'll pick you up at your place at eight. Wear something sexy."

She walked back to her office still disturbed by what he said. She sat at her desk for quite a while thinking about how she would question her best friend. At noon, she came to the lobby and saw Wendy there waiting for her. At the café, they were seated by a large bay window. Soon after, in walked Tony Rodgers and Geraldine. Tony was embarrassed but just walked by, following the waitress to their table. His only sign of recognition was a slight nod of his head as they passed their table. Wendy had a coy smile on her face,

"That one is a bitch," Wendy whispered to Marie. "I heard her talking to one of the girls bragging that she had a thing going with Tony. Looks like she was telling the truth. God help him if his wife ever finds out."

Wendy glanced toward their table. Geraldine noticed them and waved her hand in recognition.

"She is brazen and she's going to cause your boss a lot of trouble," Wendy said.

Marie was nervously picking on her salad with her fork but wasn't eating. She wasn't sure how to broach the topic with Wendy.

"This morning Rocky noticed you talking to Pat Fager," Marie said. "Are you going out with him?"

"Did Rocky put you up to this?" Wendy asked. She shook her head in disgust. "Rocky should know better. Pat is my brother. Rocky and my brother were in the same caucus for years. He should do his research before sending you to investigate."

Both were silent for a moment.

"You know, all you had to do was go into my files in Tony's office and you'd see that my maiden name is Fager," Wendy said.

Marie felt completely embarrassed. Wendy was her closest friend and she didn't want to jeopardize her friendship.

"I'm so sorry for this line of questioning," Marie said. "I would never go behind your back and look at your files. I just am worried that your brother might know about Rocky and my relationship."

"Marie, I didn't tell Pat anything," Wendy said. "But I guess I should tell you now. He told me all about you and Rocky staying at the hotel on the beach. He got this information from Johnny who saw both of you coming out of the hotel one evening."

Marie was shocked and felt her face become hot. Wendy paused before she continued, placing her hand over Marie's.

"You should know something else," Wendy said. "Everyone knows that Rocky is a lady's man and loves to play the field. Apparently he is having an affair with Geraldine along with seeing you."

Marie felt tears running down her cheek.

"I'm so sorry you had to find out this way," Wendy said. "He's not a good guy and it's clear as day now. Not only is he is two-timing you, now he's asking you to do his dirty work?" Wendy stopped talking when she noticed how upset Marie was.

Marie had a look of shock on her face and sat there silent. The waitress interrupted them with a tray of two chilled long stem glasses and a bottle of expensive white wine.

"Compliments from Tony Rodgers," the waitress said. "He told me to tell you to enjoy the wine and don't hurry back to work."

Marie felt like she had been punched in the heart. She didn't know what to say. Wendy reached out to grab her hand.

"We've had a friendship for many years," Wendy said. "I hope that me being Pat's sister and you being with Rocky won't affect that. I also want you to understand that there isn't a thing that happens in the plant that Johnny isn't aware of. He knows all about Rocky's shenanigans. Johnny found out a week after the election that Rocky was asked to run for president from the opposition. He also was ready when Lou Sargent tried to manipulate him into shutting down the plant because of the Roger Hansen issue. Johnny came out on top regarding the Hansen situation. Lou and Rocky will never be able to live that down."

"I'm going out with Rocky tonight," Marie said quietly. "I'm not going to tell him that Pat is your brother. If he found out, he'd insist that I stop talking to you."

"What are you going to say then?" Wendy said. "He watched Pat and me talking for a good ten minutes. He recognizes that we aren't just casual acquaintances. Just tell him we share the same hometown. Now, what are you going to do about you and Rocky?"

"Wendy I love him so much and I don't want to lose him," Marie said. "I knew in my heart that he was seeing other women but I didn't want to face the truth."

Wendy had never seen her friend look so sad.

Over at the other table, Tony and Geraldine were just getting their food. The waiter brought over their steaming steaks and placed the largest one in front of Geraldine. She gulped down her drink.

"Honey, I'm starved," Geraldine said, pulling the plate toward her. "That drink gave me an appetite."

She began cutting her steak and asked the waiter for a refill of her drink. She then leaned over to give Tony a kiss. He immediately reared back, nearly causing her to fall out of her chair.

"Damn it, don't do that," Tony snarled. "I don't want those two over there knowing about us."

He looked and noticed the two women looking their way.

"Honey, neither of them are goody-goodies," Geraldine said. "They know all about what we're doing. There are a lot of others doing the same thing that we're doing. "

She cut into her steak and chewed quickly. She seemed completely unaffected by Tony's frenetic energy.

"You wanna bet?" Tony said. "My job is on the line and you don't really seem to give a shit. I don't even know why we are sitting here together when those two women are here to begin with."

Geraldine reached over to gently pat his hand.

"I'll be more discreet from now on," she said. "But I believe the whole office knows we're having an affair."

Tony lost his appetite and pushed away his plate. He was frowning when he noticed the waitress bring the bill over to the two women.

"We've got to go," Tony said, panicking. "I don't feel comfortable leaving after those two do."

"Honey, don't rush me," Geraldine said, chewing. "I know those two. They won't say anything about us."

"Bullshit," Tony said. "If there is something that I know about you ladies, it's that you talk. And you talk a lot. Now hurry up and finish that steak. I gotta get back before people start looking for me."

He wiped his mouth with a napkin and discarded it on top of his unfinished meal. He had barely touched his plate. He glanced at his watch.

"Come on, Gerry," Tony said. "We've got to get the hell out of here."

He signaled to the waiter for the check.

Geraldine just kept eating the steak, like she didn't have any other care in the world.

"Maybe we could go over to some place where we won't be recognized," Geraldine said. "I know a nice motel just down the road. I could get that nervousness out of your system."

Tony was thoroughly annoyed at this point and trying to hold his temper. He ignored what she said and pulled her out of the restaurant. Thankfully they were just behind Marie and Wendy. As soon as he hit the highway he began to burn rubber, clocking 90 miles an hour. Even though he was going fast a Corvette passed him. He then noticed a police car with flashing lights zooming behind the Corvette. He attempted to slow down but the police car had already turned on the overhead lights, signaling him to pull over.

"License and registration please," the policeman said.

"Officer, that Corvette you were chasing was going faster than I was," Tony said.

He had slipped a $20 bill in between his license and registration.

"Doesn't matter," the policeman snapped. "I clocked you at 90 miles an hour in a 50 mile per hour zone." The officer looked at the license and registration before scowling.

"If you don't want to get hit with an additional summons for attempted bribery, you better only hand me your driver's license and registration," the policeman said.

He dropped the $20 bill in Tony's lap.

The policeman walked back to his car. He then returned with the summons and Tony's identification documents.

"I'm letting you off light this time," the policeman said. "I better not catch you speeding again."

Tony waited for the policeman to retreat before reading the summons.

"That lying son-of-a-bitch didn't give me any break, he ticketed me for going 90 miles an hour," Tony said.

"He could have ticketed you for attempted bribery," Geraldine joked.

"That isn't funny," Tony said. "This whole day has been a mess."

As he drove he noticed the police car following him from a distance.

That night Marie allowed Rocky to pick her up like they had planned. He took her to the Moonlight Club, where they ate dinner and danced the tango. When they were heading back to their table, a young man and his wife approached them.

"Hi Rocky, I'm surprised to see you here at the club," the man said. "I thought that you'd instead be at the caucus meeting tonight."

"What meeting?" Rocky said. As soon as he said the words, he wished he hadn't. It made him look terribly out of the loop that he didn't know about the meeting.

"It's the caucus meeting at the church, like we always have," the man said.

"Oh, right," Rocky said, lamely. The man and his wife walked away.

"Does he not know that you're running against Johnny?" Marie asked.

"That's hard to believe," Rocky said. "That's one of Johnny's fighter friends. He has to know we split up. I wonder why he came over to talk to me?"

Rocky sat at the table and pulled out a cigarette. With this other hand he took out his gold monogrammed lighter. As he took a few inhales, he grew irritated that he wasn't notified of the meeting and his close supporters didn't inform him.

"By the way," Rocky said. "What is the relationship between your friend Wendy and Pat Fager?"

"Oh, uh, they're just old friends from her hometown," Marie quickly said. "I asked her if she knew Johnny Romanek and she said that she didn't."

"You can never be too careful," Rocky said. He motioned for the waiter to bring the bill. "I know a little motel down the road," Rocky whispered.

"Sweetheart, I can't," Marie said. "It's been a long day and my parents are waiting up for me. Maybe some other time."

"Too bad, I was really in the mood," he said. He was annoyed and unable to mask his disappointment.

"Should I take you home now?" Rocky asked.

"Well, I was hoping we could stay here a little while longer," she said.

"We better not, the waiter is already coming with our bill," he said.

He was in a rush to drop Marie off so he could see if Geraldine was available. Marie noticed his impatience and realized he was probably going to meet up with Geraldine later.

"We'll do this some other time next week when you're able to stay out later," Rocky said.

"Sure," Marie said. "That'll be fine."

When she got into the car she turned her face away from Rocky so he couldn't see the tears falling down her cheeks. It was beginning to feel awful to be around him, but the thought of letting him go was agonizing. When he dropped her off he didn't even kiss her goodbye. He instead slammed the passenger door closed and zoomed away.

* * *

During the bargaining of the new local agreements, Freddie McCoy supported Johnny on every demand pushed across the bargaining table. Rocky and Lou met with Johnny on numerous occasions to encourage him to slow down. The reason was that if Johnny won all of his demands in the local agreement, he would be hard to defeat in the upcoming election.

One evening Rocky and Lou approached Freddie to meet at a bar to discuss certain aspects of the union.

"Freddie, I'm all for the membership like you are," Rocky said. "We have to look to the future, our election is coming up this spring. If the company gives in on most of Johnny's demands, he'll be a shoo-in when it's time to win the election. We can't afford that. We need your help to slow him down. He's coming across as real strong with the company. We have approached you because of your expertise with previous contract meetings in the Chester plant. Lou and I want to run you for the plant committeeman job, Lou for vice president and me for president. With the three of us in office, we could accomplish a lot. What do you say? Are you with us to dump Johnny?"

"Look, Rocky, I've been with this union a lot longer than both of you," Freddie said. "The demands that Johnny is pushing are something I've been trying to get ever since I was a union official. At this time I'm not going to sell the membership down the river. I'm going to do my best to get those demands into the agreement. After the contract talks are over, we can talk about my role in getting us all elected."

He turned to address Lou.

"If it wasn't for you I wouldn't have gotten elected as a committeeman," Freddie said. "That was your old district. I'll make one thing clear, I won't hurt you in the upcoming election. I'm here for you. Ok guys, I'm ready for the next drink."

As Freddie went to the bar, Lou turned to Rocky.

"Listen, Rock, don't worry about Freddie," Lou said. "He's one of our staunchest supporters and he'll never go over to Johnny's side. I know what I'm talking about."

Securing the new local agreement went well for Johnny. He got all of his tentative demands in cooperation with the company, subject to the membership approval. Freddie was true to his word. He supported Johnny all the way and won the respect of the company after his presentation. After the meeting with the company concluded, Johnny took Freddie aside.

"I got a call from the international union informing me that the National Ford Council will convene Thursday in Detroit," Johnny said. "The call stated that we're entitled to three delegates but I talked to Ken Bannon and he agreed to allow you to come along as an extra delegate. Rocky or Lou don't need to know about this, so please don't tell them. I'm going to tell the executive board that the entire bargaining committee will attend. My caucus members will go along. I booked you a flight already, everything is set. All you have to do is agree to come."

"I got some inside information that Rocky and Lou are going to support the national agreement even though we didn't get the work standard provision in it," Freddie said. "I'm aware of the blood pack made at the sub council to knock down the contract if it didn't support our resolution on work standards. I'm sticking all way with you on this. You better make sure I'm a voting delegate on this. But is there some way you can drop Rocky as a voting delegate? He's the one trying to make a deal with the international union to switch our vote. I might be able to get Lou to go along with us."

"Let me worry about how our local will vote," Johnny said. "After the last membership meeting they won't have the balls to switch. Remember it was one of Rocky's supporters who made the motion to poll the bargaining committee on our position to reject the contract if we didn't get the work standard provision in it. If they dare vote for the national agreement without the work standard provision in it, I'll make sure they never get elected again."

Johnny noticed some of the men glancing over at them.

"If they ask you what we were talking about, just tell them we were discussing the flight time to Detroit," Johnny whispered.

Freddie accepted Johnny's offer and they all flew to Detroit for the National Ford Council meeting. On entering the lobby of the Cadillac Hotel, the entire bargaining committee were met by a large group of delegates who were emphatically opposed to the negotiated national agreement that the United Automobile Workers leadership was proposing. The delegates gathered around Johnny to urge him to lead the fight on the council floor to knock down the tentative agreement and force the negotiators to return to the bargaining table to get the work standard provision into the contract as part of the agreement.

"When we were meeting with the resolution committee is when I proposed the work standard provision and they accepted that," Johnny said. "I'll lead the fight to try to get the negotiators to add something in the contract to give some relief for the operations on the moving line. Our only chance is if the delegates don't approve the contract. At our membership meeting my bargaining committee promised the members that we're committed to that demand for relief."

Johnny stopped to look at Rocky and Lou and waited until they acknowledged his comment.

"We made our blood pact and we can't deviate from it," Johnny said. "Before the meeting tomorrow, why don't we all gather in the Rose Room to discuss the position that we'll take?"

They all nodded their heads in agreement. Johnny looked down at his watch.

"We have just about every local here so why don't we meet tonight at 6 p.m.?" Johnny said.

Johnny picked up his bag and headed to the lobby's reception desk. Nicky Commers, an international representative, who also was checking into the hotel, approached him.

"I see you're taking the same position against the contract," Nicky said. "Johnny, we got the best pension plan. Better than any other union in this contract, plus a substantial raise for everyone. There's also an additional raise of 50 cents per hour for the skilled tradesmen to bring them to equal standing with outside contractors. In the last hour before the strike deadline, the company agreed to the pension plan that effects every member working at Ford. It was an offer we couldn't refuse. We made more gains in this contract than we ever did before. The international union hopes when you meet tonight, you'll support their agreement. You gotta realize that we represent all locals."

"Nicky, I agree that the UAW won a lot for the members, but we were assured by the international that we'd get some relief on the work standards," Johnny said. "All the assembly plants went out and committed themselves to this resolution. We got our members up in a pitch. How can we now go back to our members and tell them we changed our minds? This contract looks good to you but for us it's a killer."

Nicky was in an uncomfortable position because his job was as a liaison between the international and the sub-council to see their demands were met to their satisfaction in the contract.

"I reported this to Ken and he told us the company was prepared to stand firm before they relinquished the right to add work to get the maximum from their employees," Nicky said. "In order to put the settlement to bed we had to do a little conceding. We're proud of this contract and we need your help to sell it.

None of the delegates would take a position on the contract until you got here. They will listen to you so we're asking you for help."

"Nicky, I'm sorry but I can't support the contract without some relief for the workers on the line," Johnny said. "I got myself pushed into a corner when I believed international when they told us that we would get some relief there. Now I can't go back to my members without that included in the contract."

Johnny looked down at his watch, eager to cut the conversation short.

"Nicky, I have to go now," Johnny said. "We have that meeting at six, why don't you come and give your pitch for international? I'll see you later."

Johnny left to go to the elevator to check into his room. Lou and Rocky watched and when Johnny disappeared, they approached Nicky.

"Let's go to the bar for a few drinks," Rocky said. They went and sat at the far end.

"Nicky, Lou and I are in a bind with this contract," Rocky admitted. "Some of my supporters thought they were putting Johnny on the spot when they heard that we didn't get the work standards agreement, so they made a motion to poll the bargaining committee to pledge that they'll knock down the contract if it wasn't there. Johnny's no dummy. He took a strong position and had the membership poll us. So we have no choice but to go along Johnny. We're both going to work on Johnny to support the agreement. If we can do that, we could sell it to the membership."

"What I need you to do is talk in favor of the agreement at the council meeting tonight," Nicky said. "Point out the good features in the agreement and suggest that the focus be on the work standards so it can be in the next contract."

"We just have to careful on how we go about this," Rocky said. "Our local election is coming up soon."

Nicky nodded his head in understanding.

"I'll go to work on Freddie McCoy," Lou said. "Maybe with him on our side, we will weaken Johnny's stand. Right now, Freddie is more adamant against the contract than Johnny is. I got to remind him that he owes me."

Lou walked over to the lobby to dial Freddie's room. Johnny answered.

"Johnny we're at the bar downstairs, would you and Freddie care to join us?" Lou hoped Johnny would decline the invitation. Johnny wasn't a big drinker so he figured he would reject the offer.

"I'm still unpacking and I want to freshen up before we go to the meeting," Johnny said. "Here's Freddie."

"Where the fuck are you guys?" Freddie said. "I called your room a half dozen times."

"We're down at the bar," Lou said. "Come down and join us. We have the international with us and we'd like to have a talk with you."

"I'll be right down," Freddie said. "Order me a double scotch and soda."

He turned to address Johnny before he headed to the bar.

"I'm going to meet those guys at the bar," Freddie said. "I'm going to let them buy me the drinks. But those guys are going to be extremely pissed when I refuse to go along with them. I'll see you at the Rose Room at 6 o'clock."

"Be strong, Freddie," Johnny said.

Downstairs at the bar, Lou waved Freddie over as soon as he saw him.

"Over here Freddie," he said. "Your drink is waiting for you."

Freddie's hand was shaking with nervousness as he picked up his drink and gulped it down fast.

"I needed that real bad," Freddie said. "Now what the hell is this meeting all about? I'm sure you didn't invite me down just for a drink."

"Nicky came to us with a request that we go along with the agreement and we need your help," Lou said, certain he could convince Freddie.

"Well, you know my position on the work standard provision," Freddie said. He immediately ordered another drink before continuing. "I made a promise to the membership and I intend to keep my word."

"Look Freddie, you're over 60 and that pension agreement was made to suit guys like you," Lou said. "The members who came with you from Pennsylvania have high seniority and I'm sure they're all in favor of the agreement. All you have to do is agree and we'll out vote Johnny 3 to 1. With the election coming up, we can't let Johnny look good. I need you now. I was there when you needed me. What do you say?"

"Sorry Lou, I stand firm," Freddie said. "I can't agree with the proposed contract. I'm going to speak against it tonight and also tomorrow."

Lou's eyes flashed with anger. He walked to the bartender and ordered him to close his tab.

"You promised me you'd have my back," Lou snarled. "Fuck you!"

He walked away from the bar, leaving Rocky, Nicky and Freddie.

"I'm not sure about you all, but I'm going to have another round," Freddie said.

Rocky and Nicky awkwardly excused themselves. They realized they couldn't convince Freddie to change his mind.

"Well that didn't go according to Lou's plan," Nicky whispered to Rocky when they reached the elevators.

"I'm hoping Freddie might change his mind at the last minute," Rocky said, though he didn't think Freddie would.

That evening when the president of the council called the meeting to order, every delegate was present. Every local president took the same position against the new contract. The only one who spoke in favor of the agreement was the international representative. His plea in favor of the agreement fell on deaf ears. Johnny leaned over to whisper in Freddie's ear.

"I thought for sure that Rocky was going to take a stand in favor of the agreement," Johnny said.

"He'd have to be a nut to speak in favor before this crowd," Freddie said. "Everyone can see that the council wants to knock the agreement down."

Nicky was completely disgusted as he threw his papers into his briefcase. He had to face the UAW Ford director with no answers as to why he couldn't swing any delegate to approve the agreement. The following day was the big meeting and the international would have their top officials selling the agreement. No matter how good the contract was, they always wanted to get 90 percent for ratification.

The following morning, Johnny walked into a meeting room and was met by Ken Bannon, Ford director, who was talking to many members of the executive board.

"Johnny, I see you got the sub-council united against the agreement," Ken said. "I was hoping that you would help us sell it. It's a damn good agreement."

"Ken, you know better than that," Johnny said. "You cut the legs out from right under us when they gave us nothing in work standards. I know Nicky reported our stance. I don't see why you're worried about us. You have all the other councils in your hip pocket and we make only one-third of what the national council makes. You'll get your ratification without any help from us."

Johnny saw Rocky waving to him from a distance.

"I better get to my delegation," Johnny said, excusing himself before Ken had a chance to respond.

As Johnny walked to meet up with Rocky he saw the UAW National Director and the executive board members were sitting on the platform to indicate their support for the agreement. There were heated debates for and against the agreement. Johnny was called upon to lead the fight against the agreement for the work standard provision and did a good job. The international delegates were roaming the floor to call in favors over the years to get the delegates to ratify the agreement.

Walter Reuther spoke fluently in favor of the agreement and commended the negotiators on doing a splendid job for Ford. Most delegates were ready to vote.

"My name is Rocky Durango, vice-president of Local 3001, representing the Clinton assembly plant in New Jersey," Rocky said. "I want to take this opportunity to commend the director and his negotiating team for doing a job well done in getting this outstanding agreement. I feel they deserve a round of applause."

Johnny was angered by Rocky's outburst. It showed a split in the assembly plants' blood pact and he was not happy.

Ken, however, was pleased Rocky acknowledged the good work he had done.

"Thanks Rocky, we appreciate your praise," Ken said. "By the way, Rocky is a delegate from sub-council 2 so we especially appreciate this statement coming from them."

The delegates rose to applaud the negotiators by clapping and some stamping their feet. Ken called the council to order by rapping his gavel on the podium desk.

"Are you ready to vote?" Ken asked.

"Ken, to make this a fair and democratic vote, I make a motion that we take a roll call vote," Johnny said. That motion was seconded.

There were boo's and protests from many of the delegates as Ken had to accept the motion.

"It takes 10 percent of the delegates present to have a roll call vote," Ken said. "If this motion is approved, we may be here for hours until each local casts their vote. Many of the delegates have planes to catch to get home. Are you ready to vote? Those in favor of the motion say 'aye'."

Johnny and all the sub-council delegates followed said "aye." Ken saw the vote was well over the 10 percent required.

"The motion is carried," Ken said. "We'll start the vote with the locals with the lowest number and go upward until the vote is counted."

Johnny was determined that they have a roll call vote. He feared that a voice call vote would not reflect the 10 percent needed. He wanted to make sure the voting would show how each delegate voted. The delegates stood fast on their vote. Local 3001 were one of the last locals to vote. Rocky leaned over and whispered to Johnny.

"You could be a hero if you vote our local in favor of the agreement," Rocky said.

Johnny shook his head. His local was called upon to vote. He walked up to the microphone that was set in the middle of the aisle.

"Local 3001 votes to reject the contract unanimously by our delegates," Johnny said.

"Mr. Romanek are you voting for all your delegates?" Ken challenged.

"Yes I am," replied Johnny.

"Yet I was informed that your local has a split vote," Ken said.

Johnny turned to his delegation seated behind him.

"Is there any delegate who wants to cast his vote separately?" Johnny asked. "If so, please come up to the microphone and vote."

One could hear a pin drop and many of the delegates stood up to see everyone's reaction. Many thought Rocky would break since he commended the negotiators on a job well done. The delegates from Local 3001 remained seated.

"The contract is passed by a vote of 66 to 33," Ken said. The hall immediately became a flood of boo's and cheers. Johnny knew this was just the first of many fights. He now needed to galvanize the members to reject the contract.

"Please, hold on and let me finish," Ken said. The room quieted.

"We have brochures available which outline the gains in the new agreement on the table at the rear of the hall," Ken said. "We have them in boxes with the local numbers on top. Take them and distribute them to your members. Every local must take the ratification vote by next week. The results will be mailed to us immediately after the votes are tabulated."

Every single plant in Ford motor had to vote on the agreement to determine if it was going to pass.

While checking out of the hotel, Nicky walked over to Johnny, who was discussing with delegates the reasoning for his position on the agreement. Nicky interrupted the discussion by handing Johnny two pennies.

"This is all you're going to get from the international union in the future," Nicky said, walking way in disgust.

"I'll save these in case I need a loan," Johnny shouted after him.

Johnny knew there were going to be many more fights, that this was just the beginning of it. The meeting was over, and now it was time to explain why the contract was rejected to the workers and other members of the union.

Back home, Johnny and the rest of the bargaining committee spent the next week explaining why the contract agreement was refused. The members understood the union leaders' position and appreciated them taking a strong stance on making sure the agreement included getting relief for the workload on the moving line. Johnny put out bulletins urging the members to reject the contract while the international union sent in representatives to try and sell the agreement to the membership.

The day before the ratification vote, Johnny's father came to the union office to see him. Frank Romanek was still a big man and sat in the chair directly in front of Johnny.

"Son, I read your bulletin about rejecting the proposed agreement," Frank said. "I read the agreement and it has a lot of good things in it. Specifically, the pension is very good, the best we ever had. I'm not a line worker anymore but I do understand your concern that the company keeps adding work to the jobs all the time after the standards would be agreed upon. Since I went to work in the powerhouse my job was easy. But I could never forgot how hard and boring the job on the line was. I appreciate your position. I was reading about the new pension plan, which would enable me to pick up an extra $100 a month. That's a lot of money for me in these times."

The powerhouse was where the fans and furnace was housed for the entire plant. Frank paused before continuing the conversation with his son. He leaned in and looked directly in his eyes.

"I wanted to talk to you in private to let you know that I'm going to vote for the contract," Frank said. "I know you're dedicated to the membership and you feel you're doing the right thing for the men on the moving line. But I got to look toward my future. I'm going to retire in a couple of months. And this extra $100 is going to help your mother and me. I didn't want to mislead you in believing that I supported your position. Do you understand?"

Johnny felt tears in his eyes as his father spoke. It wasn't ideal that his father and him didn't see eye-to-eye on the contract, but he understood the position his father was in.

"Pop, I can appreciate your position and I'm grateful that you came to talk to me," Johnny said. "I don't blame you for voting in support of the contract. I hope you understand my position. I was the one who proposed we get a work standard agreement in this contract as our prime demand. The international promised us some relief in that area but that didn't happen. I was one who led the fight to knock down the contract. You worked on the line for many years and you know how managers hide behind the racks to time the workers when they think there is a way to do the job faster and easier. That has to stop somewhere."

"Son, I understand that you have to do what is right for the membership but I'm looking out for myself and your mother," Frank said. "I hope that there won't be any hard feelings between us for me taking this position."

His father stood up and shook hands with his son.

Johnny realized there were many in his father's age group who probably felt the same, especially those nearing retirement age.

"Pop, you gotta do what is best for you and Mom," Johnny said. "And I have to do what is right for the membership. Also, pop, tell mom that I'll be over for dinner tonight. Ann has a P.T.A. meeting. How does that sound?"

His parents always were pleased whenever he stopped by to see them. They were so proud that their son was the president of the union.

"Mom will be thrilled," Frank said. "In fact, she said she was going to make your favorite, pierogies, the next time you came for dinner."

Chapter 20
Year 1966

Johnny worked at the union office until six p.m. getting an agenda prepared for the ratification meeting that was taking place on Saturday. Then he drove over to his parent's home which was less than a mile away.

He pulled his car into the driveway of a white and brown Cape Cod home that his father had bought when they moved the plant to a new place in Clinton. He had painted the trim of the house in black, with black shutters. A dark green lawn caressed the front and rear of the house which was surrounded by a mixed assortment of flowers and shrubs that blossomed from early spring until the frost set in.

At the rear of the property was a large retaining wall that had two levels. The ground was all sand but Frank Romanek was a farmer for many years before he worked at Ford. He treated the ground with the needed fertilizer and cow manure. He had a green thumb and was able to grow all kinds of vegetables. The neighbors didn't know how he did it because their gardens never produced anything. Frank always said what you put in the ground is what you got out of it.

Johnny walked into the house and there seated at the kitchen table were his three children.

"How did you kids get here?" Johnny asked. "I thought your mother had to go to a P.T.A. meeting tonight?"

"Mom did go to the meeting tonight," Wayne said. "When Grandpa called and said that Grandma made pierogies we insisted to come here for supper. You don't think that you were going to have all those pierogies to yourself now did you?"

"Dad, you know we all love grandma's cooking and yet you only invited yourself," Saundra said. "We would have been stuck with hamburgers or something like that."

"I was only coming over to see grandpa and grandma, I didn't know she was cooking pierogies," Johnny explained, laughing. "I was expecting something light for supper. Wayne, I thought that you had to work at Frank's Sweet Shop tonight?"

Wayne tucked his napkin under his chin to protect his Midland School sweater from getting soiled while his grandmother placed a steaming plate of pierogies in front of him. This was a specially prepared Polish dish made of heavy dough, then filled with a seasoned beef. The dumplings were first boiled in water, then fried to a golden brown color with bacon and served with homemade *chow chow*, a Polish relish.

"Dad, I called the shop up and told them I was going to my grandmother's for something important," Wayne said. "There's no way I was going to pass pierogies up."

Wayne started eating his food like someone was going to take it away from him. He did no more talking until his dish was clean.

Frank Romanek sat there beaming at his grandchildren. He always was thrilled when they came to visit.

"I called Ann on the phone to invite her but said she was unable to come," Frank said. "She did say that if I picked up the children, they were welcome to come for supper. I promised that I would take them right home after they ate so you could go into the plant tonight. Mother put aside a large plate of pierogies for Ann."

Frank turned to the children, only half-joking.

"Those pierogies are only for your mother so you guys better not touch them," Frank said.

"Hey Grandma, how come you never made these for me before?" said Frankie, stuffing his mouth. "These are real good."

"The last time I made these, you were at a camping trip with your Boy Scout troop," Anna said. "I didn't realize you never tasted them before. I'll tell you what I'm going to do, I'll put a couple extra on your mother's dish for you."

The other kids chimed in.

"Hey, that's not fair," Saundra said. "He could have been here the last time you made them but he wanted to go camping. How come he gets special treatment now?"

"Saun, you've had these a lot of times," Frankie said. "You're not being fair. I've never tasted these before and if Grandma is giving some to take home, what's it to you? Why don't you save some of your pierogies from your plate to take home?"

"Grandma, I'm just really hungry and I know I'll be in the mood for pierogies tomorrow too," Saundra begged.

"Grandma, please don't let Saun steal my pierogies," Frankie pleaded.

"Ok, ok," their grandmother laughed. "I made a lot more when Grandpa told me he was picking you guys up. So there'll be enough for all of you tomorrow, sound good?"

The children stopped arguing and turned their attention back to the food.

Johnny got up from the table rubbing his belly.

"Mom, that was delicious," Johnny said. "It really hit the spot."

He took his jacket off the back of his chair and pulled it on.

"Ok kids, don't give your grandfather a hard time," Johnny said. "He has to take you all home so you can do some homework and go to bed. I don't want you to talk your grandparents into letting you stay so you can watch T.V."

After Johnny left, Frank asked Wayne about college. He was concerned Wayne wasn't thinking about his future enough.

"I don't know yet," Wayne said, shrugging. "I applied to a few colleges but they didn't respond. I was hoping I would get a baseball scholarship or a call from one of the major league clubs."

"Well, a baseball or a football scholarship would be great," his grandfather asked. "But playing pro sports is unpredictable. The only way to get anywhere is with a college education."

His grandmother stopped washing dishes to join the conversation.

"Your grandfather is right, sweetie," his grandmother said. "We both came from Poland and we went through terrible hardships because your grandfather didn't have a formal education. Look at your own dad. When he came back from the war, he went back to work at Ford's and didn't get anywhere until he went back to school. He went to college for two years and now he's president of the union."

"I've read a lot about ball players getting hurt and the owners let them go because they can't play anymore," his grandfather said. "If you have a college education, you have the tools to go into any business and don't have to depend on sports to make a living. Go to college and you can become a doctor or a lawyer and become a millionaire."

"You're right, but I don't like school," Wayne said. "It's too hard to study. I told mom I'd like to go to work for a year and then go back to school. Also, mom has to wake me up every morning and it takes 15 minutes to get me out of bed. If I go to college, there'll be no one to wake me up and I'll flunk my classes and it will be a waste."

His grandfather laughed.

"Son, that's no reason to stop considering college," he said. "Your father was the same way. Your grandmother had to call him 50 times before he got out of bed. Then he went into the Army where he had no trouble getting up. If it's something that matters to you, you will wake up."

"Grandpa, it's a little different in the Army," Wayne said. "If you don't get up, the corporal throws you out of bed. I was talking to a friend of mine who went to college and missed half of his classes and he flunked out. What if that happens to me?"

"Did you tell your father how you feel about college?" his grandfather asked.

"No, grandpa, he'd blow his top if he heard I didn't want to go," Wayne said. "A baseball scout from the Cincinnati Reds came to see me play. He said I have the moves of a big league catcher and I should go to college to play against qualified pitchers to get the experience. That way I could get more money if the big league drafted me. I did talk to mom and dad about working for a year before going to college."

"Wayne, once you stay out of school, you never want to go back," his grandfather said. "While you're working you get a taste of money and you don't want to give that up. College-educated men come into our plant with poor work ethic but they become bosses because the company recognized their education. A college education means everything these days. When your father worked at the battery plant, he tried to start a union there but the workers didn't listen to him. They felt he was a cocky young man with no education. It was only after he went to college that he became president of the union."

"That's enough talk for tonight," his grandmother interjected. "It's getting late so you should get the kids home."

"Wayne, just think about it," his grandfather said. "Whatever you chose, we all will support you."

* * *

The membership meeting held no surprises and happened as Johnny planned. The international representatives were effective with the old timers in the plant but the young workers turned the contract down overwhelmingly. The final vote was 1501 against the ratifications and 155 for the agreement out of five thousand members in the local. The rest of the members didn't vote, but Johnny knew there would be complaints from them as well.

After the meeting, the members gathered around Johnny to congratulate him on the outcome of the vote. Mikey Ryan, a night shift worker, took Johnny aside.

"Mr. Romanek, Freddie McCoy has been knocking you real hard lately," Mikey said. "He's been telling groups of workers that he was the one who won the local agreement and that he was the won who projected the demands at the meeting with the company while you just sat there and let him do all the work. He's also been telling us that Rocky would be a better president than you."

"Thanks for this information Mikey," Johnny said, letting the information settle.

"Freddie is hard to believe because he's always drunk," Mikey said. "I don't know if it's the drink talking but I was also told by some of his friends that he's getting a lot of extra money from the union. He's slandering you a lot and some of the workers are listening to him."

"I expected blowback from Freddie, but this is more than I thought," Johnny admitted. "I assure you, he won't be getting any extra money from the union from now on."

Johnny shook hands with Mikey. Then he pulled together an impromptu meeting with his night shift committeemen.

When all the men had gathered in their meeting space, he addressed the issue of Freddie.

"I thought you guys had a commitment from Freddie that he wouldn't play politics during our contract talks?" Johnny said. "I had a gut feeling when you guys suggested him for the night shift plant committeeman position that he was the wrong person. I was against that but I felt you guys knew what you were doing because I trusted your insight. He stood by me during our contract talks but now that he's on Rocky's team, it's a different ball game now. He's done a complete 180. He's not on our side anymore."

Johnny paused before continuing.

"If Freddie wants to play dirty politics, I'm a master at that," Johnny said. "He doesn't realize he's in the big league here and not some shit-ass union where he came from."

He stopped for a moment and turned to Burt Landers.

"Burt, as of Monday, I'm going to assign you as the night shift plant committeeman," Johnny said, effectively replacing Freddie McCoy.

Monday night, Johnny went into the night shift and directly to Freddie McCoy's department. There he saw Freddie standing against the wall in a drunken stupor. He was talking to his constituents and Johnny could hear him.

"You guys better not forget me in this coming election," Freddie slurred. "If it wasn't for me we wouldn't have shit in this local agreement. I intend to be running the show when Rocky gets elected president of this union."

While Freddie was talking to the workers, the foreman came over.

"Freddie, you can't take the workers off their jobs to talk to them," the foreman said. "This line has been down for three minutes now and we've lost three jobs this hour. I'm asking you to tell the men to go back to work or I'll have to take them to labor relations for a work stoppage. That could result in severe discipline."

Freddie almost fell as he lunged for the foreman who easily moved away. Freddie held onto the wall to keep his balance.

"You're a motherfucker, you're not taking anyone to labor relations," Freddie yelled. "I'll have your ass fired and out of the plant. Now get the fuck away from me, can't you see that you're bothering me?"

No one noticed Johnny observing the fiasco taking place between Freddie and the foreman. Johnny was aware that the company wouldn't charge Freddie with a work stoppage but they would go after the workers for work stoppage, to make the union look weak. Johnny approached the workers who then noticed him for the first time.

"What's happening"? Johnny asked.

He turned to Freddie who was unable to stand and was now trying to sit on a bench but kept nearly falling off. Johnny grasped Freddie by the arms to steady him.

"Are you alright?" Johnny asked. "I think I need to take you to the medic. Men, go back to work while I take Freddie to be treated."

Johnny helped Freddie down the aisle toward the medic department. Freddie attempted to pull away from Johnny who held a strong grip on his arm.

"Leave me alone!" Freddie yelled. "I'm all right. I want to go back and kick the shit out of that foreman."

Johnny held onto Freddie tightly. They were out of sight from the workers on the line.

"You drunken fool, you want to play politics so I'm going to play with you," Johnny sneered. "You promised the night shift committeemen and me that you wouldn't do dirty politics while we were in contract talks, yet I was told you were talking shit about me the entire time. Tonight I heard it for myself. I'm taking you off the floor as committeeman and putting Burt Landers in your place. Your pay with the company stops right now. You're a disgrace to our union by coming into work in this drunken condition. You've been selling your members down the river and getting away with it. If one of the workers on the line were in your condition they would have been sent home for a week without pay as discipline."

Freddie shrank back and realized he was in no power to do anything. Johnny dragged him to the plant exit door.

"I'll be back every night to check on you," Johnny said. "If I find you with the slightest trace of liquor on your breath, you'll be taken off the floor."

Freddie tried one last time to fight off Johnny.

"Get your fucking hands off of me or I'll deck you right here," Freddie said.

"I'll keep my hand off you but you better remember that you're not dealing with a foreman on the line," Johnny said. "Try to lay a hand on me and it's your ass that's going down. If any of the workers gets disciplined due to your actions tonight, I'll bury you as a union committeeman."

Freddie then tried a different tactic, since he realized he wasn't winning the fight.

"Come on, Johnny, I didn't mean anything by it," Freddie said. "You've been a politician for a long time and during election time everyone talks crap about the opposition. You should be used to it by now. It's going to be the same way until the election is over."

Johnny pressed his finger into Freddie's chest to further his point.

"You made me a promise that you wouldn't play politics during the contract negotiations," Johnny said. "You also said you were no fan of Rocky's because he was a sneaky union official. You're nothing but a fucking liar and a scumbag. I can take your shit-talking but when you put our members in jeopardy by causing them to be disciplined, that's where I draw the line. You want to be known as some great opposition to the company but you aren't going to be disciplined for causing a work stoppage, our workers will. If any one of those workers that you took off the line to campaign get disciplined for it, I'll cut the legs out from under you."

Just then they came upon Franklin Todd, of labor relations.

"Johnny, I got a call from Mr. Gorley me that Freddie took some workers off the line to talk to them causing the company to lose three jobs," Franklin said. "They men need to be brought in for a hearing. I'd like you and Freddie to be there to represent them."

"Franklin, Freddie's not feeling well so I want to put Bryan Dill on the floor to represent the chassis line," Johnny said. "He's the alternate committeeman. It's 4:30 presently and I want Freddie's time to stop now. I'll see that he gets out of the plant safely."

"Also, Franklin, please delay the hearings until you hear from me," Johnny said. "It won't be longer than a half hour. I'll make sure Bryan and I will be there. I'd like to talk to Mr. Gorley to explain what happened. The men aren't at fault in this case. All they did was listen to their committeeman who wasn't in any condition to give advice."

"I'll delay the hearing but no longer than a half hour," Franklin said. "I'll notify Bryan's foreman. If you can't get to the hearing we'll do the hearing with Bryan instead."

"That's fair enough," Johnny said. "Thanks."

When Franklin disappeared, Johnny pulled Freddie by the arm through the plant exit door.

"Okay fuck face," Johnny said. "I'm going to get one of the workers here to drive you home. Then Bryan and I are going to clean up your dirty work. You're a disgrace as a union official."

Johnny saw one of the workers taking a smoke break and motioned him over.

"Please get this fool home," Johnny said, giving the man some cash. "I'll talk to your foreman and let him know I sent you on a task outside the plant."

Johnny returned to the chassis line and saw Matt Gorley talking to another foreman. He went over to him and explained that he took Freddie off the floor for the night and replaced him with Bryan. Matt explained that he went along with Freddie's shit talk during negotiations because he didn't want to do anything to interrupt the negotiations. Now it was a different ball game, he wasn't going to allow Freddie to cause a work stoppage and do nothing about it.

Now Johnny had to address the hearings with Matt. When Matt started to work at Ford, Johnny was his representative and helped him on many occasions, pulling a lot of strings and doing a lot of favors. Matt owed him one and he knew it.

"Matt, I'm gonna get right to it," Johnny said. "How about calling off these hearings? The men weren't at fault. All they did was listen to that drunken fuck. I'm going to make it a point to see that he comes into work sober from now on."

"I was wondering when you'd catch him talking all that shit about you," Matt said, smirking. "I felt it was only a matter of time before you'd catch him. I know I owe you one, Johnny. You saved my job years ago when I blew my top with the foreman. I'll call labor relations to cancel the hearings. You can go over to the line to let the men know that you stopped the hearings. I'll call my foreman in the area and instruct them to say nothing to the men."

"You won't regret this, Matt," Johnny said.

"I better not," Matt said.

Johnny walked over to the line to address the men.

"I just talked to foreman Gorley and he agreed to call off the hearings and drop the charges," Johnny said. "The next time Freddie comes in her drunk and runs his mouth, come directly to me. Men, I put Bryan Dill on the floor for tonight."

"Johnny, Freddie has been hitting the bottle heavy lately," one of the workers said. "It's only a matter of time that the company is going to clobber us for listening to him."

He pointed to a worker standing there.

"When that guy Joe came in under the influence, he was sent home for two weeks as discipline," another worker said. "Freddie told him that suspension was the normal penalty for being drunk on the job. How come Freddie can come into work and nothing happens to him?"

Johnny waved his hand.

"Listen, I did you all a favor calling off the hearings," Johnny said. "Least I could get is a thank you. If you want to worry about Freddie's drunk ass, go ahead, but it's not gonna get you anywhere. I told you I would handle him, and I will."

Johnny excused himself to go find Burt, who was just walking into the plant.

"Listen, I found Freddie drunk on the line, I told him you'll be taking over as committeeman," Johnny said to Burt.

"I heard," Burt said. "He was pretty sauced when you found him."

"Listen, I can't talk long, my family will disown me if I'm late another night," Johnny said. He shook hands with Burt and left.

Johnny walked into the kitchen while his wife was having a cup of coffee. She saw that her husband was visibly upset. She got up from her chair and went over to him, kissing him on the cheek.

"Do you want to talk about it?" Ann asked. "Or do you want me to sit here and be quiet?" Ann placed a cup of water in front of Johnny.

"I caught Freddie in the plant doing a political job on me," Johnny said, loosening his tie. "What burns me up is that I had a feeling he would backstab me the first chance he had. But instead I went along with the other guys, thinking they might be right about him, and I was wrong. I was hopeful he would stay neutral until the election."

Johnny took a few sips of water.

"I found Freddie drunk in the plant, running his mouth of tonight," Johnny said. "I came so close to punching him out, but I kept cool. Rocky is sneaky enough, and now I have Freddie to deal with. Enough of me talking, how was your meeting with Wayne's teacher?"

"I spoke to Wayne's English teacher and he told me that if we have any intention of sending Wayne to college, he better bring up his grades up," Ann said. "He's a 'C' average right now and he needs to be at least a 'B' to get accepted into college. His teacher said Wayne has a natural ability to write and that should be cultivated. His writing is apparently very descriptive with a lot of meaning. But unfortunately he has a habit of not turning in his homework even though he's completed it."

She paused and took a sip of her coffee before continuing.

"Another thing she said was that Wayne doesn't want to go to college," Ann said. "I believe he's afraid of being away from home. You're going to have to build up his confidence some way. He tries to please you in everything he does. It's going to be up to you to encourage him in his school work like you did with his sports."

"I'm so wrapped up in this president's job that I have no time to live up to my responsibilities here at home," Johnny said. "I'm sorry I haven't been here for Wayne. At least when I was a committeeman, I was home every evening. Now I'm hit with problems on three shifts. I wonder if this job is worth the effort?"

"You love your work and I don't know what you'd do without it," Ann said. "You get angry when things don't go your way but I see the gleam in your eyes when you talk about the union and what you've accomplished. Take tonight for an example, you're angry with Freddie. You knew from the start you had to watch him. Once this resolves, I'm sure you will feel good about the president position again."

"Hon, let's go into the living room and relax," Johnny said. "There's a heavyweight fight on T.V. tonight."

"I'm not interested in watching the fight," Ann said. "You go ahead and enjoy the fight while I clean up this mess. I picked up a good book from the library that I want to read. You go and relax."

The following morning when Johnny arrived at union hall, Mike Ferrera, midnight committeeman, was waiting for him in the parking lot. Mike was always aligned with Johnny ever since he was elected midnight committeeman even when he was a millwright with the grueling job of handling the heavy steel construction at the plant. He was a powerfully built man at six feet tall and always with a pleasant disposition until someone took him on. He walked alongside Johnny as they approached the headquarters.

"The Freddie McCoy incident is all over the plant and the talk from the chassis line workers is that it was about time you put Freddie in his place," Mike said. "One of the workers is really on your side. He's been giving an earful to everyone that Freddie was a drunk and is harmful to the members that he represents. Freddie is a mean son of a bitch and this is just a sign that you'll have to watch him closely."

"Yeah but Freddie is a drunk and he'll make the same mistake again and then I'll get him," Johnny said.

"Johnny, the night shift has your back solid but the day shift committeemen are blasting you every chance they get," Mike said. "Leroy in the commercial department is blaming you for all the grievances that Rocky has associated you with and they're pissed off at you. I hate to tell you this shit but it's better you know so you can work to correct these slanderous comments. Dominick Long, the committeeman in freight, hates you with a passion. He's been telling his members that you knocked him off on weekends and placed your name on the sheet to represent his men. But that's not even the bad part. He spread a rumor that you don't even come into the office. That instead you go watch your son play football every Saturday. The men believe this because they read the newspapers that are always writing about Wayne as an outstanding athlete."

Johnny angrily threw his briefcase onto the sofa.

"Dominick Long is an ungrateful bastard," Johnny said. "I made arrangements with Cliff, to carry Dominick whenever freight worked on weekends so he could get overtime. Our bargaining committee rotates the overtime work every three weeks and Dominick gets to come in every weekend. I guess I'll have to work on my opposition."

Johnny picked up his briefcase from the sofa and placed it on his desk.

"Let's change the subject for a moment," Johnny said. "I have an important question to ask you. I'd like you to run as my vice-president in this upcoming election. What do you say?"

"What about Burt Landers?" Mike asked. "He's in a position to help you more than me. I'm buried on the midnight shift and don't see that many members."

"I thought about that," Johnny said. "Burt and I have been working a lot of overtime on both shifts and members overlap into your shift for more than two and a half hours each shift. I'd like you to get into the plant problems especially with the foremen's hourly jobs. Blast them when they move in to pick up missed operations. That happens a lot on both shifts. When you call out foremen like that, members notice. Be sure to be loud enough so that members hear and see what you're doing."

"I'm not a union rep on their shifts and the company would stop me from doing that," Mike said.

"That's even better," Johnny said. "When labor relations comes down, raise holy hell and demand they call for me to come. I'm sure they won't but if they do, we can shut them down for a violation of the contract. Labor relations know that."

Mike began to smile.

"I think I'm going to like running as your partner," he said, shaking Johnny's hand.

"Well then brace yourself for this," Johnny said. "I'm going to put Otto Brodwick for plant committee on our ticket."

"You know you're asking for trouble," Mike said, frowning.

"I realize that, but for the last year, I've been talking about having a black man on the bargaining committee," Johnny said. "So I better put or shut up."

"What about the dayshift," Mike said. "They still have a bitter taste in their mouth about the demonstration. They still feel the blacks took away some of their jobs with the Good Will Committee."

"That's not true," Johnny said. "All the Good Will Committee did was stop the foreman from harassing both whites and blacks from both shifts."

"What made you select Otto?" Mike asked.

"He's a level-headed black man and he won the respect of everyone when he helped to put the demonstration to bed," Johnny said. "We might lose a few white votes, but if we handle this right, we could convince white workers that we're doing the right thing."

"All together, how many black workers are working at the plant?" Mike asked.

"A little over two thousand and it's growing every day," Johnny said. "When the company hires workers, you know that the white man quits quicker than a black worker. The black worker likes the job because of the higher pay than other plants offer."

"Johnny I know that you're doing the right thing for the membership," Mike said. "But they're fickle people. They will take all the support you give them. Will they in turn offer you their support?"

"That's going to be Otto's job to convince them, with us coaching him," Johnny said. "I'm sure we'll get the majority of the blacks behind us. All we have to do is wait and see."

"I'm not going to try to change your mind, but if Rocky runs a good white man in that position he'll win," Johnny said. "It only takes a majority vote to win that position. Otto should take every black vote for that position and he could win."

"I hope you're right," Mike said. "Listen, I'm heading home right now since I've been up through the morning and I'm exhausted. I'll be here tomorrow to campaign."

Johnny completed his work at the headquarters and went into the commercial department to begin his campaign later that morning. He couldn't plan on his approach until he assessed the damage that was caused by the committeeman. He walked into the paint area and noticed Terry Walker talking to a group of his constituents at the far end of the department. Johnny was pulled aside by one of the workers who complained that the line speed was too fast and requested that it be checked. Johnny took out his time study watch and found that the line was going faster than the agreed speed. He immediately phoned the time study department and requested that the time study engineer come out to slow the line down. Jim Malvey, the time study engineer, came and stood next to Johnny as he checked the line.

"It's only going a hundredth of a minute fast," Jim said. "Terry usually let's us have that."

"Jim, I don't care what Terry agreed to," Johnny said angrily. "I want the line sped exactly on the money now. We agreed that our manpower is set for a certain speed per unit so each operator can complete his job within his time allotted. I want you to go to the panel box and slow the line to the proper speed. Even if that means lowering it to the hundredth of a minute."

"Johnny, we wouldn't gain a half job over an eight hour schedule," Jim protested.

"Jim, get your ass up there on the ladder and go into the panel box and slow this line down to its proper speed," Johnny roared.

Johnny motioned for Terry to come. When Terry got there Johnny spoke loud enough for all the workers to hear.

"Terry, this line is running fast and Jim told me that you agreed to his faster speed," Johnny said. "From now on I want this line to run our agreed speed and not a second faster. If you're afraid to fight for our members properly, I'll send someone who will protect our workers right. Am I clear?"

Terry was deep red from embarrassment.

"Johnny, it was only a hundredth of a minute faster," Terry said. "That doesn't amount to anything."

Johnny was hoping for that answer from Terry. He now had the opportunity to show the men in his department that he wasn't a good committeeman who instead agreed to allow the company to increase the line speed to get more than the allowed jobs at the end of the day.   "Terry, how come the company won't agree to run slower than the time allowed?" Johnny asked. "If you can agree to allow them to go faster, you can agree to have them go slower, right?"

Many of the workers came close to observe if the time study man would go up to the panel to slow the line down. They knew that was a big no-no.

"Jim, slow the line a hundredth of a minute slower than the agreed line speed, to make up for the time that the line was faster than the agreed time," Johnny said.

"I can't do that," Jim said, shaking his head. "If I did I would get fired."

Johnny got the answer he wanted. He looked around at the workers.

"Remember, this is the guy you elected to protect your rights," Johnny said. "Terry, don't ever let me find the line speed faster than the agreed time or I'll have your ass in a sling."

The workers applauded as Terry tried to explain but Johnny interrupted him.

"Don't bullshit me like you do all the other members," Johnny said. "I want you to check the line speed every morning and every afternoon. They better all be right on the money."

Johnny also had another bone to pick with Terry.

"Also, what grievances are you telling the members that I was supposed to have withdrawn?" Johnny asked Terry.

Terry was flustered because he realized that someone had told Johnny what he had been saying. He had been spreading lies around the department about Johnny.

"I don't know what you're talking about," Terry stuttered. "I did mention that you ordered Rocky to settle all the third-stage grievances by getting the good ones granted and withdrawing the bad ones."

"That's not the way I'm hearing about it," Johnny said. "You told the aggrieved that I personally withdrew his grievance which is a bold-face lie.

Terry was upset over the confrontation, noticing all the workers now gathering around and listening. Everyone knew Terry as the compulsive liar he was.

"Whoever told you that must have misunderstood my reply," Terry said. "Tell me who it was and I'll straighten them out."

"Terry you're a fucking sneak and a company stooge," Johnny said, waving his hand dismissively. "You better start telling the workers the truth. Make sure that you keep the line speed on the agreed speed. Now get the fuck away from me and go do the job you were elected to do."

Johnny turned to the workers before leaving the scene.

"If I were you, I'd buy a stopwatch to keep this guy honest," Johnny said.

Johnny was satisfied with how he handled the situation and now was on his way to the freight department. His goal now was to have a confrontation with Dominick Long, who was spreading rumors and falsehoods about him. He walked the crane way and was stopped by a group of forklift operators. Ed McKenna, who was one of the top senior employees in freight, was denied the right to work the weekend. He asked which union representative handled overtime on Saturday. Johnny was confused by the question.

"Rocky Durango was the representative last Saturday but what does that have to do with him?" Johnny asked. "Dominick Long is your committeeman and he was here last Saturday. He's the one you have to see. He's the one who picks the men to work off of the overtime list that is posted on the board. If you have a grievance, go see Mr. Long. He's the one who controls the rotation of the overtime list."

"I saw Mr. Long and he told me that he wasn't in on Saturday because you knocked him off and had the company put you on as the representative in the freight department instead of him," Ed said.

The workers all noticed Dominick coming down the crane way as Ed continued speaking.

"Mr. Long told me to go to the union office to put in a grievance in order to get paid for Saturday," Ed said.

Johnny noticed Dominick out of the corner of his eye trying to sneak away.

"Dominick come here," Johnny said. "Ed tells me it was his time to work overtime on Saturday, yet Cliff brought in a man with more overtime on the list than him and he has a lot less seniority than him. How could this happen?"

"What's Ed crying about?" Dominick snapped. "I just left Cliff's office and asked why Ed wasn't in last Saturday to work. He told me that Ed sneaked out of the plant last Friday and wasn't around to come to work on Saturday. I got him scheduled to come in first next Saturday."

"You know that's a fucking lie," Ed cried. "I saw you at quitting time in the parking lot when you were getting into your car to go home. I called out to you about why I wasn't coming to work the weekend. I know you heard me because you jumped into the car before I could get to you. You must have made some good deal with Cliff to keep me out. I always thought you were a good committeeman but now I see that you're nothing but a liar and a prick."

"Ed be a man and stop being a fucking cry baby," Dominick said.

Johnny had the opening he needed.

"Dominick why did you tell the men that I was full-time Saturday and that Ed should go over to headquarters to put in a grievance for Saturday's work?" Johnny asked.

"These guys are all fucking liars," Dominick raged. "I'm not going to stand here and be humiliated by them."

Dominick walked away while all his workers jeered at him.

Johnny had proved his point in both departments. Now a large group gathered around him when they heard the confrontation. They all heard Dominick blasting Johnny for months and now they wanted to hear the other side.

"I want to set the record straight," Johnny said. "Mr. Long has been working every weekend all year long and had Cliff assigned him to work weekends so Mr. Long wouldn't have to be bothered representing his workers for any problems. If Mr. Long denies that he wasn't coming in, ask him to show you his pay stub. That was all the money he received all year. Better yet, let's call the warehouse while we're at it."

Johnny dramatically walked over to the phone on the desk and picked it up.

"Hello, yes, this is Mr. Johnny Romanek, union president," he said. "I have a question about Dominick Long. Did he work every weekend these past few months?"

Johnny held the phone out so the workers could hear the affirmative answer. He then hung up the phone and clapped his hands together.

"So now you all know that Dominick Long has been fucking with you for the last two years," Johnny said. "The election is coming up so don't let him screw you for any longer." Johnny caught sight of Larry McCormick walking down the line. He pointed to Larry.

"There's the guy that should be your committeeman," Johnny said. "He was the best committeeman that you ever had. I'd appreciate you men voting for him in the next election."

"Larry you heard what I said to the group," Johnny said, approaching Larry in the crane way. "How about you running for committeeman?"

"What about Dominick?" Larry said. "I thought the workers liked him."

Johnny laughed and turned to the workers.

"He's not as strong as he once was, right men?" Johnny said, with the workers cheering. Johnny turned back to Larry.

"We just caught him in a bold-faced lie in front of the workers," Johnny said. "I assure you that this latest update will go all around the department. I'll see to that. You got everything working for you. With Ed McKenna on your side, you'll win in a landslide."

"With you in my corner, I'll have a good chance of winning," Larry admitted. "You know that Dominick is supporting Rocky and has been smack talking you, right? I want to warn you that you have only one committee supporting you. So you have an uphill battle to win. But we'll do it. I'll see you Saturday at the caucus meeting."

Chapter 21
Year 1966

Johnny was all smiles when he entered the house after a long day of handling grievances and other issues at the plant. He felt things were going his way and his re-election would be seamless. He started to push Duke around the room while the dog was biting at his pant cuffs. The dog needed roughhousing to tire him out since the children were in school and Ann had enough work to keep her busy all day. Duke nipped at the sleeves of Johnny's jacket as he continued to play and growl. Ann heard the ruckus and came into the room.

"Dear, you're in a good mood for a change," Ann said. "Did everything go well for you in at the plant?"

"Today was the first time I had the opportunity to get back at the day shift committeemen who have been smack-talking me," Johnny said. "Before I was tied up with meetings on negotiations. Now I'm going to be roaming the plant, campaigning and protecting myself from my opposition. I also spoke to Mike Ferrera and he's willing to run for the vice president position. He's not happy about Otto Brodwick running on the ticket with us, since he feels we may lose the white vote. But I'm hoping with Otto on the ticket we can convince the white voters that having a black worker on the bargaining committee will enable us to relate to the black community and bring more harmony to the plant. He did a good job helping to dismantle the black uprising. Maybe with him on the committee we might have peace in the plant. Only time will tell."

"John, you're starting something new in the plant bringing in a new worker into a key position on the bargaining committee," Ann said. "Your position has always been that you have to work your way up in any position to get promoted to a key role. He has to prove to the members that he has the ability to handle the bargaining job. You're going against your theory. Think about that, it's important to prove to the membership that Otto is right for the position. Do you think that the whites will accept a man to represent them who is going to be learning on the job?"

Johnny had spent the past 12 years discussing union matters on his wife. He knew how brilliant she was with political strategy.

"It's going to be a hard fight but we can't continue denying blacks their own representative," Johnny said. "I'm counting on Rocky to run Freddie McCoy for plant committeeman. Freddie is smart as a union representative but he's an alcoholic who can't control his liquor and temper when he's drunk. He's made a lot of wrong moves lately."

He leaned closer to Ann and paused.

"No more shop talk," Johnny said. "Let's you and I go out to dinner alone tonight. I'm not going to have any free nights during the campaign."

"Dear, I would love to but not tonight," Ann said. "How about a date on Saturday? Perhaps a Broadway play in New York? I have a roast in the oven and my hair needs to be set."

At that moment the phone rang. Ann walked to the phone to retrieve it.

"Dear, it's Burt Landers," Ann said, handing Johnny the phone.

"Hi Burt, what's up?" Johnny asked.

"Johnny, I hate to bother you after spending the whole day in the plant campaigning, but we have a serious problem," Burt said. "Freddie is soused to the gills and instructed an hourly man named Sully Jones to miss part of his operation because a foreman was helping him to complete the job. When the operator let the job go, they took him to labor relations and gave him two weeks off without pay."

"Was there a standard problem with the job?" asked Johnny.

"No," Burt said. "As a matter of fact, Sully was on light duty and was only performing half of an operation."

"Sully is a utility man and has been around a long time," Johnny said. "He knows better than to refuse an operation."

"I saw him after the hearing and I asked him about it," Burt said. "He told me he wanted the night off but he never expected to get hit with a two-week penalty. Matt Gorley was the one who insisted they give him the severe penalty because of the incident with Freddie McCoy the night before. Freddie was slobbering all over the place and cursing out Matt Gorley and labor relations. I tried to quiet him down but he won't listen to me. I'm in the next office in labor relations and I could hear Freddie screaming through the walls as if he were next to me. Johnny, he's completely out of control. You're the only one who can take Freddie out of the plant. It's that bad."

"Burt, I'll be right in," Johnny said, looking at his wife and shrugging. He placed the phone on the cradle.

"Hon, I'm sorry but I have to go back into the plant," Johnny said. "Freddie is drunk again and the company disciplined a man for listening to his bad advice. Keep the plate hot for me. I'll be home as soon as I can break away."

"It's a good thing we rescheduled our date," Ann laughed, kissing her husband goodbye.

Johnny went directly to labor relations and he could hear Freddie cursing all over the place through the thin walls. He was calling Matt Gorley "bastard" and threatening to shut down his production. Matt Gorley was standing against the wall while Franklin Todd was sitting behind his desk. Freddie was walking up and down the room in a drunken rage. Johnny sat down on one of the empty chairs.

"Freddie, what's the problem?" Johnny asked. "I thought that we had an agreement that you wouldn't come in the plant under the influence again."

Freddie dismissed Johnny's remarks.

"Johnny, this fuck, Matt Gorley," Freddie slurred. "He gave my best worker, Sully Jones, a two-week dismissal for missing part of an operation. I warned Matt a hundred times that I wasn't going to tolerate any foreman performing an hourly operation but he doesn't give a fuck. I caught Harry Peters doing a part of Sully's operation so I told Sully to let Harry do the operation for the rest of the night. The next thing I know, Matt brings Sully to labor relations and disciplines him."

Matt was thoroughly incensed by Freddie's behavior.

"There's a procedure in the contract to follow if our foreman performs an hourly function," Matt said. "The union doesn't have the right to take matters into their own hands by ordering an hourly employee to miss part of his operation."

He pointed his finger at Freddie.

"You pissed me off because your president sent you home because you were under the influence yesterday and I agreed to drop the hearings on the members that listened to you, but not tonight," Matt said. "You got away with it yesterday but not a second time."

"Where is Sully Jones now?" asked Johnny.

"I sent him home an hour ago," said Franklin Todd. "I ordered him out of the plant in 15 minutes. Harry went to the line to put away Sully's tools and brought back Sully's lunch box. We had security escort Sully out of the plant."

"Freddie, I'd like to talk to you alone in the next room," Johnny said. They sat down in the next office that was vacant.

"I don't know what you're trying to prove," Johnny said.

Freddie was squirming all over the place.

"Don't get up or you'll fall flat on your face," Johnny said. "I heard Matt's side of the story. Smarten me up so I can understand why you had Sully miss the operation?"

Freddie's hand was trembling while he took a pack of cigarettes from out of his shirt pocket. He put a bent cigarette into his mouth but couldn't get a match to light it. He threw the cigarette into the wastebasket.

"You know that these foremen are always working," Freddie said. "When I came to the area and saw Harry helping Sully, I told him to get off the fucking job and he told me that he was showing Sully how to do the operation. Sully knows every operation on the line so I got pissed off and told Sully let Harry do the operation for the rest of the night. Then I walked away. I didn't think that Sully would take me seriously."

He took a handkerchief from his back pocket to wipe his brow.

"Johnny, I'd appreciate if you could get Sully back to work," Freddie said. "I didn't realize he was on light duty and was performing a job that he didn't know how to perform."

Johnny then realized that Freddie wasn't as drunk as he was pretending to be.

"You pulled the same shit yesterday when I had to go to Matt to have him drop the charges," Johnny said. "I don't appreciate going to management to cop a plea when you instructed a man to violate the contract. Tonight you did the same thing and now Sully Jones is on the street. There's no way I can get him back without offering something I can't afford to give. Freddie, you leave me no choice but to remove you from the floor and place Bryan in your place. You need to leave the plant right now."

Freddie realized he was in a bind with the membership over his foolishness. He took the bent cigarette out of the wastebasket and lit it up.

"Okay, I'm not as drunk as you thought, but I feel bad about Sully Jones," Freddie admitted. "I'd like you to get him back to work. All I wanted to do was make the foreman look bad and it backfired on me. The most I figured would happen is that Sully would get a reprimand and a warning but not a loss of pay. I'll make a deal with labor relations so they give me the penalty time off instead of Sully."

Freddie knew there was little Johnny could do with Sully Jones out of the plant but he felt if the company gave him the time off instead, it would play well with the membership. Johnny wasn't buying any of what Freddie had to offer. He merely shrugged his shoulders and walked out of the plant.

Johnny went to Franklin Todd's office.

"Franklin, I just sent Freddie home and I'd like you to contact Bryan Dill's boss to tell him Bryan is the committeeman for the rest of the night," Johnny said. "Stop Freddie's time as of now."

He turned to Matt next.

"I know you did me a favor last night but giving Sully Jones two weeks off is a harsh punishment," Johnny said. "Why don't you ring him back tomorrow, we'll let the penalty remain on his record and loss of pay for the time off. I'll make sure there'll be no grievance."

"Johnny, I can't do that," Matt said. "Sully got hurt at the start of the shift and the medic department placed him on light duty for three days. When he returned from the medic department, he asked me to send him home for the rest of the day thinking medic would pick up his time for the rest of the night. I couldn't do that because the plant doctor made it clear that Sully can do a one-hand operation for the rest of the night. The job I put Sully on was the easiest one in the chassis department and all I gave him was one-half of the operation. I spoke to Sully after the hearing and he said that he expected to get the night off only. When I hit him with the two-week penalty, he started to sing a completely different tune. Too bad Sully has to suffer due to Freddie's bullshit but I gotta start somewhere."

Matt looked toward Franklin Todd for a moment before continuing.

"Johnny, let Sully Jones stay out for tomorrow so he understands that he can't violate the contract and get away with it," Matt conceded. "You can call him up and tell him he can come back the day after tomorrow. Let him know this incident will remain on his record. Our biggest job is to make sure that Freddie gets the message."

"Matt, thanks again," Johnny said, shaking his hand. "I'll call Sully tonight to tell him to come back the day after tomorrow. I'll explain to him that he should have known better than to listen to a drunk when he knew what he did was wrong. I'm going out on a line to tell them I put Bill Bryant on the floor tonight because of Freddie's condition. I'll also make sure to tell them that when Freddie's drunk and tells them to violate the contract, don't do it."

"You're going to have your hands full with Freddie," Lou said. "He can't stop drinking. Maybe with the loss of pay, he won't have the extra money to buy drinks, although that's wishful thinking on my part. Again Johnny, I couldn't bring Joe back any sooner. If I did, Joe would have gotten his wish and he wouldn't have gotten the message."

Johnny thanked him and went directly to the area where Sully Jones was working. He told the members what happened during the hearing. He explained that he took Freddie off the floor because of his condition and that Freddie told Sully Jones to let the foreman do his job and abandoned it. As a result, labor relations gave Sully two weeks off as discipline for refusing to complete his operation. Freddie knew better than to tell Sully to let the job go to a foreman and gave him bad advice.

"When Freddie is drunk, he acts like a tough guy and does things that are flat out wrong," Johnny explained. "I'm going to have to come in here more often to keep Freddie honest. Freddie was getting away with a lot of violations while we were in contract talks because the company was afraid we would strike the plant. Now it's a different game, the contract is settled and we're going into our local elections. The best I could do was get Mr. Gorley to bring Sully back to work the day after tomorrow. That's the best I could do under the circumstances."

"Freddie was a building chairman in the Chester plant for one year and he knows we're going to get clobbered when we refuse to do an operation," said one of the older workers. "He was always drunk there and he's doing the same thing here. Maybe the company should discipline him when he comes to work in that condition. Then he'd learn to sober up."

The worker made a lot of sense but Johnny didn't want to encourage the company to have a hearing on one of his committeeman.

"I took Freddie off the floor yesterday and today for being under the influence and stopped his pay," Johnny said. "I'll continue that until he gets the message. If he doesn't, then I'll have to take drastic measures."

The men were satisfied with his explanation except the older worker.

"I'm going to circulate a petition to force Freddie's resignation since he keeps coming in drunk," the older worker said. "He's going to kill us all if we don't do something. I know how he was in Philly and we were all hurt by his actions."

During the week the petition was circulated throughout the night shift chassis department and car delivery asking for Freddie's resignation. Normally it was difficult to get the workers to sign a petition against their committeeman, but in this instance, the workers were furious because Freddie was never disciplined because of his drunken behavior. Freddie continued his abusive attitude toward management whenever the company brought in a union member for a hearing due to a violation.

The night shift chassis workers came to the union headquarters demanding the bargaining committee come into the plant to resolve their problem. Rocky Durango and Lou Sargent were the only ones present at the time, listening to the workers' complaints. They immediately went into the plant to meet with Matt Gorley to request that he rescind the penalties dealt to the workers that were assessed during the week. Lou Sargent who was the previous committeeman in the area approached Matt Gorley about the number of penalties. Matt Gorley explained the events that transpired between Freddie and Johnny. He was at his wit's end and couldn't take Freddie's abuse anymore.

Rocky tried to use his position as vice president to get Matt Gorley to rethink the penalties.

"Matt, I was told you wouldn't even listen to the man's explanation when you had him in the office," Rocky said. "That's not a fair hearing."

"Rocky, you're right," Matt Gorley said. "When we had the hearing in labor relations, Freddie would call us all kinds of names so we had no choice but to impose the next penalty for the violation."

"Even if the man might be innocent?" asked Rocky. "Those men aren't abusing you, Freddie is."

"Rocky, you know me for years, I've always been fair but I'm not going to be abused by a committeeman," Matt Gorley said. "I'm not going to straighten out Freddie, that's the union's job. Freddie gets a thrill in taking us on. He has no intention of stopping. If I let Freddie get away with what he's doing, I'll be out of a job."

Rocky was aware that Matt Gorley was assigned by the company to improve the conditions in the chassis department. If he didn't do his job, they would just put someone in the position that would. Marie, who was the labor relations' secretary, warned Rocky that Freddie McCoy was out of control during negotiations and was causing the company to lose production but Rocky paid no heed. He felt that dealing with Freddie was Johnny's responsibility not his.

"We have men on the street out on discipline because of Freddie," Rocky said. "Bring them back and I'll straighten Freddie out."

"Rocky," Matt Gorley said. "I'm sorry, but Freddie has been nastier than ever. If he continues along these same lines, more men will get punished if they listen to his bad advice."

Lou Sargent and Rocky knew Matt Gorley was in no position to move on disciplinary cases so they walked away. They proceeded down the aisle and saw a chassis man carrying a recall petition from worker to worker who took the time to sign it. Lou Sargent walked over to the man.

"Dan, what the hell are you doing with this petition?" Lou asked. "You know that Freddie's the smartest committeeman on the night shift, right?"

"Lou, I know that Freddie is your friend but a lot of our members are getting hurt on account of him," Dan said. He was flustered getting caught red-handed with the petition.

"We didn't mind him doing the things he did as long as no one got hurt," Dan said. "But now it's different. Freddie comes in every night drunk and we're getting clobbered because of his big mouth. I just came from an operation where Freddie told the guy to let part of his operation go so it would come to a head. The guy has a work standard grievance on his operation and if he listens to Freddie, he'll get time off without pay. What are you two guys going to do about this? Wait until someone gets fired?"

"Dan, if I get Freddie off the juice, will you drop the petition?" Rocky asked.

"If you can get him off the juice," Dan said. "But that's a long shot. There's Freddie over by the wheel-mounting operation. Straighten Freddie out and I'll rip up this petition."

Dan pointed to Freddie who was leaning against the table so he wouldn't fall down. Lou and Rocky walked over to Freddie.

"Freddie, we'd like to talk to you a minute," Rocky said.

"If you're here with the same bullshit that Johnny pulled on me, you're wasting your time," Freddie slurred. "I got a problem with this job and I want to get it resolved tonight. The foreman added more work to this and I feel that it's too much."

"When did they add this work to the operator?" Lou Sargent asked.

"They added this spare wheel to him two months ago," the operator said. "I just asked Freddie where my grievance was so he told me to stop putting the spare wheel into the trunk. I'm for that but I don't want any bullshit that will send me home for missing my operation. If you guys tell me to miss the operation, I'll go along."

"We're not in a position to tell you to let the work go," Lou said. "But we'll set up a meeting with management to get the grievance heard and to see if we can get it corrected. Let's go over to the coffee machine and talk."

"Rocky, let's not bullshit this guy, tell him how it is," Freddie said, not moving. "He's been doing the job for two months without missing a job. If he really has a problem let him skip the spare wheel and we'll have everybody looking at the operation."

"Freddie, you know better than to tell Jim to miss the operation," Rocky said. "Let's go over to the coffee machine so we can talk."

"Fuck you both," Freddie yelled. "Why don't you get the fuck out of my district so I can do my job!"

Freddie walked away to the next operation to talk to the operator there. Rocky and Lou were embarrassed as they were insulted in front of the union members who were standing nearby.

Dan watched the confrontation take place and knew Freddie wasn't going to change his ways.

"Sign this petition so we can get Freddie a new job and save ours," Dan said to one of the workers.

There was nothing more Rocky or Lou could do to save Freddie.

On Friday afternoon, the night shift was buzzing with excitement to see what action the chassis members would take against Freddie McCoy. The members knew Lou Sargent and Rocky would do everything in their power to prevent Freddie from being recalled. They were also aware Freddie was smack talking Johnny every night for the last month. The members were anxious to see what position Johnny would take and what position Rocky and Lou would take to counter it. A few of Lou Sargent's diehard backers were trying to get members to suspend the petition but were unsuccessful. When the shift ended, most of the workers drifted over to the union hall and it was completely filled in 15 minutes.

Johnny walked into the hall and had to push his way up through the crowd to the podium. Rocky was standing on the platform with Lou Sargent at his side. Johnny opened the petition that had 450 signatures on it from the chassis department. It looked like every member signed it. Rocky leaned over to Johnny.

"Looks like this is going to be a hot meeting," Rocky said. "Isn't there some way we could get the members to drop the petition? We all owe Freddie a debt of gratitude for the way he helped during the local agreement. Most of the members here are your supporters. One word from you and you can cancel this whole affair."

"There's a lot of unhappy members out there," Johnny said. "Freddie was riding high on the hog during the negotiations when the men loved the diversion while he clobbered the company. Now the shoe is on the other foot and the company is clobbering our members with discipline for his bullshit, while Freddie is riding high on the hog and the company can't discipline him for his actions. I've been called at my home almost every night over Freddie's bullshit. We have 20 members out on the street on discipline because they listened to him. Both of you were in the plant trying to talk to him and he told you to go fuck yourself and get out of his department in front of the members standing by. If Freddie doesn't give a shit, neither do I. Rocky, I'm not going to push the membership one way or the other. I'm going to leave it to the membership to decide what they want to do with Freddie."

"Johnny, we know you're pissed Freddie was bad-mouthing you ever since the local agreement was adopted by the membership," Lou said. "But for the sake of the union, let him finish out his term as committeeman. I'll see to it that he doesn't run for office in this coming election."

"Lou, I don't give a damn if he runs in this election or not," Johnny said. "I didn't take up the petition, his members did. I think they were right in doing it. He hurt a lot of people out there. They're the ones you should be talking to, not me."

The hall filled to capacity, causing the men to wrap up their conversation. Johnny took the microphone in his hand and called the meeting to order. He had the petition in his hand, holding it up and preparing to say something. Before he could say anything, Freddie McCoy pushed his way through the crowd.

"Mr. Chairman, I request a special point of privilege," Freddie said.

Johnny nodded his head, allowing Freddie to come forward.

Freddie staggered toward the podium with his hair falling over his eyes. He had to lean on a member standing in the aisle to keep from falling. He was helped up the steps to the platform to the microphone. Freddie leaned against the podium and the hall came to a complete silence. He started to sway and almost fell before Lou Sargent caught him and held him in place.

"I don't see why Johnny called this meeting tonight to have me removed," Freddie said. "I already notified the company that I was going to retire."

Johnny immediately stepped forward and took the microphone away from Freddie.

"Freddie, I'm sure the sponsors of this petition weren't aware that you are retiring," Johnny said. "This new information sheds a different light on this meeting. You were a dedicated union official in Chester and when you came to Clinton you were forced to drink because you were under constant stress. I'm going to ask the members to withdraw this petition so you can retire and go out in dignity. I'd like to take this opportunity to have a motion to rescind the petition."

There were seconds for the motion throughout the floor. Johnny called for the vote and it passed unanimously.

"I'd like another motion to have our union place Freddie on vacation for a week while he waits for the pension to come through," Johnny said. The members also voted to approve this.

"As of now, Bryan Dill is the committeeman in the chassis department," Johnny said. "To make this official, let's vote that you approve of Bryan taking over as committeeman."

The members voted unanimously to approve. Johnny placed his arms around Freddie's shoulders.

"Freddie, I want to be the first to congratulate you on your retirement," Johnny said. "Besides the vacation that we're giving you, I'm going to ask Bryan to take up a collection from your chassis members to get you an appropriate gift."

He shook hands with Freddie who stood there with a befuddled expression on his face.

"I'd like to be the first one to donate," Johnny said. "Here's a 20 dollar bill from me to start the collection. Good luck Freddie."

Johnny saw the members were satisfied with the results and called the meeting adjourned. He also realized he surprised Freddie with the latest turn of events. Johnny's goal was to disperse the tension as best he could.

"Rocky we have to make the old man happy," Johnny said. "I see Bryan Dill coming up to the podium, so how about you two putting up 20 bucks along with me?"

They were too embarrassed to refuse and realized they were outfoxed by Johnny's action. They had caucus members lined up to speak on behalf of Freddie. All their planning went to waste when Freddie was placed on vacation. They were now faced with realigning the candidates who were going to run with them in the election.

Johnny's caucus members gathered around him to congratulate him for the handling of a sticky political situation. Pat Fager came forward with a hand extended.

"Johnny you're a master when it comes to politics," Pat said. "We all know Freddie had no intention to retire but was only going to say that to throw everyone off. You never gave him a chance to detail his plan. You killed that when you took away the microphone. I saw the dazed look on Freddie's face but there was nothing he could do to stop the momentum."

"Let's get out of here before we see a grown man cry when he realizes what happened to him," Johnny said.

Freddie didn't recover from the shock when he turned to Lou Sargent.

"What the fuck just happened?" Freddie asked. "Before I could finish speaking, Johnny took the microphone away from me and now I find out that I'm retiring. That's not the way we planned it. Lou, it was your idea that I start off by saying I was going to retire but you didn't say anything when he took away the microphone. Now what do I do? I can't go home to my wife and say I retired because I was drunk and didn't know what I was doing."

Lou was embarrassed by being outfoxed by Johnny. Freddie had no choice but to retire after his opening statement. Lou kept his eye on Bryan Dill as he went from man to man to get their donations. He knew in his heart that he made a mistake in underestimating Johnny. He placed his arm around Freddie attempting to comfort him.

"I'm sorry," Lou said. "I was taken by surprise by Johnny's actions but once the members got riled up there was no stopping him. Maybe Rocky and I could get the international union to give you a job. I'll give Marty a call."

"Lou, you know fucking well that Marty isn't going to give me a job when we went against the international on the contract," Freddie snapped. "Marty's like an elephant, he never forgets. What am I going to tell my wife? Only last week, I told her that I was going to run for plant committeeman. Is there some way we could meet with Johnny to explain that I can't afford to retire and get him to reverse the membership's action?"

"Freddie, I spoke to Johnny before the meeting to intervene on the petition and he refused," Rocky said. "I wish you guys told me what you were planning before announcing it for everyone to hear. I know him better than anyone in the union, including his close friends. I wouldn't have let you make that opening statement. I told you, Johnny's a shrewd politician and he proved that tonight. There's no turning back the clock, you have to live with it."

Freddie pushed Rocky's hand off of his shoulder.

"I knew I made a mistake by teaming up with you two bastards," Freddie sneered. "You gave me bad advice and now you tell me that's how the cookie crumbles. I'm going to meet with Johnny myself to stay on as committeeman."

Freddie got up from the floor and started to stagger down the steps. One of the members caught him and assisted him to his car which was parked nearby. Freddie saw Bryan Dill talking to a group of members while making the collection for his retirement gift. Freddie staggered over and asked Bryan where Johnny was.

"The last time I saw Johnny, he was walking out of the parking lot with Pat Fager," Bryan said. "They might have gone to Club 7-11 for a drink."

Freddie thanked him and staggered to his car.

Meanwhile Johnny and Pat walked into the parking lot as Freddie left.

"Pat, we have to go somewhere to celebrate Freddie's retirement," Johnny said. "Get our caucus members together and we'll go to Luigi's rather than Club 7-11," said Johnny.

They walked over to where Bryan was standing.

"I ran into Freddie and told him that you went to Club 7-11," Bill said.

Both Pat and Johnny laughed out loud.

"I guess we better make it Luigi's for sure then," Johnny said, slapping Pat on the hand.

Chapter 22
Year 1966

After the frenzy of Freddie's forced retirement died down, Johnny got back to union business. The first thing he did was call a special meeting on a Sunday afternoon to discuss the newly won pension plan and how it would affect their future.

The members and their wives were excited as they entered the local union hall. When the members entered the lobby, local union secretaries who were dressed in long blue gowns greeted them. They pinned a lovely corsage on each of the wives and escorted them through the hall to tables that were set in front of the speaker's platform, facing the speakers.

Along the east wall, tables were laden with all kinds of food. It was evident that the executive board spared no expensive to make the affair a memorable one. There were endless platters of roast beef, chicken, Polish kielbasa, Italian sausage and peppers, assorted breads, olives, tomatoes and bowls of assorted salads. The last table had an array of cakes, chocolate layer cakes, banana cream cakes, Italian pastries, strawberry short cake loaded with whipped cream and pots of coffee and hot water for those who preferred tea.

There were young high school girls who volunteered to serve food to members at the tables and assisted them with their choices of food. Many of the wives placed their plates on chairs and went up to one of the speakers to ask questions about how the plan would affect their family's future. Most of the men were content to enjoy the feast and waited until the meeting started. They knew the speakers would go into all the details of the new agreement and how it would affect them.

After most in attendance were through eating, Johnny called the meeting to order.

"I'm sorry we had to take you away from your families on this nice Sunday afternoon," Johnny said. "This was the only day we could get everyone together. I hope all of you enjoyed the buffet which was provided by our local union."

The members and their wives applauded.

"The reason we had the wives here at this retirement meeting is because retirement will effect them the most and bring a change to their day-to-day," Johnny said. "For years your home was your workplace, now you'll have your husband at home and this might upset your daily routine. The other reason we invited the wives is that they're the ones who usually call the union office for information and questions. I also noticed while you were eating that many wives went up to the speakers with questions related to retirement and what the coverages were."

He turned to the speakers who were from the international union.

"I would appreciate if the speakers addressed those questions and answered them to everyone assembled," Johnny said. "I'm sure many of those questions are on the minds of all the members and their wives."

Johnny introduced each representative and asked each to stand when he called out his or her names. The first one to speak was Joey Price, the expert on the retirement plan. He spoke for two hours explaining the fine details of the plan. He answered all questions that were asked by the members and their wives. The next speakers were three from the social security department who explained that if retiring at age 62, workers would only get 80 percent of the social security amount they contributed and if they pushed their retirement age to 65, they would get the full amount. They went into fuller detail on how Medicare would work. The next speaker was a woman from Blue Cross health insurance who explained medical coverage and how it would affect them. The meeting went on for hours, with the wives mostly asking the questions.

As the meeting broke up, many of the retirees and their wives came over to congratulate Johnny on his foresight in calling such a meeting.

"Mr. Romanek, my husband has been a member of the union since its inception and this is the first time wives were invited to a union meeting," a wife said. "I want to personally thank you. This meeting was so enlightening to all of us. I had a number of questions and they were answered to my satisfaction. I thank the good Lord we have a union here at Ford and have such good benefits. I hope and pray that you stay in office for many years. You're good for the union."

"Thank you," Johnny said, extending his hand to shake hers. "That is why I am president, to ensure families like yours are taken care of."

Many of Johnny's caucus members gathered around him to praise his handling of the meeting.

"Johnny you really outdid yourself this time," Pat said. "All we heard while we circulated the floor was praise for what you did here today. The speakers did a fabulous job and convinced a lot of the members to take advantage of retirement. I heard one of the members say that retirement would bring him about 80 percent of his basic weekly pay and he's going to take advantage of it."

Pat then started to laugh as he remembered something.

"I noticed Rocky became green around his gills as the members had so much praise for you," Pat said. "Maybe he'll reconsider and not run against you."

As they were talking an elderly black couple approached him. Marion Bland politely interrupted Pat and Johnny's conversation.

"Johnny, my wife and I want to thank you for this meeting and going down to Alabama to march with Dr. Martin Luther King," Marion said. "It was nice of you to take time out of your busy schedule as president of the union to go on our behalf to advocate for the black community."

"Marion, you must tell Mr. Romanek the talk going on about him during the day shift," Mrs. Bland chimed in. "He's a fair man and did so much for our people. He should know what they're saying about him."

"Well Johnny, you know that it's election time," Marion said, hesitatingly. "Rocky and Lou have been bad mouthing you to the workers in my department. They have their stooges going around to the white workers in the plant saying that you were only interested in going on the march to get the black vote at the plant. They were also criticizing the pension plan because you had the members vote against the new contract and the pension. Now you're trying to capitalize on the good benefits that the international union got for us. A lot of people are listening to them but I'm not. I know Rocky got elected on your team the last election but he's trying hard to make you lose this next election, which I don't understand."

"Marion, I never said the pension wasn't good," Johnny said, trying to keep his calm. "Rocky, Lou and I put out a bulletin saying that the international union didn't get us the promised work standard provisions that we needed. I assure you, I will remind the membership that Rocky and Lou were involved in turning down the last contract. As for my involvement in the march, I believe in what Dr. Martin Luther King is doing for his people. He's going about it the right way. We can't stop there. In our local we must elect a black man on the bargaining committee to represent the black members in the plant and speak out for their rights. Black workers would feel more comfortable having a black man speak out for their rights."

"Johnny, we're not as dumb as the politicians think we are," Marion said. "We know that they're spreading lies but I warn you that many workers are listening, including the black worker. I'm only telling you this because I like what you've done since you got elected president. Your program is helping everyone in the plant and a good example is what you did here today."

"I appreciate you telling me this, Marion," Johnny said.

"You're welcome but I'd like to add that bad words go further than good words," Marion replied.

"What do you mean?" Johnny asked.

"I've been working at Ford for more than 30 years and I've seen many presidents do good things, but the members only remember the bad things," Marion said. "I just hope the old-timers remember all the good things you did for this local."

"Marion, let me ask you about the young black workers in the plant," Johnny said. "What are they saying about me going down to participate in the Selma march?"

"Well it's a little mixed," Marion admitted. "Most of the young blacks are saying that if you're really interested in them, you'd get them assigned to some of the good jobs in the plant, regardless of seniority. They say they were denied these good promotional jobs for many years and the union should see that black workers be placed in equal proportion on choice jobs and in choice departments."

"We aren't able to ignore seniority like that," Johnny said. "How do you feel about the way I helped black workers at the plant?"

Johnny wanted to see if Marion was sincere wanting to help him.

"Johnny, I believe in seniority and I saw a lot of high seniority black workers get good promotional jobs since you became president," Marion said. "That's the first time I saw a radical change in the plant operations. Not only that, you opened up prime departments to all of us, both white and black."

"Are black workers campaigning against me?" Johnny asked, scratching his chin.

"No," Marion said. "They're listening right now and waiting to hear what's going to be said by the politicians during the campaign. The young black workers are impatient and want all the changes to happen right now. We know the changes aren't going to happen overnight. What you have to watch out for is the promises that Rocky makes behind your back. He's been promising some of the young black workers that he'll take care of them when he gets elected president. He's careful about how he words things so it won't get quoted and used against him if it gets back to the membership. He's tricky."

"Marion, I was working here before there was a union and we had to fight for all the benefits that we receive today," Johnny said. "The new members were handed these on a silver platter. They don't know about the hard fight we went through to get these benefits. We suffered hard times with strikes and loss of money to achieve what we have today."

"That's why the old-timers appreciate the union," Marion said. "We were in that fight to get all that we enjoy today. Those young fellows believe that the company gave them all the benefits and the union is holding them back from getting these good jobs. I heard through the grapevine that you're going to run Otto Brodwick for plant committeeman. That could help you with the black vote in the plant."

"You heard right," Johnny said. "I expressed my feelings all along that I felt we had to have a black man on the bargaining committee."

"Otto is a good choice," Marion said. "He's always been an outspoken advocate for the black man, but a level-headed activist. He knows how to work the system and is respected by young and old black workers. You better make sure you get him out there to spread the good work you did for everyone in this local, especially what you did to help the black workers. I like what you did for us and I'm going to campaign for you all the way."

He thanked Marion and his wife for the information and shook hands before leaving. Johnny then turned to Pat who was standing there listening to their conversation.

"Pat, they're crapping on us from all sides," Johnny said. "I'd like to get one shot at Rocky to see if we can keep the campaign clean. I know Lou Sargent will never let up on me. He's the one who has Rocky all keyed up and using him in every way because of his high vote in the last election."

Johnny then noticed Rocky hurrying toward the exit and he cupped his hands around his mouth.

"Hey Rocky, can I see you for a minute?" Johnny hollered.

Rocky had an expression on his face indicating that he had hoped to avoid Johnny.

"Johnny, we've been here for eight hours and I got a date tonight," Rocky said, looking down at his watch. "Could this wait until tomorrow?"

"I know how long we've been here," Johnny snapped. "This will only take a few minutes."

"Okay, let's go to your office before someone else comes over to talk," Rocky said with resignation.

Johnny led him to his office and closed the door behind them. He sat down on the sofa as Rocky plopped himself down beside him.

"I'm going to cut to the chase," Johnny said. "The election is a short time away. I've been told that your caucus members are bad-mouthing me pretty hard. They're calling me a nigger lover for going on that march. They're also spreading lies that I was the only one who voted against the contract in Detroit. They're saying you supported it."

Rocky had a smirk on his face as he waited for Johnny to continue. Johnny rose from the sofa and then sat on the edge of his desk facing Rocky.

"How about from now on we have an agreement that we campaign on the facts only and keep the election clean," Johnny said. "I don't want to see an unknown slip in and dump the both of us."

"You got to be kidding," Rocky sneered. "We're the only two powerful groups in the plant."

"Rocky if you don't stop your guys from mud slinging, I'm going to go to work on you," Johnny said, pointing his index finger at Rocky's face. "I'll hit you with every dirty issue in the plant. I don't want to get in the gutter with you guys but I will if you don't stop with the dirty politics. You know I can be a vicious son-of-a-bitch when I go after a guy. Let's keep it clean so we don't knock each other out of the box."

"Johnny, you're getting thin-skinned," Rocky said. "You did vote against the contract. Where's the lie in that?"

"We voted against the contract as a group, not me alone," Johnny snapped. "You were heard telling the old timers that you voted for the pension plan and I was the only culprit that voted against it."

"Johnny, you know damn well that the members always distort what is actually being said," Rocky explained.

"Let's cut the bullshit," Johnny said. "If you continue to distort the facts, I'll hit you so bad that you'll never recover. I only called you aside so we should stop cutting each other up. If a novice wins this election, Tony will eat him alive. We could lose all the benefits that took us years to get."

"I don't see it the way you do," Rocky said, shifting in his seat. "We're the only strong leaders in the plant. I don't consider Bryan Dill or Lou Sargent a threat."

"Listen, I don't want to hold you up any longer since I know you have a date," Johnny said. "What do you say, can you get your caucus to keep it clean?"

Rocky was uneasy as he saw the anger flash in Johnny's eyes. He knew Johnny's capabilities and determination.

"You and I were in the same caucus for many years and you know that I'm forced to run for the top job," Rocky explained.

"Come on Rocky, give me a straight answer and stop beating around the bush," Johnny said, irritated. "If you're the leader, you call the shots."

"I'll talk to the caucus to try to get them to tone it down," Rocky relented. "You know that they hate you with a passion for many reasons. They're pissed about what you did to Freddie McCoy. Taylor Wicker is still being rapped about the line speeds in his department. Dominick Long can't walk the crane way without someone asking him about the overtime list that he let management control. I could go on all night," Rocky continued. "Look at George Plassard, he's still getting forty cents an hour while we're all making a good buck. It's going to be hard to get those guys to ease off."

Taylor Wicker was a committeeman in the commercial department.

"Rocky, those guys asked for it," Johnny said. "George started blasting me right after the election and wouldn't let up until I cut him off from all those goodies. Long was rapping you as much as he was rapping me."

"Let me continue," Rocky said. "Allen is pissed at you because you got rid of Freddie McCoy and Bryan Dill stopped his overtime. Don Byrne is angry because you beat him in the election. You see, you made a lot of enemies from our camp. I'll try to stop the mudslinging but they're not like our old group. They play for keeps and they don't care who they hurt." Rocky shrugged his shoulders dismissively.

Johnny got up from the edge of his desk and finally could see that Rocky wasn't the one calling the shots. He was merely a follower and Bryan Dill's caucus was using him because of his high popularity during the last election and they were hoping to take votes from Johnny's caucus. Don Byrne's caucus was determined to dictate how the election was going to be run.

"Rocky, keep in mind that I haven't started to sling the mud yet," Johnny said. "You know I'm a master of that and if you guys don't change, I will. Think about that."

Rocky just nodded and left the office. As Rocky was walking out, his only hope was that if he won the president job, he would assume complete control of his group. Right now he was completely dependent on Don Byrne's caucus.

Later on that night when Johnny arrived home, he was forced to park in front of his neighbor's house because there were 10 motorcycles parked in his driveway, cars parked in front of his lawn and also in front of his neighbor's lawn. Ann had notified him that Wayne was having a meeting with his high school friends.

Walking into the living, he heard Sammy Ritter, the quarterback, talk about getting a gift for Coach Casaro.

"The annual football dinner is next Saturday and we still haven't decided on what gift we should give," Sammy said. "We got to get him something. We were undefeated and won the state championship."

"Sammy, the coach wasn't good to us," complained Ned Heedy, the 200-pound fullback. "He never gave a damn about the players. He only cared about how well we did in the game. Look what happened to me when I missed a hand-off. He came over to give me a kick in the ass and an elbow to the ribs."

Jim Groupe, co-captain, was standing in the doorway and agreed with Ned.

"None of us went out for the team to get knocked around by the coach," Jim said. "The coaches were paid to teach us how to play, not beat us up when we made a mistake. I'm going to vote that we give him a big nothing."

"We can't do that," Sammy protested. "I don't like him any more than any of you. But how would it look in front of our parents if we didn't show our appreciation for the good job he did in helping us to win the championship?"

John Doty, the wide receiver, was sitting on the sofa. He got up to make his point.

"Sammy, I don't want to get anything for the coach," John said. "I remember the time I missed a block while in practice. Coach then put me on the line as a tackle against Rick, who is 260 pounds to my 140. Rick almost killed me when I tried to stop him from getting in on the next play. There was no need for coach to do that. He just wanted me to get hurt. I have no respect for him."

Everyone started to laugh as they looked over at Rick, who had a sheepish expression on his face. He stood over 6 feet tall, with a barrel of a body.

"I'm sorry, John," Rick said, throwing his hands up. "That was the time I tackled Ned with the ball and you got caught in between us."

"I'm laughing now but it wasn't funny when it happened," John said. "I was knocked out for over a minute."

Sammy felt helpless when he realized none of the players wanted to give the coach a gift. He turned to Wayne.

"You were the star of the team and the coach always respected you," Mike said. "What do you think we should do?"

Wayne was always the quiet one who did more listening than talking.

"I never appreciated the way Coach Casaro treated the players, especially when he slapped Bob around for horse-playing with the wet towel while we were in the showers," Wayne said. "I realize Bob was wrong but coach had no right to lay his hands on any student. No matter what."

The group nodded their heads in agreement.

"Since I knew before going into this meeting that no one wanted to get coach a gift, I met with one of the past coaches that we all respected," Wayne continued. "I explained our problem with Coach Casaro and he suggested that we present coach with an empty envelope. The parents will all think there is something in the envelope, and then when Coach Casaro opens it in private, he will know how we really felt about him."

"That's the best suggestion I heard today and I'm all for it," Bob Reed said.

The players talked among themselves but no one could come up with a better suggestion.

"It seems everyone is in favor of Wayne's suggestion," Sammy said. He noticed Wayne's dad standing by.

"Mr. Romanek, what would you do in our case?" Sammy asked.

"You're all getting to be men and must make your own decisions," Johnny said. "Make your decision and stick to your guns. I thought I was the only one who had problems," he laughed. "I better join Mrs. Romanek in the kitchen and let you guys go about your business."

Wayne laughed at his father's response.

"Sammy, my father is the best quarterback around," he joked. "Look at how you handed him the problem and he handed it right back to us without batting an eye. I still think the empty envelope is the best solution for us."

Sammy looked around the room and saw all the players nod in agreement.

Johnny walked into the kitchen where his wife was preparing a large platter of assorted cold cuts, potato salad and soft drinks.

"How was your meeting, dear?" Ann asked as she continued to prepare the platter.

Johnny hung his jacket on the back of the chair. He told her about the meeting and his discussion with Rocky. He went on to tell her about after meeting with Rocky, he called the regional director, David Bard, at his home to ease the tension between Rocky and himself. Johnny explained to David that the fight between them could lead to an unknown candidate coming in and taking over. Someone who never held a union position could get elected and they could lose all the benefits they earned over the years. David promised that after the UAW convention, he would be able to place either Rocky or Johnny on the international staff. David's only concern was to keep the election clean so that members wouldn't reject both candidates. Johnny was confident that he could beat Rocky in a clean head-to-head election.

"Based on my conversation with David, I'm going to set up a meeting with Rocky to see if he would give up running for the president job to take the international job," Johnny said. He reached for some black olives on the platter.

Ann gently slapped his hand away.

"Doesn't the international job pay more than the president's job?" she asked.

"Yes, but you're not the boss when you're in that job," Johnny explained. "You have to follow orders. The president of the local has a lot of power, especially during contract negotiations."

"Do you think Rocky will accept the international job?" Ann asked.

"I know that he would like to accept the job but I doubt that his caucus would allow him to," Johnny sighed. "He's been selected as their leader now and if he dropped out, their caucus would fold and their candidates might lose. Another thing is that Rocky doesn't have a say in their caucus and he's afraid to rock the boat. Lou Sargent has his hooks in so deep he watches Rocky like a hawk. Over the years, I saw Lou pull him into some bad situations and he fell for it completely. Rocky is not the smartest guy around but he has a way with the membership. He's afraid to buck his caucus but I'm going to offer him the job."

"Dear, if the loser will get the international job, we have nothing to worry about," Ann said. "You'll only be changing jobs."

"It's not that simple," Johnny said. "If we get dirty in the campaign, the membership could vote both of us out. That has happened before in other locals. My biggest aim is to get Rocky to keep his caucus members in line and campaign on the issues."

"Dear would you consider taking the international job?" Ann asked.

"No, I have too many caucus members to take care of," Johnny said. "I'm the president and I have the best chance of winning the election. Rocky's old caucus members would come running to my side if he lost. My guys would never back Rocky, they hate him with a passion."

"What do you mean by old caucus members?" Ann asked.

"I'm talking about the old original caucus members while Rocky was in our caucus when we ran together in the last election," Johnny said. "Don Byrne's caucus has no real power at all. They're depending on Rocky to garner the votes for them. What I'm worried about is if there's a third party in the running for president and we split the membership because of our fight, that third party could be in the run-off election and one of us would be out. If Rocky wins in the run-off, our caucus members wouldn't vote for him. If I was to win, I know that his old caucus never lose respect for me and would come back to our caucus," Johnny said.

He sighed and rubbed his eyes. He had another long day.

"That's enough about the union," Johnny said. "What are we going to have to eat? Cold cuts?"

"This is for the gang of vultures in the living room," Ann said. "The kids and I just voted that you were going to take us out to dinner. I worked hard enough making up this tray and I deserve the night out."

"Mom and dad, let's go out to some place nice so I can wear my new dress," Saundra said, entering the kitchen.

"How about McDonald's?" Johnny joked. Ann teasingly hit him with a wooden spoon.

"Saundra was such a big help to me," Ann said. "I'd never have gotten this platter together if it wasn't for our daughter."

"Yeah, all Frankie did was taste the food," Saundra said.

"Well someone had to tell mom how it tasted," said Frankie who had entered the kitchen after Saundra.

Johnny put his arms around his daughter.

"Don't get upset," Johnny said. "You are right. My two ladies both deserve the night on the town. Let's go to Hawaiian Moon. Now go upstairs and put on that pretty new dress. The food is fabulous and the music is great."

Saundra's eyes lit up.

"I'll take a quick shower and be ready in in no time," she said.

Wayne walked into the kitchen looking for the food.

"Wayne, I prepared a large platter of cold cuts and all the trimmings," Ann said. "And there's plenty of bottles of soda in the pantry. I don't want to see a mess when I come home. I expect the fellows to put their paper plates and cups in the garbage can when they're done eating."

"Mom, I'll make sure that we eat in the kitchen," Wayne said, picking up the platter. "Most of these guys act like pigs when they're away from their own homes. I'll make sure they won't make a mess here."

"I heard about some of your football parties from other mothers," Ann said. "I'm leaving you responsible so I expect nothing gets broken."

Wayne noticed his sister coming into the room dressed in her pretty flowered dress. He knew this was the perfect moment to tease her.

"Saundra, why don't you stay and help me out?" Wayne teased. "You like to give orders and I'm sure you'll be able to keep everyone in line to make sure the house doesn't get messed up."

"If I stayed behind, I'd make sure all of you ate in the backyard," Saundra said, punching her brother's shoulder playfully. "But since I'm not going to be around, you better set an example instead of being your dirty old self. Mom and I don't want to come home and clean the house all over again."

Wayne just shook his head as he disappeared with the platter into the other room.

"Remember to eat in the kitchen!" Ann called after him.

* * *

After Rocky had met with Johnny, he drove over to Marie's to pick her up. She came running down the porch steps in graceful strides even though she was wearing high-heels. He couldn't help but admire her figure as she ran toward his car. He slid across the front seat to open the door for her.

"I like the way you move when you run," he teased.

"You're fresh," she said, pinching his cheek playfully. "The last time we went out it took me an hour to get your dirty finger marks off my bra. This time I wasn't taking any chances so didn't wear one." His face turned red from excitement.

"Where are we going tonight?" she asked.

"I was told they're having a fabulous show at the Hawaiian Moon and their food is outstanding," Rocky said, pulling away from her house.

"That's swell," she said, powdering her nose. "I like that music they play. It gives me a reason to snuggle up close to you when we're dancing."

While driving through the center of the town, they stopped for a red light.

"We were tied up with that damn meeting Johnny called for almost eight hours and after that, he asked me to meet with him in his office to talk politics," Rocky explained. "I was pissed, I wanted to spend more time with you."

"I hope he realizes you're going to be the next president of the local," she said.

"It feels funny to run against him after being together for so many years," Rocky said.

He took a cigarette out of his shirt pocket and placed it in his mouth. Marie moved over to light the cigarette.

"He's quite upset that our guys are rapping him pretty hard," Rocky said. "I believe it's going to be a dirty election."

"What's the difference between this election and the ones in the past?" Marie asked, staring out the window.

Rocky took a deep drag on his cigarette before answering.

"I never like to campaign the way Lou and George do," Rocky said. "They like to go into departments and blast away at the opposition. I rather pick my fights and let the members do the blasting. They're giving Johnny the ammunition to attack us in the same way. I have to be careful not to have the membership be too sympathetic of Johnny."

"You're heading the ticket, why don't you run the campaign your way?" Marie said.

"I can't do that," Rocky said. "The caucus hates Johnny with a passion. They're coming out saying he's a nigger lover, strike happy and a president who looks for any reason to shut the plant down."

"Tony says the same thing about him," Marie said. "If it's true, what's wrong with Lou and Don bringing that up to the members?"

"Those guys don't know Johnny like I do," Rocky said. "He's vicious when he's on the campaign trail and very effective."

The light changed and Rocky continued driving.

"If my memory serves me right, you won your election with a high margin in the last election," Marie said. "Show your caucus that the way to run an election is your way. It was very effective."

"I'm going to try but I know they won't stop blasting Johnny for any reason that I give," Rocky said. He took another puff from his cigarette.

"What I think would help is if I got Tony to help me in this election," Rocky said. "He hates Johnny as much as my caucus does."

"What can he do?" Marie asked. "If the members found that out, they'd be against you. Isn't Tony supposed to stay out of union election matters?"

"I'd like to use labor relations to secure things for the members and make sure they don't give Johnny anything," Rocky explained. "The company could make Johnny look good or bad, depending on how they act toward him. When you go in on Monday, tell Tony I'd like to meet with him."

"Certainly," Marie said. "I heard Tony tell Jay Cannon on numerous occasions that he would like to see you as president. I know that he'll help you but it has to be on the sly. He has to be careful to not be charged with collusion of the union. He could lose his job."

"Tony knows we're dating," Rocky said. "I'd like you to drop a hint that Johnny is going to run Otto Brodwick for plant committee. Once Otto gets elected, there will be no stopping the blacks. They'd demand all prime jobs, want to be in the skilled trades and insist on salaried jobs."

"Do you think he could win?" Marie asked.

"No," Rocky said. "Johnny doesn't know who will be running against Otto. The word is that Don Byrne is going to quit and go into a private business venture. Since Johnny forced Freddie McCoy to retire, we convinced Don to stay on and run for the plant committee job. He'll win in a landslide. He has everything going for him. He's a past president with complete knowledge of the contract whereas Otto has no experience at all."

"Do you want me to tell all this to Tony?" Marie asked.

"Yes," Rocky said, nodding. "And another thing that you could pass on is, ask Tony to have his reps take a poll on what the members think of the candidates. My guys tell me what I want to hear and not what the members are actually saying. Johnny told me something that is very disturbing."

"What's that?" Marie asked.

"He feels that we could knock ourselves out of the box and an unknown could win the election for the president's job if we don't keep this election clean," Rocky said. "I know Johnny has a lot of dirt on Lou and George and I'm afraid that he'll lump me in with them. I'm going to need Tony to help."

Marie snuggled up close to him and he placed his arm around her with his hand on her breast.

"I was a lot safer while you were just talking," she said, teasingly pushing his hand away. "I'll tell Tony that you have to meet with him. I'm sure there are going to be a lot of questions that only you can answer."

"We're here sweetheart," Rocky said, as they pulled into the parking lot of Hawaiian Moon.

The Romaneks had already entered Hawaiian Moon and were met by the maître d' who was dressed in a black tuxedo. He asked Johnny if they had a reservation.

"Yes, Mr. Romanek for a party of four," Johnny said, helping Ann and Saundra take their coats off. "I would like to have a table somewhere near the dance floor so my daughter can have a good view of the floor show. It's her first visit here and I'd like it to be a memorable one for her." Johnny placed a 10-dollar bill in the maître d's hand.

The maître d' was all smiles as he led them through the restaurant and to a table that was the perfect distance from the band. The table also had a clear view of the floor for a show that would take place.

"Dad, this is some place," Saundra said. "We have the best seats in the house. How were you able to get these seats when the place is so crowded?"

"Sweetheart when the maître d' saw the two most beautiful women enter this place, he figured that he'd add class to the joint by placing you two close to the dance floor for everyone to see," Johnny said. "The old cliché was that the front row of any entertainment establishment was filled by old men with bald heads and their beautiful women. We sort of changed that tonight since I'm not bald."

"I overheard the coat check girl say that tonight's floor show is the best one they've had in years," Saundra said. "We hit the jackpot tonight, thanks Dad."

While ordering food from the menu, Ann observed Rocky and a beautiful blonde being escorted to a table near them.

"I see Rocky and a beautiful blonde coming toward the table near us," Ann said. "Wave them over so we can say hi."

Rocky noticed Ann looking toward them and decided it would be best to introduce Marie rather then dodge the Romaneks. They had all clearly seen them at this point. Rocky pulled Marie over to the Romanek's table.

"Marie, you know Johnny but I'd like to introduce you to his wife, the beautiful Ann Romanek," Rocky said. "Here is his beautiful daughter, Saundra and his second son, Frankie."

Marie was all smiles until she realized Ann was the same woman she met in San Diego. Marie felt the blood rush to her face. But Ann stood up without any trace of recognition.

"Marie, I'm so pleased to meet you," Ann said.

Marie felt a little uneasy but she realized Ann was too much of a lady to give her away.

"Rocky always said Johnny had the most beautiful wife and he wasn't kidding," Marie said. "I'm pleased to meet you as well."

Marie bent forward to kiss Ann on the cheek.

Rocky embraced Ann and kissed her on the cheek.

"You're still as stunning as ever and Saundra is the spitting image of you," Rocky said. He put his hand out to shake Frankie's.

"You're getting so big," Rocky said. "I never would have recognized you if you weren't with your parents."

Rocky finally turned to Johnny, who had an amused expression on his face.

"It's a surprise to see you here," Rocky said. "They tell me that the floor show is fabulous."

"Marie, you look radiant tonight," Johnny said. "Ann wanted a night off from cooking and I was able to snag a reservation last minute."

"Supposed to be a good show tonight," Rocky said.

"Yeah," Johnny said. "Listen, after the show why don't you meet me at the bar? I have something that could be of interest to you."

"Sure, that'll be fine," Rocky said.

He led Marie back to their table. He was confused by Johnny wanting a meeting. He felt that the discussion they had in the office ended any idea of compromise.

"Daddy this is our night out," Saundra huffed. "Don't spoil it by talking politics with Mr. Durango."

"You're right, this is your night out," Johnny said, grabbing his daughter's hand. "It'll just be a short talk with Mr. Durango, after we've had our fun here."

Ann smiled as she observed her daughter trying to determine which dish was the best on the menu.

"Dear, let me order for you," Ann said. "Otherwise you're going to sit here all night staring at the menu. I'll order different platters that we will all share. You take the one you like best. I know Frankie hates vegetables, so we will order the platter for him. It's barbecued meat with sweet sauce. I know he'll enjoy that."

They placed their order then relaxed while they listened to the music. They drank water and picked on the assorted appetizers that were on the table. In a short while the waiter arrived with the food and placed it on the rack next to them. He served Saundra first and placed a small portion of each dish on each plate.

As Saundra began eating she couldn't make up her mind which of the dishes she liked the best. Frankie dug into all the dishes, vegetables and all. The dinner was beyond all their expectations with Saundra being the most impressed. She wiped her mouth with her napkin and sat back in her chair.

"Dad, I'm stuffed," she said, patting her belly. "This is the best restaurant that we've ever been to. Every dish was tasty and I could eat all the food they brought. Plus, Frankie ate all the vegetables."

The group then enjoyed the floorshow, which was excellent. After the show Johnny called the waiter to bring the dessert menu for the kids and coffee for Ann. He then excused himself to meet Rocky at the bar. Ann asked Johnny to have Rocky send Marie to their table.

Johnny got to the bar as Rocky was ordering his drink.

"I ordered a gin and tonic for you," Rocky said. "You're still drinking the same?"

Johnny nodded his head and picked up his drink.

"Here's mud in your eye," Johnny said. Rocky returned the drinking greeting with a nod.

"You asked for this meeting," Rocky said. "What's up?"

"After our meeting concluded, I called David Bard at his home to ask him if he could put you on the international staff," Johnny said. "He agreed and said there wouldn't be an opening until after the UAW convention and at that time, he would put you on staff if you wanted it."

Johnny took another sip of his drink while watching for any reaction from Rocky but he sat there, expressionless.

"His brother, Roy, wanted to wait until after the convention so he could qualify for the new additional benefits," Johnny said. "You always said that your ultimate aim was to be placed on the international staff. Do you want the job?"

Rocky was interested in the job but couldn't let on that he was. He kept his eyes down and played with his drink.

"I can't Johnny," Rocky said. "My old caucus members would call me a quitter. I let them down the last time when they were pressuring me to run against you in the caucus. They felt I should have been the one to run for the president job rather than you. That's water under the bridge now, but if I quit at this point, it would come back to haunt me. You had a taste of the presidency, why don't you take the job?"

"You're forgetting that as president I made too many commitments to people in the plant, including black workers," Johnny said. "All that I accomplished would go down the drain. Marty gave me his word that one of us would be at the helm of international after the election. But we have got to keep this campaign clean. If we get into a dirty election, neither of us is going to get elected, an unknown will get elected president."

Rocky called the bartender for another round of drinks.

"We spent a lot of time in that plant since we got elected," Rocky said. "If we were paid for all that time, we would have had a good salary."

"You can thank George Plassard for that," Johnny said. "Right after the election he kept writing letters saying he was trying to stop spending money to build up the treasury, then he leaked those letters to the membership blaming me."

"He's still pissing and moaning about that," Rocky said.

"He'll never be on your side." Rocky laughed in spite of the tenseness of the conversation.

"I still don't think there is anyone in the plant who could knock the both of us out of the box," Rocky said.

"We differ again," Johnny said. "I was told Stan Kaplan threw his hat in the ring. He's strictly campaigning on the fight that's going on between our groups and the members are listening to him. I'm the one who's getting hit the hardest because I didn't start working on you guys. When I do, the tide will turn against you."

"You're losing sight of the fact that I pulled a few hundred votes more than you in the election," Rocky said.

"Don't remind me of that," Johnny said. "When I run with a guy, I support him all the way."

Rocky couldn't afford to get angry at this point. He knew Johnny was aware of the double-crossing tactics that he pulled with his group.

"Getting back to Stan Kaplan, he never held any union position in the plant," Rocky said. "He knows little about the contract. The membership would never vote for a newbie like him."

"He has a college education and is capitalizing on our split as a fracture of the leadership in our union," Johnny snapped, losing his patience. "He made a point of looking up all the members who were disciplined. He told them we were too busy fighting against each other to take care of these grievances. He's earning brownie points and the members are listening. One of us can win this election only if we stop fighting and stick to a clean campaign."

"I haven't heard anything about Stan," Rocky said. "The only word I got is that you're a dead duck on the day shift."

"Rocky, you're committeemen on the day shift and those guys are telling you what you want to hear," Johnny said, leaning close to Rocky. "Lou is priming them up to build up your ego so you go along with his fight. He knows that he's a dead duck without our support. Look how I destroyed two of your committeemen with one day of campaigning in their department. Another thing I hear is that Mark Fords is resigning as a committeeman. He can't take the heat and that's not going to help your election."

Rocky was pissed to be put on the defensive and didn't like it one bit.

"He's resigning not because of what you said," Rocky sneered. "He has family problems. His wife is pissed off at him for working too many hours in the plant and not getting paid for them."

"Again thank George for that," Johnny said. "He did me a big favor there. Your committeemen were going around knocking my brains out and putting in vouchers for overtime work. The day shift committeemen were bleeders, that's why our local was going broke."

He paused before continuing again.

"We're getting off topic," Johnny said. "I think you're passing up a golden opportunity in not taking the international job. I could put out a good word that you were given a promotion join the international staff and the membership would respect you for that."

Rocky was afraid to cross Don Byrne's group and was reaching for straws. He wanted the international job more than the presidency but feared what the caucus would do to him. He again tried to persuade Johnny to take the job. Johnny became more annoyed and saw that he was getting nowhere in the conversation.

"Your committeemen didn't do their jobs for the last two years and I intend to see that they'll be working on the line after the election," Johnny said. He pushed his drink away. "We're going around in circles here, just try to get your guys to stop the mud slinging."

Rocky was well aware that he was merely a figurehead and had no power to get Don Byrne's caucus to run a clean campaign.

"I'll do my best to get them to tone it down," Rocky said. "It was good that we had this talk. It cleared up a lot of points."

"The membership is going to read every piece of literature to determine who is telling the truth," Johnny said. "Monday, I'm going to start campaigning in the plant and the first slanderous word I hear from your caucus, no matter how small, I'm going to come out swinging. I know these issues inside and out and I won't hold back."

Rocky swallowed hard and realized how threatening Johnny could be when provoked.

"Think about what I said," Johnny said. "I have to get back to my family. See you in the plant Monday."

Johnny came back to the table and caught a glimpse of Saundra watching the couples on the dance floor. He tapped Ann on the shoulder and asked her to dance.

As they approached the dance floor Ann leaned to whisper into her husband's ear.

"I can see this is going to be a stormy election," Ann said.

"What makes you say that?"

"Dear, I've seen that look in your eyes when you are ready for a fight," Ann said. "You'll never be a successful gambler. Your eyes give you away. What did Rocky say?"

"You're right as usual," Johnny sighed, pulling Ann close as they began to dance. "I explained the facts to him but his caucus has him so pumped up that he thinks he can't lose. He'll fold from the pressure when I go after him. What surprises me is that he's so afraid of Don Byrne's group. Tom Romeo told me that Rocky is a big time racketeer here in Clinton. That's hard to believe after I had a talk with him. We'll see after the nomination meeting. I'll be able to analyze the situation and act accordingly at that time."

"John, there's a good chance that both of you could lose," Ann said.

"That's true but that leaves me no choice," Johnny said. "The one thing is if I lose, I'll come back stronger than ever but they'll be buried for life."

"What make you think that?" Ann said.

"Lou Sargent made the mistake of getting hit by a foreman and did nothing about it," Johnny explained. "All I have to do is refresh the members memories' and lump Rocky right into the center of it. That's enough politics talk, let's enjoy the music."

"In spite of your problems, tonight was a lovely evening," Ann mused. "I have never seen Saundra so thrilled. Look how beautiful your daughter is. Her eyes are sparkling with joy. I hope Rocky didn't spoil your evening."

"Politics will never spoil my evening," Johnny said. "Let's go back to the table so I can ask your daughter if she cares to dance."

Johnny and Ann returned to the table and Johnny tapped Saundra on the floor.

"May I have the pleasure of this dance?" Johnny teased.

"Dad, what took you so long?" Saundra linked her arm with his as they walked to the dance floor. It was an incredible night for the Romanek family, but Johnny couldn't help but feel nervous about the future of his presidency.

Chapter 23
Year 1966

The nominations for candidates for the 1966 local union election were being held on a Sunday. The regional international union was conducting the meeting and accepting nominations for all union positions. The meeting had all indications that the election was going to be a stormy one. Johnny Romanek was nominated to run as an incumbent for the president position. He received a standing ovation from his followers. Rocky Durango was nominated to run for president representing Don Byrne's old caucus and they shouted in applause, stamping their feet and shouting. Finally, Stan Kaplan was nominated to run for president, representing the independent group. He received a mild applause.

After the nominations were completed, all the caucuses marched around the hall carrying banners of their choice. They called out their chosen candidates for president, shouting and chanting. Some had drums which they were banging as hard as they could, others were carrying placards with slogans on them and others were dancing. The police were in the hall to make sure order was kept. The marchers paraded in front of the podium where Johnny and Rocky were standing and watching the procession. When Rocky's group came marching in front of the podium, one of his staunch supporters shouted while pointing a finger at Johnny.

"Motherfucker we're finally getting your ass back on the moving line where you belong," the man yelled. Johnny just smiled, unperturbed.

Directly in front of the podium, Bummy Harris and a group of Johnny's supporters stood to protect him from any attack. As the heckler continued to shout obscenities at Johnny,

Bummy moved in quickly and threw a haymaker directly to the jaw, breaking it and knocking out his front teeth. It happened so fast no one really caught on that it happened. The heckler was thrown back into the crowd of marchers while Bummy shouted.

"Please get this man some help, he's hurt," Bummy yelled. "He's bleeding from the mouth."

Bummy picked up the man's jacket and held it to the man's mouth to absorb the blood. The police were there in matter of seconds and asked the man what happened. He just shook his head, explaining that he didn't know.

One of the policeman looked at Johnny.

"Mr. Romanek, did you see what happened?" the policeman asked.

Johnny shook his head.

"No officer, I didn't," Johnny said. "All I saw was the man waving the banner and cursing at us. Then he went flying backward into the crowd of marchers."

Rocky jumped down from the platform to assist the man who was standing there with blood coming out of his nose and mouth. He spit out one of his front teeth. Rocky took out a clean handkerchief from his pocket and applied it to his mouth.

"Officer, one of Romanek's goon's did it," Rocky said.

The policeman was still holding the man to steady him from falling.

"Did you see who did it?" the policeman asked.

"It happened so fast," Rocky said. "But I know it was Johnny's men who were all standing in front of the platform. "

Rocky was angrily eyeing Johnny's supporters who stood at attention in front of the platform. They had sly grins on their faces.

Members came from all corners of the hall came to see what was going on. The officer tried to keep people back to sort out what happened.

Rocky's parade dispersed. Rocky then climbed onto the platform next to Johnny.

"Johnny, roughing up the members that are against you is uncalled for," Rocky said.

"You're right, Rocky," Johnny said. "Do you condone your guys calling me a motherfucker?"

Rocky was embarrassed and had nothing to say. Lou Sargent joined the two and leaned toward Johnny.

"Johnny, you got a bunch of slap happy guys who you better control or we'll make it a free for all," Lou said.

Johnny's eyes were blazing with anger as he stepped toward Lou but Rocky stepped in between the two, restraining Johnny. Johnny reached over Rocky's shoulder to point a finger at Lou.

"If it's a fight you want, we're ready any time," Johnny threatened.

Rocky was well aware of the ex-fighters Johnny had in his caucus and wanted no confrontation. He pulled Lou away.

"Lou, let's forget it," Rocky said. "We were both wrong."

Some of Stan's supporters wanted to join in the argument but were restrained by Stan.

"Let them fight," Stan said. "This will just give us more ammunition."

At the conclusion of the meeting, all the groups held a meeting to outline their strategy and the type of literature that would be handed out to members. Their main objective was to protect the programs that would benefit the membership and point out all the weaknesses of their opponents.

Monday morning Rocky, Lou and Don Byrne met in the plant union office to discuss the strategy they would use while campaigning. Lou listed the departments and the topics they would address with members.

"Let's hit the car delivery first," Lou said. "We'll rap Johnny on the changes he made in the local agreement in the car delivery that effects members." Lou smiled at the thought.

"I used to represent members on nights and we screened every one who came into the department," Lou continued. "We made sure the men coming in had less seniority than our regular supporters who wanted to be protected."

Lou turned to Don and asked him what members were saying about Johnny.

"They're pissed off at him," Don said. "Especially now that all the jobs posted are being posted plant-wide. This brought in a lot of high seniority men. Like you said, they're afraid of being bumped from the department."

Lou slapped his notepad against his thigh.

"We have to put the fear of God into those members," Lou said. "Let's rap Johnny hard with these issues. The members make good money in car delivery and will destroy anyone who wants to take their positions away from them."

This wasn't Rocky's way of campaigning because he knew the danger of inciting Johnny. For years Rocky's philosophy was to speak to members on a one-on-one basis and not in groups. He didn't believe in giving Johnny the opportunity to point a finger that he was running a slanderous campaign. Rocky instead liked to blame members for misunderstanding and distorting his statements. Rocky attempted to dissuade Lou from pursuing his tactic.

"Let's be careful how we handle this," Rocky said. "If there are any blacks around, don't let them hear us blasting the agreement. You know they benefited from the agreement. Talk only about the issues, including that high seniority men could be dumped on nights in the event of a cut back in the work force. Let's concentrate on the pool area and drivers who are looking for promotional jobs they always got before the new agreement. Let's tell them Johnny's motive was to get his caucus members and friends into the car delivery department and other key jobs in the plant."

They all agreed readily.

"That's a good point," Lou said. "Let's get started."

Even though Rocky would much rather campaign on a one-on-one basis, he was talked into the latter approach. The first group of workers they approached in car delivery was a small group who were on break and standing around the coffee machines. Rocky walked up to them and immediately began talking.

"Hi fellas," Rocky began, "you all know we were nominated to oppose Johnny and his goons who took away many of our good benefits that we enjoyed in car delivery for many years. If you want those benefits back, then we can help. But in order to beat him, we're looking for your support."

"Rocky, I thought Johnny did a good job for us," one of the workers said. "What are you going to do to help us?"

"A lot of things that Johnny changed in the plant that Lou and I oppose," Rocky said. "Look at the local agreements. We used to have all the promotions come from within the department where all you guys could work your way up to a better job, like repairs, inspection and auto mechanic. Now that's all changed. Currently a guy with 30 years from another department can bid on a job and he carries full seniority into the department with him. Then to top this, you fellas have to teach him how to do the job. If the company decides to cut back on production, you guys that carried the department for years could be dumped on nights or in some cases be sent back to the chassis department while the new workers with more seniority remain on your job. We don't think that is fair to you old timers from car delivery. "

A black worker was with the group of men surrounding them and had been promoted from the body shop into a repairman's job. He stepped forward to share his opinion.

"I feel that was a fair change in the local agreements," the worker said. "We all belong to the same union and we should be able to get better jobs with seniority."

He looked at his watch before excusing himself.

"Rocky, I'd like to stick around to hear how you guys are going to do better but my relief time is up and I have to get back to my job," the worker said.

Rocky waited to resume talking after the black worker left.

"I can see that Roy sides with Johnny because he's one of his caucus members that got one of the repairman job you fellas were entitled to," Rocky said. "That is precisely what I'm talking about. Rocky turned to a driver who had been in car delivery for years.

"John, look at you," Rocky said. "You're a better repairman than Roy will ever be. I remember you always filled in on repairs during vacation and when a worker was absent or sick. You got 25 years in this department. Can the new guy with more seniority do what you guys have been trained to do all the years that you worked here doing the job that you're familiar with? I think the answer is no."

John Cleary was in a rage with anger when reminded of the job that could have been his.

"I worked hard at my job in car delivery and I was good at repairs," John said. "I busted my ass because I was told by my foreman that I would get the next repair job when it opened up. Johnny fucked me and the whole department real good when he changed the local agreements. Even my boss took me aside and told me that I was a better repairman than Roy but he was forced to put him on the job because of the new promotional agreement. It's clear to see Johnny's only interest is the fucking black workers in the plant. He'll never get my vote. I'm going to vote for you Rocky."

John then turned to Lou.

"You used to be the committeeman on nights," John continued, "let these guys know how we used to take care of each other and how we worked up the ladder to get these promotional jobs. All we had was a few black workers in this department but look at what we got now. Pretty soon the black workers will be taking over and we'll all be out on our asses."

Lou had a huge smile on his face as he kept nodding his head in agreement. This conversation was going just as he planned.

"John is right," Lou said. "John is an excellent repairman but he was passed over to make room for one of Johnny's cronies. We need your support to bring back the good old days."

Rocky was all smiles as he thanked the men for listening to them. When the men dispersed and were out of earshot, he whispered to Lou and Don.

"The seed is planted," Rocky said. "Let them spread the word. I'll bet that will get around like wild fire."

Don also was pleased. He realized that this kind of talk would easily get him elected over Otto Brodwick. However, he was nervous about bringing race into the campaign.

"Rocky, I don't want this election to turn into a racial affair," Don said. "If that gets around, we could have a riot on our hands."

Lou slapped Don on the shoulder in reassurance.

"Don, you're a shoo-in," Lou said. "We have no control what the members say. And remember it was John who called Johnny the nigger lover, not us."

The men then walked into the repair booth where there were a few black workers working on the same unit. They stopped working to listen to what the candidates were saying. Rocky made the same pitch that he gave to the other group but left out the racial issues. Darnell Summers was wiping his hands on a towel. Darnell, who was black, was interested in the election and the candidates.

"I hear you're running against Otto for plant committeeman," Darnell asked Don. "Don't you feel we should have a black worker representing the black community on the bargaining committee?"

Don was at a loss of what to say. Lou took over quickly.

"We all feel like you do," Lou said. "A black worker should represent blacks on the bargaining committee. But who gave Johnny the right to pick what black member should run for the job? The black members working here should have done this. We believe Johnny selected Otto to use him as another Uncle Tom."

Darnell wasn't persuaded that easily.

"I didn't hear or see your caucus nominate any black worker to represent us on the bargaining committee," Darnell said. "Instead your group put Don Byrne, an ex-president, to run against Otto."

"Brother, you're wrong," Rocky interjected. "We have Benny Fields running for recording secretary on the executive board, which is the highest power in the local union after the membership."

Darnell was visibly annoyed for being taken as a fool.

"Rocky, that's bullshit and you know it," Darnell said. "The bargaining committee is the real power in the local union. And we need a black man to represent and speak up for us. You're only throwing us a bone by putting Benny up as a candidate. You put him up against Pat Fager who has been in office for years and is solid. Pat is respected by all the blacks for the things he did for the black community in this union."

Rocky put his hands up in the air to calm Darnell down.

"We're going to groom a black man to become a committeeman and give him the experience to know the contract and to be able to negotiate with the company," Rocky promised. "I know black workers want a competent man to represent them, not one hand-picked by a white man. We have Frank Roland running for committeeman so he can get the experience to lead black workers."

"Aren't you doing the same thing as Johnny by putting Frank up as your spokesman for black workers?" Darnell said in disgust.

Rocky knew he was skating on thin ice. Lou quickly took over.

"That's not what we're doing," Lou said. "What we're doing is making sure the black man gets the experience to represent workers. He will have to prove himself in the eyes of the black community. When you have your black caucus meeting,

you'll select the best man to represent you, not us. All we're
trying to do is help a black man like Frank learn the trade."

Darnell waved his arm in disgust and walked back to his
job.

After Darnell departed Rocky turned to Don and Lou.

"What Darnell doesn't understand is that whoever gets
elected as plant committeeman must represent all the members,
not a select group," Rocky said. "If he makes any mistake the
whole plant will suffer. Don Byrne is our candidate and he has the
experience. He was the past president and has the experience to
handle the job. While he was in office, he proved that he's not
prejudiced and helped many black members get ahead."

Another black man spoke up.

"We admit Don has the experience but he's not black and
can't speak for us," the man said. "I like what you said about
black workers picking who they feel is most qualified to represent
us. That's the only fair way to do it."

"Thanks for listening and we appreciate your support,"
Rocky said. He waited until the group of men left to continue.

"This last guy gave us a good note to leave on," Rocky
said. "Let the workers get around that they should pick who they
want to represent them. If we're lucky, they might brand Otto as a
Uncle Tom."

Meanwhile, Johnny entered the administration building
where Mike Ferrera, Otto Brodwick and Pat Fager were waiting
for him.

He removed his tie and suit jacket and placed the jacket on
the rack that the company provided for visitors coming into the
plant. He wanted to look like one of the workers and not dressed
as a union official. Johnny was ready for campaigning.

"Where should we start?" he asked, rolling up his sleeves.

"Let's hit the maintenance and freight departments," Mike
said. "They're not confined to the moving line. They could spread
the word about our platform."

Pat hesitated.

"I can't go through the plant with you," he said. "I'm on a
short break and have to go back to my job. But before I go, I
wanted to fill you in on the shit that Rocky and his group are
spreading. They're hitting you hard on the black issue. The word
getting around is that you are running Otto for one of the top jobs

in spite of the fact that he has no experience as a union official and that you have an attitude with management."

"What attitude do I have with the company?" Johnny asked.

"They're spreading the idea that you're the first president who took three strike votes while in office," Pat said. "Also that you refused to sign a good agreement with the thought of shutting the plant down. They're planting the seed that if you get re-elected, we'll be out on the street with a long strike."

"On every strike vote I took, we won every one of them and forced the company to back off," Johnny snapped. "We proved to the company that we had the membership backing us all the way in spite of Rocky and his group trying to sabotage us. If we didn't take those strike votes, the company would have worked our workers to death."

"Johnny, don't get pissed," Pat said. "You've got to remain calm. All I'm telling you is how they're hitting you with every dirty trick in the book."

Pat then turned to Otto.

"They're also spreading the word that Johnny is using you to get the black vote as his Uncle Tom," Pat said. "Word is that Johnny will still be calling the shots, regardless if there is a black committeeman elected."

"I'd like to hear them say that in front of me," Otto seethed. "I'd bust their fucking heads in. I'm no Uncle Tom for anyone."

"Well we all know what we have to do," Johnny said. "This is going to be a dirty campaign. Let's go to work and hit them with everything we got."

Their first stop was the maintenance department where they encountered a group of workers prepping a project that was scheduled to be installed over the weekend. This was Johnny's old department that he had represented for 10 years, as a committeeman where he won their respect and support. The workers gathered around him shaking hands and slapping him on the back.

"How are things going with you guys?" Johnny asked.

"Damn good since you knocked out the outside contractors doing our work in the plant," said Ted, one of the workers. "We've been working daily overtime hours and weekends thanks to you."

"I'm going to get right to it then," Johnny said. "I need you to support our entire team in this election. Ted, you know Otto Brodwick is our candidate for plant committeeman."

They all reached over to shake Otto's hand.

"If you don't know Otto, I'd like to tell you a bit about him," Johnny began, "he's been working at the plant for 10 years and was mainly responsible for putting the demonstration to bed. We're at that period of time where we feel black workers at the plant have to be represented by a black man on the bargaining committee. Otto is knowledgeable of their problems and knows how to deal with them. Black workers want someone on the bargaining committee who has been subjected to the prejudices that they've faced for many years. They want someone in there they could trust who understands their problems and suffered like they did."

Otto, a welder, took his welding shield from his head and placed it on the bench. He nodded his head in agreement.

"Johnny, I agree that we have to change our ways," Otto said. "The black demonstration opened all our eyes to the problem the black workers have. I believe the committee that was formed did a fabulous job. This is the first time that we have good working relations in the plant."

"The committee did resolve many of our problems but they're all the way in Detroit," Johnny said. "You noticed that the committee consisted of only blacks from both sides and they brought peace to the black community. We're now in a position to elect a black man to carry out the work that the committee started. We need the white vote for that to come about. We feel that Otto is that candidate."

"Johnny, we're with you all the way," Otto said.

Jack Levy, an electrician, joined the group.

"Johnny, I just came from car delivery where Rocky and Lou are campaigning," Jack said. "They're really knocking the hell out of you. They're calling you a nigger lover and that you changed the local agreement to suit your needs. A lot of workers are believing what they're saying, especially the whites who have been working there for a long time."

"Let's go down there and confront the bastards," Otto replied, turning red from anger.

"No," Johnny said, placing his hand on Otto's arm to calm him. "We'll continue according to our plan. We're going to go

through the maintenance and then the freight departments.
They're really lowering the broom on us with their dirty campaign
and we are not going to stoop to their level."

Jack smiled as he reached over to shake hands with
Johnny.

"Johnny, we're a team," he said. "We'll do our job to
knock the shit out of them before the campaign is over."

Jack then turned to Otto.

"I hope I didn't offend you by telling you the words they
are using," Jack said. "That's the expression they're saying."

"I want to hear the exact words they are using," Otto said.
"I appreciate you telling it like it is. Thanks Jack."

"I'd appreciate you guys talking up our ticket in the
departments you're working in," Johnny said. "We're going to
need every vote that we can get."

Johnny headed the group to the freight department. He
turned to Otto and addressed him.

"Otto, you're going to have to convince the whites that
you'll represent them equally and not favor the blacks," Johnny
said. "We're going to support you but you also have work to do."

As soon as the men hit the crane way, the drivers stopped
their vehicles to gather around. Other workers who were
unloading the freight car also came over to hear what Johnny and
the group was saying was going to say.

"The first thing we have to do in this department is to get
rid of that two-timing committeeman," Johnny said. "Dominick
Long is letting the department go to waste and is a stooge for the
company. Here's Mike Ferrera who is the committeeman in
maintenance. He's the one who picks the people to work from the
overtime list on the board for daily and weekend overtime, not the
foreman. Dominick Long is only interested in taking care of
himself, not the workers. He's making sure he gets everything he
can get from the company to let them do what ever they want. The
superintendent brags that he has Dominick in his pocket for a few
pieces of silver. If he denies what I'm saying ask him to show you
his paycheck. Let's get Larry McCormick back as committeeman
in this department. He proved that he could do the job when he
was here. We're looking for your support for our ticket in the
coming election."

Over half the workers in freight were black and were very much interested in who was running on Johnny's ticket. They gathered around as Mike spoke.

"We need everyone's support to get Otto elected to the bargaining committee," Mike said. "Johnny is the only one who feels that black workers need a black plant committeeman who understands their issues. Otto is new but he was there during the demonstration and helped to put it to bed."

One of the black drivers had just come back from the car delivery department.

"Otto, how come we didn't have a black caucus called for us to have us select who we wanted to represent us on the bargaining committee?" the man asked.

Otto walked up to the man and placed his hand on his shoulder.

"Look my good man, we had a nominating meeting on Saturday and I was the only black man who was nominated for the plant committee position," Otto said. "Not only am I black, I feel I'm qualified to run for this position."

The man nodded his head so Otto continued talking.

"Johnny came over to me and asked if I would run with his group," Otto said. "I agreed. He's the only candidate running for president who is concerned about the black workers in the plant. Rocky has made no attempt to offer a black candidate and now he's making excuses for his shortsightedness. Just by his actions you can see he has no interest in black workers at the plant. Johnny Romanek is different. Not only does he care, he puts action behind his words. He went down to Selma to march for black civil rights and now he is including a black man on his ticket. Rocky nominated Don Byrne to run against me. What does that tell you, brother?"

The men could see that Otto made some valid points.

"I hear you talking, brother," the worker said. "We'll get the word around. Johnny, I want to thank you for going down to Alabama on that march with Dr. King. That took a lot of guts. I shouldn't have doubted you. I'm with you guys all the way."

Johnny noticed Larry McCormick walking down the aisle.

"If you want justice in your department, here's the guy who you should elect for committeeman," Johnny said. "Mr. McCormick was rated as the best committeeman you ever had before he became president. The guy you got now as committeeman is a bum and it is time to get rid of him. Let's get the union back in this department."

The men gave a rousing cheer as Larry raised his hand in a victory salute.

Johnny thanked them and led his candidates toward the body shop which was his strong hold. Evidence of this was seen he entered the body shop, everyone stopped working and gave him a rousing cheer.

"Johnny, you know we're with you all the way," a metal repairman said. "You were the best committeeman we ever had and a great president. If it wasn't for you, we'd be busting our asses here."

"Thanks fellas," Johnny said, beaming with a smile. "I need you to support my entire ticket in order for our programs to get enacted."

He raised Otto's hand up in the air.

"Fellas, this is Otto Brodwick, my candidate for plant committeeman," Johnny said. "You have my word that he will represent all the members equally and fairly. When Don Byrne comes here for your support, ask him why he saw it appropriate that you would be confined to the body shop forever. Don't let him bullshit you that he did a great job as president. He knew he couldn't get elected as president so he joined the status quo by hooking onto Rocky Durango's group to run for plant committeeman."

Johnny and his ticket hit every section of the body shop and received the same response. At the end of their campaigning in the body shop, Otto had a confused expression on his face.

"I heard many members say you're a dead duck on the day shift," Otto said. "We hit three departments and it looks like they're behind you all the way."

"I purposely took you through my stronghold on the day shift," Johnny said. "Last month I rapped Dominick Long pretty hard, that's why the freight department has turned around in our favor. I did the same thing in the commercial department. I caught Taylor Wicker allowing the company to run the line faster than the agreed line speed. Now we have to go into other departments to turn things around. Taylor Wicker did some job on me while I was tied up in negotiations."

"Johnny, what's our strategy when we got to the next department?" Mike asked.

"Let's hit the trim line where Al Carter is the weakest committeeman in Rocky Durango's caucus," Johnny said. "His guys were disciplined quite a bit and he didn't know how to help them. He kept rapping me, saying that for two years I was strike happy and that Rocky and Lou were the only ones who kept the plant working. Let's play it by ear and talk about all the gains we made with my ten-point program. Let's listen carefully, the members will give us an opening."

Johnny was optimistic and excited to campaign in a department where he was hit the hardest.

As soon as they entered the department, some of the opposition members were waiting.

"It must be election time, I see our illustrious president," a dissident member snarled. "The last time he came into this department was when he was looking for support for a strike vote to shut the plant down."

Many of the workers clapped their hands together and began laughing.

"Jimmy, I believe you're right," Johnny said. "Also, wasn't that the time Lou Sargent got knocked on his ass by foreman Hansen while Rocky was standing by? If memory serves me right, they didn't do a thing to foreman Hansen except come running into my office to ask me to do something about it."

A crowd of workers were milling around now.

"Yeah man, I remember that," one worker shouted. "Wasn't that right after we had our membership meeting where Rocky said he would have kicked the shit out of foreman Hansen but the lunch bell ran and saved the foreman?"

"Jimmy, you're right, I did call for a strike authorization then," Johnny said. "I asked the membership to back me up when a member of management hit Lou Sargent, a union official, and knocked him on his ass. You should know that was Lou Sargent who wrote the bulletin to shut down the plant to get foreman Hansen fired."

More workers continued gathering around, curious about Johnny's explanation. One worker spoke up.

"Johnny, I supported you on that issue," the worker said. "I was at the meeting when you explained the settlement was a good one but you refused to sign it because you wanted it to include firing foreman Hansen for knocking Lou Sargent on his ass. I respected you for that."

"I was also at the meeting when Rocky and Lou got up to support the settlement even though they did nothing to foreman Hansen," another worker said. "I give the black workers a lot of credit, at least they stayed out until they got Superintendent Acuff got fired. I got to agree with Johnny, those two running against him, Rocky and Lou, are gutless."

"At least Rocky and Lou kept their cool about them when they saw they got a good settlement on the strike issue," Jimmy said. "They made sure we didn't lose any time. If Johnny had his way we'd have been on the street with no pay until he was satisfied."

"Jimmy, you're right, I was standing next to you at that meeting and you were the greatest supporter and shouted the loudest in favor of the settlement," one of the trim line workers said. "I remember your exact words. You yelled, 'fuck Sargent, I'm not going to lose pay for that gutless bastard!'"

Jimmy was embarrassed for being singled by his fellow workers and tried to defend his position.

"You got to admit that Rocky kept his cool by recommending that we settle," Jimmy stuttered. "He knew Johnny was a hot-head and looking for a reason to shut the plant down since he wasn't getting his way. I'm still supporting Rocky as president."

Johnny placed his arm around Jimmy's shoulder.

"Jimmy I don't blame you for supporting Rocky," Johnny said. "Wasn't he the one who got you the utility promotion even though you didn't have the seniority to qualify?" Jimmy turned even brighter red.

Johnny then turned to the other workers to further his point.

"I know you fellas aren't in favor of bypassing seniority," Johnny said. "Jimmy, did you have to pay for the promotion or was the agreement that you would blast me whenever you could?"

The crowd booed as Jimmy walked away in embarrassment.

"Let me ask you, do you want a pair of gutless union representatives to represent you on the top level?" Mike Ferrera asked the men. "They didn't have the backbone to stand up to management when Lou Sargent got belted. Whatever anyone says about Johnny, you've never seen him take a backward step in any fight with the company. You all better think long and hard about who you're going to support in this election to lead our union."

"Let's get out of here and let them think about what we said," whispered Otto in Johnny's ear.

He was getting a lesson in campaigning and he felt proud of being part of Johnny's ticket.

"Most of those guys used to be in Don Byrne's caucus," Otto said as the men left to campaign another department. "Let Rocky and his men try to explain why the gutless fucks are afraid to take foreman Hansen on. We should come back another time to see their reaction."

"Otto you're thinking like a true politician," Johnny said. "You're learning fast. Let's get out of here before they try to get us on other issues."

Now it was time for Stan Kaplan to campaign. He hit the trim line first. His main idea was to stress the importance of unity within the leadership of the union to achieve their goals.

"How are you going to do that, when you've never held any union position before?" one of the workers asked.

"You're right but it's time for change," Stan replied.

"What kind of change?" a worker shouted.

"A change for the worst!" another answered.

Stan ignored the question.

"I hear that Johnny Romanek is blasting Rocky Durango as a weak leader," Stan said. "Here's where I agree with him. Rocky proved that he is weak. You know I feel these guys are telling the truth about each other. I was in car delivery where Rocky and Lou Sargent stated that Johnny is responsible for all the bad things that happened there over the last two years. I believe Rocky, but he neglected to tell them that he was part of the leadership who failed the membership. They all were responsible for the failures."

"Cut the bullshit, Stan," a Rocky supporter shouted. "What are you going to do to make things better for us?"

"If you let me talk," Stan said. "I'll tell you."

The crowd quieted down.

"The first thing I'd do is make sure the bargaining committee concentrates on the company and not on each other," Stan said. "You know the company loves it when the leadership fight amongst themselves, like they're doing now. The company is able to then get away with murder, especially when they're overworking men on the line. An example is in the trim department. Right now the foreman gets away with choosing workers to get promoted and ignoring the promotional agreement."

"You're referring to Jimmy Mack, I hear," one of the workers said. Jimmy turned a crimson red and walked away.

Stan saw that the message was hitting home and continued.

"Jimmy is just one of many," Stan said. "I hear complaints all over the plant. How long are you guys going to be asleep on this? Wake up! Now is the time for a change in leadership. Let the company know that we're not going to give them a free pass to let them do what they want. Our membership deserves a change in the leadership for the good of the membership and our union."

"Johnny was here a short time ago and he said Rocky and Lou are gutless," a worker asked. "How do you feel about them?"

"They're doing a pretty good job given the conditions," Stan said. "But I will say this. If I was president when foreman Hansen knocked Lou on his ass, I wouldn't have settled until Hansen was fired. I blame both parties for that blunder."

The men nodded their heads in agreement.

"A vote for Kaplan is a vote for unity," Stan said, waving as he walked away.

Chapter 24
Year 1966

Marie Collin's desk was cluttered with piles of paper. One listed the nominations of the committeemen in all departments, another listed the candidates running for the executive offices, the candidates for the UAW convention and the sub-council #2 delegates. She was in the process of pulling all this information into a single page, so Tony Rodgers would know who was running for each position. Tony's prime concern was to see how teams lined up after the votes were counted.

Marie was busy typing when Tony walked in. She had a pencil in her hair and sunglasses perched on top of her head. He looked outside the window and noticed it was dark.

"Marie, what are you doing with sunglasses on top of your head?" Tony asked, chuckling.

"I was looking for them a while ago but I couldn't find them," Marie said. "I placed them there when I got out of my car in the parking lot. I've been working on this candidate sheet all day and didn't know they were still on my head. Mr. Rodgers, I'll be through with this union list in a moment."

"Put that aside for now," Tony said. "I'd like to talk to you for a minute."

Marie shut her typewriter down and went over to pick up her steno pad to follow him into his office.

"Don't bring your pad," Tony said. "I want to talk to you about something privately."

Marie became flustered and placed her pad back on her desk. She was fearful she was going to be reprimanded. She walked behind Tony into his office, closing the door behind her. Tony was seated behind his desk and took a cigarette from his pocket, offering her one but she refused. Tony never invited her in to talk privately. She sat up straight, and then crossed her legs one way, then the next. She couldn't calm her nerves.

"Marie, are you still going out with Rocky?" Tony asked.

Marie was caught off guard. She didn't know Tony knew about her and Rocky.

"What happened?" Marie asked, turning a bright crimson color. "Did I do something wrong?"

Tony noticed her embarrassment and tried to back track.

"Marie, I'm sorry," Tony said. "I don't mean to pry into your private life. I was hoping you still were in good standing with Rocky because I want to set up a meeting with him without anyone in the union or the company knowing about it."

"Oh, uh, Mr. Durango and I go out occasionally for a drink but nothing serious," Marie said. "That's the extent of our relationship. But I'm sure I could set up a meeting with you and Mr. Durango discreetly."

"If you could, I'd like a meeting with him as soon as possible," Tony said. "Tonight would be ideal. Tell him we could have a meeting in my private country club where no one knows us and we could talk in secret. Assure him there is no one at the club who's from Ford so it'll just be us."

"I'll phone around to a few departments to track him down," Marie said. Tony nodded.

She got up to leave his office and make the calls from her desk. As she walked away, she was glad she described her relationship with Rocky as casual.

Tony then focused his energy on his next task. He had an important meeting set up with the plant manager and his top staff. It was important for him to have all the important information he needed. He dialed Franklin Todd's office.

"I got a meeting at two this afternoon and I need all the information you can get on the candidates and how the campaign is progressing," Tony said.

Franklin was well aware that Tony was deeply concerned about the union election and wasn't happy one bit with the power that Johnny wielded while in office.

"I just got a report that Rocky and his group is in car delivery where they're rapping Johnny and Otto Brodwick real hard," Franklin said. "The good part is that the workers are listening to their pitch. Tony, there's one area that could be dangerous. It's the part where they are calling Johnny a nigger lover. That could polarize the members and we could have another strike on our hands."

"I thought that Rocky was a smarter politician than that?" Tony griped.

"It's not Rocky, it's Lou Sargent," Franklin said. "He's got an ax to grind with Johnny over the Roger Hansen affair. He wants some of Johnny's blood. One of the foremen was nearby and heard their conversation with the workers. He told me that Lou was planting the seed with the old timers that they were denied the promotion because of the way Johnny changed the local agreements. He's getting them steamed up over the changes by saying that Johnny is trying to get his black friend into the car delivery department. As soon as Lou got them riled up, he told Rocky that they should leave the department so his followers could rake Johnny over the coals when he came to campaign. He said their hands would be clean when the workers spread the word that Johnny was a nigger lover."

"Well, there's nothing we can do now," Tony said. "What burns my ass is that during every election, we end up losing valuable production time because workers leave their job to listen to the candidates. Did you hear anything from what Johnny or Stan Kaplan said?"

"All I got on Stan is that he doesn't know anything about the union contract," Franklin said. "No one seems to be taking him seriously. I got a call from the administration building that Johnny's been making the rounds with Mike Ferrera, Otto Brodwick and Pat Fager."

"Franklin, I appreciate you filling me in on the candidates," Tony said. "If I'm not in the office, give this information to Marie. She'll pass it on to me. If any issue that comes up can make Rocky look good, let's let our labor reps play it up, but with discretion. We can't afford to have two more years with Johnny Romanek as president."

"Will do Tony," Franklin said. "I'll definitely call you before your meeting with a blow-by-blow description on what's going on. Good luck with your meeting."

As soon as Tony hung up, there was a light tap on his door and Marie entered.

"Mr. Rodgers, I contacted Mr. Durango and he said he could come to the White Plains Country Club at nine tonight," Marie said. "The reason for the late hour is that he's committed to campaign at least four hours this evening on the night shift. I informed him that the dress code at the club is suit and tie."

"I'm glad you told him, the dress code slipped my mind," Tony said. "Thanks for everything. I really appreciate all that you're doing. Oh by the way, I told Franklin Todd to pass all the information that he gets on the candidates, to the office. If I'm not here, take it and pass it on to me later. I want to see that Rocky gets elected but I have to be discreet or I could be charged with collusion with the union. If anyone asks about our position on the union election, tell them we're strictly neutral."

"I'll be discreet," she said, smiling. "Whenever any reports come in I'll place them in my top drawer which I keep locked at all times."

"Thanks again, Marie," Tony said.

A few minutes before two o'clock, Tony entered Jay Cannon's office suite. His secretary, Jane Carroll was typing a report.

"Is he in?" Tony asked.

"Yes Mr. Rodgers, also, Chip O'Neil just got here," Jane said. "They're waiting for you to arrive."

Chip was a production manager for the plant.

Tony walked into the office which was elaborately decorated with mahogany paneling and a deep red plush carpeting that was bordered with a black stripe encasing a beautiful flowered design of red and gold. Along the draped wall was a large sofa made of soft brown leather. The center of the room had a knee-high tall polished table that held many automotive books and news magazines.

Tony sat on one of the matching chairs at the opposite end of the room so he could look at them without turning his head.

"I just got off the phone with Franklin Todd and he tells me that this is going to be a stormy election," Tony said. "Rocky's group is hitting Johnny real hard on the fact that he's strike happy and looking for ways to shut the plant down. We all know the day shift doesn't want to lose any more pay."

They all nodded in agreement. Tony took out a pack of cigarettes from his shirt pocket. He offered one to Jay and Chip but they both refused. He lit one and sat back down to relax.

"I'm a little concerned about how the candidates are conducting the campaign," Tony said. "I have to talk to Rocky about the remarks that Lou is making about Johnny."

They both looked up quickly at Tony.

"Rocky's team is framing Johnny as a nigger lover," Tony explained.

Chip was sitting on the large sofa as he took out a cigar to smoke.

"Why should that be of concern to us?" Chip asked, a smug expression on his face. "What they say about each other should have no bearing on us or the outcome of the election. No matter who gets elected, they'll try to hamper our production when they don't get their way."

Tony shook his head in disagreement.

"I'm concerned about derogatory remarks that could lead to a riot," Tony said. "We'll have another demonstration on our hands."

Tony took another puff of his cigarette to let the statement sink in.

"We have to get a union president who understands our needs and will not hamper production," Tony said.

Chip wasn't buying Tony's suggestion that the company get involved in the union election.

"Tony, getting involved with the union election could get us charged with collusion and jeopardize the efficiency of the plant," Chip said. "I suggest we keep our hands clean of that."

Jay understood Chip's concern and responded before Tony could reply.

"Chip, over the past two years, we were able to speed up the lines controlled by Rocky's committeemen," Jay interjected. "That stopped now because one of the time study engineers made the fatal mistake of telling Johnny."

Jay mentioned that committeeman Taylor Wicker had allowed them to increase the agreed line speed when they had a breakdown. He looked at Tony for agreement.

"Tony, why don't you tell Chip about the rest," Jay said.

"Johnny took issue with increasing the speed of the line and threatened to remove Taylor from the floor," Tony said. "That spread all through the commercial department and word was that Taylor was a dead duck in the commercial department. As a result of this, the entire committeeman now refuse to give their consent to increase any of the line speeds due to a breakdown. That's the reason that we're working the department an additional two or three tenths of an hour each day."

"Did anyone attempt to talk to Johnny and explain the facts of life to him?" asked Chip.

"You're kidding, right?" Tony said. "I spoke to him on numerous occasions but it did no good. I went so far as telling him that those production lines paid all our salaries, including the union officials. He's a hard guy who wants to follow everything by the book. Rocky is different. He'll play ball with us if he gets elected."

"We can't afford to have a guy like Johnny as President," Jay said. "We know we can't change his ways but we could help to get him defeated if we play our cards right."

At this point, Chip was convinced.

"What do you need me to do?" Chip asked.

"We want you to line up your production managers on both shifts to cooperate with the Durango ticket," Tony said. "They have to be discreet in the way they do it. We can't afford to have the employees aware of the fact that we're playing along with Rocky."

"I understand," Chip said. "What are you going to do if Stan Kaplan gets elected? My intel is that he's making strong inroads in this election for president."

"We have nothing to fear there," Tony said.

He put his cigarette out in the ashtray on the polished table.

"It'll take him two years to learn the fine points of the union contract," Tony said. "I'll guide him down the primrose path."

"Chip, we don't want to get involved in this election but we have to," Jay said. He stood up to conclude the meeting.

Before Tony left, Jay asked another question.

"Tony what does the international union think about the candidates?" Jay asked.

"They're annoyed with Johnny especially since he opposed the last contract agreement," Tony said. "They feel he was the one responsible for the blood pact throughout the assembly plants. But they also believe he tried hard to get the contract rejected but they understand where he was coming from. They're not too happy with Rocky either. They feel he didn't have the guts to publicly vote for the contract even though he made the motion to congratulate the negotiators for a job well done on the contract. All he gave was excuses that his hands were tied. He tried to change his position and was fearful of what Freddie McCoy would do. On Stan Kaplan, they don't know a thing about him. They called here to get some background on him. Of the three, they think Johnny would do the most for the union membership but he has to become more flexible."

Tony then left, closing the door behind him.

"I'm going to our management meeting and I'll explain our discussion to them," Chip said to Jay. "I'm going to stop by Tony's office first. Then I'll line up the rest of the guys and tell them to be very careful in their dealings with the election."

"Thanks Chip, we're doing the right thing," Jay said.

Chip was well aware that they were skating on thin ice when they involved themselves in a union election. He was hoping that Tony's hatred toward Johnny wouldn't jeopardize any future relations with the union, including the possibility of Johnny winning. When he got to Tony's office, Chip stopped and placed his hand on Tony's shoulder.

"I hope this doesn't come back and kick us in the ass," Chip said. "A word to the wise, concentrate on a course of action that we should take in the event that Stan gets elected. Mark my words, he's a dark horse who's going to sneak in."

Marie was sitting at a far end booth of the Clinton Diner enjoying a cup of coffee while waiting for Rocky. Through the window she saw him pulling into the half-empty parking lot. She began to pour him a steaming cup of coffee from the pitcher the waitress had left. When he entered the diner, she stood up to get his attention. He walked over and sat across from her.

"I'm dying to know, what happened last night with Tony?" Marie asked.

"He didn't spare any expense last night," Rocky chuckled. "We ate like kings and talked politics over a few drinks. He is worried that someone will find out about his involvement in the union election and had me swear to secrecy. He said he has everyone lined up in management to give me what I need to win the election. That should wrap up the election for me."

"I'm so happy for you," Marie said. "The election can't get here soon enough for me."

"I got Tony to get the security guards to remove Otto Brodwick from the plant if he tries to campaign on the night shift," Rocky boasted.

"How could they do that?" Marie asked. "Otto is a candidate for a plant wide election."

"It's a company rule that when the plant shuts down, those workers on that shift have to leave in 15 minutes," Rocky said. "This doesn't apply to union officials but he's not an official."

"Wouldn't that also apply to Don Byrne then?" she asked.

"Not really," Rocky said. "My plan is to show Otto as a weak candidate when security escorts him out of the plant in front of membership. Meanwhile when they try to do that with Don, I'll make an issue of it and force the guards to leave. It's a little political trick to get the members on your side."

"Doesn't Johnny know those same tricks?" Marie asked.

"Yes," Rocky said. "I asked Tony to do that only if Johnny isn't around. Tony also agreed to dump all the hot disciplinary cases on Johnny when they come up. That should keep him busy during the election."

"I doubt very much that Johnny would allow himself to be tied up in hearings," Marie said. "He's much too smart for that."

"I know that," Rocky said, visibly annoyed. "I asked Tony to have the labor representatives who are conducting the hearings to tell the aggrieved that they're trying to get Johnny to represent them. Then they will tell the affected parties that Johnny is too busy campaigning to come to the hearing. Believe me, Johnny will blow his top when he gets back to his job after the hearing."

Marie was getting an education on dirty politics and smiled.

"There's so much to know when you become a union president," Marie said. "I'm going to enjoy dealing with you directly after the election. My job will be so much easier."

He finished his coffee and bun with a smile on his face. He picked up the check and thanked Marie for setting up the meeting with Tony.

"I have to run now," Rocky said. "I'll be tied up every day and night until the election is over. I'll give you a call when I'm free and we'll get together."

Marie kissed him on the cheek when they left the diner.

* * *

The campaign became vicious. Rocky and Lou walked the lines and blamed Johnny for all the problems in the plant. They portrayed him as a president who lost touch with the needs of the membership and became an ineffective leader. Rocky continued his tactics of meeting behind the racks so he wouldn't get blamed for carrying the dirt. He also instructed followers to harass Johnny at every opportunity that came up.

The reports of dirty politics came back to Johnny swiftly who in turn instructed his followers to go on the offensive. His strong hold was the night shift where his caucus members began to instigate problems for the opposition.

One day some of Johnny's followers stopped Rocky and Lou as soon as they entered the plant. They complained they were denied a medical pass even though there was a utility man available. They became vocal and raised all kinds of hell when they had to wait. Rocky knew Johnny started all this. He was helpless to get any of the problems resolved. There were also catcalls from behind the racks calling Rocky and Lou gutless and company stooges. It got to the point where Rocky and his team dreaded campaigning on the night shift. There were cartoons posted in all the work areas showing Lou knocked on his ass with a superintendent standing over him while Rocky was standing by wiping his brow with a handkerchief. A caption over Lou's head read: "Saved by the Bell."

Rocky's team was made the laughing stock of the union. The harassment became so bad Rocky went over to the union office to meet with Johnny.

"Is he in?" Rocky asked Betty one day, smiling nervously.

"His door is open," Betty said. "He's working on some reports. He told me he was available to anyone who wants to see him."

Rocky tapped softly on the open door.

"Can I see you for a minute?" Rocky asked.

Johnny covered up his papers and placed several folders on top of them.

"Sure," Johnny said. "Come in and take a seat. What's on your mind?"

"Johnny, your guys are hitting us below the belt," Rocky complained. "I don't mind name calling, but when the members degrade the union officials by putting cartoons all over the plant to make us the laughing stock in the eyes of the membership and the company, that's going too far. Some of your guys also are calling the union officials from our group company stooges. Some of the foremen are laughing at us when we're trying to get problems solved and several tell us the workers don't take us seriously.

We're not able to get any problems solved, no matter how serious they are. The union is going to weaken if they don't stop."

Johnny was pleased that his tactics were finally getting to Rocky and his team. He leaned back in his chair, while placing his feet up on the edge of his desk.

"Give me some specifics," Johnny said.

"At the end of the chassis line, you have an inspector by the name of Russo," Rocky said. "Whenever we get to his area, he stops work to lift up a cartoon and shouts for everyone to hear, 'saved by the bell.' Then everyone starts to laugh. They shout the same thing over and over. That's not only happening in that area but all over the night shift."

Rocky took out a cartoon from his jacket pocket and placed it on the desk.

"This is the dirtiest piece of literature I ever saw," Rocky said.

Johnny picked up the cartoon and looked at it for a moment.

"Rocky, you have to admit that we did a pretty good job here," Johnny joked. "The likeness of you and Lou is perfect. I don't see anything wrong with it."

Johnny removed his feet from the desk and walked around to sit in front of Rocky. He handed the cartoon back to him.

"How about you keep this for safe keeping," Johnny said. "And don't worry, I have a lot more where this came from."

Johnny turned away from him, indicating the conversation was over.

"You know I had a taste of being booed by your caucus so I know just how you feel," Johnny said. "Not too long ago one of your followers was caught booing and got the shit kicked out of him."

"I never heard that," Rocky said.

"I'm surprised to hear you say that," Johnny said. "The day after it happened, I saw him come to your office to complain. He was with you for quite a while. I'm sure he didn't come to see you for a cup of coffee."

"I don't recall," Rocky said.

"Rocky, you're full of shit," Johnny said, as he stood up to face Rocky, who was now standing. He pushed his index finger into Rocky's chest.

"You guys set up the rules for this election and I'm playing by them," Johnny said. "Remember, I'm the guy who came to see you about keeping the election clean but you didn't give a shit. Now I don't give a fuck one way or the other. I'm going to knock your brains out every chance I get."

Rocky pulled on his coat as Johnny continued talking.

"I just started and it's going to get worst," Johnny said. "You haven't seen anything yet. Wait until I get started on you."

Rocky wasn't looking for a fight with Johnny and was hoping to ease some of the tension.

"Don't get so hot, we'll both be officials when this is over," Rocky said.

"I wouldn't count on that if I were you," Johnny said. "I see that little talk at the Hawaiian Moon had no effect. I have some hard-hitting bulletins coming out on you and Lou. Since you wouldn't keep it clean, I'm getting into the gutter like the two of you. I'm going to refer to how Roger kicked the shit out of Lou and you hid in the racks until the lunch bell rang to save you from doing anything."

"That's hitting below the belt, isn't it Johnny?" Rocky said.

"Yes, but it's no worse than you telling members I'm a nigger lover, a strike happy president and the only one who stood up to vote against the national contract," Johnny flared. "You have the nerve to talk about mud-slinging. When I get through with you, you won't be able to get elected to run anywhere, let alone president of this local. At least I don't hide behind the racks to do my campaigning. Be on notice that I'm going to go after you with everything I got. Now get the fuck out of my office, I have a lot of work to do."

"Johnny, you're getting thin-skinned lately," Rocky said, attempting to assuage Johnny. "All I'm doing is politicking the best way I know how."

"I don't think I'm the one who's thin-skinned," laughed Johnny, "you're the one who came crying into my office about being rapped on nights. Wait until after this week is over, you'll probably have trouble working the day shift."

Immediately after leaving Johnny's office, Rocky went over to see Tony. When he got to the office, he merely nodded his head at Marie and walked into the office. He was still upset about his meeting with Johnny and detailed to Tony the entire exchange.

Tony had a plan already formulated and felt he could beat Johnny. He took out a cigar from his pocket and lit it, placing his feet on the edge of his desk feeling confident Rocky's team would win.

After Rocky finished detailing the incident, Tony took a bulletin from the folder on his desk and handed it to him. It was addressed to all the local retirees. In it he outlined all the gains won for them in the last contract giving Rocky and Lou credit for their position and promised they would continue to fight for their future needs and benefits. Rocky's face broke out in a smile.

"This is terrific," Rocky said. "We could hand it out when the retirees come to vote."

"No," Tony said. "That's not the way to do it. I'll run off a list of all the retirees' addresses and we will send them this bulletin and our slate card so they know who to vote for. There are over a thousand retirees out there. Their main concern is to get the candidates elected who are going to do the most good for them. Getting their votes is a nice cushion to have and could ensure you win the election."

"How soon could you get us the list of the addresses?" Rocky asked.

"I'll have the night man run them off tonight and give them to you in the morning," Tony said. "What you better do is go to a printer tonight to run of a thousand copies so you have them ready for tomorrow's mail. You only have a week before the election to do this so you better start hopping."

"I'll have it in the mail by tomorrow," Rocky said. "Tony, are your guys sure Stan is making headways in this election? A week ago no one was saying anything about him."

"That changed when Johnny came into the plant campaigning," Tony said. "Stan is taking advantage of the fighting between your and Johnny's team. Stan is a very effective speaker and he's rapping both of you on the Roger Hansen affair. You're pretty strong on day shift because your committeemen are defending you, but on nights it's a different ball game. They hate you with a passion and you're in trouble there. But with your edge on the dayshift and the letter to the retirees, I think the presidency is yours."

"Thanks for your help," Rocky said. "I'm sure the bulletin will put me over the top. I'll get George to get this to the printer the first thing in the morning."

Rocky pulled on his jacket and slipped the bulletin into his pocket.

"Do you and Johnny use the same printer?" Tony asked.

"Yes," Rocky said. "It's the only union printer in the area."

"You better look for another printer," Tony warned. "If the bulletin gets into one of the wrong hands, say one of Johnny's men, then you'll lose your edge. We need to surprise them and win over the retirees."

Johnny was true to his word. The following morning, he put out a humorous bulletin blasting Rocky and Lou as being gutless. It took Rocky and Lou two days to recover from the bulletin and to feel respected again as union officials.

Meanwhile Stan kept drumming the same beat of unity, promising that he would restore cohesion within the union leadership. He was slowly being considered a serious candidate for president.

Johnny continued being a good fighter and showed no fear in dealing with the company. In spite of that, the membership disapproved of the fight that was going on between the leadership.

* * *

The night of the election, tension was high in all groups and the membership. The Clinton police was out in full force to see that order was maintained during the tabulation of the votes.

As the count came in Johnny and Stan were running neck-and-neck. Stan had a 200-vote advantage over Johnny while Rocky was behind by 300 votes. The voting machine tallied Stan with 1305 votes, Johnny with 1150 and Rocky with 853. There were still 400 paper ballots from the retirees to be counted.

Johnny left the hall to go to his office to make preparations for a run-off election between Stan and himself. He was happy Rocky and his team had little effect on his re-election. He also was confident he could get Rocky's caucus members to rally behind him in spite of the fact that Lou was in the run-off with Mike Ferrera vying for the vice-president position.

While Johnny was working on the run-off bulletin, Rocky came into Johnny's office with his hand extended.

"Johnny, I want to congratulate you on making the run-off," Rocky said. "The results of the committeemen election show that you swept every position on both shifts. That should give you an edge on those shifts in the run-off."

Johnny looked up wide-eyed and reluctantly shook Rocky's hand.

"Here's hoping you win," Rocky said. "I'm looking forward to the international job."

"Too bad you didn't take my advice to keep the election clean," Johnny said.

Of course Rocky was in there with an ulterior motive. It irked Johnny that after running a dirty campaign and losing, Rocky had the nerve to ask about the international job.

"You were right about Stan," Rocky said. "Who'd ever believe that an unknown could come in and dump one of us? He's nothing but a dipshit and knows nothing about the contract and negotiations."

"Well, let's hope he doesn't get elected or the whole union could go down the drain," Johnny said. "Will you come out with a bulletin supporting me for president?"

"I can't do that," Rocky said, swallowing. "Lou is in the run-off against Mike. I still owe my allegiance to him, publicly. What I'll do is meet with my guys secretly to tell them to vote for you but let them know I support Lou and the rest of my group that's in the run-off. That's the best that I can do."

Johnny smirked with annoyance.

"Still the same old guy, hiding behind the racks," Johnny said. "I'll get your old caucus members to help me regardless of your support. I did them a lot of favors over the years and they're beholden to me. Now excuse me, I have a lot of writing to do."

Johnny heard a commotion outside his office coming from Rocky's group.

"I'm going to tell that fucking Johnny Romanek that he's a no good son-of-a-bitch," a man said, charging at Johnny.

Wayne intercepted and came charging at the man with his fists up in the air, ready to strike. It took three of Johnny's prizefighters to restrain Wayne. The man going after Johnny noticed Wayne and shrank back.

"Who the fuck is that kid?" the man asked. "He looks like he wants to kill me."

Rocky looked over to see Wayne being restrained.

"That's Johnny's kid," Rocky said. "I wouldn't tangle with him if I were you."

The man looked scared and uneasy as he noticed Wayne and the other fighters on Johnny's team watching him.

"Rocky, all I wanted to do was needle Johnny because he was so sure he would beat you in this election," the man explained. "I better get the hell out of here before they do a job on me."

Johnny came outside his office to see the man running out of the union hall in fear. Johnny put his arm around Wayne.

"Son, I appreciate your concern but nobody has to fight my battles," Johnny said. "I was hoping that guy would come over to take me on. I could have taken the frustration of my day out on him."

"I couldn't help it, pop," Wayne said. "He was coming at you and I couldn't just stand there."

"It's OK, son," Johnny said. "I'm proud of you. Now I need to speak to my men, so stay out of trouble."

Johnny addressed his caucus members.

"Let's go to my office," Johnny said. "We still have a run-off election for Mike and the rest of our ticket."

They all crowded into his office. Some sat on chairs, others on the floor and most stood against the wall. Justin Lowen came in with the results of the election.

"The retiree votes came in," Justin said. "They all voted for Rocky."

Groans and sighs moved through the room.

"Let's listen to what Justin says," Johnny said.

"We got Mike in the run-off with Lou," Justin said. "We lost Otto to Don Byrne in a lopsided vote. Pat Fager won in a landslide vote while George Plassard also won. I was told by some of the retirees that George was responsible for getting Rocky the votes."

"Johnny, do you think they fixed the retiree's vote?" Pat asked. Pat was closely scanning the tally sheet.

"I'm the one responsible for that blunder," Johnny said. "I knew the retiree's had to get their paper ballots from the financial secretary's office in order to cast their vote. Well I never gave that much of a thought or I would have had one of our members stationed there. Not only did Rocky's team give the retiree's their ticket's slate card, they also had a well-written bulletin addressing all the gains won for retirees under the new contract. When the retirees came to pick up their ballots, they had all that information from Rocky's team, we gave them nothing."

Justin referred to the tally sheet again.

"We won two trustees positions and the sergeant-at-arms on the executive board," Justin said. "The other trustee and guide positions are in the run-off."

"Right now we have four positions on the executive board," Johnny said. "When we get Mike elected as vice president along with the other two positions, we'll have complete control of the board. We won every committeeman position except two, so this gives us a big edge in the run-off. I need every one of you committeemen to work your hardest to get our guys elected. The one satisfaction I got out of this was that we got every committeeman of the opposition team dumped. The only one we missed was George. But we'll get him next time."

Johnny turned to Pat who was emotional and had tears in his eyes.

"What the hell are you crying about?" Johnny asked. "I still gotta job. All I did was lose the union position to Stan. You should be all smiles, you won your position in a landslide."

"What the fuck is good about that when we lost the head of our union," Pat said. "It's like a chicken running around with his head chopped off."

"What do you guys want to do about the president's position?" Johnny asked his men. "We have a problem here. Rocky is a back-stabbing bastard and Stan Kaplan doesn't know the first thing about running a union."

Every caucus member shouted: "Dump Rocky Durango and Lou Sargent!" The hate toward those men was so deep that they were determined to see that both of them would go to work back in the plant.

The run-off election took place the following week. Johnny was in the plant every day on each of the shifts speaking for the candidates on his slate. When he was asked by members who he supported for president, Johnny just smiled and told them they would have to decide who was the better candidate and let their conscience be their guide.

The night when the election was tallied, Stan won with a resounding majority of the votes cast. Mike Ferrera won the vice presidency in a lopsided vote along with the two trustees positions.

After the election results were announced, Johnny's caucus all gathered in his office.

"I want to thank all of you for a job well done," Johnny said. "We have full control of the executive board and all the committeemen positions but two. I want all of you to support Mike in everything he needs, to help get the membership back in the fold. My biggest concern is that we don't allow Stan to give away any of the benefits that took us years to earn."

"Johnny, what are you going to do?" Mike asked.

"I'm going to go back to work in the body shop and start campaigning for the president's job," Johnny said. Johnny's team broke out into applause.

"Johnny, the talk around the plant is that the company is going to offer you a management position," Pat said.

The caucus members became unruly and grumbled at Pat for even asking that question. Pat held up his hand in defense.

"I know that isn't going to happen," Pat explained. "But when our bulletin floated around saying that Johnny went to college and majored in engineering, a lot of members said, 'he's too smart to go back to work as an hourly worker. The company is going to snatch him up to work for them.' They all know Johnny is a sharp guy."

Johnny raised his hands up in the air.

"Let me make this clear, a leopard can never change his spots," Johnny said. "I'm indoctrinated with union ideals which would never change and the company is aware of that."

The caucus members were relieved by Johnny's statement.

"I want you all to know I'm still available to anyone who needs my advice," Johnny said. "Even though I'm no longer the president, I'll continue to work for our caucus. I want everyone to rally behind Mike. He'll be the spokesman for our caucus until I come back as president."

Mike stood next to Johnny and placed his arms around his shoulders.

"Johnny, you are still our leader," Mike said. "We'll be meeting with you as much as we can in and out of the plant. We all thank you from the bottom of our hearts for what you did to get us all elected. I'm going to work hard to get you a decent job at the plant. You can't go back in the body shop. That's the hardest department in the plant."

"Mike, I'm no Don Byrne," Johnny said. "I'm going back to my old classification and will wait for a promotional job to open up like any member. I want to thank all you for your concern. I'm a survivor and I'll do just fine."

All of Johnny's caucus shook his hand before departing.

When Johnny returned home that night, he arrived to smell Ann baking his favorite: leg of lamb roast. Ann and his children were waiting for him to come home. Ann wiped a tear from her eye as she kissed Johnny.

"What are going to do now?" Ann asked. But before he could answer, Ann remembered something.

"You know, dear, this reminds me of World War II when I asked you the same question," Ann said. "And the answer to that changed my life for the better. Our life will continue just the same. Now wash up, we're going to eat everything I made special for you and the kids."

"You're right," Johnny said, kissing Ann on the cheek. "We made that decision years ago and it made me the happiest man in the world. Ann, we'll make it. I'll probably drive you up a wall because I'll be around a lot more."

"John, the kids and I are going to love having you around," Ann said. "Now we can do things when we want to without the union always taking you away from us."

Johnny and his family had a scrumptious dinner full of laughter and stories. Johnny went to bed relaxed and happy.

On Monday morning, Johnny came in a little later than usual. When he arrived the secretaries stood up from their desks to greet him. Betty and Mary came over to hug him and said that they were sorry he lost the election. He acknowledged their concern.

"I want to thank both of you for your services here," Johnny said. "I don't know what I'd have done without your help."

"Oh, I should tell you," Betty said. "Mrs. Kaplan is in your office, cleaning it up. I told her that her husband wouldn't have possession of the office until after the installation meeting. She just waved me off and went in. I'm sorry."

Johnny walked in as Mrs. Kaplan was cleaning the office and moving the furniture around. Johnny placed his briefcase on the desk.

"I'm sorry, are you the new maid?" Johnny asked sarcastically.

"Well," Mrs. Kaplan replied, "I'm the new president's wife, Mrs. Kaplan."

She was a well-groomed lady, yet slightly on the plump side. She was dressed in a white flowered blouse and a tight black skirt with a silk scarf tied around her hair.

"Your husband doesn't have possession of this office until after the installation meeting," Johnny said. "I have a lot of work to do, so I'm going to have to ask you to leave."

"Well, I'll be!" Mrs. Kaplan said in a huff, gathering her broom, rags and other items. She left quickly.

Johnny laughed as he started to complete his final paper work. He sat back in his chair and thought about the secretaries. He knew Mrs. Kaplan would probably be bossing them around. He then went through his desk to remove his personal things and the pictures of his wife and family off the desk and placed them in his briefcase. He took one last look at his office, vowing to win back the presidency. But today, he closed the door and walked toward the body shop department.

It was his first day back as an hourly employee.